VALPOLICELLA VIOLET

FRANKI AMATO MYSTERIES BOOK 7

TRACI ANDRIGHETTI

Limoncello
Press

VALPOLICELLA VIOLET

by

TRACI ANDRIGHETTI

***

❀ Created with Vellum

To Madeline Mrozek, my narrator-partner in crime, who prevented me in a moment of creative crisis from sinking Valpolicella Violet like I did the Death in Venice book in chapter one

1

"Venice is hauntingly beautiful, isn't it?" Veronica Maggio, my best friend and boss and an imminent bride-to-be, gazed at the serene canal water.

I shifted uneasily on the elevated walkway. I wanted to agree with her, but there were a couple of problems. One, we weren't *in* Venice, we were *underneath* it in the permanently flooded crypt of the Chiesa di San Zaccaria. And two, the tranquil canal water she was gazing at reflected vaulted alcoves with eerie white tombs. "It's definitely haunting, but I struggle with the beautiful graveyard concept."

She rolled her eyes, making me think of people rolling in their graves. "I think it's gorgeous, Franki, especially the way the tombs are framed by the partially submerged columns."

I tried to see the beauty, but those columns raised questions, such as were they holding up the Gothic-Renaissance church over our heads? If so, how much longer could the tenth-century pillars withstand the eroding effects of the salt water? And what about the brick walls?

My concerns weren't unfounded. The crumbling plaster on the low ceiling might have escaped her notice because she was barely five feet five. But I had five inches on her, so the disrepair was in my face. And with potentially rising water, I felt boxed in.

In a subterranean cemetery.

I tugged at my turtleneck and tried to distract myself from the claustrophobic conditions. "Who do you think the statue on the tomb is? A Roman god?"

Veronica tucked blonde hair behind her ear and pulled a guidebook from her floral Gucci bag. "I doubt it. From what I've read, Venice didn't come into being until ancient Rome was on the verge of collapse."

"Then who were their influences? Mermen?"

She turned to a bookmarked page. "This says the Venetian Republic began in 697 AD and drew inspiration from Byzantine Constantinople and Islamic Cairo. You can see their influence in the architecture of the Basilica of San Marco and on the Grand Canal."

I'm dying to, I thought, *but I'm stuck in this burial basement.*

She proceeded along the narrow walkway, moving deeper into the crypt. But I stayed put. The old brick was covered in an inch of water and surrounded by looming pools, which evoked walking a wet plank.

I checked my Goldon's Boots, the reusable plastic shoe covers made in Venice for *acqua alta*, the high water caused by storm tides. I'd wanted to take them home to New Orleans for the bimonthly floods that besiege the French Quarter where Veronica's PI agency, Private Chicks, was located, but this pair had a date with the garbage. Because the odds were as high as the floodwater that they were steeped in bone broth.

Now that I thought about it, that dank, earthy odor probably wasn't just from the wet, decaying building. I pulled a lock of my brown hair over my nose.

Ripples marred the surface of the pool.

And I got queasy. *Was something swimming in it, like a rat? Or was more water pouring in?*

I speed-trod to catch up with Veronica to find out whether she needed me to stick around for an as-yet-unknown maid-of-honor duty. If not, I intended to get the hell out of the creepy catacombs. "What's the plan after this?"

"As soon as Dirk is done paying Father Festin, we're going to dinner."

I imagined the three of us at a table for two in a charming trattoria and, given our surroundings, plates of cold osso buco. "I'm exhausted from the trip, so I think I'll get room service at the hotel. Besides, I wouldn't want to ruin your romantic dinner."

"You wouldn't. We've already been here for a couple of days, so we'd enjoy the company. We're going to the Cantina do Spade, near the old Red Light district, where Casanova once took his lady friends."

My lips flattened like tomb lids.

Veronica's cornflower blue eyes grew guarded. "Any update from Bradley?"

I pulled my phone from my coat pocket, hoping to find a text from my fiancé. No reception. "The last I heard, the snowstorm was really bearing down."

"At least he's safe with his family."

I was happy about that, but not about the timing. Given the December weather, I'd worried that the long layover he'd scheduled in Boston would result in a delayed connecting flight, and sure enough, it had. "I just wish he'd waited to surprise his mother on the way back from the wedding. Venice is for lovers, and I'm here alone."

"You are not. You've got Dirk and me."

"And I love you both, but not like Casanova loved his lady friends."

She exhale-smiled. "The ceremony is in six days. You'll have plenty of time together before your family arrives."

Thanks to the rippling water, my reflection fluttered like a ghost, ironic considering that Veronica's wedding would haunt me if Bradley didn't make it. My mom and my eighty-one-year-old Sicilian nonna thought he'd been slow to propose, and if he were a no-show for Veronica's wedding, two things would happen. They would interpret it as a sure sign of cold feet for marriage in general, and my nonna would go into manic-match-maker mode.

Splashing footsteps drowned out my anxiety.

Veronica's soon-to-be groom, Dirk Bogart, strode up the walkway. Although he was named after English matinee idol Dirk Bogarde, his reddish-blond hair, blue eyes, and strong jaw were reminiscent of a young Robert Redford. "We're all set, and Father Festin is going to give us a quick tour of the crypt as soon as he finishes up with a communion wine delivery. You'll like him, Franki. He's quite a character. Italian, but grew up in England."

Unless his tour came with a complimentary glass of that wine, and I was confident it didn't, I wanted no part of it. "I'll meet him at the wedding. Right now, I think I'll head out."

He glanced at Veronica. "Are you sure? I made a dinner reservation for three."

Dirk was a gentleman, but I was tired, and I had no desire to be the third wheel in a city that used only boats for transportation. "I appreciate the invite, but the nap I took on the plane has worn off."

Veronica's brow furrowed. "I hope you'll come with us to the Palazzo Ducale at nine tomorrow morning. We're taking the Secret Itineraries tour of its prisons and the torture chamber."

Most couples took a gondola ride, but to each their own.

"Oh, and we have to be at the hotel restaurant at three

o'clock. The chef is going to let us sample the dish she created for the reception."

Food was more like it. "I will definitely make that. See y'all tomorrow."

I maneuvered carefully around Dirk on the narrow walkway, because I had no desire to take a dip in the tomb soup, but a priest in a black robe, presumably Father Festin, blocked my exit. His head was lowered, and when he raised it, I got a shock. Deathly pale, he had pronounced under-eye circles and a head so bald it might as well have been a bare skull. And Dirk was right when he'd called him a character, because Father Festin looked like Uncle Fester from *The Addams Family*.

The frightening father clasped bony hands. "I trust you're enjoying the crypt."

I didn't know what surprised me more—the questionable use of *enjoying* or his "Monster Mash" voice.

Veronica peered around Dirk. "We are, Father. It's like a reflection pool."

"When the water isn't up to the ceiling, yes."

Way to literally put a damper on the tour, pal—uh, priest. I checked the ripples to make sure they hadn't become waves.

Dirk slid his arm around Veronica's waist. "Who's buried down here, Father?"

"Eight doges, all of whom died the most savage deaths."

Father Fester was chock-full of downer details.

His gaze wandered to a tomb. "Three were assassinated here at San Zaccaria."

I started, which was precarious considering where I was standing. "That's a lot of murders...for a church."

"They were violent times." He practically sang the statement. "And it was a small number given that one hundred twenty doges ruled *La Serenissima*, the Most Serene Republic of Venice, until Napoleon forced the last doge to abdicate in 1797."

Dirk rubbed his chin. "That would've been during the French Revolutionary Wars, before he sold Louisiana to the United States."

"Yes, money he used to fund the Napoleonic Wars. He was a warmonger and a thief who left devastation in his wake."

Just like my Cairn terrier of the same name.

He frowned at the water as though that was also Napoleon's doing. "Before the dissolution of the Republic, the Chiesa di San Zaccaria was a monastic church with great influence, as the abbess was always a relative of the doge. Napoleon took away its power, plundered its art, and banned burials in this crypt and upstairs in the church."

My head tipped forward. "People are buried there too?"

"Of course. The church was founded in the ninth century when the Byzantine Emperor Leo V the Armenian gave Doge Giustiniano Participazio the gift of the body of Saint Zechariah, the father of John the Baptist."

"Oh, *man*." I threw up my hands and looked at Veronica. "That's what I was going to get you for your wedding."

Her eyes widened, and Father Festin looked as though he wanted to shove me in the bone-water moat.

Catholic guilt pricked at my skin, and I scratched my neck. The joke might have been in poor taste, but so was giving corpses as presents.

Dirk wiped a grin from his face. "Did Napoleon ban burials throughout the city?"

"Yes, because of the flooding he said it was unhygienic to bury the deceased anywhere on the main island, so he commissioned a cemetery on the island of San Michele, which is still in use today."

A sound policy.

"He tried to remove our relics, but the Church resisted. In

return, he closed our adjoining monastery and gave it to the Carabinieri." He shuddered. "A crime."

I disagreed. Between the murders of the doges and the unsafe burials, the Chiesa di San Zaccaria needed police protection—from itself.

Veronica flipped through the guidebook. "I thought I read that the monastery burned down."

"It caught fire in 1105, but it was saved. Unfortunately, one hundred nuns who hid in the cellar died from smoke inhalation." His hummed words hung in the air like a shroud.

I would've sworn the ceiling lowered, and I struggled to breathe. The church and its priest were more suited for a funeral than a wedding—or a TV show about a family that was creepy, kooky, mysterious, spooky, and all together ooky. Either way, that was my cue to leave. I'd come to Venice to celebrate the joining of two lives, not ruminate on murder and dying.

"Do you mind if I slide around you, Father? I've got a date with death." My jaw dropped at my disturbing slip of the tongue. "I mean, my bed."

He held up his hands to let me pass, and I sucked in my gut to squeeze past his. As I climbed the worn marble steps, my nerves were as rattled as the bones in the tombs. I didn't know why the "date with death" remark had popped from my mouth, but I certainly hoped it wasn't a premonition.

I emerged inside the vestibule, which had closed a half-hour before at 6:00 p.m., and took a life-affirming breath.

But I was met by more death.

Two gold-and-glass caskets were on the wall before me— one identified as Saint Athanasius was held aloft by giant angel sculptures, the other, Saint Zechariah, rested at their feet. Because of dark woodwork, black columns, and somber Renaissance paintings, I hadn't noticed them when I'd arrived an hour earlier. But now that darkness had descended, the caskets and the white-robed corpses that rested inside gleamed in the glow of sconces and candles, as though sending me a grave message.

"It's official," I said aloud in the sacred space. "This church is killing my excitement about my best friend's wedding."

But that was irrational. The exhaustion and stress about Bradley were getting to me. I needed sleep and the safe arrival of my fiancé, and all would be well.

I passed the pews and hoisted open the old wooden door. Clouds obscured the moon, which didn't promise anything positive for the walk back to the hotel. I stepped into the brick piazza known as the Campo di San Zaccaria and pulled out my phone in case I needed the flashlight—or the *polizia*.

"Chill, Franki," I whisper-muttered. "Like Father Fester said —I mean, Father Festin—the Carabinieri are next door in the convent."

A shuffling sound pricked up my ears, and I scanned the crypt-like darkness. An elderly man in an elegant *tabarro*, a Venetian cloak that dated to the medieval period, walked toward a public drinking fountain with a grocery bag.

Relieved, I smiled. "*Buonasera.*"

Ignoring my "good evening," he stooped to take a drink. Then he rose and thrust his cane at the building. "*Non entrare. Non entrare!*"

I'd heard Italian at home and had studied it with Veronica at the University of Texas, so I knew he was telling me not to enter the church, probably because it was after hours.

He bared yellowed teeth. "*Quella è la Chiesa degli Omicidi, capito?*"

I understood, all right. The Church of Murders. I looked at the massive, five-story structure with its tall Gothic windows, colonnades, and curved gable. *Was that nickname a thing of its past—or part of its present?* I turned to ask, but he was gone.

Spooked, I pulled up the hood of my coat and headed for the

Hotel San Marco. My romantic notions of Venice had vanished, like the old man. In their place were thoughts as dark as the starless night.

"YOU SERIOUSLY PICKED *NOW* NOT to work?" I glared at my phone, but it wasn't to blame for the fact that I couldn't find my way back to the hotel. The culprit was the sketchy reception among the narrow, building-lined streets. I had no GPS, no way to call anyone, and no one to ask for directions. And to top it all off, I had brain fog from sleep deprivation, so I couldn't get my bearings.

As time wore on, my stomach sank further and further, much like Venice itself. The city had six main districts called *sestrieri*, which came from *sesto*, or *six*, and I feared that I'd strayed far from San Marco, and my hotel. It didn't help that fog as dense as the one in my head had rolled in, or that my footsteps echoed in the empty city, making me worry that I was being followed.

Voices came from an alleyway a few yards ahead.

My body tensed, and I hugged my hobo bag as I peered around the corner.

It wasn't an alley, but a bookstore set back from the street. The name, Libreria Acqua Alta, struck me as ironic both because books and flood water didn't go together and because I felt like I'd found a life raft in a lagoon.

The inside of the store was as damp as the streets and equally devoid of people. Books were elevated off the concrete floor, some stacked in shelves, and others piled in a variety of unlikely containers, a bathtub, a canoe, a chest of drawers. Nevertheless, many were warped and wet. A hodgepodge of light fixtures, plants, and a stray cat gave the space the look and smell of a garden center at a home repair store.

I entered an adjoining room that had a gondola overflowing with books. A straw-and-ribbon gondolier's hat hung from the curved metal bow, and a male and female mannequin in Carnival dress stood in an amorous pose behind a red heart-shaped seat. Below them were copies of Giacomo Casanova's *The Story of My Life*, which added to my depression. His life was synonymous with erotic adventures, whereas the story of mine was being apart from my fiancé. What I wanted was to be with *my* Casanova, aka Bradley Hartmann, and to kiss him in a gondola like the one before me under the Bridge of Sighs.

A wistful sigh escaped my lungs, and I wandered into the next room in search of the travel section. Forest green double doors opened onto a canal that threatened to spill into the store. An old-school life preserver hung from one of the handles, and on the door frame beside it were the words Fire Exit and a comical image of a person diving for the water. An olive green armchair completed the scene. Unlike the flooded crypt, it was the perfect place to sit and reflect, and a reading spot too tempting to resist.

I reached into a wine barrel and grabbed a random book —*Death in Venice* by Thomas Mann with a cover from the 1971 movie starring Dirk Bogarde.

The nape of my neck tingled. *Is it a sign that something's going to happen to Veronica's Dirk? Is that why I've been on edge in this floating city?*

I sank into the armchair.

"Don't sit there!" A thirty-something woman dived for me like the diving figure on the door frame. She slammed into the chair, tipping it on two legs, and seized my arm, sending *Death in Venice* sailing to its demise in the dark water.

Panicked, I latched onto the door handle, preventing my own

canal catastrophe.

She pulled me from the seat with a strength surprising for a five-foot woman with the curves of a snowman. "That chair's as wet as a sink sponge."

I would've appreciated the warning before I sat down—and before the tackling—because my derrière was drenched and my bicep had taken a beating.

"You all right?"

She was shouting as though I was hard of hearing, and it was turning my brain fog to hazy headache. "Yeah, I'm good."

"Well, you look pretty rough."

I eyed the life preserver. The canal catastrophe I'd prevented might have been the better option. "I flew in from New Orleans today, so I'm worn out."

"The Big Easy, eh? Know it well. I'm from Screamer, Alabama."

That explained her high volume.

"Last name's Helper." She shook my bruised arm up and down. "First name's Shona, like Mona. Just drop the 'm' and add a 'sh.'"

I'd like to add a sh. A couple of them, actually. "I'm Franki Amato." I put my hands on my hips and looked around the room. "Any idea where the maps are?"

"Beside the register on your way out, but I have a better suggestion." She tied her stringy brown hair into a top knot and pulled a book from a shelf. "*Venice Legends and Ghost Stories: A Guide to Places of Mystery in Venice* is a fun way to get to know the city. I read it twice before I came. We've got it at the library where I work."

A loud-talker librarian? The next thing you know, she'll dog-ear a page. "It doesn't mention the Chiesa di San Zaccaria, does it?"

"Sure does. The Church of Murders. It had quite the history back in the day."

Let's hope it stays in the past.

She flipped through the book and held it up. "This one's my favorite, the bell ringer of San Marco. It's a true story about a seven-foot-tall man who sold his skeleton to the Museum of Natural History in the eighteen hundreds before he died. You should go see it."

"I was at a crypt earlier, so bones are out."

"Okay, but you might regret it. The bell ringer certainly did. Legend has it that every night just before midnight, he slips from the museum in a black cape, rings the bell at Saint Mark's bell tower twelve times, and wanders the streets, ringing a hand-held bell and begging for money to buy back his skeleton."

I didn't believe that nonsense, but a part of me was glad that it was only seven forty. "Thanks, but I'm a PI, so when I'm on vacation I like to get away from mystery and take it easy. Speaking of which, I'm falling asleep on my feet, so I'd best be off."

"I hope you have a restful stay!"

I did too, and that started with getting away from her.

On my way to the register, I got sidetracked by a tiny, walled courtyard. Wet, disintegrating encyclopedias were stacked like stairs against the back wall with the ungrammatical sign, "Follow the Books Steps Climb."

Curious, I climbed to the top and looked over the wall. The canal lay below. In the daytime, the water was a turquoise color, but without the sun it was deep purple-blue. I looked left and drew in a breath.

A woman with wavy blonde hair in a flowing white dress and lace gloves stood on a bridge, staring at the water. Her face, hidden behind a white facial mask, reminded me of Jason's hockey look from *Friday the 13th*, but it was clear she was distraught. She wrung her hands and looked behind her. Then she glanced in my direction and went rigid.

"Ahem."

I spun around.

A middle-aged man in suspenders tapped his wristwatch. "We close now."

I took one last look at the bridge. The woman had vanished as abruptly as the old man at the church.

How do Venetians do that? Are they all ghosts?

With a shudder, I went to the register and picked out a street guide, but I couldn't get the ghostly woman or the *Death in Venice* book out of my head. It was irrational, but something, a sixth sense, had me spooked.

My phone rang, and *amore mio* appeared on the display. *Bradley!* I handed the man twenty euros to cover the map—and the drowned book—and rushed from the shop. "Hey, babe," I answered as I headed for the open air of a canal to keep my phone reception. "Did you find a flight?"

"Everything's canceled until tomorrow. The snowstorm's a full-on blizzard."

I wanted to shout à la Shona, *Our days are numbered before my family arrives and goes into meddling overdrive! Hire a private plane! Charter a boat! Take Santa's sleigh!* But that wasn't safe—or entirely realistic—and the dejection in his voice silenced my objections. "It's only one more day."

"I know, but I miss you."

My stomach gave a flutter kick. "I miss you too."

"How's La Serenissima?"

"You mean, La Scarenissima." I cast a glance behind me. "Venice doesn't have street lights, and it's practically a ghost town at night."

"How is that possible? It's one of the most visited cities in the world."

"The manager at our hotel said that wealthy foreigners who don't live here year round own most of the property, and it's so expensive the people who service the tourists live outside the city. So when the shops close, Venice empties out."

"Where are you now?"

I wish I knew, I thought, as I scanned foreboding buildings. "On my way to the hotel."

"After dark? Are you sure it's safe?"

I glanced over my shoulder, quite sure it wasn't. "Don't worry about *me*, Bradley Hartmann. You should be worried about yourself."

"Why's that? The flight?"

"No, I've got big plans for you when you arrive."

"I like the sound of that." His serious tone had turned as smooth as Venetian silk. "I'll call before the plane takes off. I love you."

"I love you back. *Buon viaggio, amore mio.*" I hung up, and the warm, fuzzy glow of the call faded back to the black night.

And then to fuzzy glow?

Thinking I was hallucinating, I blinked hard. But no, yellow-orange lights floated down the canal. *How?*

In the fog, it was hard to tell.

Entranced, I walked toward the water.

The woman I'd seen on the bridge emerged from a side street, her white gown swirling at her feet. She raised a lace-gloved arm as though pointing at the light.

Was the floating glow the thing she'd been looking for on the bridge? I picked up my pace, and my heels smacked on the street.

Her masked face jerked in my direction, and she ran the way she'd come.

What's going on?

The source of the canal lights came into focus, and it was more haunting than the woman in white.

Floating down the water with a lit candle on each of its four corners was a coffin—the kind vampires sleep in.

"*coffin?*" Veronica repeated into the phone. "The tapered type that vampires use?"

I crossed the Piazza San Marco, wondering how her questions were going down at our hotel's breakfast buffet. "Precisely that kind. It was black and fairly small."

"Oh." Her tone softened as though the size made the sighting less relevant. "So it was for a child."

I stopped at the Caffè Florian's outdoor seating area, searching for a table farthest from the grand piano outside the entrance. "Child vampires can do just as much damage as adults, Veronica."

"Here we go again with your irrational fear of Claudia from *Interview with a Vampire.*"

"In my defense, that vampirette was more bloodthirsty than Lestat."

At a table on the last row, an attractive young man and an older woman in a black chiffon headscarf and white sunglasses looked up from their newspapers.

I flashed a smile to reassure them that I wasn't a nutjob—

and that my canines were non-vampire—and sat a few seats away with my back to them.

Veronica sighed. "And like Lestat, she's a fictional character from the Anne Rice books."

"Yes, but as we know from that fraternity murder I investigated, there are real people who live as vampires." I glanced behind me at the couple, who frowned at their glasses of blood-orange juice.

"Well, maybe the coffin was for a festival or funeral."

"With no one in attendance except the woman in white?"

Dirk murmured something unintelligible, and the clink of a spoon striking a porcelain cup assailed my ear.

"Franki, can we talk about this later? The chef is on her way to our table, and I want to make sure she's still planning to serve us a dish from the reception menu today at three."

"Fine. I'll think better after I down some espresso, anyway."

"We'll meet you at the Palazzo Ducale ticket booth in half an hour." Veronica hung up before I could object.

I put my phone in my bag and pondered the funeral angle. If the coffin and the ghostly woman were connected, then she could have been having a memorial for a lost child, but it didn't seem likely given her attire. Her mask and white gown were reminiscent of a New Orleans voodoo ritual. *Had I witnessed Venetian black magic?*

A chill snaked down my spine. I turned on a table-side heat lamp and reached for the menu.

Pigeons descended in front of my table, and we eyed one another uneasily. They were wondering whether I'd give them something to eat, and I was wondering whether they'd eat me. The pigeons of Saint Mark's Square were notoriously aggressive, so much so that not only had they survived multiple removal attempts by the city, their population had grown to almost double that of the Venetians.

I was tempted to move inside to one of the café's historic tea rooms, but I wanted to have that experience with Bradley. I opened the menu and held it up so that I couldn't see the beady bird eyes. My gaze went straight to *cioccolata in tazza.* "Chocolate in cup?" I translated aloud. "Why, yes. I believe I will."

Beneath the tantalizing drink was a picture of something even more enticing—hot chocolate with a mint cream topping and chocolate shavings named after none other than Giacomo Casanova. I sighed and closed the menu. The guy was all over Venice, but my Casanova wasn't.

A waiter with the bone structure of a model and a nametag that read 'Ambrosio' approached in the café's signature uniform, a white dinner jacket with black pants and a black bowtie. "May I take your order, miss?"

He must've heard me speaking English. "A croissant, an espresso doppio, and a Casanova."

The corner of his mouth twisted upward.

My face grew warm, and it wasn't because of the heat lamp. I'd meant to order the drink, not the man. "I meant, a *Cioccolata* Casanova."

He nodded and left the table, no doubt thinking that I was a hard-up American hitting on him.

I shot an embarrassed glance at the couple, relieved to see that they were deep in conversation, and turned to admire the beauty of the piazza dedicated to Saint Mark, or San Marco, as he was known locally. The domes of the basilica with its gold mosaics, the red-brick bell tower, and the pointed arches of the Palazzo Ducale, visible from the piazzetta that branched off the main piazza, transported me back to the Renaissance. Everywhere I looked, I saw the symbol of Venice, the winged lion with the gospel of Saint Mark under his paw. And for the holidays, there was an enormous Christmas tree made from strands of white lights.

My plan was to people-watch, but I had to pigeon-watch instead. They strutted around with puffed chests and tensed wings, and every few seconds one would rush me and retreat. I stood up to drag the heat lamp in front of me to threaten them with a roasting. While stooped over, I saw the hem of an ankle-length black tabarro and men's boots with a tiny skull on each heel. As I returned to my seat the wearer pulled out a chair at the couple's table.

The skulls and the cloak reminded me of the bell-ringer legend. I stared at the columned belfry of Saint Mark's tower and imagined a seven-foot skeleton ringing the bell. I snorted. Now that I'd had some sleep, my fears from the day before seemed almost comical.

"*Dopo mezzanotte*," one of the men behind me quasi-shouted.

I turned my head an inch, curious to know what he thought should happen "after midnight."

A hushed but heated exchange followed in a dialect of Italian, probably because the couple-turned-trio realized I was eavesdropping. Nevertheless, I recognized the odd word, *vero* for *true*, and *palla d'oro* for *golden ball*. I wasn't sure what the latter referred to, but it wasn't a Christmas ornament because that was *addobbo*.

The waiter returned with my order—and a cheeky twinkle in his black eyes.

Avoiding his gaze, I shot the espresso. When he was gone, I took a sip of the Cioccolata Casanova. My hand went to my lips. If the real Casanova was even half as seductive as the sumptuous drink, I would've succumbed to his every whim.

The man behind me slammed a hand on the table. "*No, la pavan!*"

"*Zitto*," the woman silenced him.

The "pavan" got my attention. It was my mother's maiden name, and her family was from the area. My last name, Amato, meant *loved*, but it had never occurred to me that hers might be an Italian word, as well.

Something hit the back of my chair, and I lurched forward, sloshing the precious mint chocolate onto the piazza. I clenched my jaw.

The pigeons.

I turned to pluck the dirty birds but discovered that the culprit was Shona Helper, who stood behind me in a green knit cap and white puffer coat jumpsuit that enhanced her snowman figure.

"Franki Amato," she trumpeted. "Fancy running into you."

I wanted to tell her that the expression was never intended to be literal, but I focused on the positive—her loud talking had scared away the pigeons.

Shona dumped a tote bag from a romance writer convention on the table and took a seat, her charcoal eyes bright with excitement. "I've been dying to come to the Caffè Florian. It opened in 1720, which makes it the oldest continually operating café in Europe, unless you believe the French, who say the Café Procope has been open since 1686. And Florian's list of patrons reads like a who's who from the history books. Goethe, Lord Byron, Charles Dickens, Charlie Chaplain, Winston Churchill..."

I looked for the waiter. Time to replace my Casanova with a cocktail. *And why not?* It was 1.30 a.m. in New Orleans. "So what're you doing in Venice?" A worrisome thought struck me. "You didn't come alone, did you?"

"Nah, I'm with my rowing club."

That explained how she'd lifted me from the wet armchair at the bookstore. "There's rowing in Alabama?"

"We have water too, you know. Although I learned to row up north in my hometown."

It occurred to me that Shona didn't have a Southern accent. "Where's that?"

"Belchertown, Massachusetts." She pounded a burp from her chest.

I sensed a pattern with her cities of residence, and I didn't like it one bit.

"Yep, my team is going to race on the Grand Canal on Christmas Eve Day."

"Wow. That sounds amazing. What's your team called?"

"The Screamer Scullers."

The name had a ring to it, and thanks to Shona's shouting, it rang my ears.

"What about you? Are you really here on vacation?" She grinned, revealing deep dimples. "Or are you investigating a case undercover? You can tell me." She leaned forward. "We librarians know how to keep mum."

Given the information she'd been rattling off, I wasn't so sure. "I'm here for my best friend's wedding at—" I decided to keep the Church of Murders location to myself for fear she'd make a scene or show up at the ceremony, "—a chapel."

"Ooh, you know what that reminds me of? A story from that book I showed you last night. It's about a woman named Tosca."

"The one from the opera?"

"No, that was about a fictitious singer Puccini dreamed up. This Tosca was a real woman from Treviso, a town thirty-two kilometers from here, which is twenty miles to you and me."

True to her librarian title, Shona was a solid resource.

"Tosca was gorgeous, probably blonde," she said with a flip of her mousy brown strands. "And because her family was poor, she agreed to marry a rich nobleman who was way too old for her. But she fell in love with a handsome young hunter, and they escaped to Venice. The enraged nobleman," she pushed up from the table and puffed her chest like one of the pigeons, "came and found them and shouted, 'If I can't have you, nobody will.' Then he killed the hunter, and *whack!*" She karate-chopped her left hand. "He cut off Tosca's ring finger."

I covered my ruby-and-diamond-engagement-ringed ring finger. The violence had caught me by surprise, but Shona's reenactment of the shouting hadn't.

She returned to her seat. "Tosca took her own life, and to this day, her ghost wanders the Castello district dressed as a bride."

Instead of Veronica's Vera Wang dress, my mind went to the masked woman's flowing white gown. "Just out of curiosity, where is the Castello district?"

"You were in it last night, at the bookstore. Tosca is often seen there on a bridge, looking for her ring finger."

Saint Mark's Campanile rang out the ten o'clock hour, and it was no peal of wedding bells. It was a foreboding funeral toll.

SHONA STOPPED on the dimly lit stairwell inside the Palazzo Ducale and turned to look at me. "It was awesome of your friend, Veronica, to let me use your fiancé's ticket."

"Mm," was all I managed, glad that she was getting to take the Secret Itineraries tour, but stressed because she was preventing me from keeping up with the rest of the group. Our retired American soldier tour guide, Alma, took no nonsense, and even though we were in a medieval prison, she didn't take any prisoners either.

Shona turned, put her right foot on the next step, and her left. Then she spun to look at me again. "I don't know if you're aware of this, but you have to book this tour *months* in advance."

I gripped the railing and squeezed. Shona's loud and steady information stream had drowned out our guide in the *Pozzi*, the basement prison cells nicknamed the *Wells* where prisoners were left to drown during acqua alta floods. And now, on our way to the Torture Room, her chatter combined with her stop-and-go stair-climbing, had the effect of a slow water drip on my forehead.

"The tour is so popular because of the Council of Ten," she droned. "They were the Venetian chamber of justice. Have you heard about them?"

"I have," I said, hoping to head off yet another info dump, "from Alma, our tour guide?"

"Right, but she should've gone into more detail about their terror tactics."

I wondered whether one of those tactics included trapping people in a narrow stairwell and tormenting them with chitchat.

"The Council was so feared because they had hundreds of informants who left incriminating notes in drop boxes all over the city that were called *boche de leon* because they looked like lion mouths. And whoever they condemned was tricked into going to a street called *Calle della Morte* where they'd be killed."

How? I wouldn't be caught dead on a murderous street named Death Alley. But I didn't dare ask Shona that question.

She exited the stairwell, and I zoomed past her and entered a doorway marked *Stanza della Tortura*. A museum guard with a severe burn scar on his neck watched from a corner as I surveyed what was no garden-variety torture chamber. Instead of the dank stone-dungeon look with wrought-iron fixtures I'd expected, the walls had rich, dark paneling, and an antique desk, cabinet, and chairs in exquisite hand-carved wood furnished the room.

"Holy mole sauce," Shona bellowed. "The Venetians certainly didn't want to be surrounded by squalor while they watched people suffer."

"Apparently not." I walked to three wooden steps placed in the middle of the room in direct view of the desk. A rope dangled above them from a vaulted ceiling. "I'm surprised there isn't a noose."

"Didn't you hear the tour guide?"

"No," I replied pointedly.

"You should listen. They know tons of information."

I laid a side-eye on her. "Like someone else I met in Venice."

"Who?"

Shona just didn't get it. "No one you know."

"Oh. Anyway," she approached the steps, "the rope was used to hang prisoners by their hands, which had been tied behind their backs. If they took too long to confess, their shoulders snapped like matchsticks."

Not that much worse than what I'm going through now.

Alma stormed the room in her combat boots and blew a whistle, and Shona and I stood at attention.

"It's against regulations for museum visitors to separate from their guides." She put the whistle in a pocket of her beige utility dress. "We'll proceed single file to the *Piombi*."

Shona touched my arm. "That's Italian for the 'Leads.' They're attic prison cells with lead roofs that are like freezers in winter and ovens in summer."

The battle-scarred lines on Alma's face hardened. "That's what *I'm* here to explain."

Shona's dimpled cheeks flushed the color of Alma's raised March! flag.

We followed her into a rustic hallway with old wood beams and paneling. As with the Wells in the basement, the Leads had low doors with metal reinforcements and windows with rusted bars.

Veronica emerged from a cell in a white wool pantsuit. "Franki, Casanova escaped from here. Can you imagine?"

No, because I couldn't seem to shake the guy, or Shona for that matter. "What year was that?"

Alma tapped the window bars with her flag. "It was 1756 on Halloween night. He and a fellow prisoner, a priest no less, made a hole in the lead ceiling, climbed into the attic, and crossed the palace roof. Then they re-entered through a palace office window and convinced someone that they were visitors who'd been locked in the prison." She shook her head. "Whoever that numbskull was, committed a scandalous breach of security that allowed Casanova to flee in a waiting gondola and escape to Paris."

It figured he'd taken a gondola. "Why was he imprisoned?"

"Public outrages against the holy religion."

Shona held a hand to the side of her mouth. "A.k.a., adultery for affairs with married women. He once called marriage the tomb of love."

Alma clicked her heels, and Shona and I went rigid. "He was also charged with being a cardsharp, a con man, a Freemason, an astrologer, a cabbalist, and a blasphemer."

She sure showed Shona.

"If you ask me, Casanova got off too easy. They used to announce executions of nefarious characters like him from the two red columns of the loggia, and then they'd hang 'em from there during a ceremony presided over by the doge and leave them for days as a warning. I tell you, that's the way to fight crime." Alma raised the flag. "Onward, to the last stop."

After that pronouncement, we marched downstairs to the middle of the palace like dutiful prisoners.

"Here we are." Alma gestured to what looked like a short, narrow hallway with a glow of light from a lone window. "The famous *Ponte dei Sospiri*, or Bridge of Sighs, so-called because the prisoners would sigh as they took one last glimpse at Venice before going to the clink. The bridge was designed by the architect Antonio Contino and built in 1614. It connects the old prison and interrogation rooms to the new prison."

Dirk took Veronica's hand and led her to the window.

Shona shouldered my side. "Aren't they adorable?"

"They are." *So why do I feel a sense of foreboding about their wedding?*

She stomped her clogs. "Whoa. Look how worn down the floor is."

Maybe that's the reason.

Alma shot her a hawkish look. "Millions of tourists' plodding feet have thinned the old stone."

My stomach nosedived at the revelation. Seeing the bridge from the water below was looking like the better option.

Veronica waved me over. "Come look, Franki. There's a gondola on the canal below, and the island of San Giorgio Maggiore is in the distance."

I sighed as though I were a prisoner going to my cell and stepped onto the bridge. The floor, uneven under my feet, caused my stomach to list like a boat in choppy water. But under Alma's commander gaze, I forged ahead and completed my mission. The window was covered with bars and decorative grilles, so I had to squint to see through an opening. I looked at the water several stories below and imagined Bradley and me in a gondola.

With a candle-adorned coffin floating behind it.

I closed my eyes to erase the image, but the woman in white appeared. *Who was she? And was she supposed to be Tosca's ghost?*

Shona bumped into me, and my stomach threatened to capsize. She peered through the glass. "Legend has it that if a man and woman kiss in a gondola under the bridge, their love will last forever."

I gave a lovelorn sigh. "Yeah, I'd planned to do that with my fiancé, but I'm not sure when, or if, he'll get here."

She took my hand.

I rolled my eyes but let her have the moment. It steadied my vertigo, and she *was* using my fiancé's ticket.

Veronica came up behind us and gazed out of the window. "Just think how awful it must've been to see this stunning view before being locked in a cell. Worse than the torture chamber."

I rubbed my unbroken shoulder, unconvinced. "I wonder whether anyone besides Casanova ever escaped from here."

Dirk strolled up, still holding his wallet after tipping Alma. "I don't know of any prisoners, but an international jewel thief network known as the Pink Panthers made off with earrings and a brooch from an exhibit on loan from Qatar's royal family."

Veronica slipped her arm through his. "Dirk's a gemologist, so he follows these things."

"Good to know." Shona nodded, filing away that information in her brain database. "And when did this happen?"

Dirk slipped his wallet into his back pocket. "Around 2018, I believe."

I hadn't heard about the crime. "That recently? Jewel heists sound so 1960s."

"They're very current, unfortunately. In fact, I read in the paper this morning that there was a jewel heist here in Venice last night, and the worst possible kind."

"What do you mean?"

His brow wrinkled. "A grave was broken into at the San Michele cemetery, and authorities believe they stole a necklace."

My head swam as though it had filled with canal water, and the flaming coffin floated front and center.

3

"See you in the restaurant in an hour." Veronica wiggled her fingers in a wave and slipped inside the Hotel San Marco's bridal suite on the second floor.

My stomach growled like the winged lion of Venice as I headed down the opulent white-and-gold silk-covered hallway. The croissant I'd eaten at the Caffè Florian had long ago gone to its grave in the pit of my stomach.

The grave.

It could've been the hunger, but a nagging in my gut told me to check the local paper for news about the jewel theft at the San Michele cemetery. As I approached my room at the end of the hall, a twentyish redhead in a crisp maid's uniform rounded the corner and picked up the copy of *Il Gazzettino* I'd left untouched outside my door.

I raised my hand. "I'd like to keep that, please."

She dropped the newspaper, her eyes wide as though I'd caught her stealing, and scurried away.

Bewildered, I picked up the paper. *The hotel must prohibit staff from fraternizing with guests.*

I inserted my key card into the door and entered the lavish

room, paid for courtesy of Veronica's parents, who were sparing no expense for their only daughter's wedding. Four-foot bronze cherubs stood on either side of aqua-and-gold damask curtains that framed glass doors leading to a balcony overlooking the Grand Canal, and from the red-and-gold bathroom on the corner of the building, the domes of Basilica San Marco were visible. A Murano glass floral chandelier hung over a sumptuous king-sized bed adorned with an aqua silk comforter and accent pillows in the same shade of gold as the antique sofa.

The only sour note was a painting over the bed of a frowning bearded man in a spotted fur cloak and the horn-like bonnet of a doge. But given that my ex-stripper landlady had furnished my New Orleans apartment like an old French brothel, a dour doge was a detail I could live with.

Glad to be free of Shouting Shona and the torture tour, I pulled off my wool coat, flopped backward on the bed, and stared at the plastered ceiling. Unlike Veronica and Dirk, who were staying in separate rooms until the wedding, I'd hoped to share mine with Bradley—until my family arrived, and he moved to his room. Even though my parents had a suite with Nonna, the mere idea of him in my room would go over as well as me wearing one of Glenda's stripper costumes to my wedding.

I sat straight up. "That was a random and terrifying thought."

My gaze landed on the front page of *Il Gazzettino*. The San Michele cemetery grave robbery was the lead story. The lid had been pried from the tomb of the Duchess Genevieve Magritte Von Leipold of Austria, who'd been buried in 1782 at the age of fifty-seven. She wasn't a child, but I still thought it was weird that I'd seen a coffin of any size the same night someone had desecrated her grave.

Authorities expressed concern that additional graves would be targeted, such as that of Catherine Bagration neé Skavronskaya, a Russian princess who had inherited a jewelry collection that included the "Potemkin Diamond," which she sold to Napoleon, and Jean Michel Schlumberger, a French designer for Tiffany & Co. who once counted Elizabeth Taylor, Audrey Hepburn, and Jaqueline Kennedy among his clients.

"Nice of the paper to flag their graves for the thieves." I turned the page to the second part of the article and discovered an interesting detail. According to local lore, Duchess Von Leipold had been buried in a gold sphere necklace covered in precious gems. It reminded me of the gold ball that one of the men at the Caffè Florian table had mentioned.

I picked up my phone and googled *palla d'oro*, but the only reference I found was to a pizzeria in Brazil.

The theme from *Jaws* erupted from the device, and I dropped it on the water-colored silk. My mother was calling from Houston. She and my nonna were upset that Bradley and I had decided to wait until after Veronica and Dirk got married to plan our wedding. The ringtone was appropriate given that the second they arrived in the "City of Water," they'd stalk us like sharks on the hunt, trying to force us to set a date.

With a Bridge of Sighs-sized exhale, I tapped Answer. "Hi, Mom."

"Francesca? It's your mother, dear."

I held the phone from my ear. Her voice was shrill, even on an overseas call. "As I said, 'Hi, Mom.' What's up?"

"I was calling to remind you that our flight arrives at noon on Wednesday." She paused. "But is everything okay between you and Bradley? You sound down."

She smelled blood. I had to keep my pitch steady. "I'm waiting to sample Veronica's reception meal, so I'm just hungry."

"Are you and Bradley getting any alone time, dear? Venice *is* a City of Love."

The obvious course of action was to lie, but if my family

arrived in La Serenissima before my fiancé did, all inferno
would break loose. The only thing to do was shift the focus. "Yes,
it *is*. Casanova and all."

"Well? What have the two of you done so far?"

I covered my chest with a pillow. She was circling her prey.
"Nothing, really—"

"Why the hell-a not?" My nonna, who habitually lurked on
the other line in my parents' house, attacked first.

"Francesca Lucia Amato," my mom bit out. "What are you
not telling us?"

I pulled my legs to my chest as though I was in an aqua silk
ocean on a raft surrounded by sharks. "Actually, there was a
problem with his flight, so—"

"He's not coming to the wedding?" Her shrill had escalated
to screech.

"I'll-a bet his-a mamma make-a him stay in-a Boston for
Christ-a-mas!"

My wounded body drifted down the aqua bedspread. The
feeding frenzy was underway.

"That Lilian Hartmann *is* a society snob," my mother hissed.
"After we made it clear that the traditional Hartmann wedding
in Boston was out of the question, she probably convinced
Bradley to call off the engagement!"

"*Madonna mia!*" Nonna wailed. "*Franki è condannata allo zitellaggio perenne!*"

A Shona-style bellow built in my lungs. Nonna had been
calling me a *zitella* for half my thirty-two years, and it struck an
artery every time. "Bradley did not call off the engagement, so I
am not condemned to perennial spinsterhood. He's just caught
in a Boston snowstorm."

"Well." My mother huffed. "There's no need to shout,
Francesca."

"She take-a after the Pavans, Brenda."

"I beg your pardon, Carmela. She takes after the Amatos, her father in particular."

"My sonny, he is a *santo!*"

"I've been married to your beloved sonny for thirty-five years, and I can tell you that the man is most definitely not a saint. Did you know that he—"

"Mom," I interrupted before she said something that permanently scarred me, "today I overheard someone say 'la pavan.' Does your maiden name mean something?"

"Yes, dear." She shifted from peeved to pleased as if she had a split personality, which would've explained a lot. "The *pavan* was an aristocratic processional dance from the sixteenth and seventeenth centuries, so I've always suspected that I have nobility in my bloodline."

Nonna gave a dry cackle. "And I'm-a the pope's-a sister! *Pavan* is-a from *padovano*, Franki."

"So, a person from the town of Padova, here in the Veneto region."

"*Sì.* It also mean some-a-one who put-a *birds* in-a ragù, instead of pork and-a veal like a normal Italian."

"That's nonsense, Carmela, and you know it."

I thought of my feathered frenemies from the piazza, and my lips wrinkled. "Yuck, Mom. Y'all don't use pigeons, do you?"

"She's talking about chicken and duck, Francesca. And at least we put the *birds* in the sauce and not their food, as the Sicilians do."

"Bird-a food-a?" Nonna shouted. "What are you talkin' about?"

The sharks were turning on one another.

"You people put *peas* in your ragù. Talk about weird."

"Birds eat-a worms, not-a peas, and you people eat-a the worm soup."

"Wait." My abs tensed, steeling my stomach against nause-ating news. "What's she talking about, Mom?"

"It's not actual worms, Francesca. The soup is called *biscia*, the Venetian word for worm, because of the pasta's shape."

My abs relaxed.

"But birds also eat fish, and Sicilians eat tuna hearts and sperm sacs."

I hunched over like I'd been gored in the gut and hung up. As Veronica's maid of honor, I had to protect my appetite for the reception food, and given my shark analogy, the shift to consuming fish parts was unsettling—and gross.

The display showed a missed text from Bradley.

All flights from Boston still canceled. Going back to bed. I'll be in touch when I know something more. Love, B

"Ugh." I hung my head off the side of the bed. "Casanova was wrong. Marriage isn't the tomb of love. *Venice* is."

I sat up. Since I'd arrived in the city, I'd seen a steady stream of tombs, caskets, and even a coffin. *What's going on with that?*

I grabbed my phone and typed "Venice coffin legend" into my browser. The second link was to a blog about local ghost stories.

My chest tightened as I began to read.

On a foggy night on November 29, 1904, a water bus known as a vaporetto collided with a gondola outside the San Michele cemetery, resulting in the drowning of several passengers. All the victims were recovered, except for a little girl named Giuseppina Gabriel Carmelo. In the years since her death, locals claim that on foggy nights a small coffin appears with a lit candle on each of its four corners. It's believed to be Giuseppina, lighting the way for boats to prevent another tragedy.

The phone dropped onto the bed. I didn't buy the legend for a second, but one thing was certain. Something dark was going on in Venice.

And I was caught up in it.

~

"ONE MOMENT, MADAME." Caterina, the twenty-something hotel reception clerk who studied an English textbook when she wasn't assisting clients, smiled at me and returned her gaze to a group of Germans checking out.

I leaned against the marble counter and scanned the lobby, a stunning room with chandeliers hanging from frescoed ceilings, candelabra sconces, and modern sofas in white leather with rows of pillows. If the gold-framed Rubelli silk wall coverings had been replaced with mirrors, the lobby would have looked like the Hall of Mirrors at Versailles down to the parquet floor. But I wasn't interested in the décor. I was on the lookout for Shona, who seemed to keep showing up.

My attention turned to a display of brochures advertising things to do in Venice, and one caught my eye. The Foodunnit Culinary Mystery Tours.

What were the odds?

I flipped through the advert. Sure enough, it was the food tourism company owned by Midge and Madge Maven, the British spinster sisters I'd met in Sardinia over the summer who dressed and behaved like they were trying to be Miss Marple for Halloween. They offered a tour of Venice's *bàcari*, local bars that sold wine and tapas called *cicchetti*, in a traditional boat called a *batela*. In addition to food and drink, participants received a rowing lesson and solved a food-themed mystery. Because the batela was a standing rowboat, with one person at the bow and the other on the stern, it would be a fun thing to do with Bradley. "I just hope Shona and the Screamer Scullers don't know about this."

"Pardon, madame?"

I looked up. Caterina was alone at the counter. "Oh, sorry." I pocketed the brochure. "I have a question about local customs."

Her bright black eyes awaited expectantly.

"Do Venetians dress in costume any other time besides *Carnivale* in February?"

"Also for party or special occasion. But tourists wear all the year to capture the experience of the Carnival."

The same was almost true of New Orleans, except that masks were legal only on Mardi Gras day, and even then they had to be removed at 6:00 p.m.

She reached for a sticky note. "You would like to visit a costume shop?"

"Yes, Ms. Maggio's rehearsal dinner is masked. Which do you recommend?"

"Near the Rialto Bridge is *La Bottega dei Mascareri*, which mean 'the shop of the mask makers.' There is also the Casanova Mask Artisan Workshop."

Of course there is.

Gaspare, the manager, emerged from a door behind the counter in an expensive gray suit that complemented his hair and neatly trimmed beard. He lowered his glasses. "Have you been help-ed, *signorina*?"

I resisted the urge to grin at his somewhat stereotypical pronunciation of the *-ed* ending of past tense verbs. "Yes, but I wanted to ask about a woman's costume I saw last night near the Rialto Bridge. She had wavy blonde hair like you'd see in a Renaissance painting, a white mask, and a flowing white gown with lace gloves."

His lower lip protruded. "That could be any costume. Do you have-ed more informations?"

"Well, she was wringing her hands and looking for something."

"Ah." Caterina tucked long black hair behind an ear. "The woman was costumed as Tosca. She lose her finger."

"Lose-ed," Gaspare *in*corrected.

"Possibly." I chewed my lip as I chewed on whether to spit out the rest of the story. *Might as well.* "But I saw her later, and she was pointing at a coffin in the canal with lit candles on each corner."

Caterina's eyes sidelined to Gaspare. He stood as still as a marble column, but air escaped his mouth like a tire going flat.

I cleared my throat. "This will sound crazy, but I was wondering whether the woman had anything to do with the little girl who drowned near the San Michele cemetery. Have either of you heard about that?"

He stretched his neck and tugged at his collar. "Indeed, signorina. But the two cannot be related, as the coffin is merely a legend."

Except that I saw it flaming in the canal.

My phone rang. *Private Chicks.* Veronica had left our two college-student employees, David and Standish, aka The Vassal, in charge of the agency. And for them to call meant that we either had a new case or a problem. I glanced at the dumbstruck duo behind the counter. "Thanks for your help."

I left the noisy lobby and walked down a side hallway. "Hey. Everything okay?"

"Not really, since I'm sitting behind this reception desk while you're living it up in The Floating City."

The dry voice was a blast from the past that literally knocked me against the wall, and gravity pulled my body, as though I was one of the piles holding up Venice, sinking into the silt at the bottom of the lagoon. "What are you doing behind that desk, Ruth?"

"Working. What else would I be doing?"

My mind dredged up an image of the fun meter badge she'd

made me wear on a steamboat case I'd investigated, and its pointer, which went from Max to Med to Min, had dropped into unmarked territory—Mis for Miserable. "Uh, not at Private Chicks."

"You owe me a job."

I grit my teeth. "I already got you *two* jobs."

"And you cost me both of them, missy."

Ruth's tone was tighter than her signature bun, and either the chains on her black horn-rimmed glasses were clacking, or it was the folds of her turkey neck. She'd never gotten over losing her admin position when Bradley resigned from Pontchartrain Bank to spend more time with me, but Veronica and I had helped her get another job on the Steamboat Galliano. "What happened to the cruise director gig?"

"Captain Vandergrift and I had grown quite fond of one another until he found out that I knew your winepress was stashed on board and booted me off the boat."

I couldn't blame the guy. The winepress that my nonna's friend Luigi Pescatore had given me used to belong to a New Orleans mobster's father, and said mobster, a spats-wearing Al Capone wannabe named Gigi Scalino, wanted it back.

"I not only lost my job, I lost my honey, my home, and the chance to find the Civil War gold hidden on that broken-down old barge."

My back slid down the white-and-gold silk-covered wall, and I imagined myself in lagoon silt to my waist. Ruth lived in the warped Wapner world of Court TV, and there was no telling what kind of justice she'd exact from me.

Ice clinked in a glass followed by a pouring sound. "I'm looking for an attorney to sue that old coot. In the meantime, I'm shacking up at Private Chicks."

"You're *living* there *too*?" I shrieked, and an elderly couple coming up the hallway appeared appalled at my lack of decorum.

"Believe me, I share your horror. This place is a dump, but it's slightly more livable now that I've moved a bed into your office."

I slid-sank into silt up to my chin.

"But far be it from me to discuss my personal life at work." She slurped what was no doubt booze she'd claim was an innocent herbal concoction. "Anyhoo, a man with an Italian accent as thick as ricotta cheese called and asked about you. He wouldn't leave a name, but based on the number, the call came from Venice."

"What did he want to know?"

"Whether you worked here as a PI."

That didn't sound right. "What did you tell him?"

"I said you did and told him where you were staying."

At last I emerged from the silt. "If Veronica *had* hired you, which she *didn't*, giving out my personal information would've gotten you fired."

"Last time I checked—every drawer in this agency—there was no policy manual. Besides, Veronica'll keep me on out of guilt for not inviting me to her wedding."

"Why would she feel guilty for that? You're not friends."

"Because she's jealous that you threw her over for me."

I snort-laughed. "I most certainly did—"

"Of course you did. The hard truth is, I couldn't afford to make the once-in-a-lifetime trip, anyway, since you cost me my job. But listen, the movers are here with the rest of my bedroom furniture, so I'll let you go."

The line went dead, and my head hit the wall. *Would she ever really let me go?*

A door opened at the end of the hall. The maid I'd scared

earlier was exiting the hotel via the jetty entrance in black street clothes.

Gripping my phone, I stormed into the restaurant and through the doors to a terrace on the Grand Canal.

Veronica waved from a corner table, the picture of happiness and tranquility. The sunshine radiated off her blonde hair, and her eyes were as sparkling blue as the water.

Spitting mad, I marched to her chair. "R...r...r..."

She glanced at the canal. "Do you want to ride on a motorboat? Is that what you're saying?"

I shook my head and tried again. "*Rrrrruth*," I ground out. "She invaded our office and made herself our receptionist. Not only that, she's using my office as her bedroom."

Veronica shook her head. "She's quite the piece of work."

"And that piece of work is working at Private Chicks." I flopped into a cushioned chair and tossed my phone on the table. "God knows what she's done with David and The Vassal. She probably tied them up somewhere." My fingers squeezed the arms of the chair. "And she'd better have, or they're gonna catch hell for not giving me a heads-up that the horn-rimmed-glasses-wearing horror has horned in on our office."

Veronica breathed in the sea air. "Franki, we're in Venice on the Grand Canal waiting to be served my reception meal by a Michelin-starred chef. Let's embrace this splendor and worry about Ruth when we get back."

I waved my hand in front of her. "Snap out of the bridal bliss, Veronica. We have to worry about her now. Ruth is like an infestation of rats with fleas carrying the Black Death. If we don't exterminate her from the building, we could end up in that crypt at the Church of Murders, instead of the altar."

Her lips curved into a smile as she pushed an Aperol spritz toward me. "I wondered how long it would take you to find out the church's nickname."

"You knew, and you didn't tell me?"

"Because I figured you'd get all superstitious and take it as a sign of your untimely demise."

"That's called logic, not superstition." I took a slug of my drink and, out of her line of vision, flashed the *scongiuri*, an upside-down horn gesture to ward off bad luck. Because in the Italian culture, mentioning my untimely demise was sure to cause it, as was having Ruth live in my office.

She plucked a piece of fig wrapped in prosciutto from an appetizer plate. "Anyway, Dirk and I didn't want to get married at the Basilica San Marco. We wanted someplace more original, and we like the intrigue of the church's history."

"Well, I'm not going to lie. It's creepy, and so is that priest with the haunted voice."

She chuckled. "He *does* sound like he sings Gregorian chants."

"More like spooky Halloween songs."

Veronica slipped on a pair of blue sunglasses. "He's just eccentric. By the way, he's the one who suggested Iona Parsons for our reception food."

I lost my lion appetite. "She sounds English."

"Very."

"What's she doing in Italy?"

"I asked her that. Her mother was from a noble Venetian family, but they apparently lost their wealth. You know how that goes."

I didn't. My family owned a deli, which made us neither royal nor rich. "So, what's she making us?"

"It's what she's making *you*. Dirk and I had it a couple of days ago. She earned her Michelin star for her *risotto alle rose*."

"Rice with *roses*?"

"Yes, with white wine and Parmigiano-Reggiano cheese. And when I told her that our bouquets are violets and your maid-of-honor dress was the same shade, she suggested we serve a variation of the dish, *risotto alle violette*."

Normally, I was against mixing my foods with my flowers, but I was all for the wine and cheese. I leaned back in my chair and scrutinized a quad scull boat coming down the canal to make sure Shona wasn't on it.

Veronica glanced at her phone. "Before I forget, Glenda will be here later today. She's arriving from Barcelona. Can you believe it?"

I couldn't. There was no logic to explain how my ex-stripper landlady's memoirs, *Like a Polecat at a Garden Party*, together with a social influencer campaign, had led to a European book tour.

"And she's bringing a mystery date to the wedding."

"Why is he a mystery?"

She shrugged. "She wants him to be a surprise, and I can't wait to see who it is. Glenda has met so many interesting men on her travels—a Spanish flamenco guitarist, a French winemaker, an Austrian duke."

I sipped some spritz. In the three years that Veronica and I lived in the downstairs apartments of Glenda O'Brien's fourplex, I'd seen a string of her dates. And there was no telling what the polecat would drag in.

"Oh." Veronica moved her appetizer plate. "Here comes the chef."

A small, busty woman in a white chef's uniform and hat that obscured her hair crossed the terrace with a tray balanced on one hand. She arrived at our table and placed the dish before me—rice in a pale purplish sauce with fresh violets on top.

I looked up, expecting her to say something about the food, or at least introduce herself, but she erupted in a coughing fit. Dismayed, I stared at my plate. Not only did it have flowers, it probably had phlegm flecks too.

Veronica removed her sunglasses. "Iona, are you all right?"

She wasn't. Her scrubbed skin had blanched to match her outfit, but her lips and tongue were purple. She hacked and held out a hand.

I stood and picked up my water glass. "Here. Sip this."

Her face contorted.

My brow was indignant. I hadn't drunk any, and even if I had, my germs were no worse than her phlegm.

Iona's coughing grew more labored, and her lips and tongue were purple. She opened her mouth wide, gasping for air, and the inside of her mouth was strangely brown. Still coughing, she backed into the railing.

And she went over.

Veronica screamed, and I catapulted over the terrace and almost took out a family of ducks as I plunged into the canal. I surfaced, already shivering, and swam toward the chef. The icy water shocked my system, as did the cold fear undulating along my spine. Too many signs had foretold a watery doom—the flooded crypt, the drowned *Death in Venice* book, and the floating coffin. *But doom for whom?*

Iona?

Or me?

Treading water, I flipped the chef onto her back and got my answer.

Because Iona Parsons was dead in the water—literally.

4

"*H*eave!" a voice boomed as strong hands pulled me from the water.

"Ho!"

"Ho!"

"Ho!"

A trio shouted in succession.

"*Heave!*"

"Ho!"

"Ho!"

"Ho!"

Was I being rescued by a sailor Santa and three of his helpers?

The hands draped me across the bow of a boat on my back, and my rescuers came into sharp focus—Shona Helper and the other Screamer Scullers. *I knew that librarian was lurking.*

My legs dangled over the side, and my teeth chattered so badly, I was afraid I'd vibrate back into the water. Carefully, I rose on my elbows and watched Shona and one of the Scullers use an oar to fish Iona Parsons from the canal and hoist her limp body toward the deck. "W-w-won't that b-b-break?"

Shona pshawed. "The cleaver is designed to bear a lot of weight."

"The *c-c-cleaver*?"

"That's the style of the oar, because it's shaped like a meat cleaver."

An awful name considering the circumstances—and the chef.

Gaspare, Veronica, and Caterina took Iona and lay her on tablecloths they'd spread on the deck.

Shona took a seat at the bow and slid forward, pushing the oars. "Hang tight, Franki. We're taking you in."

I gripped the edge of the boat with half-frozen fingers and saw Iona's white chef hat floating on the water like a coffin. A *Heave!* beckoned to the bile in my stomach, and each Ho! Ho! Ho! hammered home the horror I'd seen.

The boat docked at the private jetty on the side of the hotel. A burly valet helped me from the bow, and Shona hopped from the boat. We ran to the lobby, where Caterina met me with a plush hotel robe. "I call the ambulance."

"*Grazie mille.*" I slipped on the robe and followed Shona through the restaurant to the terrace.

Veronica stood with arms crossed, pressing a cloth napkin to her mouth and watching a woman in a white lab coat pump Iona's chest while Gaspare looked on.

Still shaking, I slipped my arm around my best friend's waist, and an arm slid around mine—Shona's. "Is that woman a doctor, I hope?"

Veronica removed the napkin. "A dermatologist from the hotel spa."

The dermatologist stopped pumping and said something to Gaspare, who gasped and crossed himself. Then she pulled a tablecloth from a nearby table and covered Iona Parsons.

Veronica faltered, and Shona and I swooped in to hold her up.

"I've got her." Dirk appeared like a superhero and scooped up his bride-to-be like a groom about to cross a threshold. He carried her from the restaurant.

"Poor Veronica," Shona breathed.

I thought about going after her, but it was best to give her and Dirk some space. "Yeah. And poor Iona."

"How'd she fall into the canal?"

"She had a coughing fit and backed into the rail."

"Oh, geez. She must've hit her head and drowned."

"Maybe." I walked to the railing and looked at the water. There weren't any rocks below, which was why I hadn't been able to get traction to lift Iona from the canal. But she could have hit her head on the base of the terrace as she fell. Still, drowning took time, forty seconds by some estimates, and I'd pulled her face from the water in less than half that.

The dermatologist was on a cell phone, so I approached Gaspare, who had removed his glasses to rub his eyes. "I'm a private investigator. Would it be all right if I look around the kitchen?"

Air exited his mouth but no words came with it.

A common reaction to the implication that a crime had been committed. "Chef Parsons was cooking for my best friend's wedding. For both of their sakes, I'd like to rule out foul play."

He sucked in his breath and slipped on his glasses. "This is not an American movie, signorina. The staff all go home, after the lunch, so the chef was alone in the kitchen. There was no one to harm her."

"Okay, but she was a young woman, and she coughed uncontrollably before she fell over the rail. It's important to find the cause."

Shona puffed up her puffer-coated chest and narrowed her eyes. "Unless you've got something to hide?"

"Certainly not." Gaspare straightened his gray necktie, but perspiration beaded on his forehead. "And there is no need to shout."

She raised her palms. "Who's shouting?"

The loud librarian might have research skills, but her perceptive abilities were sorely lacking. "Did you see anyone enter or exit the kitchen? Or hear anything unusual?"

"No, but Caterina and I do not have-ed a view of the restaurant from the lobby."

True. So anyone could have passed through unobserved.

Shona glanced at Iona's covered corpse. "Did the chef have any medical conditions?"

His lower lip protruded. "*Sano come un pesce.* Healthy as a fish."

She jerked a thumb at him. "We got ourselves a wise guy, Franki. After the woman dies in a canal, he calls her a fish instead of a horse."

I cleared my throat. "It's a common Italian saying."

"Oh." She flashed her dimples.

Gaspare grabbed a cloth napkin from a table and dabbed his face. He'd begun sweating so profusely that he almost looked like he'd fallen into the canal. "The chef is a celebrity in Venezia. You must be discreet or the hotel could be ruin-ed."

"Obviously," Shona shouted.

My eyes met Gaspare's in a moment of pained understanding. "I'll need a hair net, gloves, and shoe covers, if you've got them."

"Me too." Shona grinned. "Petite."

I looked at her as Gaspare set off for the supplies. "It's best if you leave the investigation to a professional."

"Don't worry. I read the library copy of *The Complete Idiot's Guide to Private Investigating* from cover to cover."

"Now I feel better." I should've given Shona the old heave-ho-ho-ho, but she'd come to my rescue and helped with Iona. Frazzled, I sat at the table I'd shared with Veronica. Her purse hung from her chair, and my phone was beside my untouched plate of violet risotto. I would never eat it now, not even at the reception—if the wedding was still going to take place.

I gazed at the lifeless figure under the tablecloth, and I thought of the white-robed corpses in the gold-and-glass caskets. *Was I right about dark forces in Venice? Or was Iona's death a tragic coincidence?*

Gaspare returned with the supplies, and Shona and I suited up. "Does Iona have family in Venice?"

He *tch*'d, an Italian sound for *no*.

"My friend Veronica mentioned a mother."

"Decease-ed. She have no one."

Shona shoved her stringy locks into the hairnet. "She must've had friends on the hotel staff, or a boyfriend. I'm friends with everyone I work with, but I'm still on the hunt for a man."

Gaspare frowned. "Chef Parsons was a professional. She did not give confidences."

Shona turned to me. "Is that another Italian expression?"

"Yes, in Italy they're not as quick to confide in people as you —I mean, we—are. Now, let's stop gabbing and get to work."

I stood and entered the restaurant. We passed an open supply closet with black uniforms and packages of gloves and hairnets and went through a door marked *Cucina*.

The kitchen was a sea of white tile and stainless steel. I headed for the stove on the back wall but kept my distance to avoid disturbing the crime scene. The risotto pan was still on a burner, as was a pot of what looked and smelled like vegetable broth. On the island across from the stove were the remaining ingredients for the dish—rice, scallions, Parmigiano-Reggiano, and a container of fresh violets. There was also a small bowl with remnants of the purplish risotto. I took a sniff, but it smelled of the cheese. I glanced in the trash, which only contained the roots of the scallions. "Nothing seems out of the ordinary."

Shona's eyes popped. "Aren't you going to dust for finger-prints or footprints?"

Great. A CSI wannabe. "I didn't bring my dusting kit to Italy."

"You can use clear tape and cornstarch or cocoa powder. They must have both in here somewhere."

My smile was wan. "Why don't we leave that for the police?"

"Suuure. If you want *them* to get the credit."

Apparently, Shona had glossed over the *Idiot's Guide* chapter on tampering with a crime scene. *But is that what this is? Or is Iona's death simply a terrible accident?*

Gaspare appeared in the doorway. "Everyting is in order, no?"

I took another look around. "I believe so, but I could be missing something."

Shona raised a finger. "What happened to the grape Kool-Aid that made the chef's lips so purple?"

"Kool-Aid's not a thing in Italy, and even if it were, a Miche-lin-starred chef from England wouldn't drink it." I glanced around. "Red wine would do that or—" The sentence died on my lips, and my head jerked toward the violets.

Had Iona Parsons been poisoned by the flowers she'd served me for lunch?

～

"*La Dogaressa*?" Shona boomed over the motor of the vaporetto. "As in 'dog?'"

My grip tightened on the handrail of the waterbus. I hadn't been able to shake the loud librarian even after a lengthy shower —which had involved a surprising number of duck feathers. "No, as in 'the wife of a doge.' I've seen it translated as 'dogaress.'"

"Are you sure it isn't duchessa? Dogaressa is so unattractive."

Admittedly, the name didn't lend itself well to English. "Gaspare said Iona bought the violets for the risotto at La Dogaressa Flowers. She made a special trip earlier today because she wanted to get them from the same place Veronica ordered her wedding flowers, which makes sense. Michelin-starred chefs are meticulous about their ingredients."

"I don't know. The word is awfully ironic considering that female dogs are called bitches."

If anything was ironic, it was that I was being dogged over the word dogaressa by a woman who'd been hounding me since we'd met. "'Dog' is *cane* in Italian, so it doesn't apply."

"I hadn't thought about that."

For a resourceful librarian, Shona could be kind of daft.

The vaporetto glided toward the Rialto Bridge, and Shona pointed to a huge black banner above a restaurant awning with the sign *No Mafia Venezia è Sacra*. "What does that say?"

"No Mafia, Venice is sacred."

She clutched her romance tote and flashed wary eyes at the passengers standing around us. "I thought *Mafiosi* were only in Sicily."

My mind flashed to Gigi Scalino and the winepress he'd tried to claim before retiring to his native Palermo. "They're everywhere, unfortunately, and there are other organized crime groups like them."

"They deal mostly in drugs, right?"

"These days, yes. And the effects are devastating." *Addiction, death, Ruth Walker living in my office.*

We passed the entrance to the canal where I'd seen the flaming coffin. Had it held heroin or cocaine? The Mafia wasn't above such a low tactic, but it was also possible that the coffin had contained nothing at all—and certainly not the remains of the little girl who'd drowned in 1904.

I shuddered and buttoned my wool coat to my chin. I wasn't cold—just unnerved.

The vaporetto pulled up to the stop at the Rialto Market, and I was anxious to get off. Even though I was on a waterbus, I was still on the Grand Canal, a body of water I now associated with death.

We disembarked among throngs of tourists, and I glanced at the maps app on my phone. "It's almost six, so the market's closed. Let's cut through to escape the crowds."

Shona trotted behind me through the empty fruit and vegetable stalls, her short legs struggling to match my stride. "I don't know why you didn't let the Screamers take us in the quad scull. It fits in the narrow canals, so they could've dropped us off at the shop."

"We heave-ho-ho-hoed to the hotel jetty, and I'm not doing that again."

"Someone's a Scrooge McDuck."

"Is that a crack about the duck family I almost took out when I tried to save Iona?"

She pressed a mittened hand to her puffer-coated chest. "For your information, I take duck safety very seriously. It was a Christmas reference."

I turned down a dark, dank street. "I got that. But what does it have to do with rowing?"

"On December twenty-fourth, hundreds of gondoliers come down the Grand Canal dressed like Santa Claus. Since the Screamer Scullers are racing before them, the heave-ho-ho-ho represents our solidarity with the gondoliers and the spirit of the season."

"It just sounded like merry shouting to me."

"I think you've got a touch of holiday depression, which is understandable after what happened with Iona and your fiancé's flight. I can recommend a self-help book."

"I might take you up on that." I'd need one if she didn't stop tagging along.

The flower shop was on the corner of a building in the Campo San Cassiano, a tiny piazza with a small stone well in the center.

"Oooh!" Her exclamation bounced off building walls. "This is the site of the world's first public opera house."

I saw an old church and some shops, but nothing else. "Where is it?"

"Gone. The building was demolished in the nineteenth century after it went to pot. Casanova said it got so bad that prostitutes worked in the seat boxes during performances. By the way, if you haven't read his memoirs," she cocked her mouth to one side and winked, "they're a good substitute for an absent fiancé."

I should have guessed from her romance tote that Shona wasn't only a loud librarian, she was a lusty one too. Shame she hadn't learned anything from Italian reluctance to confide in people.

"You were right." She pointed to a glass storefront with La Dogaressa Flowers painted on the window.

I kept an 'I told you so' to myself for fear of know-it-all librarian backlash. "Before we go in, let's not mention what happened to Iona. We don't want the shop owners to think we're accusing them of poisoning her."

"Mum's the word." She giggled. "Get it?"

I sighed and opened the door.

A woman who looked like a 1970s Sophia Loren—wide cheekbones and mouth and eyes enhanced with huge glasses—beckoned for us to enter. She was on the phone behind the register, so Shona headed for the flower refrigerators.

I went to the counter and browsed a list of the shop's services—bouquets, wreaths, and something called the Pala d'Oro, the phrase I'd heard the trio at Caffè Florian mention. *Pala* was spelled with one *l* instead of two, which explained why I hadn't found it with my online search.

"Over here." Shona's bellow startled the woman, who juggled the phone and knocked her glasses askew.

I flashed a "sorry" smile and went to the cooler.

Shona opened the door to the cooler. "These are the violets Iona bought. The common blue variety, which isn't poisonous."

"They're in Veronica's and my bouquets, so I'd rather not take your word for it."

"Suit yourself." She raised her perky nose. "But in my library, I specialize in the gardening section."

What topic didn't she specialize in? "Then tell me whether the violets turned Iona's lips purple."

"I'll do better than that." She grabbed a handful and stuffed them in her mouth.

I gasped and grabbed her arm. "Are you crazy? Spit those out!"

"I'm showing you that the violets are safe to eat," she said between chews.

"The jury's still out on that." I glanced at the woman behind the counter, who was still on the phone. "And you could've just answered me with one of your many facts."

"No, because you're one of those silly skeptical types."

I resented the character assassination from a blooming idiot who ate potentially poisonous flowers. "FYI, I'm not paying for the violets."

"Thanks a lot, tightwad. This is your investigation, and I live on a librarian's salary." She swallowed and stuck out her pink tongue. "But no purple, right?"

Only my cheeks, which were probably purple with anger, because Shona was not only a thorn in my side, she was a spine in my behind. About to return to the counter, I stopped to look at a bouquet of roses with a bottle of wine in the center.

Shona gave a sonorous snort. "If you won't spring for a few violets, that's definitely out of your cheapskate price range."

The look I gave her was more toxic than an oleander.

She took a step back. "But the arrangement is a cool concept. It reminds me of that old expression 'the days of wine and roses.'"

It reminded me that white wine was in Iona's rose risotto. *Was it also in the risotto alle violette?* I pulled out my phone and texted the question to Veronica.

The sales clerk hung up. "I am Rosa. Please, how may I assist?"

I returned to the counter. "We came to ask you about some violets. But first, what is the Pala d'Oro?"

"We weave a tapestry of flowers. *Molto bella*. The name is in honor of the Golden Pall, an altar cloth at the Basilica di San Marco."

So that's what those people were talking about. "Does it come from Padova, by any chance?"

"No, signorina. It is here in Venezia."

Shona trotted over. "The Pala d'Oro hangs above the altar in a double-sided frame that rotates. It's a series of religious Byzantine enamel panels that have been decorated with gold and silver and jewels."

In that case, they'd better keep it under wraps. If the jewel thieves were willing to rob graves, they wouldn't think twice about looting a church.

Rosa picked up an ordering pad. "Would you like a tapestry of violets for a special event?"

"No, my friend has ordered flowers from you for her wedding, and this morning the chef at our hotel purchased some in the shop."

"Chef Parsons, *sì*. I remember. She wear a necklace—'Violet' in gold letters."

"That's weird. Her name is Iona."

"Perhaps it is the name of a child."

Shona lowered her chin. "My money's on a secret lover."

It would be. Iona didn't have any kids, so I didn't know what to make of the name. "Anyway, the violets are for a risotto dish for the reception, and I wanted to be sure they're safe to eat."

Rosa's enlarged eyes went on the defensive, and she clutched a crucifix necklace. "Of course they are safe. The root of the violet can cause the nausea and the vomiting, but for cooking we sell only the blossom."

Based on the container of violets in the kitchen, Iona hadn't eaten the roots, and she was coughing, not vomiting. Meanwhile, Shona was as fresh as a daisy after her bout with the violets, which made me think that the most likely explanation for Iona's death was a severe allergy that had caused her throat to swell.

My text tone dinged, and I glanced at Veronica's reply. *Iona used red wine, not white, in the risotto. The Valpolicella for my reception.*

Was that why her lips were purple?

But there was no Valpolicella on the island with the other ingredients, or next to the broth on the stove, or even in the trash. *Did Iona put the wine in a fridge or cabinet? Or had someone taken it?*

∽

"Pew!" Shona wrinkled her nose and sniffed her armpit. "I need a shower!"

My alarm increased like her over-sharing because she'd followed me into the rotating door to the Hotel San Marco. Letting her use Bradley's ticket to the Secret Itineraries tour was one thing, but using my shower was another. I waited for her to emerge into the lobby. "So, where are you and the Screamer Scullers staying?"

"I just realized that I didn't introduce you to them. Dena, Gena, and Lena."

The names fit since they'd all looked the same—rather plain, tall, and broad-shouldered. "Triplets?"

"What? They're not related."

That was mildly terrifying. There was something odd about the people from Screamer.

"They work at the library with me. We got into rowing because it builds our book-shelving muscles."

Made sense. The Scullers looked like librarians, albeit large ones. And librarians were known for their job dedication.

"Anyway, we all went in on a room together so we could stay at a fancy hotel." She gestured to the elevator. "We're on the third floor."

My head screamed *No No No*—followed by *Ho Ho Ho*.

"I'm gonna take the stairs." She patted a chubby thigh. "Good for the rowing muscles. If anything develops in the case, give me a shout."

It figured she'd use that expression. "I appreciate the offer, but I need to work this investigation alone."

"I won't hear of it. My last name's Helper, and that's what I do." She trotted down the hallway.

The woman took names way too literally.

"There you are, Miss Franki."

My sixty-something ex-stripper landlady's sultry voice

wafted across the lobby like smoke from her signature cigarette holder. I turned to see her exiting the elevator and imagined the strum of a Spanish guitar when I saw her red-and-black number. She wore a silk rose in her long platinum hair, castanets for pasties, and a choker with a fringe to her waist. In terms of the skirt, the rose-adorned ruffle was there, but she'd left the rest in Barcelona.

"I know what you're thinking about my look, sugar." She whipped open a black lace fan and stomped a flamenco shoe with a six-inch stripper heel. "It's an *olé!*"

Actually, it was an *oy vey*. And to back me up on that, Caterina at the reception desk had buried her face in her English textbook.

Glenda sauntered toward me with the controlled grace of a dancer about to break into a flurry of stomps. "It was a parting gift from Raúl Tango, the famous flamenco guitarist."

Sounded like Raúl had studied the wrong music.

"He begged me to stay in Spain with him." Her face took on a pained look that was as fake as her flower. "But I told him that I have a book signing here tomorrow night, and my fans need me as much as his need him. We give so much joy to the world."

Caterina lowered her textbook. "Like the Christmas song."

More like the Three Dog Night version. "That sounds rough, Glenda. But have you seen Veronica? I'm worried about her because—"

"I heard all about that poor chef, sugar. I just came from Miss Ronnie's room, and she's fine. She's calling it a night and wants to meet us for breakfast in the morning."

I hoped it wasn't in the hotel restaurant. I'd be dining elsewhere after what had happened to Iona.

A maid emerged from the hallway. "Ah, signorina." She pulled a small box from the pocket of her uniform and handed it to me. "I find at your door."

"Really?" I examined the red-and-green wrapping for a card, but there wasn't one. "You don't know who left it?"

She shook her head.

"Would you please ask the maid I saw earlier, the one with the red hair?"

Her face clouded, as though she didn't understand what I'd said.

Caterina looked up from a computer. "Pardon, madame. We do not have a maid with red hair."

"But I saw her at around two o'clock this afternoon in uniform."

Caterina recoiled. "It is very strange. I do not know what to say."

I didn't either. I couldn't fathom why anyone would pose as a maid unless they were up to something they shouldn't be.

Glenda fanned herself. "Maybe it's a gift from an admirer, sugar. Your own Casanova."

"My Casanova is stuck in Boston. It's probably a maid-of-honor gift from Veronica." But I couldn't quite believe that she would have left it in the hallway where it could be stolen. I unwrapped the package.

A porcelain lion's head box.

The lions' mouths that Shona had told me about roared in my mind—the ones that led the condemned to Death Alley. I opened the lid and found what I'd expected, a piece of paper similar to one in a fortune cookie.

"What did I tell you, Miss Franki? It's a love note."

I knew it wasn't. Nor was it an incriminating tip from an informant. I smoothed the paper.

Roses are red, violets are blue, the chef is dead, and so are you.

5

"**D**on't start with me, pal. I had a rough freakin' night."
I rose from my chair outside the Caffè Florian and
yanked off my coat to show I meant business.

The puffed-up pigeon ruffled his feathers and rejoined his
flock.

"That's more like it." I draped my coat on the back of the
chair and returned to my seat, but I kept my eye on the fierce
fowls. They seemed to be the same gang from the day before,
and I didn't want any trouble.

A text from Veronica appeared on my phone, letting me
know that Glenda was on her way to meet me, and she was right
behind her.

I gazed at the Basilica di San Marco and thought about the
jeweled altar cloth, the Pala d'Oro. From there, my mind went to
the jewel theft at the cemetery, the flaming coffin in the canal,
and Chef Iona Parsons, who'd gone to a watery grave like the
Death in Venice book. Then my gaze shifted to the two red
columns on the Palazzo Ducale loggia, and the threat in the
porcelain lion's head box came roaring.

The incidents didn't appear related. I couldn't connect jewel thieves to the chef, and the only person who would threaten me —besides Ruth Walker, of course—was the ex-Mafia don, Gigi Scalino. He'd recently sent me an ominous greeting during a short trip to Sicily, but he had supposedly retired from a life of crime, and I had no reason to suspect him of a hit on Iona.

There was one other person who wanted me dead. He, too, had fallen into a body of water, but unlike Iona, he hadn't resurfaced. At least, as far as I knew.

A shiver rose up my spine, like a body surfacing from the bottom of a canal. *Why do I have a sinking feeling that I'm out of my depth in Venice?*

Ambrosio, the waiter, arrived with the drinks. He didn't say a word, but his gaze was as steamy as the cappuccino I'd ordered for Veronica.

In reply, my gaze was as chilled as Glenda's champagne.

When he was gone, I shot my double espresso, hoping it would make up for a semi-sleepless night and looked at my phone. It was too early to call Bradley, so I turned my attention to his stand-in—Cioccolata Casanova. I swallowed a spoonful of the chocolate-mint aphrodisiac and closed my eyes to savor the sensual flavors.

"Giacomo Casanova, at your service."

My eyes bolted open.

A thirty-something male in pancake makeup and a white wig with a rolled curl above each ear bowed before me. As he rose, I took in the rest of his outfit, a red frock coat and waistcoat, a cream shirt with lace cuffs, and pink satin breeches. I didn't have to look at his feet to know they were clad in stockings and eighteenth-century man heels with bronze buckles.

Had I summoned him, or something?

"Adios, fiery flamenco guitarist. Ciao, legendary Latin Lover." The saucy, sultry voice of my landlady caught Casanova and me both by surprise.

He turned to face her and almost flipped his powdered, pony-tailed wig, and I understood why. Her sheer black trench revealed a Gucci outfit that curled my hair—GG pasties and for a thong the signature red-and-green stripe held aloft by horse bits.

He bowed. "*Enchanté, mademoiselle...?*"

"Call me your next conquest," Glenda drawled. She sat, crossed her bare legs, and held out her cigarette holder.

He produced a very un-eighteenth-century Bic and lit more than her cigarette. "You must sit inside, *cara mia*. The Caffè Florian was the first establishment in Venezia to permit the entry of women, so it has always been my favorite."

The owner must be paying him. "We're good in the piazza."

"Napoleon called it one of the world's most beautiful drawing rooms." His shifty eyes shifted to Glenda, who exhaled a smoke heart. "It will only become more beautiful with your presence."

Nope. I had to pay him. He was the Venetian version of the Roman centurions who hustled cash from tourists outside the Colosseum. I gave him five euros to get lost, and he took my hand. As he bowed and planted his full lips on my knuckles, his eyes met mine—not in a seductive stare, but in a studied one. I lowered my lids to let him know that the buck, or rather the euro, stopped there.

The cash-hungry Casanova gave a flourished farewell, turned on his brass-buckled heels, and went in search of his next victim—as had Glenda, who was practically champing at her horse bits to get the attention of our male-model waiter.

"My, my, my." A puff of smoke followed each of her extremely possessive pronouns. "Who is that long, tall drink of Italian water?"

I sipped my Cioccolata Casanova, which had cooled like my interest in the conversation. "Ambrosio."

"Like ambrosia, the nectar of the gods?"

I saw where this was going. "Uh-huh."

"I'll have to see about trading in this champagne for a glass of that sweet stuff." She slipped off her coat in an attempt to get the exchange underway—and she wasn't thinking drinks.

It was maybe fifty degrees out, but I didn't ask whether she was cold. Her skin was hardened, similar to weathered leather. "You know, the Gucci stripe is usually a decoration, and not a lone item of clothing."

"This is a cheap knockoff, sugar."

No kidding.

Veronica crossed the piazza. Her head was lowered, but she was as pale as her white belted wrap coat and scarf.

I couldn't read her expression as she took a seat. "How are you feeling?"

She untied her coat. "Still stunned about Iona, and now I'm worried about you. Glenda told Dirk and me about the threat this morning. What's going on in Venice?"

"I know, right? I just got here, so why am I a target?"

As if on cue, the top-dog pigeon rushed my chair, and I stomped my foot. He retreated but flapped his wings to let me know we weren't done.

Veronica emptied a sugar packet into her cappuccino. "That poem is proof Iona was murdered. Did you call the police?"

"I'm going to let Gaspare do that when he comes to work."

"Good, because I don't want you investigating this."

I hadn't expected that declaration. "A woman died right in front of us, and for some bizarre reason, my life was threatened because of it. How can I not investigate?"

"By leaving it to the authorities, Franki." Her pitch had risen to keep stride with her stress level. "I can't help you with this. I have guests arriving today, and now Dirk and I need to figure out what to do about the wedding."

"There's nothing to figure out. Iona's death doesn't have anything to do with you and Dirk, so you're getting married."

Glenda ashed her cigarette on the flagstone. "She's right, Miss Ronnie. You worry about your guests and getting hitched. I'll help Miss Franki investigate."

A pigeon pecked at the ashes and gave Glenda the stink-eye.

I did too. "I've worked plenty of murder cases," I half-huffed. "I think I can handle this. Besides, you'll be busy with your book signing."

"That's only going to take a few hours, then I can be available full time," Glenda licked her lips, "when I'm not kissing Casanova or embracing Ambrosio."

Apparently, the horse bits on her thong weren't there to rein her in.

Veronica touched Glenda's arm. "That would take a huge weight off my mind."

And place it squarely on my shoulders. The threatening note weighed on me, but not as much as the thought of both Shona and Glenda helping me to investigate in their respective snowman and birthday suits. Unfortunately, I had to grin and bear the burden because I didn't want to add to my BFF's stress.

Glenda swirled the champagne in her flute. "Why do you think the murderer threatened you, Miss Franki?"

"Evidently, I saw something I shouldn't have."

"It has to be the coffin with the candles that Miss Ronnie told me about."

"Probably. The woman in white looked me right in the face, but Ruth said an Italian man called Private Chicks to ask about me."

A crease on Veronica's brow deepened. "He could be the woman's accomplice. You need to call Ruth back and get more information."

"Not on your life—or mine, in this case. Ruth already gave

the caller the name of our hotel, and if she thinks he's out to get me, she's likely to wire him money to finish me off."

Veronica wrinkled her lips. "She wouldn't do any such thing."

"Oh, no? You're talking about a woman who threatens me every time she loses a job. If I thought she knew about Iona's murder, then I'd be inclined to believe she was the one who sent the threat in the porcelain lion box."

"She knows." Veronica pulled *The New York Times* from her purse and tossed it on the table. "Iona Parson's death is international news."

The front page image turned the cold Cioccolata Casanova in my belly into a two-pound bonbon. Shona and either Dena, Gena, or Lena were fishing Iona from the Grand Canal while I lay on the bow of the quad scull. "Who took that?"

Glenda took a deep drag. "The paparazzi hail from Italy, sugar."

I stood and shot a silent *scram* at the pigeons. "I need to find Gaspare."

Veronica looked up from her cup. "I hope it's to report the threat."

"I'm sorry, but I'm going to investigate Iona's death, and you don't need to worry. This won't be much different than working a case in New Orleans."

"That's exactly what I'm worried about."

She had a point. Solving crime in The Big Easy was really hard.

"Relax, Miss Ronnie. I'll go with her." Glenda moved to stand, and her horse bits jangled.

"No!" The last thing I wanted was horse and human bits jangling and dangling while I questioned Gaspare. "You stay and get your Ambrosio. I'm just going to ask about the bottle of wine

Iona used in the risotto. After my visit to the flower shop, I'm positive the violets didn't cause Iona's purple lips."

Veronica leaned forward, her cheeks had paled. "What are you saying? That the Valpolicella for my wedding was poisoned?"

I returned to my seat. "Only the bottle Iona used."

"But Dirk and I ate the risotto, and it didn't turn our lips purple."

"Iona made yours days ago. Mine was a fresh batch."

She loosened the scarf at her neck. "This is all so unreal. Iona substituted the roses in her risotto recipe for violets, and the threat uses that old 'Roses Are Red' children's poem. I hate to think that this is happening because of me."

I squeezed her hand. "You're no more connected to this than violets are blue."

Glenda raised her flute. "Did either of you see anything strange at the hotel?"

I nodded. "The redheaded maid impostor you heard me ask the legitimate maid about. She was outside my suite yesterday, trying to take my newspaper."

"What would she want with an awful thing like the news, Miss Franki?"

"Good question. I saw her again later when I went to meet Veronica in the restaurant. She was going out the side door to the jetty in black—" A realization struck me like a cleaver oar.

Veronica straightened. "What is it?"

"She was wearing a kitchen uniform."

"Are you sure?"

"Yes, I thought it was street clothes. I didn't make the connection earlier because Iona wore that white chef outfit. But when Shona and I went to inspect the kitchen, I saw black uniforms in the restaurant supply closet that were the same as the one the redhead was wearing."

Glenda put out her cigarette in her glass, and it sizzled. "You know what that means, sugar."

I did. The impostor maid outside of my hotel room might have been the killer.

"YOU WERE THREATEN-ED? With a note in a lion head?" Beads of perspiration hid behind the whiskers of Gaspare's mustache as though they were scared, and his wide eyes locked onto mine through his lenses. "Do you have-ed enemies in Venice, signorina?"

The pigeons, but I doubted they were behind this. "The only person I can think of is the blonde in the Tosca costume I saw on the bridge."

Air rattled from his lungs like breath from a dying body. "But this does not make-ed sense."

"You're telling me." I leaned against the reception counter. "I came here to witness a marriage, not a murder."

"*Sss!*" He waved his arms and scanned the lobby. "Frightening the guests is a violation of the Hotel San Marco policies."

And slapping an *-ed* on every verb was a violation of English speakers' policies, but you didn't hear me sss-ing him. "What happened to Chef Parsons is in newspapers around the world, so you can blame reporters for scaring the guests."

He stiffened and adjusted his tie in an act of composure, but he had sweat stains under his arms the size of the Venetian lagoon.

"Now, where did Chef Parsons put the Valpolicella that she used to make the violet risotto?"

"As I tell-ed the inspector, the bottle has disappear-ed."

My suspicion about the wine being poisoned moved toward confirmation. "Where did the hotel buy the wine?"

"Chef Parsons was the kitchen manager. She purchase-ed the ingredients." He sucked in a breath. "However, I did not find-ed the receipt for the Valpolicella among her records."

"The wine receipt was the only one missing?"

"Sì."

That was more than odd. In Italy, it's illegal not to provide a receipt at the time of purchase. "What about the kitchen staff? Do they know where she bought it?"

He pulled a handkerchief from his suit jacket and dabbed his cheek. "They do not."

The wine was definitely the murder weapon. *But what was in it?*

My phone rang. *Bradley* was on the display, and relief welled in my chest. I needed him, and Gaspare needed time to recover. Not only had his mustache sweat come out of hiding, his lenses had fogged. "I've got to take this. But do me a favor and let the police know about my note."

Gaspare pressed the handkerchief to his mouth and nodded, and I thought I heard a sob.

I tapped Answer. "Hey, babe. Did you—"

"Tell me that's not you on the bow of the boat."

My stomach dropped just as it had when I'd leaped over the railing. "I take it you've seen the *Times*?"

"*The Boston Globe*. But my grandmother called from Paris to tell me you're on the front page of *Le Monde*."

I sank onto a leather couch. That quad scull was really traveling. "Bradley, I—"

"Save your breath." The calm in his tone spoke of his extensive experience with my escapades. "The only question I have is, how deep are you in?"

I measured my depth in canal water, the obvious choice. "Up to my nostrils."

"I'll find a flight ASAP, even if I have to drive to another state."

A painting of a gondola caught my eye, and a sigh caught in my throat. I didn't want to put him through that, especially when helping me could land him in hot canal water. "You know I want you to come more than anything, but I'm not sure it's safe."

"Franki, I haven't been safe since the day I met you in the lobby of Pontchartrain Bank, and I've never had a moment's regret."

Tears welled in my eyes.

"One way or another, I'll be there tomorrow. In the meantime, please, stay safe. And keep away from the canals."

I pulled the phone from my ear. *What kind of way was that to end a call?*

Caterina emerged from the office door behind the counter. "Ah, madame." She smiled and tucked her hair behind her ear. "A woman inquired about you a half-hour ago, but she did not leave a name."

I rose and went to the counter. "It wasn't a redhead, was it?"

"No, a brunette."

Had to be Shona. "Tell her I moved to a new hotel."

Caterina's brows went up. "Pardon?"

"Just a joke. If she asks again, tell her to try my room."

"There is no need." Caterina gestured to the rotating door. "She has arrived."

Repressing an eye roll, I turned. The face that stared back at me wasn't Shona's. It belonged to a tall, slender thirtyish woman with long dark waves, dressed like an Italian in a beige coat and heels with a cream cowl-neck sweater and orange skinny pants.

"Stella Di Stefano." She gave me a solid American handshake. "Can we talk somewhere in private?"

Given that my life was being threatened, I needed some background. "What is this about?"

"Chef Iona Parsons. If I'm right about her death, you're in trouble. Deep."

"PI WORK MUST PAY WELL." Stella Di Stefano's oversized coat flared as she did a three-sixty in my suite. "The penthouse at The Venetian in Las Vegas can't compare to this."

I knelt to grab a couple of San Pellegrinos from the minibar, but I kept my guard standing straight up. Since she'd known where to find me and what I did for a living, she could have been in cahoots with the Italian man who'd called Private Chicks, and maybe even the redhead. "I haven't been to Vegas, and I'm not paying for the room."

She arched a brow.

Ignoring the implicit question, I put on a poker face, handed her a bottle of sparkling water, and waited for her to show her hand.

Stella scrutinized me for a moment and then stepped onto the balcony and stared at the Grand Canal, which glowed green in the 10:00 a.m. sunshine. "Well, trust me, this suite is almost as fancy as the Sala del Collegio at the Palazzo Ducale. It even has a doge."

I glanced at the portrait above the bed. "Any idea which one he is?"

"Giustiniano Participazio."

His name took me back to the flooded crypt. "The one who used Saint Zechariah's body to found the Church of Murders?"

"That's him," she took a seat at a marble table, "although he's most famous for having Venetian merchants smuggle Saint Mark's corpse out of Egypt."

The sip of water soured in my mouth—like bone broth. I'd been right about the signs of a watery doom, so I didn't welcome the recurring grave-robber theme. "What was the guy's deal with saints' corpses?"

"He used them to build the prestige of the Venetian church. He replaced the city's original patron saint, Theodore from Greece, with Mark since he was an evangelist with ties to Saint Peter and Rome. To justify the theft, Giustiniano claimed he was fulfilling the prophecy of an angel who'd told Mark that Venice would be his final resting place. Then he had the basilica built for Saint Mark's remains—except for his head, which got left during the tomb raid."

I grimaced and glanced toward the dodgy doge. And I jumped.

Shona was behind me in a fluffy Sherpa sweatsuit.

She let out a shout that echoed across the water and gripped her chest. "You like ta scared me silly."

If only I'd scared her silent. "That's going to happen if you enter people's hotel rooms and creep up on them."

"You left a message at the front desk telling me to come to your room, so I did." She turned to Stella and extended her hand. "By the way, I'm Shona, like Mona. Just drop the 'm' and add a 'sh.'"

Stella gave a sly smile. "Stella, like Bella but with a 'st.'"

Shona withdrew her hand and pressed her palms to her forehead. "Hey, Stellaaaaaa! Stellaaaaaa!"

Why hadn't I anticipated her A-Streetcar-Named-Desire *impression?*

The tense corners of Stella's mouth said she wasn't a fan of the Marlon Brando scene—or of the one with the shouting librarian from Screamer, Alabama.

I pulled out a chair. "You were saying, Stella?"

"About Saint Mark? That was it, really. But stealing his corpse was a brilliant marketing scheme for Venice. I wish I could think of something along that scale for my family's business."

Shona slid into a seat. "Funerals?"

"Food tourism."

I studied my sparkling water. I should've picked something stronger. "I'm sorry, but did I miss a link between Saint Mark and food?"

Stella glanced over the rim of her sunglasses. "Everything's linked to food, don't you think?"

"She's right." Shona held up her hands in surrender. "Dating, friendship..."

I almost said, *And saints' corpses?* But I was in a country that was notorious for celebrating dead saints with feasts, not to mention my family's history of making food for a St. Joseph's Day altar in New Orleans—and, on one infamous occasion, of making me steal a lemon from it.

Stella placed her hands on the table. "I know it sounds incredible, but to smuggle Saint Mark out of Egypt, the merchants had to cover his corpse in cabbage leaves and pork so that the soldiers, who were Muslim, wouldn't inspect the shipping container. I love stuff like that."

My lips tried to pull into a smile but fell flat. Stella's food tours would not be on my itinerary. "Is that how you knew Chef Parsons? Because of your business?"

"Actually, my great aunts own the company, and they're the ones who knew Iona and her late mother, Barbara, in England. They know you too, from a trip to Sardinia. Midge and Madge Maven?"

My poker face fell away. "*They're* your great aunts?" I half-laughed and shook my head. "Working with them must be a wild ride."

She nodded. "The X-Scream. It's a single roller coaster car on a short piece of track that seesaws on top of The Stratosphere Hotel to make you feel like you'll plunge to your death."

That seemed like a dramatic description given that the Mavens were elderly spinsters. But then again, my interactions with my nonna often left me feeling as though I'd been bungee jumping with a chain.

Shona leaned in. "Are you from Sin City?"

"Yes, my mom was British, but I was born and raised there around my father's Italian family."

Shona licked her lips, hungry for details. "You must have some stories."

Her eyes shifted to a boat on the canal. "What happens in Vegas…"

"Stays in Vegas," Shona squalled.

Not if Shona has anything to do with it. I sat up in my seat. "How did Midge and Madge know I was here?"

"They saw you on the front page of *The Daily Mail.*"

My stomach bottomed out like a see-saw with a sole rider. That picture was everywhere, which could impede my ability to investigate.

Shona's mouth twisted toward me, as did an eye. "Odd that you mentioned pork earlier, Stella. I was in the picture too, but you'd never know it because a prima donna PI hogged the camera."

"What?" My chin pulled back. "I didn't know there was a reporter in the area."

"As someone who catalogs stories for a living, I'd file that under Fantasy."

Stella grinned, and I straightened my sweater, trying to retain some dignity. If anything, the experience was bad Psychological Thriller, but the psych case was Shona, not Iona's killer.

"Miss Franki?" Glenda called.

"We're outside." I sank in my chair. Now I'd never get to hear

Stella out. "That's my landlady from New Orleans, Glenda O'Brien."

Shona peered over her shoulder. "Whoa. *Laissez les bons tatas rouler.*"

While I appreciated the substitution of *tatas* for *temps* in the *Let the good times roll* expression, I questioned the decision to leave in *bons*. Glenda had been dancing braless since she was a teenager, and she was in her sixties.

My landlady sashayed onto the balcony in gold stripper go-go boots and struck a pose with a gold mask on a stick. "I didn't bring my sleuthing suit, so I asked myself what a PI would wear in Venice. The answer was obvious."

I stared at the little gold masks on her lady parts. *Yeah, super undercover.*

Stella didn't appear fazed by Glenda's outfit, probably because she lived in the land of strippers and showgirls. But Shona's mouth was fixed in a huge O as though she were poised to let out a holler worthy of Screamer, Alabama—or a burp befitting Belchertown, Massachusetts.

Stella removed her sunglasses. "My great aunts didn't tell me you had an investigative team."

"Because I don't."

Glenda stretched out on a lounge chair. "We're helping out in a pinch."

"Yup." Shona flashed her dimples. "We're both helpers, like my last name."

I wouldn't have described it that way. In fact, if I had to pick a ride to characterize working with them, it would be The Twilight Zone Tower of Terror at Disney's Hollywood Studios. And we hadn't even gotten started on the case.

Stella folded her arms on the table. "Then I don't have any issue with you all hearing the personal information I'm about to share with Franki."

Had she even been listening *to Shona?*

"My aunts sent me today because they can't get here until after midnight."

Glenda lowered her mask—just the one on the stick, thankfully. "They're going to miss my book signing." She tapped Shona's arm. "It's for my memoirs, *Like a Polecat at a Garden Party*, and judging from your sheep suit, you could use a pole in your life. Drop by the Libreria Acqua Alta at 11:00 p.m., and I'll give you a copy."

Startled by the location—and more than a little confused by the pole reference—I didn't mention seeing the woman in white or the flaming coffin. I wanted to know why the Mavens had sent their great-niece to see me before I shared that information. "Go on, Stella."

"Well," she tucked hair behind her ear, "Midge and Madge read about the jewel theft from the tomb at San Michele cemetery, and they think Iona was murdered over a crucifix necklace that belonged to one of her ancestors."

I blinked. "Iona was related to the Duchess whose tomb was desecrated?"

"No, not the Duchess Von Leipold. This woman was a patrician, which was the only noble title used in Venice. She was buried in the necklace in 1798."

Glenda held her mask to her face. "Have you checked the cemetery to find out whether her grave was robbed?"

"I can't because it's unmarked, and I haven't been able to get in touch with anyone at the cemetery. But my great aunts visited the grave with Barbara before she died, so I was planning to wait and go with them."

Shona gripped her chin, probably running through her mental card catalog. "What about Find a Grave?"

"I assumed that was only for the United States."

"Lucky for you, I'm a librarian." She pulled a phone from her Sherpa pants pocket.

I thought of my conversation with Rosa at the flower shop. "Was her name Violet?"

"No, Lucrezia." Stella pulled hair from her eyes. "Why would you think that?"

"The day she died, she was wearing a gold necklace with the name."

Her lips wrinkled. "That doesn't make any sense."

I watched a vaporetto glide up the canal. The necklace made sense to Violet, whoever she was. I had to find her. *But how?*

Shona tapped her phone. "Okay, so Lucrezia Parsons?"

"No, Pavan."

My head snapped toward Stella. It was the second time I'd heard my mother's maiden name in Venice, and it wasn't a coincidence. *Had the trio I'd overheard at Caffè Florian been talking about Iona's ancestor?* If so, that raised all sorts of red flags. But the bigger question was, *Are Iona and I related?*

"What is it, Franki?" Stella's dark eyes searched mine. "I hate to use the cliché, but you look like you've seen a ghost."

Supposedly I'd seen two, Tosca and Giuseppina Gabriel Carmelo's coffin, and I wondered whether a third, Lucrezia Pavan, was haunting me. I went to the balcony railing and gazed at the Venetian Gothic palazzos lining the Grand Canal. Then I looked down, where Iona Parsons had met her end. "Pavan is my mother's maiden name."

"No," exploded from Shona's mouth like a cannon shot.

Glenda expressed her surprise with a smoke O from a cigarette she'd lit. "I thought that name sounded familiar, sugar."

Shona smacked the table. "I'll bet that's why you got the threatening note. It's from the jewel thieves, and they don't want you to claim the necklace as your inheritance."

Stella's eyes grew to the size of Glenda's smoke ring. "You've been threatened?"

"Yesterday." I returned to my seat. "I assumed it was because the night the Duchess Von Leipold's tomb was broken into, I saw a woman who might've been masquerading as the ghost of

Tosca near a coffin with lit candles in a canal. Now I'm not so sure."

"Where was this?"

"Behind the Libreria Acqua Alta."

Stella breathed in deep and scanned our faces. "If the coffin came from San Michele cemetery, it could've been holding artifacts stolen from the Duchess and others."

"I thought that too, but I couldn't tell you which direction it came from. Venice is a maze of canals and streets." I turned to Shona. "Is Lucrezia on Find a Grave?"

She held up her phone. "No matches found."

Stella fiddled with the cowl neck of her sweater. "You might try searching 1735, when she was born, but the omission is most likely because her grave is unmarked. According to Midge and Madge, a lot of people have tried to find the necklace over the centuries, so even if someone at the cemetery knows her burial site, they might keep it secret."

I chewed my thumbnail as anxiety chewed my gut. "Why all the interest in the necklace? Is it just the value?"

"Several reasons. It's a gold crucifix with three large rubies, for one thing. And it was a gift from Casanova, who won it in a gambling match."

The Latin Lover—who I lumped in with his counterfeit counterpart from the Piazza San Marco—was getting on my nerves. "What was her relationship to Casanova?"

Glenda lowered her handheld mask. "Honestly, sugar, she wasn't playing the roulette wheel with the man."

"She could've been. I resent the implication that women were merely men's playthings, even in the 1700s."

My landlady was so shaken that all of her masks wobbled. "Bite your tongue, Miss Franki."

Stella smirked. "Glenda's right. Lucrezia Pavan was rumored to be one of Casanova's conquests, especially because he was notorious for giving expensive clothes and jewels to his lovers."

"Oof." Shona propped a heartsick face on her palms. "Why can't I meet a man who lavishes me with gifts?"

Glenda inspected Shona through her handheld mask as if it was a magnifying glass. "Take off that sheep suit and maybe you can."

Shona pressed her lovelorn love handles. "Do I look fat in this?"

"That's the point. No one can tell because you're drowning in fleece. If you ask me, child, it's time for a shearing."

She unzipped her Sherpa jacket—an inch.

But I was only half-paying attention. I still had questions about the crucifix necklace. "Hey, Stella—"

"Hey, Stellaaaaaa!"

Shona's Brando outburst coincided with a cruise ship horn, and it was hard to say which was louder. Since she was sitting next to me, that was a problem. "Do that again, and I'll personally shear your Sherpa and shove it down your shouting throat."

Shona went silent, and I turned to Stella, who looked grateful. "You said there were several reasons that people had searched for the necklace, but you only mentioned two."

"There's some religious legend associated with it, but Midge and Madge will have to fill you in on the specifics. All I know is that the rubies are at Christ's wrists and feet and symbolize his blood. There was a jewel above his head, but it's gone."

"Another ruby?"

Stella shrugged. "No one knows, not even Iona's mother, Barbara, knew that."

I touched my engagement ring. "If the rubies symbolized blood, then the stone above his head could've been different."

"That's what I think too. I wonder how we could find out?"

Shona put a finger to her cheek. "Hm. If only there were

buildings that housed historical archives with books and documents and newspapers."

A thought struck me that literally straightened my spine. "*Il Gazzettino*."

Shona frowned. "That's one option, although not very interesting."

"No, I just figured out why the impostor maid tried to take the copy outside my hotel room—it had an article about the jewel theft." I looked at Stella. "An hour later, I think the same woman might've poisoned some wine Iona was cooking with."

Her mouth hardened. "So, that was the cause of death?"

"I can't prove it, but Iona was coughing and her lips were purple, and she'd just used Valpolicella in a violet risotto dish. She created the recipe for my best friend's wedding reception, which is why we're all here."

Shona pressed plump hands together. "I'm invited?"

"No."

Stella pulled her coat tighter. "That's awful."

"Right?" Shona's tone was indignant. "You'd think that putting my life on the line to solve the murder of the bride's chef would get me an invitation."

"Um," Stella scratched her temple, "I was talking about Iona's murder." She cleared her throat and looked at me. "Do you think this woman poisoned the wine here at the hotel?"

"Most likely, but the bottle could've been poisoned with a syringe before it was delivered. The problem is, no one on the hotel staff knows where Iona bought it."

"If you find out, I might be able to help with the investigation. I have to be back in Rome tonight for a gelateria crawl, but on Thursday, I'm doing the Mangia Mavens' Venice rowing tour and—"

"Rowing?" Shona clasped her hands in prayer. "On a scull?"

"A *batela coda di gambero*, which is a shrimp-tailed batela boat that you stand on like a gondola to row in the Venetian style known as *voga alla veneta*. They used to be common in Venice, but there are only seven replicas in existence now, and two of them are ours."

Shona gave little claps. "Count us in."

The "us" was exactly what I'd feared when I saw the Mavens' brochure in the lobby. Shona had already used Bradley's museum ticket, now she was honing in on his wedding invite and his seat on the boat too. "How would your tour help the case?"

"We visit bacari bars for cicchetti with an *ombra*, so we could check out the wineseller undercover."

"If it comes to that, I'll take you up on the offer. But I'm confused about something. Doesn't ombra mean 'shadow' or 'shade?'"

"It does, but Venetians also use it to refer to a glass of wine. It came from the practice of selling wine in the shade of church towers to keep it cool."

Glenda stretched out on the sun chaise. "If New Orleans has taught me anything, it's that Catholics know how drinking is done."

The drinking Catholics comment made me think of Father Fester—er, Festin. He'd been unpacking communion wine while Veronica and I were in the flooded crypt, and Veronica said that he was the one who'd recommended Iona Parsons for the reception food.

A powerful shudder ran through me. *What if there was a connection between the poisoned Valpolicella and the Church of Murders?*

～

THE VAPORETTO LURCHED as it docked at the S. Zaccaria *pontile*, an enclosed floating wharf behind the church. With one eye on the waves and the other on the rocking platform, I leaped from the waterbus and latched onto the doorframe to prevent a spill in the lagoon. Carefully, I made my way across a ramp that rose and fell with the swells to the covered portico that led to the church, thanking God that I hadn't ended up in the water like Iona—and that rowing practice and the book signing had kept Shona and Glenda from tagging along.

I walked the length of the street, ignoring the shops and focusing on the Benedictine monastery that Napoleon had given to the Carabinieri. The former convent was rather picturesque with its crumbling terracotta walls, exposed brick, and potted plants, but its large grilled windows seemed at odds with the building's cloistered past. *Surely passersby hadn't been allowed to peep at the nuns?*

I turned into the Campo di San Zaccaria and was immediately creeped out by the Church of Murders. With its small, curved top floor and the rounded corners of the story below, it cast a shadow over the courtyard that resembled a hulking cloaked figure.

Like the bell ringer of Venice.

My gaze shifted to a bell tower above the old monastery that I hadn't noticed when I'd first visited with Veronica and Dirk. I pursed my lips. "Really poor timing."

As I crossed the campo, I thought about the tradition of selling wine in the shade of church towers. Based on the shadow of San Zaccaria, on any given day, they could sell enough for one hell of a party in the French Quarter.

I entered the church, surprised by the light shining through its tall Gothic windows. Without it, the place would have looked like a giant tomb—which it was.

A short, fiftyish woman in a drab gray dress rose from the

last pew with a dust rag. She had a long nose and high eyebrows, like Joan Crawford, and a natural frown to her mouth.

Something about her looked familiar, but I couldn't place her. "Padre Fester—uh, Festin?"

She turned and moved to another pew. "*La cripta.*"

Crypt didn't sound any better in Italian, and especially not in the woman's harsh, German accent.

I went to the right to a door marked "please close door behind you," which I didn't do for fear of being locked in a creepy crypt that flooded, no less. As I began my descent into hell—the watery Hades version—I almost wished Shona and Glenda were with me.

Wait. No, I didn't.

My legs were unsteady on the stairs, and I told myself that it was a lingering effect of the vaporetto, not nerves. The hard truth was that I didn't entirely trust the priest. Recommending Iona as the caterer was a long way from being a murderer, but I couldn't rule out anyone who knew her as a suspect—especially not a guy straight off the set of the movie *Addams Family Values*. So I didn't relish the thought of being alone with him with water and tombs.

As I approached the bottom step, Father Festin was in his black robe, pushing a squeegee across the brick walkway. My stomach sloshed. He was removing sludge that I fervently hoped was seafoam.

"I warned your friend not to get married on a Friday, but she wouldn't listen." His statement resounded in the room like a chant. "So, if you're here to change the day of the wedding, it's impossible."

I covered my nose and mouth. The squeegee was really kicking up the dank odor, and I didn't want to inhale any bone particles. "What's wrong with Fridays?"

"In Italy, Sunday is the luckiest day to wed for obvious

reasons," he paused to shoot me a look that said he wasn't sure whether I'd grasped the religious reference, "whereas Fridays are believed to be the day evil spirits are created."

My hand went to my hip. *Veronica was really throwing caution to the wind, wasn't she?* "Actually, I came to talk to you about Chef Iona Parsons. I was at her restaurant when she fell into the Grand Canal."

"I thought that was you on the front page of *Il Gazzettino.* Horrid picture."

My hand went to my hair. *Is he talking about me or the situation? Because those Uncle Fester eye rings are hardly photogenic.*

"At any rate," he slid the squeegee across the brick, "I don't see how I can help you. Chef Parsons only recently joined the parish."

"A lapsed Catholic?"

He eyed me like he knew one when he saw one. "Veronica told me what you do for a living, so I'm certain you're aware that a priest never reveals what parishioners tell him in confession."

My skin pricked from guilt, and I began to itch—a psychosomatic hazard of the religion.

He scooped some sludge. "However, as it's a matter of public record, I can tell you that her family has a history with San Zaccaria."

"You mean, the Pavans?"

"Precisely."

"Have you heard of a Lucrezia Pavan?"

He deposited the sludge into a bucket with a *whack.* "More times than one should have to bear. A most common woman."

Well, aren't you holier than thou? I thought. Then my face grew hot. *He actually is holier than thou, Franki. He's a priest.* "I'm confused. I heard that the Pavans were a patrician family."

"Nobility does not equate with virtue, and Lucrezia Pavan was one of the more storied sisters at our convent."

"She was a *nun*? That would explain why she was buried with a crucifix necklace."

He snorted. "Hardly. Most of the nuns were whores."

My eyes darted from left to right. *Was I being punked by a priest?*

"Why do you look so scandalized?"

Maybe because a priest was talking about sex, not to mention speaking ill of the dead in front of the dead? "I don't typically think of nuns as wh—er, loose women."

He exhaled and pursed his lips. "Allow me to enlighten you about Venetian convents."

I descended to the bottom step, but not to that sludgy walk-way. "Please."

"For centuries, to avoid paying expensive dowries, patrician families forced their daughters into convents, especially if they had more than one. By some estimates, sixty percent of noble women were made to take the veil."

"That's terrible."

His dark-circled eyes lowered. "There are worse things than joining the Church."

"Oh, uh...I meant the fact that they were forced." I scratched my neck and wondered whether lying to a priest in a church crypt was the same grade of sin as lying in the church itself.

He pushed the squeegee. "Many of the sisters shared your view of the situation, so they rebelled. The convents had parlors for meeting with family and visiting clergy, but the nuns often used them to lure men to the windows with makeup, trans-parent veils, and revealing dresses. Some even crept out for trysts or brought lovers into their cells."

That explained the grilles, which were also in keeping with the unfortunate name of their rooms. "Why did the Church allow this?"

"The nuns were the daughters of patricians, so they had

political power, particularly at San Zaccaria, which was the most elite and ancient convent in Venice. And some clergy looked the other way because they felt a measure of sympathy for the women. But, make no mistake about it, their sins were not only a betrayal of their office, they were also considered treasonous."

"Treason? What did politics have to do with sinning?"

He dumped another pile of sludge. "I suggest you consult a book on the subject. *Virgins of Venice* is quite good. Essentially, sinful behavior compromised Venice's relationship to God and therefore her prosperity and security."

Normally I would have questioned the characterization of a city as a person, but I'd met Venice, and she was as deranged as Ruth Walker. "Besides Lucrezia, was there a Violet Pavan in the convent? Or did Iona ever mention anyone by that name?"

"Not that I recall." He picked up the bucket. "Now, if you'll excuse me, I must prepare a sermon on the Virgin." The corners of his mouth twitched. "None of the ones in that book I referenced."

If anything should be a betrayal of God and treason against Venice, it's his church humor. "One more thing. Where do you buy the communion wine?"

"Why should you want to know that?"

"Uh, my nonna is Italian and super devout. It would make her happy if I brought her a bottle to...donate to her church."

He beamed like Uncle Fester when he put a light bulb in his mouth. "How lovely. We have a volunteer, Perpetua, who handles the ordering. She was polishing the pews earlier."

"Oh, right. I'll go ask her."

We climbed the steps to the vestibule, but apart from tourists, the church was empty.

"Wait here, and I'll see if Perpetua's in the office." He set off toward the altar.

I glanced uneasily at the golden caskets on the wall and

thanked the heavens that I'd come up with a truthful reason for wanting to know the wineseller. Because if I was going to be struck down for lying to a priest in a church, San Zaccaria would have been the place.

With a shudder, I headed for the altar to find the father and speed him along. An enormous painting, sixteen or seventeen feet in length, caught my attention. According to the placard, it was the *San Zaccaria Altarpiece* by Giovanni Bellini from 1505. It depicted the Virgin Mary with the baby Jesus, an angel playing a violin, and Saints Catherine, Peter, Lucy, and Jerome. The female saints were virgin martyrs who had been put to death for choosing their faith over forced sex.

"A not-so-veiled message to the nuns," I punned. And one that Lucrezia Pavan hadn't received even though she would have seen the painting countless times.

In light of what I'd learned about the plight of Venetian noblewomen, I couldn't help but wonder whether Lucrezia had been forced into the convent by her parents. It was a possibility since she'd apparently hooked up with Casanova. What I couldn't fathom was how she'd come to meet the notorious womanizer or why he'd given her a crucifix, of all things. But none of that mattered as much as whether the necklace was linked to Iona's death.

"Here we are." Father Festin sailed past the altar, clutching his robe and holding up a bottle. "I couldn't find Perpetua, but I did find this. For your nonna, compliments of San Zaccaria."

I took the communion wine and read the label—Valpolicella, the same brand and vintage that Veronica had ordered for her reception.

And that Iona Parsons had used to make the violet risotto.

As I EXITED the Chiesa di San Zaccaria, the campanile above the monastery struck 1:00 p.m. I paused in the campo to stare at the bell because the lone toll felt like a warning. *Were the ghosts of the noble nuns telling me to stay away from the godforsaken church? Or was it that Veronica and I wouldn't live to see our weddings?*

The fact that the communion wine was Valpolicella had only increased my unease about Veronica getting married in the murderously nicknamed venue, not to mention my suspicion of Father Festin. *Was he the man who'd called Private Chicks to ask about me?* He could have faked an Italian accent, but I sincerely doubted he could have disguised the Boris Karloff in his tone.

There was only one thing to do—take Veronica's advice and call Ruth. I threw my head back and rolled it from side to side in utter despair. "Whywhywhywhy?"

A middle-aged brunette in the campo grabbed a young boy's arm and yanked him from me. "Come on, Joey," she said in a New York accent. "That woman's not well."

I straightened, incensed. "Lady, I'm a freaking *beacon* of mental health compared to the woman I'm about to call."

The brunette scurried ahead, pulling the boy and scowling over her shoulder.

My hand went to my hip. Surely she could tell that I was upset and not unhinged? Although, in all fairness, I *did* suspect that ghost nuns were sending me messages through a church bell.

I headed back to the vaporetto, and the *Jaws* theme surfaced from the depths of my purse. "Oh, hell no. I'm not taking a call from my mom and nonna right before I have to talk to Ruth."

Spinning on my heels, I did an about-face. It was best to return to the hotel on dry land. I didn't know what dark force had made me reliant on Ruth Walker for assistance, but if she made another announcement along the lines of moving into my office, I might throw myself off the waterbus. I checked my maps app. Venice had ten main canals, and the narrower waterways were called *rii*, or *rio* in the singular. Ironically, I was headed for the *Rio del Vin*, short for *vino*. Exhaling as though it was my last breath before I drank a poisoned bottle of Valpolicella, I dialed the office.

The line picked up. "Help us—"

It was our part-time investigator, David, and a scuffling ensued as if he was in a struggle for the receiver.

My heart fell from my chest. "Stay strong, David. I'm calling 9-1-1."

"Weeell," Ruth drawled, "if it isn't Marco Polo, world traveler."

I should have known she was David's assailant.

Ice clinked in a glass. "On second thought, Marco Polo's a bad comparison. He took his friends on his voyages."

'*Friends*' *being the operative word.* "The historical accuracy of that assertion is questionable under the circumstances. Now, what are you doing to David and The Vassal?"

"Imposing order. I run a tight ship."

Captain Vandergrift hadn't thought so, but I didn't dare say that. Ruth had already taken over my office. I couldn't risk her occupying my apartment too. "Go easy on them. They have nothing to do with your beef with me."

"Hey, I'm easy peasy as long as people take responsibility for their actions."

She was hard pard even when *I* took responsibility for her actions—every time something went wrong. "Just remember that Veronica's the boss at Private Chicks, which brings me to the reason for my call. She wanted me to ask you whether the Italian man who phoned the office had a spooky voice, along the lines of the 'Monster Mash' singer."

Snickers and snorts ensued, followed by the clacking of her horn-rim chains, and possibly her turkey neck.

"What's so funny?"

A lengthy peal of laughter was followed by a "Hooo" as she came down from her hilarity high. "The song, that's what. Still cracks me up."

It was just more proof that *she* was cracked up. The "Monster Mash" had been around since the sixties, and no one sane still thought it was that hilarious. "So, back to the Italian guy—"

"I tell you what, the funniest part is when Bobby Pickett says the name of the rock group, the Crypt Kicker 5." She snorted and resumed the snickers.

"Yeah. I'm dying."

The snickers stopped. "Is that supposed to be funny?"

I turned down a small winding street. "More so than the Crypt Kicker 5."

"You never did have a sense of humor."

I couldn't argue with her. When she was around there was zero to laugh about. "So, that Italian guy—"

"I haven't had my breakfast yet." A cabinet door slammed. "Good thing there's a jar of Nutella in the office, even though I don't care for the stuff."

My fingers squeezed the phone. That was my chocolate-hazelnut spread she was planning to spite-eat, but I couldn't protest or she wouldn't give me any information. "Could you please just tell me—"

"While we're talking about kicking the crypt, I've been reading up on Venice. Since you cost me my job and an invite to the wedding, I've been reduced to living vicariously through you."

And in my office, I thought.

"You know what I found out? That city is a death trap."

The church tower bell echoed in my head, and Iona's face flashed before me. I also realized I'd taken a wrong turn. "Why would you say that?"

"Because Venice is half empty, so criminals lie in wait in the narrow streets to ambush tourists. They even do it in broad daylight."

She *would* tell me that when I was lost. "I haven't heard about this."

"You think Italy's going to let word get out that lurking bands of hoodlums in Venice are mugging and murdering tourists?"

Murdering? I turned to retrace my steps.

"And to think you've dragged poor Bradley into a death sentence."

I scanned my surroundings for lurking figures. "He's not even here yet, Ruth."

"Well, if he wants to visit a city with water, he'd be better off coming home to New Orleans. The swamps are safer than those canals."

I bristled. Given the threat I'd received, she might have had a point. "I think you're exaggerating a little."

"Am I? What would Chef Parsons have to say on the matter?"

"The canal didn't kill her. It was something else."

"Nevertheless, there are bodies in those canals, like the nobleman from 1598. Legend has it that he rises from the water holding his wife's severed head."

I was right. Venice is deranged, and so is Ruth. "Thanks for the advice. Now—"

"No problem, and if Bradley ever asks, I know nothing about your Italian Casanova."

I stopped in the middle of the street. "I don't even know who the guy is, which is why I'm calling you."

"Maybe not, but you sure are interested in finding him."

"Because I'm working a murder investigation, and I've been threatened." I'd shouted out that information, which wasn't smart. I lowered the phone and looked around. The street was empty, and surprisingly dark because of the tall buildings.

I put the phone back to my ear, but the line was dead. *Did Ruth hang up?* I looked at the display.

No reception.

"Super. No maps app." I'd have to look for a shop to ask for directions, but the area looked residential, and one o'clock was the lunch hour, so nothing would be open, anyway. I clutched my purse tighter, now haunted by Ruth's warning, and continued along fully expecting to hear the footsteps of a roving band of muggers and murderers.

The street came to a dead end at a small canal. "Not auspicious."

Retracing my steps, I turned a corner and pulled back in shock.

Had I just seen that?

Pressing my back flat against a damp stuccoed wall, I turned my head and peered around the corner.

Next to a shrine to the Virgin Mary stood the counterfeit Casanova in full eighteenth-century dress—and he was in an animated conversation with none other than Perpetua from the Church of Murders. Her back was to me, her hair covered with a white scarf, but I recognized her drab gray dress.

I strained to hear what they were saying. From what I could tell, they were speaking German, which explained Perpetua's accent. They sounded angry, but all German sounded angry to me, so I peeked around the corner to check their body language.

Casanova looked over his shoulder, and Perpetua did the same—in oversized white sunglasses.

I pulled back and gripped the wall. I knew why she looked familiar—she was part of the trio at the table behind me at Caffè Florian. And I was willing to bet that underneath Casanova's curled white wig and pancake makeup was the young man who'd been sitting with her that day.

If I was right, then Casanova hadn't approached my table

with Veronica and Glenda to earn five euros. He'd been watching me, and he was probably the Italian who'd called the office. Not only that, his and Perpetua's meeting with the man in the traditional tabarro cloak took on a whole new meaning—as did the man's reference to *la pavan*.

7

"That was my mistake, Veronica." I pressed the phone to my ear and lay flat on the aqua silk bedspread, imagining that I was floating on a sea of calm. "When the man in the tabarro yelled 'la pavan' at Perpetua and Casanova at the Caffè Florian, I assumed he was talking about an aristocratic dance or a woman from Padova. But he meant 'la Pavan' with a capital *p*, as in 'la Signora Pavan.'"

"Italians do refer to people that way, but you can't know for sure what he meant. And there are other people in the Veneto with that last name."

"Yeah, like my mother. Although, she's not here yet, fortunately." I closed my eyes and envisioned myself on a raft with a spritz in the cupholder.

"Let's say they *were* talking about Lucrezia. How would they have found out your name? Did you pay the waiter with a credit card?"

"Ambrosio? No, cash. And I never introduced myself to him, either. He would've taken it as an invitation to come to my room." I tilted back my head to look at the dour doge, who looked doubtful. I couldn't blame him. Given Ambrosio's under-wear-model looks, I was probably flattering myself, but Italians were notorious womanizers. Hence Casanova.

"Hm." A clicking sound came through the receiver, suggesting Veronica was tapping a tooth with her fingernail. "Maybe the woman who posed as the maid got your contact information from the hotel registry. If you're right about these people being jewel thieves, she could be working with them."

"I'm sure she already knew who I was when she came looking for me."

"Why do you think that?"

"Because this has to have something to do with the woman in white and the flaming coffin. I saw her the night I arrived, and then I sat by the trio at Caffè Florian the next morning, before I came to meet you and Dirk at the Palazzo Ducale with...*Shona!*" The sea of calm grew stormy, and I shot up. "That loud librarian is the reason they know who I am. She shouted my name across the piazza and even asked me if I was investigating a case undercover."

"And you think they heard her?"

"The woman's got lungs like a foghorn, Veronica. Of course they heard her."

"It's not like she outed you on purpose."

I paced in front of the antique sofa. "Nooo, she's a *helper*, just like her last name. And she's going to help me right into my coffin, probably with a poisoned bottle of Valpolicella."

Veronica groaned. "Please don't bring that up around my parents. They're arriving tonight, and they're still reeling from the news about Iona and the Grand Canal. They can't know about the wine."

"You know I'll keep it quiet, but Shona won't."

"I'll talk to her." She paused. "Listen, Franki. I know you came here for a vacation, and I hate to put this on you, but given the revelation about the wine, well...I *do* want you to investigate Iona's murder, and I'll double your usual rate."

"This is your wedding. There's no way I'm taking your money. Besides, my life has been threatened, and for all I know, Iona was a relative."

I lay back on the bed, and we both went silent, reliving the horror of her death.

"Well," Veronica breathed, "I appreciate you. Now I have to find Shona and then get ready to greet my father's college roommate and his wife. They're arriving from Boston within the hour, which reminds me, any word from Bradley?"

I cradled a gold pillow and sighed. "He said he'd find a flight today one way or another."

"Oh, Franki, I hope he did."

She had no idea how much I hoped so too. "Something has to go my way on this trip, right?"

The door to my suite opened, and the sea of calm turned tsunami. I dropped the phone and whacked myself in the head with the gold pillow. *When, WHEN would I learn not to jinx myself?*

My mom entered in what looked like a Princess-Grace-of-Monaco fur wrap, no doubt inspired by her long-suspected noble origins, and my nonna shuffled in after her with a Sophia-from-*The-Golden-Girls* black handbag. "*Buongiorno*, Francesca!"

It most definitely, positively, absolutely was not a good day. I was glad they'd arrived safe and sound, but I would have preferred that it was two days later. "I thought you were coming on Wednesday."

"Change of plans, dear." She peeled off her wrap with gloved hands. "The manager, Gaspare, gave us a key card. A lovely man."

Nonna removed her black coat to reveal the mourning dress

she'd worn almost exclusively since my *nonnu* died twenty years before. "It's-a too bad about-a his-a breathing problem."

"Yes, we introduced ourselves, and he opened his mouth and started gasping."

Gaspare had obviously hyperventilated at the thought of having more Amatos in the hotel, much like I was doing at the moment. "He's on edge about Chef Parsons—"

"We read all about it in the *Houston Chronicle*. Such a tragedy."

"Eh, *sì*." Nonna crossed herself and then brightened. "But that-a photo of-a you in a wet-a shirt really showed your goods-a."

I covered my goods-a with a pillow and shot her a scowl. She'd been in the United States for sixty years, but her mind was still in Old-World Sicily, where women were bartered like goats. "So, I'm guessing you two want to freshen up."

My mother checked her updo. "That would be nice. Where's the bathroom?"

"I meant, in your room."

Nonna stuck out her lower lip, pinched her fingers toward the heavens, and bobbed them up and down. "This is-a our room-a."

That explained the key card. I should have known from the minute I'd spotted the dour doge above my bed that my Palazzo Ducale dream suite would go from sumptuous Sala del Collegio to terrifying Torture Room.

My mom sat beside me on my aqua silk sea of discontent. "The hotel is booked solid for the wedding, and since we came early, we have to stay with you. It's a good thing you got such a spacious suite."

Was it?

A knock on the door rattled me even further. *Who was it now? The killer?*

"Come in," my mother shrilled like a castrated drill sergeant.

The door opened, and the burly valet I'd seen at the private jetty deposited suitcases near the bed.

I leaped up and grabbed my wallet. "I'll take care of the tip." I followed him into the hallway and closed the door behind me. "Find them a room," I said in rapid Italian, "and I'll give you a hundred euros."

"The 'otel is-a fool." He pushed the cart down the hall.

"You can't find good help even in Italy." I returned to the room and found my mother examining one of the four-foot bronze cherubs.

"Look at these statues, Carmela. They could be Franki and Bradley."

Not with you and Nonna in my room.

My mother laid a look on me as though it was my wedding week, and I'd just been jilted at the altar. "Or maybe I should say, 'could have been,' since he's not coming to the wedding.'"

I lay back on the bed. From the way this conversation was going, I'd end up there anyway. "He's coming, Mom. He told me this morning, so stop worrying."

"How could we not worry about your future?"

"Your mamma is-a right." My nonna sat on the sofa, clutching her handbag, ready to do busybody business. "It's-a our job-a to make-a sure you're *sistemata*."

"It's *my* job to make sure I'm settled. So, both of you, please be normal wedding guests and don't go do anything crazy where my relationship is concerned."

"What have we ever done that's crazy, Francesca?"

I put a pillow over my face. "Uh," I said, into the fabric, "let's start with showing up in Italy two days early and work our way backward."

"It was-a necessary, and it-a cost-a us a lotta money. But we save-a some on-a the hotel-a room, *grazie a Dio*."

I wasn't sure what money Nonna was talking about, except maybe the flight-change fees, but there was no time to ask because I had to drill down on the last part of that statement. "Technically, you won't be saving money since you'll still move to your room on Wednesday." I paused and peered from beneath the pillow. "You *will* still move to your room on Wednesday?"

"We can't, dear. Bradley's room was canceled when he didn't show, so I told Gaspare to give him ours when he arrives."

I sat up. My sea of discontent had turned into a sea of sorrow, and I had to do something to keep from drowning in it. "Why don't you take the room, and Bradley can stay with me?"

My mother's gloved hand went to her chest. "Francesca Lucia Amato! What would Veronica's parents think?"

"I tell-a you what-a they think-a. They think-a Franki is a *buttana*."

Since she'd used the Sicilian word for *whore*, it probably wasn't the time to mention that my mom and I could be related to a noble whore nun. "They will not, Nonna. They know Bradley and I are engaged, so when he arrives, I'll stay with him."

"Nothing doing, Francesca. We didn't relinquish the room entirely. That's where your father is going to stay."

It's definitive. Venice is the tomb of love. I slid off the bed and went to the door.

"Where are you going, dear?"

"To jump off the Bridge of Sighs." I closed the door and marched to the elevator. On the way down, I didn't bother to check my phone for an update from Bradley.

The elevator doors opened, and Gaspare waved me to the front desk. He leaned forward. "I have a message for you."

I didn't ask if it was from my fiancé. I went straight to, "Another death threat?"

He broke out in an instant sweat. "Signorina, *per favore*." He fanned his face with a Mavens brochure. "We spoke-ed before about frightening the guests."

If anything would send them running, it was the twin rivers of sweat pouring down his cheeks. "What's the message?"

"The Commissario Lucifero call-ed. He expects you tomorrow afternoon."

My brain had stopped at Lucifero. An interview with an inspector named after the devil promised to be an inferno. "Is he at the Carabinieri station in the old San Zaccaria convent?"

"The Carabinieri do not investigate murder, signorina, unless it pertains to terrorism or Mafia. You must go to the questura, the police headquarters in the former convent of Santa Chiara."

What the hell is up with cops and convents in Venice? I turned from the counter and contemplated the white couches. With my mom and nonna in my suite, I might have to sleep on one. I leaned over to test a cushion and caught a glimpse of a blonde passing by a window overlooking the street.

Stella had said I looked like I'd seen a ghost, and I was afraid I just had.

I ran for the rotating door and jammed my ring finger on the handle. "Ouch!"

As I massaged the aching joint, I thought of the legend of Tosca, who lost her ring finger and doomed to never marry. But the woman in white wasn't the blonde I'd seen passing by. It was Sheilah.

Bradley's ex-wife.

~

"HOLY GHOST FROM THE PAST!" Shona's shout surged through the Libreria Acqua Alta like water though a flooding canal. "Bradley was *married*?"

Luckily, it was 10:45 p.m. and we were in the back by the green chair overlooking the opening onto the water, so there were only a handful of customers. "Yes, to Eilah with a 'sh,'" which brings me to a request. Could you *not* announce his private business to the entire bookstore?"

She clutched her romance tote. "It's shocking."

What was shocking was her decibel level. "It isn't. People get divorced."

"Sure, but why did the divorcée come to Venice?"

That's what I wanted to know. But I'd ducked into the elevator before Sheilah could see me. She was a society snob who'd crashed my first date with Bradley, during which she'd announced that she was his wife, so we weren't exactly friends. "I didn't talk to her. She was with an older man—much older. Her second husband, I think."

Shona balled her hands on the hips of her pink quilted jumper and kicked out a clog. "Did you at least ask Veronica if Sheilah's with the wedding party?"

I shook my head as a terrible thought struck me, even more awful than the reality of my mom and nonna showing up two days early. *What if Sheilah is married to Veronica's father's college roommate?*

If she were, she'd keep coming back to haunt me at Veronica's future functions, like a baby shower. I pressed my fingers into the sides of my head. "What are the freaking odds that something like this would happen?"

"I'd be happy to calculate those for you, as well as the odds that she came to reclaim Bradley."

If there hadn't been potential witnesses browsing the shelves, Shona would've sailed into the canal like the *Death in Venice* book. "No, thank you. Now, I need to talk to the cashier."

I stomped to the entrance. Shona wasn't a helper, she was a hindrance.

The middle-aged man I'd seen on my first visit sat at the register wearing a pair of readers. He rose and adjusted his suspenders. "I am Riccardo. How may I service you?"

The double entendre took me aback, but I didn't correct him for fear of having to explain the risqué meaning. "Do you have the *Virgins of Venice*?"

He removed his readers, bit the tip, and sized me up from chest to pelvis and back. "The...nuns?"

The lust in his tone indicated that the double entendre might've been intentional. Proceeding with caution, I slow-nodded.

"I do not." Riccardo leaned forward, and a corner of his mouth curved lasciviously. "It sell like-a the hot-a cakes."

Must be some spicy reading. "Do you have any other books about them?"

He sly-eyed me and stopped short of a wink. "You wait." He went to a shelf, pulled a book from behind a plant in a bucket, and brought it to me. "*Forbidden Fashions.*"

"Sexy title." I regretted the slip. Riccardo had clasped his hands and his lips trembled, which told me he could become a problem when Glenda arrived for the book signing. I cleared my throat and flipped suspiciously well-thumbed pages. I heard wheezing, and my gaze traveled up.

The lip tremble had spread to his body.

I stepped back. The dam of his repressed desires had better not break while Glenda was in the store, because she was likely to ride the flood in front of the customers. "Uh, I'm going to look through this in the back room."

"*Peccato.*"

I turned from the counter with a smirk. Italians used the word to mean *it's a shame*, but its literal meaning was *sin*, which was appropriate on a couple of levels.

After making sure the green chair was dry, I browsed

Forbidden Fashions. From what I read, there were two options for women in Venice—*maridar* or *monacar*, local dialect for *marry* or *monastery*. For a woman forced into the convent, the investiture ceremony, when she wore a habit for the first time, symbolized her funeral. This sentiment was borne out by the rite since it celebrated the birth of the novitiate's new life with God by marking the death of her former self.

My hand went to the neck of my black pullover. It felt tight.

I turned the page to a Francesco Guardi painting from 1745 called *Il Parlatorio*, and its English title caught my attention —*The Parlor of the Nuns at San Zaccaria.* Women in habits and ball gowns mingled with men as visitors watched through the grilled windows I'd seen on the Carabinieri station. According to the author, the windows had been installed to keep an eye on the nuns. "That backfired."

Lowering the book, I stared at the canal. *Had Casanova visited Lucrezia at one of those windows? Or did he go inside? If so,* I swallowed and tugged at my collar, *what did nuns do for birth control?*

"I'm here for the signing, Miss Franki."

I covered the book like I'd been caught with porn by a Mother Superior instead of Glenda, and the comparison wasn't too far off the mark. Okay, it was miles off, but Glenda's outfit was in the vicinity. The hood of her sheer black trench coat covered her head like one of the transparent veils Father Festin had mentioned, and she'd wrapped her body in strategically placed black-and-white ribbons. The effect was that of a nun in a deconstructed habit—with serious skin showing.

Glenda strutted to my chair, flanked by Shona and the Screamers, and unbuckled her coat. "What do you think of my gondola pole look, sugar? It's a play off the polecat theme in the title of my memoirs."

"That's really clever. It's also kind of Goth-candy-cane stripper pole."

"Why, that's genius, Miss Franki. The minute we get home, I'm going to choreograph a holiday striptease to go with this look."

Just the thing for a New Orleans Christmas.

She pointed her cigarette holder at the copy of *Forbidden Fashions*. "Is that my book you're reading?"

Close, I thought. "It's a history of Venetian nuns."

Glenda started as though it was *The Satanic Verses*. "Why in God's name would you read that?"

"Because I went to the San Zaccaria church today and found out Lucrezia Pavan was in their convent."

She started again and dislodged a pole stripe, and I looked around for the cashier to make sure his damn hadn't sprung a leak.

Glenda repositioned the rogue ribbon. "How the hell did Sister Lucrezia catch Casanova?"

"I don't know that yet, but I think she was forced into the convent, like a lot of other noble women."

Glenda cried out and collapsed on the chair arm.

I patted her back. For a woman like my landlady, being forced to take the veil—monasterial or marital—in a world full of men was an existence too painful to bear. "If it makes you feel any better, not all of them obeyed their vows. They wore makeup, perfume, and low-cut dresses with high-heeled clogs, kind of like your Garden Hos."

She managed a wan smile at my reference to the green stripper Crocs that she gardened in, so I decided to continue. "They also rode with men in gondolas and went to parties. Some even had lovers."

"It still hurts, sugar. Those nuns were my people."

I kept my mouth shut. The truth in black and white was that the heavenly harlots had more religion than she did.

Shona gave a solemn sigh. She had a faraway look in her

eyes, and her fingers formed a steeple. "Almost makes me want to join a convent."

The three Hos nodded and murmured among themselves.

Glenda leaned in. "By the way, sugar, who are the Amazons with Miss Shona?"

"Her rowing partners, the Screamer Scullers, but I call them the Hos." I glanced at the tall, muscled trio. "Not to their faces, though."

Shona perched on the book barrel beside my chair. "What else did you find out at San Zaccaria?"

"That a Casanova impersonator and a church volunteer named Perpetua might've had something to do with the jewel theft, which reminds me, would you tap into your library network for information about the crucifix necklace Lucrezia Pavan was buried with?"

"No problem." She puffed out her quilted chest. "You want Dena, Gena, Lena, and me to investigate the ruffians too?"

Glenda caressed her exposed bosom. "I'll take Casanova, Miss Shona. But first I have to see about a man outside in my fan line. Contrary to popular opinion, business *does* mix with pleasure."

The way my Venice trip was going, I wouldn't know. "There's a line?"

Shona squeezed her romance tote to her chest. "All desperate men, hungry for autographed books."

Given the author, I was confident their appetite wasn't for the signature. Or the book.

Riccardo the cashier appeared in the doorway, still atremble. "Signora Glenda, I let-a the fans inside."

"Showtime, ladies." She whipped off her trench and showed her stripes. Some other things too.

Riccardo crossed himself, grabbed a copy of her book from a stack by the door, and dropped to his knees at her feet.

I see what Shona means by desperate.

Glenda cackled. "Riccardo, honey, I appreciate the enthusiasm, but you've got to let the others inside."

"Stay down, Riccardo," Shona barked. "I've got this."

My text tone beeped. Hoping it was Bradley, I pulled my phone from my bag. It was Stella Di Stefano telling me to meet Midge and Madge Maven at Harry's Bar at nine in the morning. Before I did, I had to figure out whether the canal behind the bookstore was connected to the San Michele cemetery. But given the threat I'd received, I was hesitant to walk outside at night.

A crowd of men rushed the room, pushing and shoving and whistling.

On the other hand, was any woman safe around Glenda's desperate fans?

I cupped my hands over my bottom to stave off any pinching and elbowed through the frenzied fans to the Screamers. "Hey, do you guys want to go with me to investigate the canals?"

Ho One turned to Ho Two. "She wants us to leave now?"

"With rooms full of Italian men?" Ho Two replied.

Ho Three crossed her arms. "You'd have to take us out of here in body bags."

"All righty, then." I turned to ask Shona, but she'd whipped off her quilted jumper to reveal a pantsuit with a neckline that showed a daring three inches of cleavage.

So much for being a helper. Anxious to escape the lusty crowd, I went to the tiny courtyard behind the store and climbed the soggy book steps to look over the wall.

A gondolier steered a man and woman down the canal on a romantic late-night gondola ride. It was a gorgeous scene, and if it hadn't been for the catcalls from inside the store, I might've heard the couple's contented sighs.

Had Lucrezia and Casanova ridden in a gondola? And would

Bradley and I do the same? Something told me that with his ex-wife in town, his flight was the least of my worries.

I descended the books. I didn't have time to think about Sheilah. I had to focus on the other blonde, the one in the white mask and gown, and figure out whether the flaming coffin I'd seen her with could have traveled to the Libreria Acqua Alta from San Michele.

At the entrance, I spotted a few people out and the street lamps were on, so I figured it would be safe to walk for a short distance. "God knows, I don't want to stay at the book signing."

Using the maps app on my phone, I identified the waterway behind the bookstore as the Rio della Tetta, or Rio of the Tit, something I'd never tell Glenda. Or Shona. I followed it to Palazzo Tetta, a tall, narrow palace surrounded by water, where the Rio della Tetta merged into the Rio di San Giovanni in Laterano. Within minutes I rounded a turn to the empty street that ran along the Rio dei Mendicanti or Rio of the Beggars. From there, it was a straight shot to the lagoon—and the cemetery island.

"I'll save that trip for daylight."

A light gleamed inside the *Sogno Veneziano Atelier*. Curious why the shop had been named Venetian Dream, I peered into the window and cringed. Masked mannequins modeled Carnival costumes. They should've called it the Oh No Veneziano. Seventeenth-century clothes were creepy enough on humans, much less on lifeless figures.

Turning from the window, I made like one of the mannequins.

Am I in a Venetian dream?

I clenched my fists and blinked.

No, a Venetian nightmare. The flaming coffin was coming up the canal.

Instinctively, I crouched behind a trash can in case the woman in white made another ghastly, ghostly appearance.

The coffin moved at a brisk pace—too brisk for the serene water. The only explanation was a motor. *But why? What was the coffin for? Was it a memorial to Giuseppina Gabriel Carmelo, the little girl who'd drowned in front of the cemetery in 1904? Or did it hold more jewelry stolen from the cemetery?*

The woman in white emerged from a side street across the canal. Her mask and flowing gown were eerie in the dark night. She raised a lace-gloved hand and pointed at the coffin, as she'd done before.

This time, I zeroed in on her left hand at her side. And I went as rigid as the coffin candles. Unless my mind was messing with me, she was missing her ring finger.

Caterina from the hotel was right. The woman in white was Tosca, the young woman who'd taken her life after the jealous nobleman had mutilated her hand to prevent her from marrying the hunter.

That's impossible. But what are the odds that whoever is posing as Tosca's ghost has lost the same finger?

"I'm sure Shona would happily calculate them for me." Despite my whispered joke, I was so scared that the creepy Carnival mannequins seemed like fun friends.

Tosca walked along the canal with her arm outstretched toward the coffin.

But she wasn't pointing. Her fingers were gripping something and aiming it.

Like a remote control.

The coffin was almost to the trash can. I wanted to dive into the canal to find out what was inside, but I couldn't run the risk of Tosca being armed.

The light inside the store dimmed. *How is that possible?*

I looked behind me. *Correction, Franki. The light didn't dim. A shadow is looming over you, and that isn't good.*

My lungs wouldn't budge, not even to breathe. But, still crouching, my feet spun me to an enormous figure, at least seven feet tall, in a black tabarro. Even more terrifying than his height—his head was obscured by a hood.

I bolted up and backed into the trash can. But I didn't feel the hit. I was too busy watching the cloaked giant Frankenstein-walk toward me.

"*La prego, signorina. Mi aiuti.*" His plea for help sounded haunted in his chest.

Stunned at the request, I opened my mouth. My lungs produced gasps worthy of Gaspare, but my vocal cords remained too paralyzed to speak.

He extended his arm and held out a cup.

Is he begging on the Rio of the Beggars?

As if to answer my question, he jingled the coins inside the cup, and the movement pulled back his sleeve.

My eyes locked onto his exposed hand and wrist. Where his flesh should have been there was nothing but bones held together with screws.

"*Spiccioli,*" he moaned, "*per ricomprare il mio scheletro.*"

His words seared my brain like hot olive oil—*coins to buy back my skeleton.*

The huge man asking me for money was the bell ringer of Venice. But based on what I was seeing, what he needed wasn't his skeleton, it was his skin. Rather than give him mine, I spun around the trash can and ran like hell.

8

M adge Maven placed the crumpled black hat she'd worn when I met her in Sardinia on our corner table at Harry's Bar. Her small mouth frowned in disapproval, and her turkey wattle wagged in agreement. "My dear girl, I realize you've had a fright, but you simply must get more sleep."

Midge Maven, a softer version of her sister—a Helen Hayes to Madge's Margaret Rutherford—patted my hand. "She's right. We have a mystery on our hands, so you'll need your rest."

That was easier said than done. After my encounter with Tosca and the bell ringer, I'd spent a sleepless night on the antique sofa while my mom and nonna slept beneath the aqua silk bedspread. Anyone who thought sharks didn't sleep hadn't heard those two snoring. "I'll get to bed early tonight."

Madge sniffed. "Out of the question, I'm afraid. At 2400 hours, we shall take our boat to the cemetery to conduct a covert investigation."

Between the military language, their heavy wool coats, and the sparse 1930s décor of Harry's Bar, I could have been in a war movie. I half-expected to see once-regular patron Ernest

Hemingway drinking the bar's famous creation, the Bellini, while penning a novel. "Why don't we go to San Michele this morning?"

"We must avoid being seen on the premises. The scoundrel posing as the bell ringer will be watching your movements, as will the alleged ghost of Tosca, the Casanova character, and that questionable church volunteer, Perpetua."

My gaze drifted to *Il Gazzettino* on the table. There was nothing in the newspaper about the coffin I'd seen the night before, which made me wonder whether it was connected to the grave robbery. "So, you think the jewel thieves have broken into Lucrezia's grave even though the paper doesn't mention it?"

Madge raised her large chin. "In light of Iona's death, I'm sure of it. Someone wanted her out of the way when they stole the necklace."

Midge shrugged. "And given what you overhead that man say at the Caffè Florian, I dare say they stole it last night."

I leaned forward. "You mean, when he yelled 'No, la Pavan?'"

"Precisely. Either he was angry that they hadn't stolen the necklace when they robbed the Duchess Von Leipold's grave, or insisting that Lucrezia's tomb was the next target."

I thought the same thing. "He also mentioned the Pala d'Oro altar cloth from Saint Mark's Basilica, which means it could be a target."

Midge glanced at her sister. "The panels *are* covered in gemstones and precious metals."

The lines on Madge's face deepened. "You must mention this to the authorities. The Pala d'Oro is said to be one of the two beating hearts of the faith in Venice, along with Saint Mark's remains, which rest in the baldachin vault below it." She paused. "Do you think this man could be the bell ringer?"

"No, he was average height, and the bell ringer was around seven feet."

She raised her nose. "A man of that stature shouldn't be hard to spot in Italy. We must all be on the lookout."

Trust me, I will be.

A waiter in a white jacket and black bowtie delivered two breakfast teas, a caffè americano, and complimentary snacks—a plate of croquettes and a small bowl of green olives, which were a suitable breakfast food in Italy.

If it hadn't been 9:00 a.m., I would've ordered a martini to go with them. A stiff drink was in order before a midnight trip to a cemetery. Instead, I gulped much-needed coffee. "Do either of you think the thieves are using the coffin to transport the stolen jewels?"

Midge gripped her teacup with both hands. "It seems much too showy a method."

"Quite." Madge puckered. "I rather think of it as a diversion, a common technique among criminals."

I looked at a long, rectangular picture of the Venetian lagoon on the wall. It was possible that Tosca had been tasked with creating a diversionary scene in the city's canals while the thieves robbed graves. *But were we correct in assuming that Casanova, Perpetua, and the bell ringer were her accomplices?*

Midge gave my fingers a squeeze. "You haven't told us what you think of our great-niece, Stella."

"She seems really nice. And thanks to the two of you, she's got a dream job."

Madge adjusted her coat. "We had to get the girl out of Las Vegas."

"And her father's family restaurant," Midge said, her kind eyes wide.

"Yes." Madge puffed her cheeks. "Ghastly business."

Based on Stella's comment about how Saint Mark was smuggled out of Egypt, I half-wondered whether they served pork and cabbage sandwiches.

Midge spread a napkin on her lap and reached for a croquette. "Stella mentioned that you were going to find the distributor of the Valpolicella Iona purchased."

"Father Festin, the priest at San Zaccaria, is going to ask Perpetua since she orders the same brand for their communion wine, but I'm not sure she'll tell the truth."

Madge frowned. "I rather doubt it as well. And any number of shops could sell the Valpolicella since it's produced here in the Veneto."

Midge gave a pleasant smile. "In the province of Verona, to be specific. It evokes Romeo and Juliette, which makes it a lovely choice for your friend's wedding."

Except that they both died before they could marry. I made the scongiuri gesture under the table to ward off the possibility of the same fate for Veronica and Dirk.

Madge bit into a croquette. "Speaking of the wine," she paused to chew, "Midge and I intend to compile a list of possible poisons. We dabble in chemistry, you know." She wiped crumbs from her fingers. "Tell us, did you happen to notice anything unusual about Iona's coloring?"

The chef's face came to me in a flash. "The inside of her mouth was brown, which was weird because her lips and tongue were purple."

Madge's eyes darted to her sister. "We shall run that through the poison database."

"Like, a British national database?"

Midge's smile was as sweet as the sugar she stirred into her tea. "No, dear. Ours."

My lips tried to match her smile but fell short. Something about having one's own poison database struck me as formidable.

Madge's eyes narrowed. "Was the purple reddish or violet?"

Her choice of color reminded me of Iona's necklace. "The

latter. And while we're on the subject, Iona was seen wearing a gold necklace that said *Violet* on the day she died. Do you know who it could be?"

"I've no idea."

"Nor do I." Midge pressed a hand to her bosom. "I do hope it was a friend, poor thing. Iona lived such a lonely life. She was never the same after a family trip to Venice when she was sixteen. She met a young nobleman there and lost her head for him. As it turned out, he'd used her as a plaything."

Madge nodded. "When the family returned home to London, Iona became so incorrigible that her mother sent her to boarding school, but I often suspected it was a home for wayward girls."

I sipped my coffee. "Why do you think she returned to Venice for work? Did she come back to look for him?"

Midge adjusted the lace on her collar. "We heard that the culinary school she attended got her the job, but it's entirely possible that she asked for a position in Venice."

A thirty-something male in a trench coat and low fedora passed our table and slid a piece of paper to Madge. Unless the guy was into women fifty years his senior, I didn't think it was his phone number.

Madge caught my eye as she pocketed the paper. She wrinkled her nose. "An unrelated matter."

I shifted in my seat. I knew from the Sardinia trip that the Mavens were investigators, but something about them told me it was just flat mysterious. "What do you know about Lucrezia's relationship with Casanova?"

Their faces turned pink—to use a British term, *quite*—and I thought they'd misunderstood the scope of my question. "Oh, I don't mean the details of their sex life."

Madge gave her tea a vigorous stirring, and Midge used a menu to fan her flaming cheeks.

After an awkward silence, Madge cleared her throat. "According to Iona's mother, Lucrezia was to marry a Contarini, one of the most powerful patrician families in Venice."

"Yes," Midge said, "you should see the Palazzo Contarini just off the Grand Canal. It has a *bovolo* staircase, which is Venetian for 'snail.' An architectural marvel. Lucrezia could have inhabited that splendid building, but alas."

"Alas, what?"

"She couldn't resist the seductive powers of Giacomo Girolamo Casanova."

Madge smirked with mirth. "That's Jacob Jerome Newhouse in English."

I'd never thought to translate his name, and I was willing to bet that his lady friends hadn't either. Because he wouldn't have seen as much action with that mediocre moniker.

Midge sighed. "The Contarini family found out about Lucrezia's dalliance and called off the engagement. Since she'd been ruined, her father sent her to the convent and gave her dowry to her only sister, Ludovica, who married Annibale Bragadin. As the younger daughter, she'd been destined for the convent since birth to preserve the family fortune."

I reached for an olive. "I'll bet Ludovica was happy."

"Undoubtedly, as was the husband, I'm sure. The dowry was quite large."

"I've heard that nuns in Venice often led scandalous lives. Did Lucrezia continue to see Casanova while she was in the convent?"

Madge sipped her tea. "She must have, because he gave her the necklace rather late in life, right before he went to Prague to work as a librarian."

I almost fell out of my chair. "Casanova was a *librarian*?"

"For the Count von Waldstein in the chateau of Dux, which

is now Duchov in Czechia." She placed her cup on the table. "After he was exiled from Venice in 1785."

No wonder Shona thinks he's sexy.

Midge's hazel eyes twinkled. "Casanova was many things— seducer, libertine, adventurer, writer, poet, alchemist, diplomat, lawyer, secret agent. He was a jack of all trades, or a giacomo, as it were."

The spinster sisters tittered.

Madge dabbed her mouth with a napkin. "Jolly good joke, Midge. And she's right, you know. At one time, Casanova was even an abbot."

Whore nuns and Lothario priests? Religion did not make sense in Venice. "That reminds me, Stella said the necklace had a religious legend associated with it."

Midge recoiled. "That's something of a mischaracterization. The necklace is allegedly shaped like the Basilica of San Marco, which was designed in the shape of a Greek cross typical of Byzantine churches, but it came from Satan himself."

By this point, I was used to Venice's ghosts, but I hadn't expected the devil. "Why do you say that?"

Madge fittingly pointed a fork at me. "The story passed down in the Pavan family is that Casanova won the necklace from evil incarnate, the Comte de Saint Germain, while playing a card game called faro. Have you heard of him?"

I had, from a vampire case I'd worked in New Orleans the year before. And legend had it that he'd somehow remained forty years of age since he'd frequented King Louis the XV of France and his mistress, Madame de Pompadour, at the court of Versailles.

～

"As if Tosca, Giuseppina Gabriel Carmelo, and the bell ringer weren't enough," I grumbled, walking from Harry's Bar to the hotel, "now there's a vampire in the mix, not to mention Bradley's ex." I picked up my pace, even though it was 10:00 a.m. and tourists were swarming the shops, because that was one scary list.

I dialed Veronica. I heard her pick up and didn't wait for a greeting. "Casanova got the crucifix necklace that he gave to Lucrezia from the freaking Comte de Saint Germain."

"The man who allegedly showed up in New Orleans in the early 1900s as a vampire named Jacques de Saint Germain?"

"Yeah, and the one I thought was my client last year."

Veronica sighed. "Think about that statement for a moment."

Rounding the corner onto a street lined with designer boutiques, I maneuvered through crowds of shoppers picking up swanky Christmas gifts. "I didn't make up the fact that the Count keeps showing up century after century."

"Wait. I don't remember that."

My eyes strained against their sockets. *How could she forget the Count's century-hopping? Besides the biting, it was the scariest part.* "First, the Comtesse von Georgy saw him at one of Madame de Pompadour's soirees in Paris in 1760 and swore he hadn't aged a day since she'd seen him in 1710. Then in 1903, he bit the neck of that woman who died after jumping from his French Quarter balcony. And in the eighties, he was in St. Tropez. The guy is everywhere. He's basically a vampire version of Shona."

"It's clearly a legend."

"I'd like to agree with you, but I'm swimming in Venetian legends, which is concerning since Iona died in water." I entered the Piazza San Marco, glad there were no canals or rios for me to fall into. "And speaking of dying, don't forget that the Count supposedly committed suicide in St. Tropez, and they found a note, but not his body."

"So, you think the Count has come to suck your blood," she said, deadpan.

"Don't be ridiculous." I made the scongiuri gesture and glanced over my shoulder, checking for anyone in a cape or a waistcoat. "It's just disturbing that his name has come up in another one of my cases because, for the record, the guy once claimed to be the son of a Transylvanian prince."

"Look, I understand that the 'Roses Are Red' threat has spooked you. It has me scared too. But getting upset over a silly vampire legend is extreme, even for you."

I stopped in the middle of the piazza and rubbed my forehead. "I'm just tired, and there's a lot going on."

"I know, and Bradley's not here. But he will be soon."

Tears threatened to run from my eyes like canals. I didn't dare ask whether Sheilah was a wedding guest.

"Franki, Dirk just came to my room to discuss a best man issue, so I need to let you go. Keep me posted, and try to get some rest. The Count is a coincidence, I promise."

I hung up and started walking. *Veronica's right. I'm making a mountain out of a molehill—or a monster out of a mortal.*

The bell in Saint Mark's Campanile tolled, as if to contradict me.

I glared up at the tower. *Is that thing trolling me?* Then I stiffened. *Or is the bell ringer sending me a* For-Whom-the-Bell-Tolls *message? I did think about Hemingway and his war novels at Harry's Bar.*

"Venice is getting to you, girl," I muttered to myself. "Church bells aren't messing with you, and neither is the bell ringer—or the ghost of Ernest Hemingway, for that matter. Also, the Comte isn't alive, and vampires don't exist." I mentally canceled the last part of that sentence because New Orleans was teeming with real-life bloodsuckers, as was Buffalo, apparently. But the undead kind like the Comte defied the laws of nature. On second thought, both kinds did.

The valet stand outside the Hotel San Marco was empty. Nevertheless, it probably wasn't a good look to go around the city mumbling about bells, ghosts, and vampires.

Or about Bradley's ex. Because when my mom and nonna found out she was in Venice, there would be another feeding frenzy. And, as always, I would be the victim.

At the hotel's rotating door, I tucked my left hand in my pocket to avoid another ring-finger mishap. I didn't believe that the Tosca sighting had doomed me to a life of zitellahood, but my fiancé *was* MIA, and I was pretty sure that having his ex in the hotel was a bad omen.

It wasn't that I was jealous of Sheilah. I'd gotten over that. She was just too much of a schemer for my taste—and for my relationship. But for Bradley's and Veronica's sakes, I was open to letting bygones be bygones. Sheilah might even be nice under different circumstances. After all, Bradley had married her, and he was a great guy. *Who knows? Maybe we'll strike up a friendship. Weddings do tend to bring people together.*

Gaspare was behind the reception counter, his glasses low on his nose. He glanced up from a computer. "Is there a problem, Signorina Amato? You are peak-ed."

Like my blood has been sucked. "Are you familiar with the Comte de Saint Germain?"

"I do not recall such a guest."

"He wasn't a guest. He's a vampire who lived in Venice."

A little girl shrieked in the elevator. "Mommy! I want to go home!"

Her mother glared at me as she ushered her daughter to the exit. "Vampires don't live here, sweetie. There's no such thing."

Gaspare didn't gasp. He removed his glasses and pinched the

bridge of his nose. "If you are to remain in good standing at the hotel, I must ask you to refrain from conversation in the lobby."

"But I—"

"*Ah, ah.*" He wagged a finger. "Guests must obey the rules, and the law. I wish to remind you that the *polizia* expect you today."

"What kind of trouble has she gotten into *this* time?" a haughty voice drawled.

Sheilah. My shoulders stiffened, and the opening for those bygones being bygones slammed shut like a coffin lid.

She strutted to the reception counter in a black day dress with roses embroidered from the bodice to the skirt, dripping with Versace bags, Shalimar perfume, and her signature snarky sarcasm. It was a more elegant version of Glenda's Spanish look, but unlike her silk rose, Sheilah's had thorns. "Franki's been in jail before, Gaspare."

The gasp he'd been repressing finally came out.

I didn't know how she'd come by that information, but I wasn't going to lower myself to ask. "Don't worry, Gaspare," I said, death-staring at Sheilah, "I haven't murdered anyone...yet."

"You're as charming as ever, Franki." She batted her lashes at Gaspare. "As a personal favor to me, please find a room in the hotel for Mr. Bradley Hartmann."

"I will do my best, Signora Kensington."

My palm came down on the counter with a smack. "No, you won't, Gaspare. I'm Mr. Hartmann's fiancée, and I've got that handled."

Sheilah's mouth slid into a smarmy smile. "Is that why he's upstairs crashing Dirk's groom suite?"

A jolt went through me. She *was* here for the wedding—and so was Bradley. *How long has he been here? And why did she know about it and not me?*

Her smarmy smile turned into a sneer. "You look surprised. Didn't he tell you he was coming?"

Not today, he didn't. "*Pff!* Obviously."

"That's good, because I'd hate to hear that you two are on the rocks. I've never been to a Mafia wedding."

Gaspare went peak-ed.

I must've turned as red as the roses on her dress. The Italian slur was infuriating, especially because it involved my wedding. Sheilah had married Bradley in a posh Boston venue in keeping with a longstanding Hartmann family tradition, and I wanted to know how she knew I wasn't doing the same. *Was she in contact with his mother, Lillian? Or...*

Was she still in contact with Bradley?

Anger welled in my chest like water in a leaky gondola. "Come to our wedding, and you'll find out what mob families do to unwanted guests."

With that, I strode onto the elevator, and to my dismay, she followed, wrecking my tough-gal exit. As we went up, I kept my gaze straight ahead, and I assumed she did the same.

The elevator door opened, and I stepped into the hallway.

She did too.

There was one problem—I didn't know where Dirk's groom suite was, but I would've chopped off my own ring finger before admitting that to her. To buy time until she gave away Bradley's room with a glance or pause, I set out down the hall at a relaxed pace.

There was a second problem—she did too.

My stride became a stalk.

As did hers.

I was afraid I'd pass his room, so I slowed down.

She stopped. "What's the matter? You don't know where Bradley's staying?"

"For your information, I've already been to his room plenty of times."

"We'll see about that, won't we?"

"We certainly will."

Sheilah and I locked eyes and matched each other step for step.

Now what should I do? Feign a sprained ankle? Pretend I remembered an important errand? Or just shove her in a maid closet?

No, none of those things would work. There was only one way to deal with a woman like Sheilah—sic Shona on her. But the one time I needed her to show up, she was nowhere to be found.

Sheilah stopped at room twenty-two and flashed a she-devil smile. "Bradley's next door in suite twenty-one."

"I knew that." I spoke in a huffy tone to make it convincing.

"Sure you did." She entered her room.

My knock matched the pounding of my heart in my chest.

Dirk opened the door, his eyes widened, and he ran a hand through his Robert Redford hair. "Franki. What is it? Has there been another murder?"

"Like I said to Sheilah," I ground out, "not yet."

Bradley exited a bedroom, and even though I could see that he was worn out from his flight, he looked gorgeous in fitted black jeans and a blue sweater that accentuated his eyes.

Which only made me madder.

He held up his hands in surrender but had a half-smile on his lips that made me want to kill him. "Franki, Sheilah was going out shopping when I got to the hotel. I found out she was a guest at the wedding, and she asked me when you and I were tying the knot. It was all very innocent."

On your part, but not on hers. "Never mind Sheilah," I said, although I did mind her a lot, and especially in the room next door. "Why didn't you tell me you found a flight?"

"I was on standby in New York and didn't know I had a seat until the last minute. I tried to call you, but it wouldn't go through. I sent a text, but you clearly never got it."

The gondola-full of welled anger in my chest seeped out, leaving me feeling like a fool for succumbing to Sheilah's scheme. Embarrassed, I glanced around for Dirk and realized he'd slipped from the suite.

Bradley looked at me from under his lashes. "Are we good?"

I fell into his arms. "I'm sorry. I trust you, but I don't trust your ex."

He kissed my hair. "Sheilah's the least of our concerns, babe. Dirk filled me in on the threatening note. I wish you'd told me."

"I didn't want you to worry."

"I've been worried since I saw you on the front page of the paper. And I'm going to help you find out who's behind all of this. Just tell me where to start."

If I only knew. I rested my head and left hand on his chest. The "Roses Are Red" threat had been weighing on me like a sarcophagus, and I was wondering whether the roses on Sheilah's dress were a sign that she was a threat too. But I felt safer now that Bradley was with me. And I had every faith that he would help me solve the mystery of Iona's murder.

As his heart beat in my ear, it was as clear as the ruby and diamonds on my engagement ring that the answer lay in one of the two beating hearts of the faith in Venice, the Palo d'Oro.

But what was it?

The only thing I knew for certain was that if I didn't figure out who killed Iona soon, my heart could cease to beat.

9

"Well, I don't know about you, Miss Franki, but these Pala d'Oro jewels have got *my* heart beating." Glenda pressed a hand to her chest, which, like the rest of her, had been wrapped in an off-white linen altar cloth by a no-nonsense nun at the Basilica di San Marco entrance. Against the backdrop of the church's gleaming gold mosaics, she bore a vague resemblance to an Egyptian mummy. "It's pounding even harder than when I first saw the moth-eaten lederhosen of my German beermaker beau."

Bradley laughed and bowed his head, but I massaged my temples. I had a headache, and not just from the church's insufferable woody incense. Glenda hadn't stopped talking about the men she'd met on her European book tour since we'd run into her in the hotel lobby. Because of her many "menscapades," we'd left for the Basilica later than we'd planned, which was just in time for Shona and the other Screamer Scullers to heave-ho-ho-ho up to the jetty in *Sculling is a Scream* sweatshirts. Not only did Glenda tag along with us, so did a Screamer, and it wasn't one of the three Hos.

I looked at the Pala d'Oro. The high altar cloth hung in a

double-sided frame above the baldachin vault that held Saint Mark's remains, and it was surrounded by four green marble columns etched with stories from the gospel. "I've never seen so many jewels in one place." I sized up Glenda's getup. "The cloth is around the same size as the one you're wearing. Maybe ten by seven?"

My eyes gravitated to their corners, waiting for Shona to rattle off the Pala d'Oro's exact measurements, but her face turned pink, and she looked at the marble floor. *That's odd. Glenda's covered for once. What's there to be embarrassed about?*

Glenda wrestled with her covering like a mummy struggling to free itself from its bandages. "You'd never know the Venetian nuns wore revealing clothing from that Neanderthal nun at the entrance."

"They only dressed that way during the Republic," I laid a look on Shona, "whenever that was."

Her cheeks went fuchsia, but she didn't utter a single numeral.

Something was amiss. A librarian who'd yell in a bookstore wouldn't hold back in a church, so she should have been shouting facts from the Basilica's domed rooftop.

Intending to tease out Shona's know-it-all nature by spouting off some trivia, I googled the Pala d'Oro on my phone. It was pure folly, but I was kind of worried about her. "Wikipedia says the cloth has a hundred and eighty-seven enamel plaques depicting Christ and the saints that are decorated with gold, silver, and around two thousand gems." I peeked at Shona, whose face was tomato, and continued. "Pearls, garnets, emeralds, sapphires, amethysts, rubies, topazes, agates, carnelians, and jaspers," I paused, "whatever those last two are."

"Mercy, sugar." Glenda fanned herself with fabric. "That jewel talk's getting me hot and anything but bothered."

Trivia time was over. My landlady was not a woman of the

cloth, so I had to do my part to keep her in one. Plus, Shona was so red from repressed knowledge that I was afraid she'd burst and unleash a torrent of dull data. But I still wanted to know what was up with her silence. *Was she mooning over a man she'd met at Glenda's book signing?*

Bradley knelt in front of the glass vault containing the marble sarcophagus. "The Church moved Saint Mark's remains here when the Republic fell. Before that, they'd been in the crypt below the Basilica for a thousand years."

Silently, I thanked the *Signore* above for sparing me another visit to an underground graveyard.

Bradley rose. "It's a good thing they moved him, too, because the crypt floods." He grinned at Shona. "Acqua alta."

Her eyes took a dive, and her cheeks flamed like the candles on the coffin.

It wasn't a local Italian she had a crush on. It was Bradley! I stifled the beatific smile that tried to erupt, but inside I glowed like the bedazzled Pala d'Oro. If Shouting Shona turned into Shy Shona around my fiancé, Venice might live up to its La Serenissima nickname, after all.

Now I can investigate in blessed peace. I practically skipped to the altar cloth. As stunning as it was, I doubted that the jewel thieves would go after such a public artifact. Forgotten graves of wealthy women were safer targets. Although, with Saint Mark's sarcophagus below, the Pala d'Oro was technically part of a gravesite.

Are the thefts connected somehow? The Duchess Von Leipold and Lucrezia Pavan could have known one another, but the theft of the Duchess's gold sphere necklace didn't seem related to Iona's murder—unless it was a diversion, perhaps like the coffin. And I didn't have any reason to link the Pala d'Oro to either of the women.

Shouting broke out behind me, and it wasn't Shona.

It was Nonna.

She shuffle-shoved her way through a group of tourists and raised her arms to the golden-domed Heavens. "*Madre santissima, aiutami!*"

Glenda threw a fold of fabric over her shoulder. "Want me to go check on her, sugar?"

I shot a pointed look at her altar cloth. "Don't. She's asking for help from the Virgin Mary, not King Tut."

"She's right, Glenda," Bradley said. "It's best to let Carmela work this out herself, whatever it is." He ran his hand through his hair, and Shona followed his fingers with eyes smoldering like the incense.

I rolled my eyes and returned them to Nonna, who shoved a tourist from the holy water basin, wet her knobby fingers, and crossed herself while she made her way to her knees. She clutched her rosary, moving her lips as she worked the beads.

Something bad had happened, and I knew what it was. "Bradley," I pulled him behind an altar column, "for the love of God, run."

"What for? I don't have anything to do with whatever's going on."

"You do, or you did."

"How?"

"Sheilah," I hissed.

Realization bloomed on his face like one of his ex-wife's thorned roses, and we peered around the column.

My mother surged inside the church like acqua alta during high tide. Her fur wrap was askew, and her big bouffant do looked as though she'd just defended it from nesting pigeons. "Have you seen him, Carmela? I saw them come in."

Nonna shook the rosary at her. "I'm-a talkin' to God-a here."

"Then I'll handle this myself." My mother's jaw tightened as she scoured the Basilica. "And when I'm done with Mr. Hartmann, we'll have a date for the wedding *and* one for the birth of our first grandchild."

"Yowza." Bradley ran his hands up and down his shirt. "She really upped the ante on me."

"Yeah, except that I'm the one who'll bear the brunt of that childbirth date."

Glenda freed herself from her binding, revealing the gold Dolce-and-Gabbana-inspired outfit she'd made with rosary beads, Virgin Mary charms, and Hold Up body adhesive. "Hide in this tent, Bradley, honey."

I tossed the fabric back over her. "Keep your cloth on. We're in a church. But she's right, Bradley. You should hide under that thing, because I'm not ready to have that grandbaby."

His eyes grew hooded. "This is taking it too far, Franki. If I explain that I had nothing to do with Sheilah being invited to the wedding, your mom and nonna will be reasonable."

My hands went to my hips. "Bradley Hartmann, when in God's name have you ever known them to be reasonable where my marital and maternal statuses are concerned?"

He climbed under the cloth.

Shona's eyes burned at the sight of Glenda and Bradley under a sheet together.

Glenda snuggled up to him like spandex on skin. "Why don't Bradley and I go on over to the Casanova Museum, sugar? I need to be in an environment that appreciates my outfit."

"Good idea," I said, although I had reservations. Glenda and my Casanova in the Casanova Museum could be problematic.

Turning toward the entrance, I saw my mother rushing the high altar like a tidal wave.

"She's coming." I pushed Glenda to get them both moving. "Scale the walls until you get back to the entrance. I'll meet you in an hour."

They flitted off like unholy ghosts, and Shona put her arm around me.

Bradley's in Venice, and I'm still Shona's date.

My mother rushed up, her eyes bright with fever-induced delirium. Since I wasn't alone, she put on what I called her "cheer-faux" face. "Francesca, I'm so glad I found you." Her breath was as ragged as her appearance. "Your nonna and I met the most interesting couple in the lobby, the Kensingtons." Her pleasant smile came off as maniacal. "Do you know them?"

As I'd guessed, she'd discovered that Sheilah was staying at the hotel, which meant that the fever-induced delirium was actually frenzied shark—just before it feasted on my carcass. "I do, Mom, and there's nothing to worry about."

She grinned at Shona. "Excuse us for a sec." She pulled me behind a column, and the cheer-faux look fell away like Glenda's altar cloth. "Your fiancé's ex-wife is in the City of Love for a wedding, and you don't think there's anything to worry about?"

When she put it that way, it did sound foreboding. "Sheilah's remarried, Mom. She and Bradley have both moved on."

"Sometimes people who've moved on move back."

I made the sign of the cross with my index fingers. My mother was like the devil tempting me not to trust Bradley. "We've got bigger things to worry about than my wedding date and a grandkid. Iona's killer may be hunting Pavans, which means you and I could be next."

Her face hardened into a tale of trial and tribulation that rivaled the gospel stories carved into the columns. "I'm on a trip to the world's most romantic city with your nonna, fighting like hell to get my daughter settled. Let him try me."

I didn't need to worry about her, or my nonna for that matter. If the killer came after them, they'd just run his life to death.

A priest reminiscent of a jolly old Saint Nick approached in a black robe. "Monsignor Meneghello," he said in impeccable English. "May I be of service?"

"My mother is looking for the confessional."

He smiled and pointed. "Around the corner, *signora*."

"*Grazie*," my mother hummed as though singing a hymn. As the monsignor turned to Shona, she gritted her teeth and grabbed my arm. "God will get you for lying to a priest, Francesca."

He wouldn't, because I was certain she had plenty to confess.

"I'm sure it's cedar," Shona boomed, having found her facts, "and, if I'm not mistaken, frankincense and myrrh?"

The monsignor grinned and clasped his hands beneath his round belly. "Yes, it's Pontifical Incense, a special blend. The fragrant aroma reminds us of Christ's suffering."

How could that be a thing? And what did it mean that I'd called the scent of Christ's suffering insufferable? "Sorry to interrupt, Monsignore, but have you heard of a jeweled crucifix necklace that Giacomo Casanova gave to a patrician woman named Lucrezia Pavan?"

The smile died on his mouth, and he crossed himself.

Why did he do that? Did he know Casanova won it from the vampire Count? "Uh, is there a problem?"

He tapped his fingertips together. "Your question reminded me of the recent jewel thefts. Venetians have always cherished their gems, but to think that any of us would rob a tomb..."

Shona clenched her lips and fists. "It's a sacrilege."

We all agreed on that point. "Why are jewels so significant to Venetians?"

A serene look settled on the monsignor's face. "They represent God and Heaven. The Book of Revelations speaks of a City of God, the New Jerusalem, descending from the heavens with a foundation made of twelve precious stones. According to a Venetian scholar, Monsignor Antonio Nievo, the jewels in the Pala d'Oro reflect the foundation stones of the New Jerusalem."

Between the crucifix necklace and the jewels, I was starting to wonder whether religion was a factor in the case. "How old is the Pala d'Oro?"

Shona's hand shot up. "Oh, I know! It was commissioned in Constantinople in the year 976, but expanded upon over the centuries. Doge Andrea Dandolo is responsible for the current version, which dates back to 1345."

The monsignor tapped his temple. "Your friend is like an encyclopedia."

I bared my teeth but my lips wouldn't rise to the occasion. "Isn't she?"

He gazed at the Pala d'Oro. "Unfortunately, Napoleon stole many of the original gems."

Father Festin had said that Napoleon plundered art, but I hadn't included jewels in his loot. "I'm surprised he didn't steal the entire Pala d'Oro."

"A clever priest convinced him that the stones were fakes."

"Whoa." Shona held out her hands to steady herself. "The priest *lied*?"

"Gracious, no," he raised a finger, "it was a clever play on language. Napoleon believed the priest was speaking dialect, when, in fact, he was not. The word for glass in Venetian is *vero*, the same as the word for true, or real, in Italian."

Shona's dimples deepened. "Gotcha. So Napoleon thought the priest was saying that the stones were made of glass, when he was actually saying they were real."

The man with Perpetua and Casanova at Caffè Florian had used the words *vero* and *Pala d'Oro*. They had to be the grave robbers, and the jeweled altar cloth was their ultimate target. "When were the stones replaced?"

"A few months later, when Austrian troops drove out the

French. Some of the gems came from the church's coffers, others were donated by devout parishioners."

Shona whistled. "You'd have to be pretty darn devout to donate one of those rocks."

I agreed with her—except for the *darn*. I'd already insulted the Pontifical Incense, so I couldn't afford to push my luck.

The monsignor gazed at the gleaming domes. "As you can see, Venetians have long understood that gold and jewels attract the highest energy from the heavens."

The Duchess's gold sphere necklace spun in my mind. "What does the gold represent?"

He gave a patient smile. "It's the color of the Divine, the image of the light that theologians and Fathers of the medieval church believed was God himself. The Pala d'Oro is a Byzantine expression of the cult of light."

I scratched my neck. The word *cult* made me uneasy because it implied unhinged, and Lord knew I already had enough of that in my life. "That wasn't a crazy religious cult, was it? Uh, not that religion is crazy."

The arch relaxed from his brow. "Not that I'm aware. It was an artistic movement that used light to raise man toward God."

The lit candles on the coffin floated through my head yet again. *That's what the cult of light was in the medieval period, but does it exist now? If so, is it something different, like a cult that promises entry into heaven or eternal life?*

Every bone in my still flesh-covered body told me that the answer was yes.

"WE'RE IN THE BACK, Miss Franki," Glenda called in a voice that was suspiciously sultry for the museum setting. "In Casanova's boudoir."

My lips spread as though stretched out on a bed. Had I known the guy's bedroom was part of the exhibit, I definitely wouldn't have let her bring Bradley. If there were a tomb of love in Venice, that was it.

I passed through a room with walls covered in jacquard as black as my mood. Beside a faceless, white-wigged mannequin in a vintage blue frock coat with lace cuffs and matching breeches was a painting of Casanova wearing the outfit. As I walked by the portrait, his seductive gaze seemed to follow me like prey. But that wasn't the disturbing part. The artist, Anton Raphael Mengs, had painted Casanova in a chair, holding an open book upright on his thigh. Behind him was a dark curtain, but to his right, a cherub floated in a blue sky that bathed him in its light.

A shiver went down my back, as though traced by the legendary lover's finger. *Am I being hunted by a Casanova impersonator who belongs to a light cult?*

I moved into an even darker room, and the shiver turned lightning strike. Behind a canopy bed draped in white silk and damask were the shadows of a man and woman about to get it on.

"Bradley?" I shrieked.

"Sexciting, isn't it, sugar?" Glenda emerged from a corner fully clothed—at least by stripper standards. She waved a lace fan and raised a glass of bubbly to the couple's image. "You and your man could show that shadow projection how it's done."

My face burned. I didn't know what embarrassed me more— her comment or the fact that a projector had fooled me into thinking my fiancé was cheating with my landlady.

Bradley entered with a champagne flute. "There you are. I heard you calling."

Glenda took a slurpy sip. "She got all worked up by the shadow show, Bradley, honey."

He nuzzled my ear. "Too bad your mom and nonna are in your suite."

I grabbed his glass and gulped the cold liquid. Between Bradley and the shadow couple, Casanova's bedroom was on fire. "Mm. This is Prosecco."

Glenda flipped her platinum hair, jangling her Virgin Mary charms. "A.k.a. counterfeit champagne. Visitors get a free glass because they sell it in the gift shop."

Bradley took the flute. "The brand is named after the Latin Lover himself."

Casanova Prosecco? The guy really was everywhere in Venice. "That reminds me, Glenda, when is your date with counterfeit Casanova?"

"Day after tomorrow."

Bradley's brow bolted. "Is he who you're bringing to the wedding?"

Glenda licked her lips. "No, but my mystery date does enjoy a good period costume."

Please let it not be the German beermaker with the moth-eaten lederhosen. "We'd better get to the entrance. I left Shona in a 3D virtual reality headset that lets you walk through Venice in Casanova's shoes, and I'm not sure she can handle his eighteenth-century man heels."

Bradley slipped his arm around my waist. "She seems like she can take care of herself, although she's quieter than the stereotypical librarian."

And with any luck, the headset will keep her that way.

Glenda paused to admire an eighteenth-century dress with beaded floral motifs. "This would be fabulous if they cut away all the fabric."

Bradley and I shared a grin as a young employee in period dress approached Glenda. She wore a powdered white wig and had a beauty mark above her lip. And if her big brown eyes were shocked by the "Dolce and Glenda" outfit, they didn't show it. "I am Zanetta, miss." She spoke with a faint accent. "Since you enjoy fabric with cuts, I can show you an item that is not on display."

Glenda batted her gold lashes. "I hope it's a pair of Casanova's tighty whities."

Fortunately, Zanetta didn't appear familiar with that expression.

We followed her through the museum to the entrance, where Shona sat in a row of chairs with an old-Polaroid-type contraption strapped to her head. Based on her slack jaw and the shadow projection in Casanova's bedroom, I figured the 3D virtual tour was of the va-va-voom variety.

"Whoa!" Shona gripped the sides of her seat. "*Buongiorno!*"

That confirmed my suspicion.

Zanetta pulled a brown leather case from a drawer in the reception desk. Inside was a pair of long black silk gloves with a slit at each knuckle. "These are called *stratagliati*, like slashed. The nuns wore them to show their jeweled rings."

Glenda ran a hand over her chest. "The hellion nuns just gave me an idea for a new outfit."

Holy hell.

Zanetta closed the case. "Casanova was quite fond of nuns."

"I'll bet." Bradley rolled his lips. "No strings."

Glenda jangled her charms. "Or zippers."

Zanetta's beauty mark twitched. "A famous chapter in his memoirs describes his amorous encounters with a nun from the convent on the island of Murano, who he identifies only as M.M."

Shona gripped her headset. "*Oh là là!*"

Either Casanova had walked his man heels to France, or something *très sexy* had happened on the virtual video. "Did he ever write about a nun named Lucrezia Pavan?"

"Yes, but only in a letter to a friend. He described his farewell meeting with Lucrezia in 1774, before he left Venice for the last time, on the Ponte delle Tette."

Glenda gasped. "That's where my Casanova asked me to meet him."

I gathered he hadn't told her that it translated to the Bridge of the Tits, or we would have heard all about it and gotten some sort of performance. "Is this letter in the museum?"

"No, in an archive, but I do not know which one. Some scholars believe that Casanova did write about Lucrezia in his memoirs, but under a false identity, possibly the nun, M.M., or his true love, Henriette, the crossdresser."

Bradley coughed on Prosecco. "Casanova dated a crossdresser?"

Zanetta nodded. "Men's clothing allowed women to be anonymous in the city. Nuns used this disguise, especially during Carnevale."

Glenda elbowed me. "We know a Carnival crossdresser, but she's not a nun."

I ground my teeth. "She's talking about her drag queen friend, Carnie Vaul, who's a Hun, as in Attila."

Zanetta's brow furrowed. "But the nuns took great care with their appearance. In the Renaissance, outward beauty reflected inner nobility."

"Oh, I believe you." I angled a glance at Glenda. "It's just that this particular Carnival queen is a commoner inside and out, and no amount of drag makeup will change that."

"Ah, I see," Zanetta said, but her doe eyes indicated otherwise.

And I could sympathize. I didn't understand Carnie either.

"Since you mention makeup, the Venetian nuns took beauty lessons from a book by Giovanventura Rossetti, *Well Known Secrets of the Art of Perfumery*. For instance, the gloves I showed you were perfumed. The nuns also bathed in water scented with rose and jasmine oils and perfumed their hair. Like the Venetian courtesans, some perfumed and painted their nipples."

Glenda gazed at her low-hanging Virgin Marys. "I've done that, child. You're better off with latex. It doesn't run when you work up a sweat."

Bradley scratched his temple. "I'm just going to take a look around."

I would have fled the conversation with him, but the perfumed hair made me think of Tosca's brassy waves. "Zanetta, did Venetian women bleach their hair?"

"It was the style during the Renaissance. Venice was represented as a blonde noblewoman because blonde hair symbolized virginity and purity."

My mental image of Tosca morphed into Society Sheilah, Bradley's ex. *That's not what it means now.*

Zanetta touched her wig. "However, powdered hair like mine was the fashion during Casanova's life. In his letter, he said Lucrezia matched the powder to her clothing, and she always wore violet."

Violet. Does that have anything to do with the name on Iona's necklace?

"*Heiliger strohsack!*" Shona clutched her head and rotated.

I didn't understand German, but that sounded pornographic.

Glenda pulled a headset from a hook behind the desk. "Excuse me, ladies. This showgirl wants in on that continental head trip."

Honestly, I kind of did too. I cleared my throat. "Do you know anything about a jeweled crucifix necklace that Casanova gave to Lucrezia?"

"Casanova was generous. He gave his lovers jewels, silk

stockings, and bonnets. He also found rich husbands for many patrician women after he stole their virtue."

I knew I didn't like the guy. "But nothing about a crucifix necklace?"

She lowered her gaze. "I do not like to speak of it. Casanova won the necklace at the Ridotto casino from a most unholy man."

Even though I knew who she was referring to, I went cold as though a ghost was present. "You mean, the Comte de Saint Germain."

Her fingers went to her throat.

An odd gesture, given that he was rumored to be a vampire. Was she protecting her neck?

Zanetta swallowed. "In his memoirs, Casanova said the Comte was a liar, but he was also astonished by the Comte, who claimed to be three hundred years of age."

Reminds me of a tangerine-haired witch I know. "I hate to insist about the necklace, but could you tell me whether the stones were all rubies?"

She fingered a pearl earring. "One was different. A diamond, perhaps. The Comte claimed to make them, as well as gold. A French aristocrat, the Comtesse von Georgy, wrote that the Comte wore diamonds on every finger, on his watches, even his shoe buckles, and he carried snuffboxes decorated with them."

The same woman from Madame de Pompadour's party who said the Comte hadn't aged in fifty years.

"He also made strange elixirs and potions and told Madame de Pompadour that he had the secret to eternal youth."

The *eternal* reference retriggered my cult fears. The way Monsignor Meneghello had crossed himself at the Basilica when I'd asked about the necklace was unsettling, and he'd never told me whether he'd heard of it. *Was the jeweled cross believed to have religious power or an occult connection? And did the cult of the light start with the Comte?*

My hand went to my throat, and I forced it down to the desk. "Do you mind if I ask how you know that one of the stones was different?"

Zanetta looked down. "A museum guest, who also wanted to know the type."

One of the jewel thieves? But why would they want to know about a missing stone? "Who was this?"

Her beauty mark quivered. "I am not allowed to disclose the personal details of museum visitors."

"How about a date?" I leaned over the desk. "It's important, life or death."

Her face turned as ashen as her powdered wig. "I will check the registry." She clicked the keys on her computer. "Friday, the seventeenth of December."

The day before the first grave robbery. I had to know the guest's name, but I couldn't let her see me looking at the screen.

"*Ay, chihuahua!*" Shona covered the lenses of her headset as though that would block the virtual view.

Glenda gave a raucous laugh. "That's no dog, Miss Shona, but it's the size of one."

Zanetta turned her head in their direction, and I stole a glimpse of the registry.

My heart spasmed as though a stake had been driven through it.

The museum visitor who'd asked about Lucrezia's necklace was Richard Chanfray, the man who'd committed suicide in St. Tropez in 1983 after claiming to be none other than the Comte de Saint Germain.

10

"I t's not humanly or aliently possible." I sat on the bench in the hallway of the Santa Chiara convent-turned-*questura* and leaned my head against the cold stucco wall of the police station. "He can't be *the* Richard Chanfray. Or an eighteenth-century vampire."

An officer side-eyed me as he passed.

And I stink-eyed him back. The guy had no right to judge me. Based on my stay in Venice, I could guarantee that he'd seen far more disturbing things in the line of duty than a woman mumbling about a centuries-old bloodsucker.

I rose and paced the stone floor, which was as worn as the one on the Bridge of Sighs. And I sighed. The questura was on the north end of the Grand Canal, and yet Bradley and I couldn't have been farther from our gondola ride. He'd offered to come with me to the station, but I'd sent him to the hotel. I had a foreboding feeling that I needed to be alone when I met Commissario Lucifero. *Maybe it was his last name?*

Whatever the reason for my unease, I wasn't sorry to be surrounded by police. Iona's case was beyond concerning. Grave robbers were the pits, but a vampire was rock bottom, especially one that kept showing up, like Shona. *What is it about me that attracts creepy-crazy repeat visits? And while I'm mulling over the subject, why am I a magnet for people with poor social skills?*

My eyes raised heavenward, somewhat accusingly. Like so many ceilings in Italy, this one was divine. I wondered what Father Festin at San Zaccaria would say about an inspector named Lucifer roaming the halls of an old convent. Maybe he'd think it was fitting given the nuns' sins. Was that why Casanova had given Lucrezia Pavan the crucifix necklace? To absolve her, or rather, them of their transgressions?

No, Christ would have forgiven them. Plus, Casanova knew the Comte was a nefarious character deemed to have mystical abilities. Surely he'd thought that the necklace had power, maybe a talisman for protection. Then again, since the noble nuns had been saddled with remaining virtuous to ensure God's favor and the security of Venice, the necklace might have been intended to give Lucrezia power.

Religious?

Or occult?

I flopped back onto the bench. I had no idea what went on over two centuries ago, and I didn't know what the devil was taking Commissario Lucifero so long, either. I'd been waiting for almost an hour. Scanning the hallway for a clock, I spotted a sign on a door.

Archivio del Convento.

I shot up. *Were there archives at the San Zaccaria convent too?*

"Signorina Amato." The deep voice belonged to a man in a dark blue police uniform who had the sculpted looks of Michelangelo's David but with a devious edge—and without the freakishly long arms and huge hands. "Commissario Niccolò Lucifero."

Perfect. Not only is he named after Lucifer, he has the same first name as Machiavelli, and he's devilishly handsome.

He ushered me into a high-ceilinged room with grilled windows, and as I crossed the threshold, I was tempted to grab the doorframe and catapult myself back out. There was a hand-carved wooden desk, lots of file cabinets, and stacks of papers, all of which I'd expected. What I wasn't prepared for were the display shelves of jars of wet specimens, once living creatures soaking in formaldehyde with eyeballs smashed against the glass.

The office was my version of hell. Although, it was still preferable to one with Ruth Walker living in it.

I took a seat. The chair squeaked a soundtrack to my apprehension. "Do you collect those, uh, specimens?"

He licked his full lips. "They are from various cases I have investigated."

My head jerked to the jars. *Were they parts left over from serial killers?*

The inspector brandished a cardboard tube and pulled out a poster. "I assume you recognize this?"

My chair squeaked again as I sighed. The poster was a picture of twenty-year-old me frolicking in the Trevi Fountain during a college trip with Veronica. In all fairness, the stunt was a result of my first encounter with limoncello, before I had such bad luck with water. Or maybe the fountain frolic was the start of my water misadventures. "I do."

"Then you're aware that it was part of a national ad campaign to discourage criminals, like yourself, from defacing our monuments."

Sharp tongue. Is it forked too? "I take it this isn't a cordial meeting."

"That is up to you, is it not?"

The guy was surly, but I gave him the benefit of the doubt. It would've been hell to have a Satanic surname in such a famously Catholic country.

He rolled the poster while keeping black eyes fixed on me. "This was sent to me by a colleague in Rome to help me remind you that all of Venice is a fountain. I believe you know her, the Commissario Boccadifuoco?"

I'd met her when I'd flown to the Eternal City to locate David and The Vassal, who'd disappeared on a spring break trip. And I wasn't surprised that a guy named after the devil would know the Roman inspector. Her last name *did* mean Mouth of Fire. "Since the two of you have been in touch, then you also know that I grew up and became a PI."

"I am aware of your profession, Signorina Amato, just as I am aware that Chef Iona Parsons is not the first person to fall into water in your presence—and die."

Conflicting emotions undulated through me. Anger that he was suggesting that I'd had something to do with Iona's death, and shock that he knew about Wesley Sullivan. Commissario Boccadifuoco, the fire-breather, hadn't told him about the detective, because his water mishap hadn't happened when I'd met with her. "Then you're also aware that I tried to save Iona. And if you're talking about Detective Wesley Sullivan, the New Orleans PD considers him a missing person."

"Tell me, how did the good detective get into the Mississippi River?"

My seat gave a sharp squeak that matched my inner scream. Wesley Sullivan was more befitting of the name Lucifer than the inspector, who knew damn good and well that I'd pushed the devil detective into the river. "You have no jurisdiction in Louisiana, so let's stick to the Parsons case."

"As you wish. However, you might be surprised by my professional reach."

Satan did *get around.*

He leaned back in his chair and crossed an ankle over his

knee. "Why do you believe you received the threat in the lion's head?"

"The morning after I arrived in Venice, I overheard a conversation at the Caffè Florian between three people I think are the grave robbers. That afternoon, a fourth person, a young redhead posing as a maid, stole a newspaper from outside my suite that had an article about the theft."

"And these people want to kill you because you can identify them."

"Either that or they think I'm related to Iona and that I've come here for the crucifix necklace they've probably stolen from her ancestor's grave."

He picked up a pen. "And have you?"

"Have I what?"

"Come for the necklace. Your mother shares a surname with Iona's ancestor, Lucrezia Pavan."

He'd done his homework. "I came to be the maid of honor in my best friend's wedding, no more, no less. So instead of wasting time accusing me of killing Iona, I suggest you question the people I mentioned. Otherwise, the Pala d'Oro could be their next target. And if I'm right that they're in a cult, they'll do greater damage to Venice than one of my dips in the city's canals."

His shoulders stiffened, and he put down the pen. "What cult?"

"I could be wrong, but I think it's related to the cult of light."

He exhaled and leaned back in his seat. "That is an architectural movement associated with Apollo, the God of light in Greek mythology, and God in Christianity."

"What if the people I mentioned learned about the cult and made it into something more, something that would guarantee eternal life? They've been going around Venice in costumes, Tosca,

Casanova, the bell ringer. Another, named Perpetua, volunteers here at the Chiesa di San Zaccaria. And I think they're all involved in the grave robbery and moving the jewels in a coffin lit with candles."

The inspector contemplated a crucifix on the wall. "Are you familiar with the nine spheres of Heaven described in Dante's *Paradiso*?"

"No, but I know his nine circles of hell really well."

He threw back his head and gave a laugh that was decidedly Machiavellian. "In Canto XXX, Dante describes the Empyrean, the abode of God. When he enters, he is enveloped in a warm light that renders him fit to see the creator."

I had to give the inspector devil his due. He knew his job—and his literature, not to mention his mythology.

"Dante likens those who enter the Empyrean to candles, ready to receive the flame of God's love."

The candles I'd seen on the coffin could have symbolized this flame, and I understood that Lucifero thought so too.

"With that in mind, I suggest that you immerse yourself in the flame of your fiancé's love and your friends' upcoming wedding. My colleagues and I will see to the people you have mentioned."

I nodded, even though I had no intention of following his suggestion—not exclusively, anyway. And I debated whether to tell him about the Comte, but it sounded too far-fetched. "There is another person you should look into—he went to the Casanova Museum right before the jewel theft, Richard Chanfray. If I'm right about him, he's Lucifer himself." I held up my hands. "Uh, no offense."

His black look indicated that some offense was taken. "Be careful, Signorina Amato."

Was he threatening me because of my slip-up? "Oh, come on," I rose with a scary squeak. "It's just an expression."

He steepled his fingers.

One of so many ironies.

"Mine was not a threat."

"Then what—"

"Missing people have been known to reappear in my country."

Despite my foreboding about meeting with the Commissario, his statement was as unexpected as his jars of wet specimens, which I would have sworn were staring at me as intently as he was. But I understood why he'd said what he had.

Lucifero wasn't trying to scare the bejesus out of me. He'd just told me without jeopardizing an investigation that Detective Sullivan had surfaced from the depths of the Mississippi somewhere in Italy, possibly among the canals of Venice.

MY HANDS SHOOK as I dialed Veronica. I'd tried Bradley, but he hadn't answered. He'd texted while I was with the Commissario to let me know that he was exhausted from the trip, so I was sure he was dead to the world. I shuddered. "Fine choice of expressions, Franki."

Veronica's voicemail came on, and I hung up. I couldn't leave news as explosive as *Wesley Sullivan's alive and in Italy and might crash your wedding to kill me* in a message. As a bride-to-be, she had enough on her plate, starting with Iona's violet risotto. "Another fine choice. You're a real comedian."

I exited the questura and buttoned my coat. It was cold, the sun was about to set, and a mist had settled over La Serenissima. The ex-Santa Chiara convent was on the west end of Venice in the Santa Croce sestiere, and it was strangely quiet for 6:00 p.m. considering that it was near the cruise ship port and the train station. I crossed the bridge to the Fondamenta Santa Chiara, the walkway along the Grand Canal, to a more populated area rather than wait alone at the vaporetto stop closest to the questura for whoever had sent the "Roses Are Red" threat to strike.

Or bite.

Who left the lion's head box outside my suite? The jewel thieves had been my prime suspects until Richard Chanfray and Wesley Sullivan had reared their ugly—and supposedly dead—heads. On the other hand, Chanfray had claimed to be the Comte de Saint Germain, so one of said thieves had probably used his name as an alias. At least, that's what I hoped—with every blood cell in my body.

Detective Sullivan was another matter. If that swamp monster had surfaced in a city of water, it was most likely Palermo to set up some sort of criminal enterprise with Gigi Scalino. Unless Gigi had summoned him to find out where I'd stashed his late father's winepress and then finish me off, in which case Sullivan was in Venice.

"It's time to give that gift back to Luigi Pescatore and let him deal with Gigi."

A water taxi sped by, and *moto ondoso*, the boat waves that erode the buildings and foundation of Venice, spilled onto the walkway. And I realized I didn't know whether the winepress was still on the Steamboat Galliano or at the bottom of the mighty Mississip'.

If I wanted to find out what Captain Vandergrift had done with the thing, I had to call Ruth. Again. I threw back my head and promptly snapped it up. I shouldn't stick my neck out with a potential vampire in town.

It was midnight in New Orleans, so I'd probably wake her up. I grinned as I dialed Private Chicks. It rang a few times, and the line picked up.

Tssssssss.

"Drink yourself to sleep again, Ruth?"

"This is The Vassal, or it was." *Tssssssss.*

Something was wrong. His breathing was raspy, and he never worked this late. "What do you mean, 'it was'? And what's that hissing?"

"It's my inhaler, and I've been demoted to Serf, without so much as a The."

Ruth had scared the kid into an asthma attack. "What's she done to David?"

"He went on Christmas break early."

"That was smart."

"Not at all. Peasants don't get vacation time, so she tried him in mock court and sentenced him to being her personal assistant."

I had to unload the wackjob along with the winepress before she demoted me too. "Don't stress about this. You're still The Vassal, David's not her assistant, and I'll personally escort Ruth out of the office once I'm back."

"You'd do that?"

The hope in his nerdy voice brought a mist to my eyes as thick as the one enveloping the centuries-old palazzos. "Just as soon as we change the locks and replace the glass in the door and windows with the bulletproof kind."

He let out a rasp-free exhale. "You're a saint, Franki."

Santa Francesca. I like the sound of that. I got a whiff of rank perfume and looked for the source. It must've come from a building window. "Is Ruth there?"

"She went to get a Christmas tree."

"Ruth's not getting a tree at this hour. She's buying booze."

"To the contrary. She's cutting one from someone's yard."

My Christmas suddenly looked very merry. "I have a solution to our Ruth infestation. Do a Find My Friends on her phone, call the cops with her 10-20, and we're free of her."

"Are you mad, milady? I'd risk a lashing."

My lips pursed. From the sound of things, The Vassal, a.k.a.

Serf, saw the whole feudalism farce as a cosplay event. "Do me a favor, will you?"

"If you need my research services, please tell me quickly. Lady Ruth is due to return any minute, and serfs aren't allowed to speak."

Lady Ruth? I imagined her tight bun loosened into curled tresses that framed her turkey neck and cat-eye glasses, and I burst into a round of belly laughs that almost brought me to my knees. "Thanks, Vassal." I wiped tears from my eyes. "I needed a release."

"I'm here to serve."

I rolled my eyes. "Right. So here's what I need. Confirm the death of Richard Chanfray in St. Tropez, and," I hesitated because the next task could frighten him as much as Ruth, "any sightings of Detective Wesley Sullivan in Italy."

Tssssssss.

"Don't worry, okay? If Sullivan is alive, I'll handle him. The thought of evicting Ruth from the office will get me through anything, even another showdown with the demon detective."

"Try it," Ruth warned in a voice that would frighten Dirty Harry, "and I'll tell Bradley about the Italian Casanova you're running around with."

My lungs closed up. I'd horribly misread The Vassal's last inhaler blast, which I could've used a shot of. "There's no Casanova, and you know—" A devious thought stopped me in mid-defense, but it wasn't mine, it was Ruth's. "Was the Italian man who called the office Commissario Niccolò Lucifero?"

"Didn't I mention that?"

The palm of my hand pressed the top of a gondola pole, and I was so angry that I was positive I'd driven it deeper into the silt. But my Ruth rage was momentarily overcome by an important question. Since the caller was Lucifero, did that mean the jewel thieves hadn't threatened me? If so, the "Roses Are Red" threat could have come from Sullivan.

Either way, now a threat was going to come from me. "Ruth, if you, your bedroom suite, and your hot Christmas tree aren't out of Private Chicks when I get back on January second, I'll have you arrested for trespassing."

"That's the thanks I get for holding down this two-bit fort while you're having a gay old time in Venice?"

"Pretty much. And by the way, there's nothing gay about my visit to Venice. In fact, in a matter of hours, I'm meeting some people at a cemetery."

"Not the one on Lazzaretto Nuovo island, I hope."

"No-o?" *Don't ask, Franki. Don't get snared in Ruth's trap.* "Why?"

"That's where they found the Vampire of Venice."

Why, WHY hadn't I hung up after I'd threatened her, like a normal person? And how come Gaspare didn't give me a heads-up about this vampire when I asked about the Comte? Despite my anxiety, I made a scoffing sound. "That's obviously a legend."

"No, ma'am. This isn't the story of the Casket Girls and the founding of New Orleans. Anthropologists found this vampire in a mass grave from the plague of 1576."

I imagined Dracula in a coffin and scanned the Grand Canal. There were several gondolas and a water taxi in the distance, but no candlelit caskets. "Then it's dead."

"Who's to say they didn't miss one?"

"'Miss one?' How many Vampires of Venice are there?"

"Scores, possibly."

I stumbled, and almost took another dip.

"Back then, people thought they were spreading the Black Death. They weren't sophisticated enough to figure out that the plague was coming from fleas on rats."

Ruth would know this history. She was a bloodsucking rat

flea who'd been plaguing me since I'd met her. "But why *vampires*?"

"Every time they reopened the mass grave to add more victims, some of the corpses appeared to be eating their burial shrouds. It had to do with decomposition processes—"

"Spare me the gory details and get to the point."

"To kill the vampires, they removed the shroud, which was thought to be their food source, and shoved bricks into their mouths."

She could've been lying to freak me out. "Where did you learn this?"

"National Geographic. They showed the Vampire of Venice's skull with a brick crammed between its teeth."

"At least you're watching something besides Judge Judy."

"I meant the magazine, but I do have a new show." She took a loud slurp of something. "Dr. Pimple Popper."

Ruth Walker had to go. I'd call an exterminator, if necessary. "Listen, I called to find out what happened to the winepress."

"You have some nerve asking me for information after you gave me an eviction notice, and during the holiday season."

"What do you want, Ruth? My first born? Because FYI, it's not looking promising."

"*Puh!* I want nothing to do with your spawn, Missy. I'll take G notes—twenty of 'em—and a Murano glass Santa-on-a-gondola ornament."

"You'll get free room and board until January second and nothing more."

"Good luck at the cemetery, Scrooge McDuck." She slammed down the receiver.

The same thing Shona called me. Why add the 'McDuck'? Before stashing my phone, I googled Santa Francesca. She was the patron saint of automobile drivers, widows, and plagues. *Was that a cosmic joke?*

I glanced at the sky.

It was glowing violet, and the mist had turned into dense fog. I hadn't even seen such a vivid color in Austin, which had been nicknamed the City of the Violet Crown because of the sunsets over the hills. I wished I was back at the University of Texas having fun—and reconsidering my Criminology major. But instead, I was investigating a homicide in Venice where the color violet was a bizarrely recurring theme. The violet risotto, Iona's lips, her Violet necklace, Lucrezia Pavan's clothes. And my maid-of-honor dress.

What did it all mean?

My gaze shifted to the Grand Canal, which was a deep purple. There was no flaming coffin, but I saw vampires in every nook, cranny, and crypt of Venice. Giuseppina Gabriel Carmelo could have been a child vampire, like Claudia from *Interview with a Vampire*. Or maybe the coffin belonged to the Vampire of Venice. People *were* smaller then. The Comte was undoubtedly short too, and probably Richard Chanfray. In theory, any one of them could have fit in the creepy coffin.

The sound of heels striking pavement brought me out of my fantasy fog.

I spun but didn't see anyone.

My stride became a scamper. "You have to stop roaming the streets alone after sunset. It would also help if you didn't talk to yourself, because your mouth is like a GPS."

I stuck a mental brick between my teeth.

"Although, who am I kidding? The killer can hear my frightened feet and probably even my heartbeat, which is as loud as the bell in Saint Mark's Campanile."

The walkway ended at gondola parking.

I detoured around a building to a dark, narrow street.

Heels echoed.

And they weren't mine.

I stole another glance behind me.

No one.

Was it the counterfeit Casanova's man heels? The bell ringer's boots?

Or was it the Vampire of Venice? Richard Chanfray? Sullivan?

I broke into a run.

So did the heels.

My pulse pounded a deafening alarm as I flew through the ancient streets in the fading violet light. But it wasn't loud enough to drown out the frightened, fantastical thoughts flitting through my head.

Why don't I see my stalker? Is he invisible? Vampires can do that —and travel in a hazy, mist-like form—like the fog.

Get real, Franki, because undead vampires aren't.

Wait. Vampires can also turn into bats.

The fog had grown heavier, and clogged my lungs, as did the stench of mold and decay. I couldn't run much farther, but whoever—or whatever—was behind me had superhuman stamina. I glanced over my shoulder.

In a flash, a small, gloved hand pulled the edge of a black-and-red cape behind a building column.

My B+ blood ran deathly cold in my body.

Am I being hunted by a child vampire?

11

M y body lumbered through the dark streets like the skeleton of the bell ringer of Venice. Stooped from exhaustion, I struggled to lift my feet. *Why hasn't the tiny vampire sunk his teeth into me yet?*

The toe of my boot caught on a paving stone, and I sprawled onto the street, which served me right for thinking something so ridiculous. Nevertheless, I rolled over to fend him off.

But he didn't attack. The *vampirino* huffed and puffed like a vaporetto engine.

A supernatural vampire wouldn't breathe like that.

I pulled onto my elbows. The caped crusader was bent over with gloved hands pressed to his skinny thighs. His top hat and tails were too old-fashioned for him to be a child. "Who are you?"

He glanced up and flashed long, yellow teeth.

Anger bubbled in my gut like lava. The money I'd cost my nonna wasn't just for her flight-change fees. It was to pay my stalker, the fifty-something Sicilian marriage broker that Veronica and I met on Mount Etna last winter when Nonna hired him to find me a backup fiancé.

He removed his top hat and gave a sweeping bow that revealed slicked hair with a bald patch the shape of his native Sicily. "Maurizio Bonsignore, *u paraninfu*."

"Oh, I remember." The words erupted from my lips. "And, believe me, 'paranymph' isn't the right term for you."

He returned the hat to his head. "In English, I prefer 'Maurice Goodgentleman, nymph-helper.' It have-a the ring-a to it, no?"

After Shona, my head was ringing at the thought of another "helper" in Venice.

He straightened and rubbed his back. "*Ahia!* My spine, she is-a broken."

"That isn't the only thing that'll be broken if you follow me again." I pulled myself to my feet. "But I'll give you some credit. You're in decent shape, all things considering."

His look was wry-eyed. "I find the husband for *zitelle*. I chase-a many groom."

My lips went tight over my teeth. As a zitella myself, I resented that. "I'm sure they're also running from that cologne you're wearing."

He sniffed. "It is-a quality brand. *Sicily* by Mancera Paris. Citrus with-a violet and-a musk."

Lemon and *violet*? I took offense to that given my past and present. I grabbed his arm. "Come on."

He dug in his little loafer heels. "Where we go?"

"To the hotel. You're going to wash off that godawful smell while my nonna books your return flight."

He wrested from my grip. "If I no find-a you the back-a-up, I no get-a my bonus."

"The bonus is that you're going to live to see the land of effeminate cologne again. And if you don't start moving those feet, I'll carry you over my shoulder."

His wiry gray brow arched, and then his eyes went sly. "Like cave-a woman?"

The petite paranymph was also a perve. "Start marching."

We returned to the hotel on foot, which took a while—not because we were far away, but because the mini marriage broker had a small stride. Fortunately, no one was at the reception desk, so I was able to get him into the elevator without anyone seeing me with a Phantom-of-the-Opera dressalike.

When I got to my suite, it hit me that it was thirteen, which explained a lot. "And they say it's a lucky number in Italy."

Resigned to my fate, I went inside. My mom and nonna were in the chairs on either side of the cherub statues with dinner trays.

"There you are, dear." My mother waved a white-gloved hand from her abdomen.

I cocked my head, trying to make sense of the odd wave angle. She was encapsulated in a bizarrely puffy gray button-down dress with an extra-wide circular collar and slits for arms at the waist. To top it all off, she'd accessorized with a bubble hat. The overall look was *Lost-in-Space* robot.

"Gaspare sent wine with local pasta called *bigoli* for you and me, and Sicilian *arancini* for your nonna, all compliments of the hotel. He's obviously paying his respects since I'm from a noble Venetian family."

Or he's afraid that we're Mafia, thanks to Sheilah saying I'm having a mob wedding. "Someone else is here to pay his respects —and get paid."

Maurizio entered with a flourish of his cape. He removed his hat and kissed my nonna's hand. He moved to my mother, who struggled to raise her fingers to his lips. "I am-a honored by your attire, Signora Amato. A vintage Pierre Cardin cape-a dress."

A cape dress? How long has she been planning the marriage-broker meeting?

Maurizio straightened and clicked his heels. "I fear I must-a relay grave-a news. I follow Francesca through Venezia, and he no get a single stare."

"*She*," I corrected between tense teeth. Italians often confused English personal pronouns, but he knew better because he'd called his spine a *she* earlier. "And in my defense, everyone was too busy gawking at your outfit to look at me."

"I do make-a the beautiful figure." He half-smiled and kissed his fingertips. Then he pulled a little black book from his cape that looked big in his small hands. "As I say, we have-a the crisis with-a Francesca. After the wedding, we take-a him to Sicily."

"It's *her*, and no, we don't. The only one going to Sicily is you, tonight."

He sank onto the couch. "But I no have-a time to enjoy the Hotel-a San Marco."

"Hang on. You have a room here?"

"Twenty-three up-a-stairs."

My gaze traveled to the two women who'd had a meeting in Gaspare's office about the hotel's bookings. "That was Bradley's suite, wasn't it? You found out his reservation was canceled and had Gaspare give it to the marriage broker."

My mother reached for her hair but gave up. "Now, Francesca, it was available, and Bradley hadn't arrived yet. What were we supposed to do, let someone else have it?"

"Yes, the two of you." I threw up my arms—in frustration, not because I was rubbing in the fact that mine were free to move. "Here's what's going to happen. I have an investigation at midnight, and before I go I'm putting the 'good gentleman' on a flight or a boat or a train, and you two are moving into his room."

Nonna slammed her hand on the dinner tray. "*Impossibile*. I spend a lotta euros on Signor Bonsignore."

He gave a sad head shake. "My fee, she is-a nonrefundable."

My lids lowered at that *she*. "Let's get something straight. You're all wasting your time and money trying to find me a backup fiancé because I'm marrying Bradley."

My mother tossed her napkin onto her plate. "Then why haven't you set a wedding date? You said you'd get married after Veronica."

"Yes, Mom, and Veronica won't be married for three more days. As for Bradley, you know he wants to find a job before we get married."

"He took a year off to spend time with you fourteen months ago, so why hasn't he found that job? As a successful ex-bank president, he's highly employable."

"He's waiting until after the holidays to start the hunt."

Nonna raised her chin. "That's-a the point, no? He always-a wait, and you are out of-a the time."

The bell in Saint Mark's Campanile began to ring as if to mock my aging biological clock. That tower was lucky I was afraid of heights. Otherwise, I'd climb to the top and sound its death knell.

Maurizio rose and picked up the wine glass intended for me. "If-a the *fidanzato* drag-a the feet on-a the job, then he drag-a the feet to the altar."

"The *fidanzato* is not dragging his feet," I said, noticing a tinge of defensiveness in my tone, "and I'm not out of time. In fact, we're taking time to enjoy our engagement."

Maurizio's mustache protruded. "Brad-a-ley is. He may be with his ex-a-wife in-a the room next-a door right-a now."

"He's sleeping," I snapped and quickly added, "alone." Then I snatched his wine glass and took a swallow.

Nonna waved a knife. "In-a the old country, we have-a *vendetta* for this offense."

I didn't want to know what the vendetta consisted of, but based on the stories my nonna told about her hometown, it would involve Bradley being paraded around town naked in the back of a donkey cart—probably after being doused with orange juice to attract flies. "Just remember, Nonna, we're not in the old country."

"*Sì,* we're in-a Venezia where-a Bradley play the Casanova with-a two women."

I took another slug of wine. "Trust me, I met a guy playing Casanova in the piazza, and Bradley's nothing like him."

Maurizio paled. "A Casanova? Is-a your virtue intact?"

My eyes turned as steely as the buckles on eighteenth-century man heels. "If you're talking about my patience, no. That's been shattered."

He sat on the couch and pulled a little white book from inside his cape.

I looked over his shoulder. "What's that?"

"The book of the *zitelle.* The color is-a for purity, but-a in your case, white is-a wish-a-ful thinking."

"Look, I'm a healthy woman of thirty-two—"

A hiss ensued as he sucked air between his lengthy teeth and scribbled a note.

"You'd better not be writing that down."

"I must up-a-date the check-a-list. I do for each-a zitella."

"Are you serious? Like a fiancée form?"

He gave a wheezy chuckle that sounded like a donkey pulling a vendetta cart. "I should-a hire you for marketing. You will need-a the job because in-a terms of-a marriage, your age is-a fourt-teen years past-a the *scadenza.*"

"The expiration date?" I tried to grab the knife from my nonna's hand, but thanks to decades of dough kneading the woman had vice grips for fingers.

"Please, signorina. Let's-a not-a get emotional." Maurizio straightened his cape. "This is-a business. It's-a not-a personal."

The *he* and *him* of earlier made me seriously doubt that.

He dabbed a handkerchief on his upper lip. "We have-a only one-a weapon to find-a the back-a-up. *La dote*."

Nonna shuffled to Maurizio. "He is-a right, Brenda," she picked up the black book, "We need-a the dowry."

My mom's head popped from her collar. "Why? You paid Signor Bonsignore to help us."

Maurizio raised the checklist. "I am-a only a man, signora. We need-a the heavy-duty incentive."

My mother muttered something and topped off her wine. Her glass was full, but her bank account was empty.

I sat on the aqua silk bedspread to watch the school of sharks circle one another. For the heck of it, I googled "feeding frenzy" and found a reference to lemon sharks. *Probably my ancestors.*

Maurizio produced a quill pen. "Signora Amato, did-a you say you are nobility?"

She gazed at the Grand Canal like a patrician surveying her palazzos. "Yes, from an illustrious family."

Of chimney sweeps, based on her genealogy research.

"*Benissimo*." He clapped. "We arrange an excellent match, possibly a *conte*."

Instead of a gasp, which would have been unbefitting of an aristocrat, she raised her noble nose. "My daughter, a contessa."

Contessa Francesca did "have-a the ring-a to it," to quote Maurizio, but given that the Comte de Saint Germain was a count, I preferred any other title. I glanced at the doge painting. Except for Dogaressa Francesca. "You have a list of these noblemen in that black book?"

"Sicily is-a full of them. During-a *feudalismo*, titles were given away like-a bottles of-a vino. Lucky for us, they are desperate."

"I think I saw some of them at Glenda's book signing."

Nonna squinted at a page. "They're not-a desperate for women, Franki. They need-a money to keep-a their land."

I was interested—not for me but for Lady Ruth. I could ship her and the winepress to Sicily, where she and a desperate count could start a winery. Naturally, I'd make sure he didn't speak English so that Ruth wouldn't get returned COD to my office.

Maurizio rubbed his gloves together. "We have-a the party and invite-a noble families." He flashed his teeth. "They need-a new blood."

I wondered whether there was such a thing as a vampire shark—or vampire Sicilian counts.

"And-a at the party, signora, you present-a the dowry in the patrician tradition."

My mother turned from the window, frowning. "What does that entail?"

"The servants enter with-a basins of-a gold."

She grabbed hold of a cherub. Not only did my parents not have servants or gold, they didn't have basins, either.

Maurizio scribbled in the white book. "Also part of-a the dowry is-a the *corredo*. The fine-a clothing, jewelry, furniture, and-a paintings."

My mother tried to grasp her pearl necklace but couldn't quite get there, and I went in for the kill. "Yes, Mom. The *trousseau*."

Her gloved hands shook. "I've put a few things away for your wedding day, but I wasn't expecting a count."

"What about that Conquistador painting you and Dad bought in Juarez in the Seventies?"

"Quiet, Francesca," she growled. "This is between me and Signor Bonsignore."

Except that I'm the one you're trying to marry off.

"There's one teensy problem, Maurizio." She poured wine into a glass on the bedside table. "My family has been noble for so many centuries that our heirlooms have been spread a tad thin." She offered the glass to Maurizio.

He didn't take the wine or the bait. "This is a big-a job-a, signora. Without-a the full-a dowry, my fee, she double in-a size." He side-ogled my frame.

My gaze went shark dark.

"And-a we no get a count. Maybe a cobbler."

Panicked, my mother waved her arms at her waist like the *Lost in Space* robot. "Let's not get ahead of ourselves. What I meant was, is the dowry really important?"

"*Assolutamente.*" Maurizio's tone was strident. "In-a the patrician marriage, the bride's dowry did-a more to enrich-a the husband's household than her virtues." He raised his brow and jerked his head in my direction. "And in-a this-a case..."

I bared my chompers. As the spawn of lemon sharks, I could do damage.

My mom collapsed in her chair. "Then what did a woman need virtues for?"

Nonna looked up from the black book. "An extra bargain chip-a to secure the best-a match."

I flopped on the bed. "I would've hated to be a patrician woman, traded like a commodity."

"Non-a-sense," Maurizio chided. "The patrician women want-a the money for fashion and parties. They scheme-a too."

Sheilah must've been descended from Venetians. "But they didn't have love."

He gave a rakish smile. "They have-a better—the *scappatelle*, or little escapes, with-a Casanova."

My mother gave him a pointed look. "Those affairs with Casanova were free."

"Indeed, Signora Amato," Maurizio's eyes locked on my mom like a vampire shark's teeth, "but he always find-a way to get-a paid."

Nonna tucked a piece of paper in the bodice of her mourning dress. "Because-a Casanova scheme like a woman."

My nonna was the maestro of schemes, as evidenced by the page she'd just stolen from Maurizio's black book. My mother, however, wasn't as adept. It must've been a skill the Pavans lacked, because Lucrezia Pavan hadn't done so well for herself. By fooling around with Casanova before her wedding, she'd lost a husband and her freedom. On the other hand, she might've been so repulsed by her intended groom that she wanted to go to the convent. Or she was out-schemed by her sister, Ludovica.

But did any of that matter? An eighteenth-century family scandal wasn't likely to have any bearing on Chef Iona Parson's death.

And yet, something told me that it did.

"If that mini marriage broker made me miss the Mavens, I'll get on a train to Sicily and break him into two tinier pieces." I paced along the Fondamente Nove walkway that overlooked the Northern lagoon and San Michele cemetery. Despite the oft-repeated saying that Mussolini made the trains run on time, the 11:05 to Catania had been twenty minutes late. I'd planned to leave after I'd loaded the little-loafer-kicking Bonsignore on board, but then I spotted his top hat moving down the aisle toward the exit. So I'd stayed to make sure he departed for the land of smelly perfume and desperate counts.

A light from the lagoon shone in my face. Shielding my eyes, I made out a small boat. I was at the ferry stop where I'd agreed to meet Midge and Madge, so they could have been sending me a signal. But I ducked behind the floating wharf just in case.

The vessel approached, and the blinking become more insistent. When it docked, I debated staying hidden. Because it wasn't the Mavens' batela, it was the Screamers' quad scull.

"What are you doing back there?" Shona foghorned. "I told you it was me in Morse Code."

I sighed and walked to the boat. *The librarian managed to be loud even with light.* "I was expecting the Mavens."

"They left for the island five minutes ago. Where were you?"

I climbed on board and sat behind her. "The Santa Lucia train station."

Shona spun, gripping her oars for support. "Bradley didn't leave, did he?"

I shook my head as a frown seized my mouth, not because of her crush on my fiancé but because I'd blown an opportunity to have Maurizio find her a match. Given that I was once again out with Shona even though Bradley was in Venice, there was a good chance she'd find a way to take his place as my wedding date. "No, it was a friend of my nonna's who, uh, doesn't like to travel."

She gave me a look over her shoulder. "Is that why you forgot to tell me where we were meeting tonight?"

"Mm," I said, omitting the confirmatory hm.

"Anyway, I went to Glenda's room to find out where it was, but she was getting ready for a triple date and didn't know anything about it."

I didn't realize Glenda had friends in Venice. "Who were the other couples?"

"Oh, they weren't couples. It's triplets she met at her book signing."

That was more like it.

"So, I tracked down Stella Di Stefano in Rome. I couldn't let you do this alone. I'm a Helper, remember?"

Yeah, because she wouldn't let me forget it. Although, truth be told, I would've missed the rendezvous if she hadn't waited.

Shona began turning the quad scull, and I gripped my seat. "Can this thing make it to San Michele?"

"It's only half a mile, and small boats go to the island all the time." She pointed to a building with the sign *Ospedale SS Giovanni e Paolo.* "For instance, over there by that hospital is where aquatic hearses and funeral gondolas take bodies to the cemetery."

Just what I wanted to hear when I was setting off in a vessel that seemed as safe as using the flaming coffin like a kayak. I reached for the oars but thought better of it. Shona had enough muscle for both of us, and I didn't want to "ho" after she "heaved." The word might be too much for my stomach, which lurched at the prospect of visiting the cemetery.

As we headed toward the island of the dead, its fortress-like wall loomed like a warning. As if to back up that message, among the odor of decay that hung in the frigid air I got a whiff of danger. The moon was full, and a hazy fog sped past it as though composed of dark spirits. I shuddered and buttoned my pea coat to my chin.

It was vampire-bat weather.

Shona slid forward to row. "Fun fact—there are almost twice as many dead people on San Michele than live ones in Venice."

That fact is about as fun as the "Roses Are Red" poem I received.

She pulled back on the oars. "The population decline is such a problem that a group of prankster-provocateurs held a mock funeral for Venice with a hot pink coffin on a gondola."

Was the flaming coffin a prank too? Or some kind of symbol?

"By the way, the architect who designed the Teatro La Fenice opera house is the one who designed San Michele."

"You don't say," I said, hoping she'd take the expression literally and stop talking. In light of the setting, I feared another one of her legend stories.

"Yeah, now it's two islands put together, San Michele and San Cristoforo. But the original cemetery was inaugurated in 1813, and lots of interesting people have stayed there."

As much as I didn't want to encourage the macabre trivia, the "stayed there" demanded a comment. "You make it sound like a hotel."

"It's more like a rental property. You can be buried for twelve years, and then they dig you up. After that, your family can have you cremated and pay to keep you in a columbarium niche for another thirty years, renewable for twenty. If they can't afford it, either you're dumped in the common ossuary, or you go to another cemetery."

I looked at the black lagoon water. Venice's burial practices were unsettling, but they weren't that different from those of New Orleans. Bones from tombs were dumped in drawers after a year and one day, and I'd once seen a columbarium niche with a For Rent sign. "Wait. If that's the case, then how is Lucrezia Pavan still buried there?"

"Iona's mother told the Mavens that the cemetery lots used to be purchased for eternity until San Michele reached capacity in the 1950s. Then they started dumping the bones on Sant'Ariano island, which other cemeteries around Venice had done for centuries. I read that there are so many bones on Sant'Ariano that the ground crunches under your feet, and it's infested with snakes and mice."

Another not fun fact. "I don't want to hear anymore."

"It's not as bad as it could've been. A lot of the bones were used in sugar refining."

It was a good thing we weren't on land, because I would've been tempted to shove a brick in Shona's mouth like they did to the Vampire of Venice. "Did the Mavens tell you where Lucrezia's grave is?"

"Not specifically, but they showed me a map of the cemetery, and she's in the Catholic section. There are also sections for Protestants, Greek Orthodox, gondoliers, military, clergy, and children."

Now the graveyard seemed like a library. "Why wasn't Lucrezia buried with the clergy?"

"I asked the Mavens that, and they don't know. But Lucrezia's in an area reserved for prominent citizens, so maybe it's because she was from a patrician family."

That didn't make sense. "The Pavan family was ruined at the time of her death, and Lucrezia was a fallen woman. Why would she be in a VIP section in Venice's most exclusive cemetery?"

Shona pulled the oars. "It's a mystery, like her crucifix necklace. Dena, Gena, Lena, and I have hit up our library contacts, and so far no one has found any information about the missing jewel."

I was afraid of that. "There was a convent archive at the police station. I'll find out whether the San Zaccaria Church has one too."

"We also need to check out the state archive near the Ponte delle Tette." She spun, causing the boat to rock. "Did you know that means 'Bridge of the Tits'?"

"I speak Italian, remember?" I grabbed the sides of the quad scull, hoping to steady it. But if she made a move like that again, I'd give her bridge body part a tweak to teach her a lesson.

She resumed rowing, and I gauged the distance to the island. From the corner of my eye, I noticed a dark mass looming on the water. *That's no island. Is it a rock formation? Some sort of wreckage?*

A light flashed from the mass.

I ducked.

"What was that?" Shona boomed.

"Where's your flashlight?"

"I dunno. I dropped it."

The light flashed again.

Is it a ghost ship—one of those boats floating around with a dead crew?

It was my turn to boom. "Keep rowing. I'll look for it."

As I felt for Shona's flashlight, another thought struck me that chilled my bone marrow. We were near the cemetery where Giuseppina Gabriel Carmelo had drowned as a child in the 1904 vaporetto accident. *Is it possible that she's lighting the way so we won't have an accident?*

"Found it." Shona aimed her flashlight on the object, and I made like a corpse.

Someone was on the boat, but it wasn't a little girl. It was a towering figure the size of the bell ringer.

12

The boat began to rock, but thanks to the giant looming on the lagoon, my stomach was already in full swing. "What the hell *is* that?"

Shona's laugh blasted like an air horn. "Funny you'd say 'hell,' because it's a bronze sculpture of Dante and Virgil in a gondola, journeying through inferno in *The Divine Comedy*. A solar panel lights it at night."

"And you knew about this?"

"I do my research before visiting a city." Her tone implied that anyone who vacationed without prior study was a slacker. "But I needed to see it to be sure that it was Dante's Barge."

"Well, I would've appreciated a heads-up." It was unsettling to come upon the flashing sculpture after my conversation with Commissario Lucifero about Dante and the Empyrean, especially given my fears about a light cult. I took the flashlight from her hand and aimed it at the cloaked figures, one of which was pointing at the San Michele cemetery. "What does it mean?"

Shona resumed rowing. "Virgil represents reason, and he's leading Dante across the Acheron River, while its water heaves with tortured souls." She grinned. "Kind of like me and you."

I didn't realize I'd asked my question out loud, but if one of us represented reason, it was me. Otherwise, the only similarity Shona and I shared with Dante and Virgil was that we were traveling through an inferno. Although, after being trapped on the quad scull with her, I definitely identified with the tortured souls in the water.

She pulled on the oars and leaned back to give me a searching look. "You sure got spooked. What did you think the statue was?"

"The bell ringer." I switched off the flashlight, embarrassed by my admission. "I mean, whoever is *posing* as the bell ringer. The guy I saw was clearly in costume because his bones were screwed together."

"A walking skeleton would have screws."

My head snapped back. "Uh, no, it wouldn't."

"Without muscle or cartilage, it would need something to hold it together."

"Not if it was supernatural." My hand flew to my irrational mouth. *What had Venice done to me?*

Shona shot me an over-the-shoulder side-eye. "I'm a librarian. We believe in facts."

I didn't call her out on the walking skeleton remark. Instead, I grabbed the oars and rowed. It was time to get off the boat.

We neared the island, and Shona turned the quad scull away from the entrance. "We're going around the back so we won't be seen from the mainland."

My arms and I were sorely disappointed to hear that.

As we rowed along the east side of San Michele, I eyed the terracotta brick wall. "The whole island is enclosed?"

"Yeah, the wall's an ossuary."

The cemetery is surrounded by skeletons? Can't wait to go in.

We rowed for another ten minutes and pulled up to a dock

where the Mavens had moored their batela. Shona leaped out and tied the quad scull.

I stepped off the boat. There was nothing but brick wall. "Where are Midge and Madge?"

She shrugged. "There's no gate back here, but they must've found a way inside."

The back of my neck prickled. "We need to find them and make sure they're all right." I motioned for her to follow me to the wall. "Come on. I'll give you a boost."

"I'm the one with rowing muscles." Shona stooped and threaded her fingers.

I didn't argue. We couldn't afford to waste time bickering, and my arms were still angry about the rowing. I stepped into her hand. "When I count—"

She catapulted me straight to the top. I clutched at the wall to steady myself but fell over the edge and landed on my side in the dirt. Pain shot through my posterior, but that was from Shona. My only real injuries were an aching hip, a scratched hand, and a bruised ego.

The cemetery was deathly silent. Not even insects were alive on the island. Cypress trees loomed like dark spirits among tangled shrubs and overgrown walkways. A meaty, earthy smell made me long for the scent of Christ's suffering from the Basilica di San Marco. I shifted to a seated position, and something crunched beneath my bottom.

Bones?

Snakes and mice!

I shot to my feet.

"Ohgodohgodohgod," I chanted as I hopped around, frantically brushing myself off. Satisfied I was reptile and rodent-free, I set off through San Michele. Unlike New Orleans' "cities of the dead," the "island of the dead" had in-ground graves, many with glass ornaments from the neighboring island of Murano. But as with the cemeteries from home, there was no shortage of crosses and creepy statues, many of which were crumbling like the tombstones.

I passed a simple grave marker for the poet Ezra Pound and figured I was in the Protestant section. The religion was foreign in Italy, which explained why the grounds were so unkempt.

As I entered the Greek Orthodox section, I came upon the grave of the composer Igor Stravinsky, a long concrete marker with flowers strewn all over it.

I scanned the area for a gate.

A swoosh of black fabric disappeared behind a cypress.

Was that a vampire cape?

I dived behind a dome-shaped tomb. I didn't know who Sergei Diaghilev was, but the pink ballet slippers tied to his grave were appropriate because my heart was dancing *The Nutcracker.*

That fabric was not a figment of my imagination, and it didn't belong to Maurizio Bonsignore. *Is it the Vampire of Venice? The Comte de Saint Germain? Or his most recent incarnation, Richard Chanfray?*

Gravel crunched.

Or bones?

Goosebumps marched up my arms. Someone could have followed us to the island. *The jewel thieves? Wesley Sullivan?*

The crunching came toward me, and I grabbed a ballet slipper. The toe box on those things could do some damage.

"Hiding again?" Shona shrieked.

I sprung from behind the dome and whacked her bicep.

She howled like a wolf in heat. "Why'd you do that?"

Let's face it—she had it coming. "Arm-jerk reaction. Sorry."

"Geez," she rubbed her muscle, "I hope I can row in the race."

"It was a ballet slipper, not a tombstone. Now how'd you get in?"

"I texted Midge. She'd picked the lock on the side gate and left it open."

My scratched hand went to my aching hip. "And you didn't think to text her before you shotputted me over the wall?"

"I forgot I had her cell number."

My eyes narrowed. I was right to whack her bicep. Shona's mind was like a card catalog, so her story was suspect. "Where are the Mavens?"

"Right here." Madge tapped a crowbar on a grave marker.

Shona latched on to me like cling wrap. "You shouldn't sneak up on people."

I peeled her off but had to agree. The sisters wore navy sailor suit skirts with matching wool nurses capes. I told myself that theirs was the fabric I'd seen, but I was hesitant to believe me. Every cell in my body sensed evil in the cemetery.

Madge's lips shriveled. "Ladies, you must keep your voices down."

Midge put a finger to her mouth. "Silent as church mice."

Surely they weren't worried about waking the dead. Although, if anyone could do that, it was Shona. "Why? Is someone out here?"

"Possibly," Midge said. "There is a florist and a winery."

My saliva went rancid. And I'd thought it was bad that Italians grew grapes on volcanoes. "Where's the winery?"

She pointed to the northwest corner of the island. "Behind the Chiesa di San Michele in Isola."

I squinted at the Renaissance church and spotted a campanile. Venetian Catholics were serious about selling wine in the shadows of church towers.

Shona pulled up her sweat pants. "It was named after the Archangel Michael, who is perfect for a cemetery, since he weighs souls on his scale and decides who goes to heaven or hell."

As far as I was concerned, anyone in the temporary graveyard was automatically in hell, and that included us. I glanced at the campanile. If that thing began to toll, I would swim back to Venice.

Madge began walking. "Let's proceed to Lucrezia's grave."

The Catholic section was immaculate, like the conception. Shrubs were trimmed, the grass mowed, and rows of graves with white crosses bearing pictures of their inhabitants teemed with fresh flowers.

The sisters stopped at a curved brick wall with what looked like inlaid marble tombstones. Madge pointed to one with a blank façade. "There. That's Lucrezia."

My gaze lowered to a pot of half-dead roses and violets.

Madge tapped the crowbar on the concrete. "The flowers caught our attention too. An odd arrangement in light of the "Roses Are Red" threat you received."

Indeed. *Had Iona left them for her ancestor? Or was it her killer?* I swallowed my concerns and focused on the task at hand. "Shona told me that this is an area for VIPs. Is it possible that Lucrezia's sister, Ludovica, could've paid for the tomb?"

Madge shook her head. "She died in childbirth, and her husband gambled away the family fortune long before Lucrezia passed."

It sounded like karma had taken Ludovica's life for ruining her sister's. "Someone else must've paid for her grave. Maybe Casanova?"

"Doubtful," Midge said. "He died penniless in June of 1798, a month before her. And he'd been living rent-free at Count von Waldstein's castle in Duchov for the last thirteen years of his life."

Shona squatted before the vault. "I wonder if Lucrezia was buried in a habit or a scandalous outfit."

Midge's eyes smiled. "I imagine her in a violet dress and an elaborate hat."

A breeze blew and brought with it an unmistakable odor.

Madge and I locked eyes. Frowning, she shone a flashlight on Lucrezia's grave.

Something glinted at the top of the vault.

"Oooh!" Shona leaped up and pointed. "That's hair."

I knelt. The blonde strands were synthetic, and my stomach rocked as it had on the boat, because I recognized the wave. "It's from a wig."

Madge worked the crowbar behind the tombstone. "The seal to the vault has been broken."

Shona reached for the tool. "Let me do that."

I didn't offer to help. Based on the way she'd thrown me over the wall, she could manhandle the vault covering from the brick. After a couple of jerks, it swung open.

The body I'd been expecting tumbled out. What I hadn't expected was the way the white lace glove with the blackened ring finger seemed to point at a flickering electric candle inside the tomb.

Or the scattered bones that lay exposed on the ground.

I took a deep breath and prepared to break the stunned silence. "Tosca's not going to haunt the streets anymore, or follow the flaming coffin."

Madge pulled on a glove and lifted the corner of her white lace mask.

And for the first time, I gasped. "It's the redhead who posed as a maid. The one who tried to take the newspaper from outside my suite."

Shona squeezed my bicep, no doubt as payback. "And she has the same grape Kool-Aid lips as Iona."

"It's so much more than that." Midge wrung her hands. "She's a young version of Barbara, Iona's mother."

Madge straightened and folded her hands. "One might say a mirror image."

My blood ran as cold as lagoon water. If true, then Tosca could be Iona's daughter, which had grave implications for the motive and for me. Because the location of the body, the candle, and the flowers suggested a cult murder.

And the poem in the lion's head box said that I was on the ritual sacrifice list.

MY ARM FALTERED as I pressed the elevator button to my floor in the Hotel San Marco, and it had every right to be shaky. As if the discovery of Tosca's body wasn't taxing enough, after the police arrived on San Michele, I had to row Shona and her ballet-slipper-battered bicep back to Venice.

The doors began to close but abruptly reopened.

Glenda sashayed onto the elevator wearing a red pastie, a green pastie, and a white thong. The deconstructed *tricolore*, the nickname for the Italian flag, was appropriate since she'd been out with triplets. "It's 4:00 a.m. Must've been some date."

"There were three of them, Miss Franki, so I had to give equal time to each one. But since you're up too, I'm guessing your ex-banker beau has the strength of three men."

The elevator went up, but my mood plummeted because my ex-banker beau was asleep, and my family and the case were keeping me from him. "I'm just getting back from the cemetery. Lucrezia's necklace wasn't in her grave, but the body of the redhead posing as a maid was."

"*Dio mio,* sugar!"

My head retracted at her unexpected Italian, and she shrugged. "My three dates kept saying it."

I'll bet.

"Did you call the police?"

I nodded. "The inspector raised all kinds of hell when he found out we were at the cemetery, which is ironic because his last name is Lucifero."

"As in Lucifer?"

"Yeah, and quite possibly the original."

Glenda braced herself against the walls. "Lawd, child. Introduce me. We'll have a devil of a time."

If he made good on his threat to arrest me for tampering with a grave and interfering with an investigation, I would.

The elevator doors opened, and I followed her into the hallway. Her white I-heart-Italians stripper go-go boots reminded me that we had logistics to discuss. "Hey, when is your date with the counterfeit Casanova?"

"Tonight at nine."

"I'll be nearby, but you'll still need some way to protect yourself."

"I'm on it, sugar. I always bring protection with me when I'm traveling."

I stopped at my suite. "Just to clarify, I'm talking about a weapon, not condoms."

"So am I." She shimmied, causing her Italian flag to wave—or ripple. "I've got detachable nunchuck nipple tassels."

If she'd been anyone else, I would've been worried. But Glenda had been swinging on poles for so many years that her nunchucked breasts would have the blunt force of dual steel maces.

"Let's get some rest, Miss Franki. We've got a big night ahead of us."

I would now that the two sharks had their own den. I

entered my suite and switched on the light. And I jumped as if I'd been shocked by an electric eel.

Someone was in my bed—snoring.

I crept closer.

It was my mother in a black silk eye mask.

My nonna wasn't with her, which was odd. I checked the balcony and the bathroom. Then I went back to the bed. "Mom. Where's Nonna?"

"I've got to go to the piazza early," she mumbled, "to make a red sauce."

God, maybe she does *make ragù with pigeons. Thankfully, the suites don't have kitchens.* I gave her a brisk shake. "Wake up. We've got a problem."

"Frisky time's on Fridays, Joe."

I pulled back my hands like they'd been singed. *Ick.*

Nonna's suitcase was on the floor, but the page she'd stolen from Maurizio's little black book was on the nightstand. I sat on the aqua silk bedspread, seasick. I didn't think she'd leave a stolen list of potential fiancés unguarded. *Is something wrong? Or did Nonna get grossed out by my mother's sleep-talking and go to their new room?*

I left the suite and got in the elevator. While it took me to the next floor, I scanned the page from Maurizio's book. Not surprisingly, the checklist was written in Italian and focused on personality and physical traits. There was one I didn't recognize —*mento absburgico.* "Hm. *Mento* is chin, and *absburg*—"

The Habsburg chin! The Austrian branch of the royal family had ruled Sicily for a time. "No wonder Maurizio said they needed new blood."

The elevator opened, and a black nightgown disappeared around the corner. *Why would anyone roam the hallway at four fifteen in the morning?*

I went to room twenty-three and knocked. While I waited for

nonna, I contemplated Sheilah's door. *Is she the one running around in the gown? If so, what for?*

My eyes narrowed to the width of a dagger and darted to Bradley's door. *No. Don't get carried away, Franki.*

I knocked again. Harder.

"*Chi è?*"

A man asking who it is? Is my nonna...? It was really tempting to get carried away, but I resisted and replied with the first thing that came to mind. "Room service."

A lock clicked. The hem of an old-fashioned men's night shirt was followed by Maurizio Bonsignore's head.

My intake of breath was so profound that I was surprised I didn't inhale the black satin eye mask from his forehead. "I put you on a train—"

"And I got off at the next-a stop." He tried to close the door, but I shouldered my way into the suite and searched every nook and cranny.

"Where's my nonna? And why is it that you and my mother both wear capes and eye masks?"

He adjusted the collar of his nightshirt as though I'd offended his honor. "Signorina, I work-a with-a zitelle. I do not need the scappatella with your mother, as I have-a plenty of-a women."

Based on his girlie nightshirt and Sicily perfume, I doubted it. "Let me make myself painfully clear, and I stress the painfully, if you try to find me a match, I will break every bone in your skeleton and deposit you in a tiny box on the island of San Michele."

"Un momento." He opened the little white book of zitelle.

"That's right. Remove my page."

He picked up a pen and began to write. "Violent, behave like-a donkey, look like-a one too."

I yelled—and to my dismay it sounded a bit like a bray—and

rushed him. He ran around the side of the bed. I lunged, and he jumped on the mattress—actually, climbed because his legs were so short—and grabbed a lamp.

"Come-a close, and I do the bop on-a the head."

"Give me that book, or I do the bop on the whole body."

He lowered the lamp, and the sly returned to his eyes. "Like savage cave-a woman?"

The 'good gentleman' was really pushing it. A body-bopping was in order even if I *did* get the book.

A strangled cry from the hallway stopped us in our tracks.

Brutti traditori, vergognatevi!

Ugly traitors, shame on you? That sounded like my nonna. Then again, those sorts of outbursts were common in Italy. I'd once seen a woman on an elegant street in Siena scream the entire hierarchy of Italian words for whore at another who remained stone-faced as she strolled arm in arm with a man.

Maurizio hopped from the bed and pulled on his pants.

"You're not going out there, are you?"

"*Sì, signorina.*" He put on his top hat and reached for his cape. "I get-a new client, who have-a better manners."

"I don't know. The hallway outburst seems like a red flag."

"Maurizio," the woman shouted, "forget-a the back-a-up! We need a new fidanzato!"

My head snapped toward the door. That was no random nonna—she was mine.

I followed Maurizio from the suite, and the first thing I saw was Nonna in the black gown I'd seen when I'd gotten off the elevator. Her handbag was draped on one arm, and the other was pointed at the ugly traitors—a red-faced Bradley and Sheilah.

My body rocked as though I was still on the quad scull. *Now you can get carried away, Franki.*

Bradley held up his hands. "Babe, this is *not* what it looks like."

I eyed his hotel robe and Sheilah's red dressing gown and thought how lucky they were that I didn't have the cleaver oars. "Then what, pray tell, is it?"

"I'd like to know the same thing," Sheilah's husband growled from the doorway of their suite.

Sheilah clasped her hands. "Ted, we were just talking."

Nonna harrumphed. "About-a what-a? Playing hide-a the *cannolo*?"

"Nonna, let me handle this." The scene was devastating enough without ruining a delicious dessert.

Maurizio produced a business card with his signature cape flourish and handed it to Sheilah. "You're gonna need-a my services."

Nonna whacked him with his top hat. "Brutto traditore! I want-a the refund!"

Maurizio covered his head. "I told-a you, my fee, she is nonrefundable."

Shona stormed the hall in footed pajamas. "What's with all the shouting?"

If I wasn't so shocked by Bradley and Sheilah, I would have laughed.

Shona spotted Bradley and got tongue-tied, but her eyes shouted volumes.

Volumes that added to my humiliation. "Maurizio, invite the bachelor counts to Venice. I might need a new date to the wedding."

Bradley grasped my hand. "Franki, please. Can we speak in private?"

I pulled away. "No, I have an investigation to worry about— one you said you wanted to help me with."

"And I do."

"If this is how you help me, then I'm better off on my own." I ran down the stairs and into my room. I slammed the door loud enough for Bradley and Sheilah to hear it on the next floor.

My mother continued snoring.

I entered the bathroom, turned on the faucet, and splashed cold water on my face. Slowly, I lifted my head to look in the mirror. I expected tears, but they didn't come. After the night I'd had, I was too numb. But there was no mistake about it—Venice was the tomb of love.

After turning off the water, I reached for a towel with my left hand and jammed my ring finger on the bar. "Seriously?" I said to the mirror. "Reminding me of Tosca looking for her missing ring finger when I've just found my fiancé and his ex-wife together?"

I perched on the edge of the bidet and stared at my engagement ring. I knew Bradley wouldn't cheat on me with Sheilah, but I was angry that he'd let her in his room, and especially when neither of them were dressed. Because she was up to something, and it was definitely no good.

Guilt surged in my chest. *I shouldn't be thinking about my love life when another woman is dead.*

A cry came from the street below.

"That had better not be Sheilah sobbing because her husband kicked her out." I glared at the mirror. "If anyone deserves to lose their ring finger, it's her."

As I massaged my aching joint, I looked out the window.

And took a step back.

A woman in a terrifying black oval mask that covered her from forehead to chin stared at my window. She raised a walking stick that reminded me of the cane carried by the voodoo loa of the dead, Baron Samedi, except that it had feathers, ribbons, and a doll in a cage.

Judging from the wide ruff collar that framed her enormous

headdress, I would've thought she was a Venetian Voodoo Priestess, or even a Vampire of Venice, but there was a problem, or really two.

Her eighteenth-century violet dress and jeweled crucifix necklace said she was the ghost of Lucrezia Pavan.

13

The door to my suite opened. "Franki," Bradley whispered, "we need to talk."

I was surprised he would be so bold with my mom and nonna in the bed. Nevertheless, I had no intention of speaking to him. I stayed still on the antique sofa pretending to sleep.

Footsteps crossed the room, clicking loudly.

Is Bradley wearing heels?

Within moments, I sensed him hovering over me and opened my eyes a crack. My fickle fiancé stood before me in the counterfeit Casanova's outfit.

Talk about desperate.

With hooded lids, I gave him the once-over—from the bow in his curled wig to his pink satin breeches and man heels. The more I saw the eighteenth-century look, the less I understood why women were into it.

My gaze returned to his face, and I gripped the edge of my blanket. Somehow Bradley had morphed into Sheilah—all whored up like Madame du Pompadour with an oddly placed beauty mark at her temple.

She pulled a knife from the bodice of her low-cut nun dress and grabbed my left hand. "You didn't even know what room Bradley was in, so you don't deserve to have him." She cut off my ring finger with a single whack and put on my ruby-and-diamond engagement ring. It glowed like a heavenly light from the slit in her *stratagliato* glove, and tiny cherubs flew around it. "Now you'll never marry Bradley, or anyone."

"Like Tosca," I muttered.

"No, like a zitella." She cackled and left the room.

Blood gushed from my finger. Panicked, I squeezed the wound shut.

Maurizio Bonsignore appeared with a flash of canines and a flourish of cape. As he came into the room with a basin, his vampire shark tail left a trail of canal water. "We have-a big-a problem. The dowry, she is-a not enough."

I held up my bleeding hand. "But I just gave new blood."

He lowered the basin, and I peered inside and huddled behind a gold pillow.

It was filled with severed fingers.

My mother made a grand entrance in a tiara and fur cape with armholes by her knees. "We don't have enough fingers to get you a desperate count, dear. And since you don't have a ring finger, I had to call for help."

She turned and gave the Queen's wave—at knee level—to my nonna, who shuffled into the suite in her mourning dress and the emergency veil she kept in her handbag for any funeral opportunities. "*Franki è condannata allo zitellaggio perenne!*"

I could no longer deny her dire prediction. Without my ring finger, I *was* condemned to perennial spinsterhood, unless my mom had a solution.

Nonna crossed herself and stepped aside.

A cloaked, hooded figure materialized and did the wedding

march to the couch. As he loomed over me, I thought of the bronze statue in the lagoon. "Dante?"

"No, Francesca," my mother chided. "The executioner from the Palazzo Ducale."

He bowed before her and pulled back his hood.

I screamed bloody-finger murder. In place of his head was a skull with a Habsburg chin and the screwed-together bones of the bell ringer.

Father Festin from the Church of Murders entered with a light bulb in his mouth. He opened a copy of *Death in Venice* and started singing the "Monster Mash." When he got to the line about the Crypt Kicker 5, Ruth Walker waltzed in, semi-stumbling from snickering, in white Keds and a Judge Judy robe. She handed me a bouquet of roses and violets and stood at my side like a maid of honor. But instead of flowers, she held a fun meter that went from Max to Med to *Morta*—Italian for *dead*.

This meeting has nothing to do with my dowry. It's my wedding date with death.

The executioner produced a bottle of Valpolicella and poured me a glass.

"I'm not drinking that. It's poisoned."

At my refusal, he raised one of Shona's cleaver oars.

"Wait! You're supposed to hang me between the two red columns of the loggia!"

My mother pointed—from knee level—to the picture of Giustiniano Participazio above my bed. "There's no need, Francesca. The doge is already here."

I watched, horrified, as the oar came down.

My eyes flew open, and I rocketed up, bathed in sweat on the antique sofa. I ran my fingers through my tangled hair. "That dream was crazy even for me. I hope I didn't get a brain amoeba from the canal water."

Even though it had all been a nightmare, I took a moment to verify that I was alone in the suite so that I could be sure Ruth wasn't stalking me on the premises. Next I turned my ire on the bronze cherub statues. "Traitors. A lot of good you're doing me. Why couldn't you inspire a romantic dream?"

The dour doge scowled from his painting to discourage my foolish question.

A knock at the door interrupted my inanimate object conversation.

That had better not be Bradley in Casanova clothes. Our relationship could survive a 4:00 a.m. chat with Sheilah, but we would never recover from that costume. "Who is it?"

"Veronica. Glenda's with me."

"Hang on." I pushed myself off the couch, and rowing pains shot through my arms. I did a quick check to make sure that the quad scull journey from inferno hadn't stretched them out like my nightmare mother's.

I opened the door and winced. My bicep hurt, but Glenda's getup was more painful. I wasn't surprised to see the black satin gloves with fake jewels protruding from slits at the knuckles, but I was taken aback by the two rubies and lone black pearl jutting from the slits in her matching bra and panties.

"This is the hellion-nun outfit I came up with at the Casanova Museum, Miss Franki." She kicked up a red stripper clog. "It tickles me to think that the sexy sisters wore these things. They must've known the old saying, 'the higher the heel, the closer to God.'"

Ordinarily, I would have scoffed at such a suggestion, but given the history of the Venetian nuns, it was possible that they'd coined the expression.

Veronica entered with a strained smile. "It's almost noon, so we wanted to make sure you were okay."

I was, until blindsided by the jewels glued to my landlady's lady parts.

Glenda sashayed in and emptied a bag with a bottle of champagne, three flutes, and a signed copy of *Like a Polecat at a Garden Party*. "These'll take away your man blues, sugar."

The only thing that would do that was a Nutella cornetto with a jar of Nutella on the side. "I get the bubbles, but how will your memoirs help?"

"It's all in the theme, Miss Franki." She popped the champagne cork. "'Don't let a man get you down when you can just go get you another one.'"

Sure. A desperate Sicilian count with a Habsburg chin.

Glenda filled the flutes, and we went to the balcony. As Veronica and I sat at the marble table, Glenda leaned over the railing, and the sip of champagne in my mouth went flat. She'd glued a black pearl on her backside too.

Veronica shot me a nervous look. "Dirk said your nonna was in the hallway last night, but how is your mother doing?"

"Fairly well, really. When Nonna came back and told her about Bradley, she fainted, and then before she regained consciousness, she fell asleep. So Nonna climbed into bed and joined her." I paused. "Even sharks need their rest."

Veronica didn't react to the fish comparison. She was all too familiar with their predatory skills.

Glenda leaned her back against the rail, jutting out her jewels. "Well, I, for one, am surprised they'd hit the hay given their mania about your marital status, sugar."

"I'm not, because they knew they wouldn't miss anything. Like sharks, their eyes register movement in their sleep."

"Anyway," Veronica said, "Glenda and I haven't seen them this morning, but I did see Bradley. He wanted to come talk to you, but I convinced him to let you sleep. Dirk took him to tour the Venetian Arsenal to get his mind off things."

"That's the last place Dirk should've taken him. If my mom and nonna find him there, they have an actual arsenal of weapons at their disposal. And far be it from me to call them off."

"So you think Bradley is still interested in Sheilah?"

"Not in the slightest."

Glenda turned from the railing—thankfully. "Then what's the problem, sugar?"

My fingers folded into fists. "I'm furious with him for letting her into the suite. He knows what a schemer she is, and that was disrespectful."

"You should talk to him about it." Veronica gave my fist a squeeze. "But I am relieved to hear you say that. Remember when I told you there was a best man issue? He had a family emergency, and Dirk asked Bradley to stand in for him."

I blinked. "So we'll be at an altar together."

Glenda sat on the lounge chair—very carefully. "If you don't want to do it, Miss Franki, I'll be your maid-of-honor stand-in."

Veronica's eyes popped like the jewels from Glenda's slits, and she grabbed her champagne.

"Thanks, but I plan to be there for my best friend. Unless..."

Veronica choked on a sip. "Unless what?"

I breathed in the salty air. "Not to be melodramatic, but another woman is dead, which makes the 'Roses Are Red' threat more pressing."

Glenda lit a cigarette in a jeweled holder and blew out smoke. "I told Miss Ronnie about the redhead."

"The story didn't end with her. Lucrezia's ghost paid me a visit last night."

Veronica slammed her flute on the table. "Come again?"

"Yeah, when Stella told me that Lucrezia's last name was Pavan, I'd wondered whether I was being haunted by her ghost. And then, sure enough, a woman in an eighteenth-century violet dress and crucifix necklace, possibly Lucrezia's, stood outside my bathroom window."

Her brow lowered. "We all know she wasn't an actual ghost, so it was either one of the jewel thieves or a prank."

My fingers flipped up in protest. "Oh, it was no prank. When I made eye contact, Ghost Lucrezia ran her finger across her neck."

Fire flashed in Glenda's eyes—and her rubies. "What did this violet vixen look like, Miss Franki?"

"I couldn't tell you. She wore a black oval mask, but she has to be one of the grave robbers. And since the impostor maid was wearing a mask too, I'm going to go to a local mask shop today to see what I can find out."

Glenda exhaled smoke through her nose. "But I thought the maid was mixed up with the grave robbers, so why would they kill her?"

"Maybe to silence her." I looked at a pink palazzo across the Grand Canal and thought of Rosa at Dogaressa Flowers. "Or, because she stood to inherit the crucifix necklace."

Veronica leaned forward. "You think she was related to Iona?"

I nodded. "When Shona and I went to the flower shop, the clerk told us that Iona was wearing a gold necklace with the name *Violet*. She thought it was the name of a child, but I dismissed that because Gaspare said Iona didn't have any living relatives. Then when Midge and Madge saw the redhead, they said she was the spitting image of Barbara, Iona's mother. So I think she was Iona's daughter."

"She could be a cousin."

"Doubtful. Madge said that after Iona had a teenage fling on a family trip to Venice, her mother sent her away, allegedly to a boarding school."

Glenda crossed her clogs. "Just long enough to have a child, I'd imagine."

I watched the bubbles rise in my glass. "Which raises a critical question—why would Iona's own daughter kill her?"

"'CASANOVA MASK ARTISAN WORKSHOP' is a misnomer," I said under my breath as I surveyed the mask-covered walls. Their vacant eye sockets, long beaks, and cruel mouths weren't seductive but straight-up psychotic. And the fact that the mask-maker behind the worktable was the incarnation of Disney's Geppetto didn't help because anyone in their right mind knew *Pinocchio* was a horror movie.

Anxious to get my info and go before the long-nosed masks started talking—or braying, I made my way through a crowd of observers and approached the gray-haired *mascarero*, whose arms were elbow deep in a bucket. "*Mi scusi.*"

His head jerked up, knocking his round spectacles low on his button nose, and he splashed papier-mâché on his apron.

"You mustn't disturb the maestro while he's creating," a deep female voice admonished.

I turned to a barrel-chested woman in a velvet floral hat, green wool dress, and brown gloves. She reminded me of a matronly 1960s TV character, like the brash leader of the Psychic Occult Society from *The Ghost and Mr. Chicken* or Aunt Bee from *Andy Griffith* if she'd been a brusque busybody with money. "Do you work here?"

"Goodness, no." Her face paled like her pearls. "I'm Eloise Maxwell, the president of the American chapter of 'Friends of *L'Arte dei Mascareri.*' We support the art of traditional Venetian mask makers, which has come under siege."

"Siege?" The masks were scary, but attacking them was odd. "By who?"

"Not *who*. *What*. The art is being threatened by," she placed a hand on her ample bosom and took a deep breath, "cheap plastic knockoffs."

"Plastic," I breathed, not expecting that answer.

"Precisely. It's unbridled evil." She shuddered, and the flowers on her hat quivered. "In 2015, the Venetian founders of L'Arte dei Mascareri were forced to retaliate. They organized a procession to the Piazza San Marco called 'The Ballad of Uninhabited Masks.'" Her eyes misted, and she pulled a handkerchief from her handbag. "The mascareri carried masks on sticks to emphasize that they had no inhabitants." She choked back a sob. "*No one* was *wearing* them."

I tried to empathize, but I couldn't get worked up about empty masks because a) it was weird, b) it reminded me of Glenda's gold mask on a stick and the ones stuck to her lady parts, and c) no one was wearing the masks on the walls, and I didn't see Eloise shedding tears for them. "How were masks on sticks a retaliation, exactly?"

"They symbolized the loss of the cultural meaning of Venetian masks, as well as of Carnival itself." She gripped my aching arm, and her wide, haunted eyes sought mine. "Don't you see? The masks were *ghosts*."

I didn't see, at least not in relation to the masks. But Venice had as many ghosts as it did bones in the San Michele cemetery. I gently removed my arm from her panicked fingers. "Listen, Eloise—"

"Please, call me Eloisa. The maestro does." She pressed her hand to her heart, closed her eyes, and scrunched her face.

I couldn't tell whether she was overcome or having a stroke. "I need to buy a mask, and I was hoping to ask the maestro what some of them represent."

"The maestro must keep working since he's competing with machines. But I've read volumes of books about the masks, and I'm happy to share what I know."

The last sentence gave me pause. I didn't know Eloise's professional background, but she showed serious signs of having some Shona in her.

"Are you shopping for an event?"

"My friend's rehearsal dinner." I didn't mention the murder investigation. She was clearly too emotional to handle it.

She led me to a wall. "These are the classic masks. As you can see, there are only eight main styles."

My gaze passed over the harlequin to the most infamous—a white one with glasses and a long beak.

Eloise frowned. "That's the *medico della peste*, or plague doctor."

"I've always wondered why the doctors wanted to look like a bird."

"It wasn't about the appearance, it was the beak. They filled it with flowers and herbs to protect them from *miasma*, which was the 'bad air' believed to cause the Black Death." She wrinkled her nose. "It wouldn't do for a rehearsal dinner."

No, but I could buy it to protect me from Ruth—if invoking my namesake saint didn't work. And from Maurizio Bonsignore's Sicily perfume.

The huge chin of a square-shaped mask caught my attention. "Just out of curiosity, what's that one called?"

"The *bauta*, which is the standard for men. The protruding chin alters the voice to further disguise the wearer. It's also known as the *Casanova*."

Funny, I would've said 'the Habsburg.'

She pointed to a white mask with painted lips, similar to the one Tosca had worn. "This is lovely. It's the *volto*, which means *face*, because it offered complete anonymity."

Obviously, the redhead hadn't wanted to be recognized. "Do you know if this was ever called the Tosca?"

"I've never heard that. It was originally called the 'larva.'"

My normal-sized chin retracted. "As in, a grub?"

"No, the word also means 'ghost' and 'skeleton.'"

I shifted onto one hip. *What is wrong with this city?*

Eloise picked up a half-mask with colorful feathers. "How about the *colombina?*"

"It's a little too showgirl." I scanned the shop for the one Ghost Lucrezia had worn. "I saw a woman in a black, oval-shaped mask. Does the maestro have one of those?"

"You're talking about the *moretta*, or *little dark one*, but I don't recommend it. There are no breathing holes, and you have to bite a mouthpiece to keep it in place."

The fact that wearers couldn't breathe or speak made the mask even creepier—and more ghost appropriate. "Why would anyone want to wear that?"

"Back then, only men and prostitutes went in public alone, so the moretta enabled respectable women to protect themselves from the charge of being immodest. They wore it when they visited the nuns or engaged in forbidden play."

The reference to nuns got my attention, but I was more interested in the latter use. "What do you mean by 'forbidden play?'"

"Oh, my dear." The corners of her mouth wrinkled, and her eyes rolled. "Masks were worn to equalize the social classes, but they gave Venetians license to seduce, gamble, and commit all manner of crimes, including murder."

And they were still doing so. Ghost Lucrezia could have been Perpetua, the church volunteer I'd seen talking to Casanova. But had they killed the redhead?

"Incidentally, the moretta is also known as the *servetta muta*, which means *mute servant*."

I knew what it meant, and I didn't like it. The name gave me cult vibes.

My text tone beeped. It was Madge Maven, asking me to meet her and Midge urgently on the Giudecca, the island directly in front of Venice, at—my eyes zoomed in on the name —*Le Zitelle. There's a place called 'The Old Maids?'*

"Whatever it is," I muttered, "I'm in no hurry to go." Stuffing my phone in my bag, I scanned the shop for a mask that didn't look like a serial killer would wear to a mass murder party. The rhinestones on a black gondola reeled me in. Since I was on the outs with Bradley, the mask was probably the closest I'd get to my romantic ride.

I waited at an empty register and looked around for the cashier. A print in a display bin almost made me drop my mask. According to the price tag, it was a 1769 painting called *The Fair Nun Unmasked* by Henry Robert Morland. The nun in question wore a black veil and frilly low-cut blue dress and held a painted mask near her face. She had jewels in her hair, around her wrist, and at her bosom, but the one that interested me hung from her neck—a jeweled crucifix necklace. "Eloisa?"

"Ah, that name." She pressed her hand to her chest, looked up, and scrunched her face.

When she recovered from whatever she'd been experiencing, I asked, "Do you happen to know who this woman is?"

"Her identity is unknown. The artist is conveying the message that everyone wears a habit that is the opposite of who they really are. In this case, the woman is dressed as a Venetian nun, but she's a harlot."

Of course, I was no expert, nor was I the president of an organization dedicated to mask conservation, but if there was one thing I knew about art, it was that the meaning was subjective. "Maybe the opposite is true. She's dressed like a harlot, but she's not one."

Eloise's eyes turned skeptical. "I'm afraid the title says it all. A nun, unmasked."

I agreed, but not in the way she thought. Lucrezia couldn't be defined merely in terms of her sex life. She, like any woman, was much more than that. And I was certain that unmasking her would help me identify the killer.

14

"Surely there's a glitch in my maps app," I grumbled, although I didn't really believe that. But something was up with the old maids on Giudecca island. I'd disembarked from the ferry at the Le Zitelle stop, strolled along the Fondamenta Zitelle walkway, and passed not only a Bar Zitelle but a Church of Le Zitelle too. I felt like Pinocchio on Pleasure Island when he learned that boys were turned into donkeys and trafficked to salt mines.

I entered the spacious lobby of the Palladio, a luxury hotel and spa overlooking the lagoon, and approached an older woman with short gray hair and a pair of blue readers at the reception desk. "I'm here to see Midge and Madge Maven."

She scowled as though I were a prostitute paying a call on a client and picked up the phone. While she waited for someone to pick up, she looked me over in the same way as my nonna and her nonne friends anytime my single status came up. "You have a visitor, Signorina Maven." She hung up. "You may proceed to room twenty-seven."

"Out of curiosity, why are so many things on the island named 'Le Zitelle?'"

"Because of this hotel." She handed me a brochure with a brief history of the Palladio. The hotel used to be Le Zitelle, an almshouse started by Venetian noblewomen in 1561, before becoming a convent.

I was annoyed to be at the source of the offensive naming trend, but if you believed my nonna, I'd already been here half my life. "But who were the zitelle? The nuns?"

"Certainly not." She straightened her dress, which I realized was nun colors. "Le Zitelle teach young girls without the dowry and women without the virtue, who were destined to be spinsters, to make the lace."

My mouth cocked at an angle. Technically, I fell under both of those categories, so if Bradley and I split, I could always move to the Giudecca and make zitella lace for my whore-nun veils.

After a polite nod, I took the elevator to the Mavens' room. I raised my hand to knock, and the door swung open with a blast of mothball smell and some sort of chemical. Madge's snow-white head emerged and glanced from side to side. "Come in, quickly."

I hurried into the rose-colored room and discovered the reason for her behavior. A desk had been converted into a mini laboratory with test tubes, a flask, and a beaker on a hot plate, all of which were undoubtedly in violation of hotel policy. There was also a platter with cuts of raw meat and fish that I hoped wasn't lunch. "Um, what's all this?"

Madge slipped her hands into the pockets of her tweed skirt and gave the smile of one who knew the nuclear codes. "Slogums Advanced Chemistry Set for Girls. We never travel without it."

I never traveled without a first-aid kit, which was way more normal.

"Ah, Francesca." Midge emerged from a bathroom in safety goggles and a white lab coat. "I'm running tests to confirm our suspicions about the poison that killed Iona. We shall have the results momentarily."

Madge clasped her hands behind her cardigan and paced in her sensible shoes. "That will give us time to discuss a development."

I took a seat in an armchair in a corner. "Has something happened?"

"At breakfast, we had a most interesting conversation with the hotel manager about the history of this building. It used to be a convent called Le Zitelle." She squinted. "Are you familiar with it?"

As of only five minutes ago, but I felt as though I'd known it for sixteen trying years. "The reception clerk mentioned it."

Madge lowered her head and resumed pacing. "Well, he was telling us the names of prominent women involved with the convent, and you'll never guess who came up."

"Lucrezia Pavan?"

"No." She clenched her teeth and stuck out her lower lip. "The Duchess Von Leipold."

"You're kidding."

Midge's eyes beamed behind her goggles. "Not at all. Genevieve Magritte Von Leipold was actually Ginevra Margarita Toderini, a Venetian from a patrician family of modest rank. She married a duke who claimed to be a relative of the Empress of Austria, Maria Teresa."

The Duchess's local origins explained why she was buried at San Michele. "And what did she have to do with this place?"

Madge raised a finger. "When Napoleon closed the convents, she made an enormous donation to the women housed here. Enough to provide dowries for the young girls and the means for the older women to live comfortably for the remainder of their lives."

That was generous, but I didn't see how it related to the case. "Nothing about her sphere necklace, I guess?"

"I'm afraid not."

Midge pulled on a rubber glove. "We did ask the manager if he'd heard of Lucrezia. He hadn't, but he provided an excellent tip. The San Zaccaria convent archives contain the wills of many of its nuns."

"I'm making an after-hours visit to the archives tonight, so if it's there, I'll find it."

"Smashing," Midge said.

Madge nodded. "Quite."

"Actually, I have a development too. A woman in an eighteenth-century violet dress and servetta muta mask stood outside my window last night and made a throat-slitting gesture. I think it was Perpetua, from the church, posing as Lucrezia's ghost."

Madge raised her chin. "Assuming this individual is, in fact, a she."

I was almost positive that Ghost Lucrezia was a woman, but Madge's comment reminded me that I needed to check with The Vassal about his research into the true identity of Richard Chanfray and the whereabouts of Detective Sullivan. "I haven't been back to San Zaccaria to ask Father Festin if he found out where Perpetua bought the communion wine, so I'll go tomorrow and try to get more info about her."

"A sound plan."

Midge used a pair of tongs to pick up the beaker and poured purple liquid over the meat. "Depending on the results of my tests, we may have to make another clandestine expedition this evening."

I already had to stake out Glenda's Ponte delle Tette tête-à-tête with Casanova before going to the San Zaccaria convent, but

I welcomed any opportunity to cut that short. I didn't relish a sighting of her nunchuck nipple tassels—although, if the German beermaker turned out to be her mystery wedding date, a breast-weapon outfit might be preferable to a stripper dirndl. "Have either of you seen a painting by Henry Robert Moreland called *The Fair Nun Unmasked*?"

Midge placed the beaker on the hot plate. "Why, yes. Moreland was British, so the painting is fairly well known in England. It reflects Protestantism's disdain for Catholicism. At one time, the word 'nun' was used as an insult meaning 'whore.'"

Madge sniffed. "Owing to their clothing and behavior, the Venetian nuns were unjustly accused of all manner of things, including wars and the plague."

That was outrageous, but if Ruth Walker and I had been alive during the Black Death, I totally would've blamed her for it. "I brought up the painting because I was surprised to see a nun wearing a jeweled crucifix necklace."

"I would imagine that it was a popular style among the sisters."

"You're probably right."

Midge clasped her hands. "What I remember most about the painting is the beauty marks. The practice originated in France, and I read somewhere that women wore as many as nine and that their location on the face conveyed a message. The most common are *la coquette* above the lip and *la passionnée* near the corner of the eye. However, my favorite is *l'assassin* at the temple."

Where the one on Sheilah's forehead was in my nightmare. I knew she was out to get me.

"What is notable about the painting is that the beauty marks are on the mask and not the face."

I moved to the edge of my seat. "Yes, which makes me think

that women like Lucrezia might not have been the nymphomaniac nuns that history would have them to be."

Madge smiled. "That's the issue with history, is it not? Its interpretation can be skewed by so many things, the story one wants to tell, the evidence one finds, or doesn't..."

Valid points. So what was the truth about Lucrezia? And would I find it?

A timer went off.

Midge inspected the meats on the platter. "Based on my testing, the poison that killed Iona was most likely potassium permanganate."

"How can you be sure?" I asked.

She removed a glove. "It fits all the criteria. It's water soluble, so it would've dissolved in wine, and swallowing causes discoloration, swelling, and corrosion of the mucous membranes, which explains the brown flesh you saw inside Iona's cheeks, as well as the coughing. Death from cardiovascular depression or collapse is typically swift, if not immediate."

I glanced at the various meats, most of which had turned brown. "What about her purple lips?"

Madge pursed hers. "Stained. Potassium permanganate is a violet crystal compound."

"Violet?" I repeated.

Midge held up a sheet of paper. "The color as described in scientific literature."

I thought of the beauty marks. "Then the killer could've used it on purpose, to send some kind of message."

Madge raised her nose. "I daresay so."

I rubbed my mouth, which tingled at the memory of seeing Iona's in death. "What's it used for?"

"Certainly not bath salts."

Midge chuckled. "Good one, Sister."

It was, because it told me to stick to showers and bar soap while I was in Venice.

Midge sat beside Madge. "In chemical laboratories, potassium permanganate is an oxidizing agent. But it's most commonly used as a disinfectant in aquariums and hospitals."

My brow wrinkled. "Maybe the redhead worked in one of those places. Or one of her associates."

Madge winked at her sister. "We had the same thought, so I made a few calls. And as luck would have it, there is an aquarium in Venice in the most intriguing place."

Please tell me it's not another San Michele. "Where?"

She puffed her cheeks. "The Museo della Storia Naturale."

The museum wasn't a cemetery, but as the resting place of the bell ringer's skeleton, it was the same difference.

"You're the best thing to happen to me since I came to Venice," I said to the paper cone of *scartosso* in my hand as I approached the Hotel San Marco. The mixed, fried seafood was so *delizioso* that I didn't care who heard me. I dumped squid tentacles in my mouth, and with my grease-free hand, I texted The Vassal a request for an update on Richard Chanfray and Sullivan. Since I was going to be running around Venice after dark, I wanted a complete list of the ghosts who'd be haunting me.

Elbowing through the hotel's double doors to avoid another injury to my already offended ring finger, I entered the lobby and choked on a fish chunk.

Bradley sat on one of the white couches beneath a gold-framed Rubelli silk of cherubs hovering over two lovers, and of course the female was blonde. But he wasn't the reason I choked. I blamed that on the surprise fish eye in my cone.

He rose, brows furrowed. "Are you okay, babe?"

I gasp-hacked. "Don't 'babe' me after your pajama party with Sheilah."

"Sorry." He held up his hands. "Force of habit."

I went around him and practically punched the elevator button, causing Gaspare to jerk behind the reception counter. "You're taking your life into your hands, sitting in this lobby."

Gaspare ducked from sight, presumably fearing a Mafia honor killing.

"I'm aware of that." Bradley shoved his hands into his pockets. "Your mom and nonna have been hunting me all day with that little man, who's either a tiny Batman or a fancy vampire."

A hand appeared from below the counter and snatched the phone receiver.

"Don't even think of calling the Commissario, Gaspare," I warned. "Lucifer's already here, and she's me."

The hand reappeared and replaced the phone.

I crossed my arms and laid a lethal look on Bradley. "So, let's hear it. What was Sheilah doing with you at four-thirty in the morning in her lingerie?"

He glanced at the empty reception counter. "It has to do with Ted."

"Oh?" I hit the elevator button again. "Does she want to leave him for you?"

Bradley sighed like a man defeated. "No, she needs my help with something."

The fish eye and I exchanged a look. "The last thing you want is to let me guess what that something is."

"While I was in Boston, a financial firm contacted me about a CFO position. Somehow Sheilah found out—"

"Because she's a schemer," I said, "but go ahead."

"—and she asked me not to take it because Ted is under consideration, and he desperately needs it."

An acqua alta of doubts I'd thought were past history

swirled at my feet. *Why didn't he let me know about the CFO position? Does he want a Boston society life after all?* "You interviewed
for a job and didn't tell me?"

He threw up his hands. "It's not like I submitted a résumé,
Franki. They called me out of the blue."

"But you talked to them."

"I listened to their offer. Who wouldn't?"

The acqua alta rose and threatened to pull me under. I didn't
know what he wanted, but I wasn't cut out to be a Boston society
wife. "I'll tell you who wouldn't." The elevator doors opened,
and I got inside. "A man who wants to start a life with me in New
Orleans."

Pain flickered across his face. "Franki—"

I held up my hand. "Don't you dare."

"Sì." Gaspare peered over the counter. "Don't you dare-ed."

"It's dare, not dare-ed," I yelled as the doors closed on
Bradley. Then I rage-ate the rest of my seafood—except for the
fish eye, which gave me a stare that was probably the same as
the one I'd just given Bradley.

The elevator opened, and I stormed the white-and-gold hallway. When I opened the door to my aqua blue suite, three
sharks were thrashing around on their cell phones, snapping at
whoever they were talking to.

My mother paced toward the balcony in a lacy blue dressing
gown that could've belonged to Princess Margaret. "Bradley's ex
is on the move, Joe, so you can't stay in Houston. Anthony will
just have to run the deli and study for his hospitality certificate
at night after it closes."

Maurizio's little loafers blazed a trail that crossed my mother's. "Ask-a someone else to carry Santa Lucia's statue to the
tomb, Tancredi. Instead of a wooden woman, I got a real one just
as-a big-a, and she want a count with a strong-a jaw."

Nonna cut off my mom and Maurizio with her slow shuffle.

"If-a you can't-a do a double wedding, Padre, it's-a no problem. We take-a the quickie after the ceremony."

The scene was a live demonstration of a phenomenon I'd seen on *Shark Week*. When three or more sharks were in a feeding frenzy, their behavior shifted from circling to rapid criss-cross passes—that could result in cannibalism.

Slowly, I backed from the room.

Nonna lowered her cell and raised pinched fingers. "Franki, where you been-a?"

"Uh, a convent," I said, wisely omitting the *Le Zitelle*.

"*Mamma mia!* We're not-a that-a desperate yet."

The *yet* was telling, and I didn't like what it said. "I'm not headed for the convent, Nonna," I quipped. "I'm on my way to meet Glenda at the Ponte delle Tette."

"*Ooh, brava!* A little peep-a could get-a some new interest."

Time to exit the shark den.

I grabbed a coat and went into the hallway. The Vassal hadn't returned my text, which was unusual for a kid who lived on his phone. Lady Ruth could've been behind the so-called serf's silence, which meant I had to call her. Again.

To prep for the conversation, first I rounded the corner in case my mom came out with an I-told-you-so about Sheilah. Then I did a warmup—some deep breaths, jogging in place, and tongue stretches—before dialing Private Chicks.

"I'm watching *Dr. Pimple Popper*," Ruth answered. "Dr. Lee's squeezing a patient's cysts, and she always compares the gunk that comes out to a type of food."

Squid tentacles tickled the lining of my stomach, threatening to resurface. "I'm calling about The Vassal, Ruth, not someone's cysts."

"Well, you should see this. The gunk looks so much like butter you could spread it on toast."

I was so glad to be in the country of olive oil. "Not to change the subject, but to change the subject, are you stopping The Vassal from contacting me with the research I asked him for?"

A straw-sucking sound followed. "Yessiree, missy. I'm gonna need my Murano glass Santa-on-a-gondola ornament before Serf's allowed to give it to you."

I eyed a wall sconce, tempted to bang my head on it. "Since I'm being threatened and all, I don't have time to wait for you to receive the shipment."

"Who said anything about shipping? I'll take a photo."

"I'm not in my suite," I said, neglecting to add that I was around the corner and that she was never going to see that ornament, in picture or in person.

Her breath sounded like fire, probably because it was full of fire water. "With the holidays upon us, I'm feeling charitable. So I'll give you an early Christmas present. The Vassal checked with a police contact, and as far as the New Orleans PD is concerned, Wesley Sullivan is dead."

Ruth was as charitable as Scrooge McDuck, who I still resented being compared to, so I didn't believe her. "Is this a setup? Because I have reason to believe he was seen in Italy."

"I beg your pardon. *Ruth* is in the word *truth*."

Ruth was also in the word *truther*, and she definitely put a conspiracy spin on the facts. "Just the same, I'll be on the lookout for him."

"Suit yourself. But you're more likely to run into Casanova than the dastardly detective."

"Oh, I already have. He hangs out in the piazza in pink satin pants and eighteenth-century man heels." I side-stepped the issue of him being a likely cult member and a killer because I made it a policy not to tell Ruth anything she could squirrel away in her nutty brain and then use against me in some wack-job way.

"Too bad Judge Judy wasn't around when the real Casanova

was alive. She would've had him castrated and sent to the hoosegow. But if you ask me, the man was impotent."

"The greatest lover in history?"

"Says who? Did any woman ever write about his prowess in bed?"

I leaned against a wall. "Not that I've ever heard of, no."

"Precisely. Casanova was a con artist who wrote his memoirs when he was old and bored and living off some count. He spent ten years cranking out thirty-seven hundred pages reinventing his miserable, thieving life. And do you know the last thing he said before he died?"

Well, it wasn't that Venice is the City of Love. "No, what?"

"That he'd lived as a philosopher and died as a Christian, so it sounds to me like he repented for his BS on his deathbed."

She had a point. As historical records went, Casanova's memoirs were about as trustworthy as she was, which brought me back to a key issue—there was no evidence that Casanova and Lucrezia had ever been lovers. And if they weren't, then someone had lied about their relationship, and my money was on her sister, Ludovica, who had a vested interest in avoiding the vestments, and possibly Ludovica's then future husband, Annibale Bragadin, who had a vested interest in gaining her investments. But none of that would explain why Casanova had given Lucrezia such a valuable necklace before he left Venice.

"Hoo! The gunk in that one looks like oatmeal."

I hung up, grateful to be in the country that served Nutella for breakfast, and rounded the corner.

A cape disappeared behind the elevator doors. Probably Maurizio's. Still, my instincts told me to look at my suite.

And the seafood in my stomach started to swim.

A small box lay on the floor.

Based on the familiar red-and-green wrapping, the odds of the box holding an apology from Bradley were about the same as it being another early Christmas present from Ruth—zilch to none.

Crouching, I unwrapped the package, removed the porcelain lion's head, and unrolled the note.

Roses are red, violets are blue, Tosca is dead, tonight it's you.

15

"Genius, Franki. You've got a target on your back, so you take the narrowest street in Venice." I would have thrown up my hands, but like my mother's cape dress, the *Calle Stretta* had my arms pinned to my sides. The aptly named Narrow Street was twenty-one inches wide, which meant that my shoulder span must've been around twenty. My hips were another matter.

Daylight was waning, so I picked up my pace. Every few steps, I looked behind me and hoped the street didn't get any tighter. Otherwise, I would've been a stuck sitting duck.

The ducks around Iona's lifeless body floated into my mind, which drifted to Tosca. I'd been so close to identifying their killer in the hotel hallway, literally around the corner. Maurizio Bonsignore hadn't left my suite. *So who was the cape wearer in the elevator?*

The bell ringer?

Richard Chanfray?

Sullivan?

Gaspare was no help because he'd been in the office, probably hiding for fear that I'd return to mow down Bradley with a machine gun. "If only I had one in this cursed, haunted city."

The street curved onto the *Rio Terà de le Carampane*, the waterway that ran beneath the Ponte delle Tette. Under normal circumstances, the quaint bridge, stuccoed buildings, and shuttered windows with flower boxes would have been charming. But after the second "Roses Are Red" threat, the exposed walkway and lack of side streets made the area a potential death trap. The only place to hide in earshot and eyeshot of the bridge was inside a moored boat.

"The owners won't mind. I'm just going to lay in it." I glanced around, tossed my purse onto the boat, and stepped a foot onto the stern.

"I've been looking everywhere for you," Shona brayed from behind.

My arms flailed, and the boat floated from the wall, sending my legs into the splits—something they did not do. With a shout worthy of Shona herself, I fell backward and plunged into the cold water like that damn *Death in Venice* book. As I sunk into the cloudy depths, one thing was crystal clear—the lunatic librarian would kill me before the killer ever did.

I surfaced like *The Creature from the Black Lagoon*, or alarming green lagoon, in this case. But my psycho-monster stare had no effect on Shona, whose face was a cross between disappointed and disgusted.

"For someone from bayou country, Franki, you sure don't know your way around a boat."

I spat some water. *This date stakeout isn't going well.*

She extended her hand. "I'll pull you out."

"I'll get out myself. My arms still hurt from rowing you back from the cemetery, but I see your bicep has recovered."

"Nicely, thank you."

My glare was as icy as the water. I swam to the boat and managed to pull myself inside despite my muscle strain.

Shona rowed up in the quad scull. "It's a good thing your granny told me where you were because I've got news."

Was it? I wondered as I removed something brown and gelatinous from my cheek. "We call her *nonna*, the Italian word for grandmother."

"Oh, like Shona with a 'nn.'"

"Nno," I squeezed water from my hair. "But since you brought it up, could you 'sh' like the 'sh' in Shona? Casanova will be here any minute, and I didn't take a dunk in the rio to come away with nothing."

"Fine. I'll whisper," she whisper-yelled.

I deeply regretted what I had to say next. "Why don't you park that thing and get under this tarp before Casanova sees you?"

"On it!"

Shivering with cold, I spread out in the hull on my stomach. The boat was shallow enough that I could raise my arm and lift the tarp—and small enough that I could smell the fish, algae, and motor oil residue that coated my body.

Shona climbed in and nuzzled next to me in her puffer coat. She might sink the investigation, but I appreciated the body heat.

"Good thing my coat is waterproof. Now for that news." She tucked hair behind her ears. "One of the Screamers got a tip from a colleague that a private library in a palazzo in Piazza San Marco has papers from the Council of Ten and records about the founding of Venice and its noble families, so I spent the afternoon there with the nicest librarian. It's the Biblioteca Andrighetti Marcello."

"What kind of name is that?"

"Zon? I think it's Venetian."

"No, Andrighetti." My lips curled. "Reminds me of Armageddon."

"It reminds me of spaghetti, and I haven't had dinner." Shona rolled onto her side and propped up her head, like we were at a sleepover. "Hey, Casanova's date restaurant, the Cantina do Spade, is nearby. You wanna go after this?"

If I didn't have to meet the Mavens at the Museo della Storia Naturale, I would've said yes. Evidently, I was destined to date Shona and make my own lace. "I'm calling it an early night," I fibbed. "But what did you find out from that library?"

"Right. I'm so hungry, I almost forgot." She patted her belly. "One of the last meetings of the Council of Ten references Lucrezia's necklace and also the sphere necklace that belonged to a Duchess Von Leipold. Apparently, they were relics of the church, stolen from Doge Andrea Dandolo in 1354. The Council had gotten an anonymous tip through one of those boche de leon that Lucrezia and the Duchess had them, and they planned on getting them back, by any means necessary."

So the necklaces were connected, and to a doge. Did this mean that Lucrezia and the Duchess knew one another? "What year was this?"

"Late 1797, right before Napoleon and the French took Venice. The Council of Ten was probably abolished before it could confiscate them."

"The necklaces must've been really important for the Council to want them back after almost four hundred and fifty-four years."

"I'm sure they had holy significance."

Or special powers that the jewel thieves wanted to coopt for their purposes.

Clicking got my attention, and I peered from the tarp. Glenda was climbing the steps on the bridge. Because of its tall, stuccoed wall, she was only visible from the waist up, which I wasn't sorry about. The sight of her sixty-something-year-old tette in the nunchuck nipple tassels was already too much.

Shona looked over my shoulder. "What's under her biker jacket?"

"Weapons." I texted Glenda my location. "The brass knuckles of boobs."

"Nunchuck? Wow. She's so stylish."

My eyes shot to the side. "How do you figure?"

"Her outfits keep to the theme. And she gave me these light-up pasties she'd planned to wear tonight." She unzipped her coat, and her ponte delle tettes tumbled out, glowing red like stop lights.

I flattened against the side of the boat. Shona had brought her romance tote on board, so I should've known to watch out. "Could you zip those up?"

"Why? I want the Ponte delle Tette experience."

"Have it outside this boat. Those two flares you're wearing will out us to Casanova, and I don't want to look at that. So after you zip up, press 'em flat on the hull."

"Well, well, well." She zipped up and rolled over. "You're not only cheap, you're a prude. I bet you'd wear a bathing suit to a nude beach."

Considering the combined repressive efforts of my parents and the nuns at my Catholic school, that was a given. "Now that you've established my shortcomings, how about we listen for Casanova?"

Shona went silent. "But just so you know, these pasties go with the area."

I lay on my hands to keep from bursting through the tarp, prying a brick from the wall, and going Vampire-of-Venice hunter on her. But the truth was that even a brick in the throat wouldn't stop Shona from info-dumping.

"It was a red light district where women lit up their breasts with red lanterns. Casanova was a frequent visitor, and he carved his name around here somewhere."

"You should go look for it," I said, face-down on the hull.

"I will, when I'm done helping you." She gave a playful punch to my sore arm. "Anyway, the city paid prostitutes to parade around with their boobs out and line up topless on the bridge to try to convert homosexuals, because they thought they were a social problem."

I had thoughts about a social problem, and it had nothing to do with homosexuals.

Rhythmic tapping prompted me to peer through the tarp.

The counterfeit Casanova approached the bridge in his eighteenth-century man heels. He wore his usual costume and a half-mask adorned with musical bars.

Time to find out what the Latin Lover's after, because it sure as hell isn't sex. The date could have been a trap, especially since I was under imminent threat. But if he intended to pump Glenda for information about me and my investigation, he'd gravely miscalculated. When it came to manipulating men, seasoned strippers were the world's wiliest women.

Casanova bowed and kissed Glenda's hand.

Her mouth slid into a naughty smile. "Do all you Venetians wear masks?"

"Even Venice wears a mask, cara mia."

"And why is that, Casy baby?"

He gazed into her eyes. "She cannot remove it because her face will show corruption."

He's talking about her, not just Venice.

Glenda ran her fingers down the front of his waistcoat. "Corruption can be fun in the right context."

"As I am aware." He took her hand and kissed her fingertips. "But there is no amusement when people hide behind causes that exploit Venice and her treasures."

Glenda wasn't hiding behind a corrupt cause, unless he was refer-ring to justice—or my investigation.

She leaned against the bridge. "Now that makes me think you're a crook, since you're wearing that music mask."

"Ah, but you also wear a mask, *ma chérie.*"

Her lady parts sure did.

Glenda pulled her Mae West cigarette holder from inside her jacket, intentionally exposing a nunchuck. "I only mask this face when I do my dominatrix dance."

His lips spread into a smile as he produced his trusty Bic.

Does he know she's doing that dance with him?

Casanova lit her cigarette as Glenda studied him through spiked lashes. "And when I wear my mask, it doesn't change the fact that I've earned everything I've ever gotten, dollar by dollar, by honest means."

He looked at the water. "The situation is different here. Our institutions have failed us. We must take matters into our own hands, like masked bandits. But I am no crook, cara mia. I do the work of God. His light will save Venice, and us all."

Light? Was he talking about Catholicism? Or a cult?

"Casanova a Christian? I don't believe it."

"We are free to believe whatever we wish, no? But enough of such serious talk." He placed a finger beneath her chin. "I'm in the most beautiful city in the world in the company of a *gioiello.*"

Glenda licked her lips. "What's that, darlin'? A joy ride?"

"A jewel, hard but not unbreakable."

A subtle threat.

"Well, I saw the most fabulous jewels yesterday on the Pala d'Oro." She leaned against the bridge and arched her back, exposing the nunchucks. "Which one do I remind you of?"

Shona looked at me. "I'd say she's a Mexican fire opal. Wouldn't you?"

I released the tarp.

"Did you hear that?" Casanova asked.

My eyes blazed like the stone she'd just mentioned, and I would've ripped the pasties from her ponte delle tettes, but I didn't dare rock the boat.

"It was just some tourists, Casy honey." Glenda grabbed the lapel of his red frock coat. "Let's get back to you seducing me."

He reached for a lock of her hair. "Your platinum hair gleams in the moonlight like the Pala d'Oro's silver panels. Or perhaps a dagger."

Glenda pouted. "You said I was a jewel."

"Indeed I did. Your lips are the color of rubies and your eyes are as blue as sapphires."

"I'm partial to diamonds, but there aren't any on the Pala d'Oro. Why is that?"

"They're not among the twelve foundation stones of New Jerusalem."

The City of God Monsignor Meneghello mentioned. Casanova knew a lot about the altar cloth. Even more proof it was a target.

Glenda ashed her cigarette. "Are you implying that diamonds are third rate?"

"Nothing of the sort. And rest assured, I have paid you a compliment. Rubies and sapphires are known to be the most divine of all jewels."

Shona and I shared a wide-eyed look, and I was certain we were both thinking about the jewels in Lucrezia's necklace—the rubies that remained and the stone that was missing.

Was it a setup? Or had the smooth-talking Latin Lover made a slip?

"ARE the buildings in Venice against me, or what?" My voice exuded outrage as the water taxi I'd exited sped from the Museo della Storia Naturale. First the flooded crypt in the murderous church, then all the old maid places, and now the natural history museum resembled the Palazzo Ducale. "I mean, pardon me for being upset, but on the night of my alleged execution, I didn't want to be reminded of the two red columns of the loggia where people were hanged and left to rot."

The nape of my neck tingled as though anticipating a noose —or the whack of a cleaver oar. Checking over my shoulder, I bade farewell to the bone-chilling façade on the Grand Canal and slipped down the side of the museum to the entrance in the back.

"Now this is what I'm talking about." The warm stucco and rustic brick together with green shuttered windows and an overgrowth of vegetation gave off a Tuscan farmhouse vibe. "Why couldn't Veronica and Dirk get married in a cathedral in Florence instead of the Church of Murders?"

Madge emerged from the shadows with the hood of her nurse's cape pulled up. "Did someone say 'murder?'"

If Midge hadn't been beside her dressed as if she'd stepped off the set of *Call the Midwife*, I would've run for the canal. Because Madge's hooded look was not an ideal sight for someone awaiting an executioner. "Ignore me. I was grumbling to myself."

Midge squeezed my forearm. "I do it all the time, dear."

Madge sniffed the air. "I don't mean to criticize your hygiene habits, Francesca, but you smell rather like the aquarium."

So much for British politeness. "I fell into the rio before Glenda's date, and I haven't had time to change."

"Ah, the perils of a city of water."

You can say that again. And again.

Madge clasped her hands behind her back. "What, pray tell, did you learn from our Casanova impostor?"

That he's a sexaholic like his assumed namesake, judging from the way he and Glenda were making out on a side street when I left. But I didn't want to mention that—or that Shona and her romance tote had stayed to watch. "He's on some sort of religious mission to save himself and Venice from its exploiters, which could support my cult theory. He also said that rubies and sapphires are the most divine gemstones, so I'm thinking the missing stone they're after may be a sapphire."

Midge pulled two headsets from a bag. "Did he mention a color?"

"Blue, but in reference to Glenda's eyes."

She handed a set to Madge and put one on. "The Pala d'Oro has sapphires in a number of colors."

"Yes," Madge said, fitting the headset beneath her hood. "I'm afraid it's too little to go on, if you're correct about the stone."

"Hopefully, I can find out something more specific at the convent archives." I gestured to the door. "Are we ready to go in?"

Midge raised her hood. "We're waiting on Stella."

"She's coming?"

"She's already inside." Midge pointed to a tree by the entrance that grew alongside a second-floor window. "She climbed that oak and slipped inside."

Madge smiled with pride. "Our hips aren't what they used to be, so Stella is our Girl Friday. She's also our security system specialist."

Not the usual skill one acquired in Vegas—unless you planned to pull an Ocean's Eleven-*style heist.* I eyed the museum. When Shona told me the bell-ringer legend, I'd vowed not to come. And yet here I was, about to meet his real-life skeleton.

Stella opened the door in a black turtleneck and skinny jeans. "Ready, Franki?"

I looked at the Mavens. "Am I the only one going in?"

Madge nodded. "I shall remain here as lookout, whilst

Midge stands watch at the front." She winked and tapped her hood. "Hence the headsets."

"Fair enough," I said, although I felt like I'd been hoodwinked.

Stella ushered me inside, and I instantly got the heebie-jeebies. The museum teemed with taxidermy, which is not what a gal wants to see when a killer is hunting her. Glass-eyed animals with claws out and teeth bared watched us as we walked, and some looked as though they could still pounce.

I kept an eye on them as I followed Stella toward a room emitting an eerie glow. I knew it was the aquarium, but all I could think of was the light cult. And the Empyrean.

Was tonight the night I'd go to Dante's heaven?

The aquarium was huge, fifteen or so feet in length. A sign indicated that the tank held more than fifty different species of fish and invertebrates from the tegnue, a rocky reef in the Venice gulf.

Stella jiggled the handle of an unmarked door. "Locked." She pulled out a nail file. "Give me second."

An old-school technique for a security-system specialist. I made eye contact with a fish, and it darted behind a rock. I could relate. Venice was a giant aquarium, and a host of predators were watching me swim in it.

"We're in." Stella opened the door, and the odor of chlorine filled the room.

My phone rang. I didn't recognize the number, but as long as it wasn't Ruth, I was willing to answer. "Hello?"

"It's...Vassal. I...a dormmate's..."

"You're breaking up. Hold on." My phone had only one bar of service. I turned to Stella. "I'm going to step out to get a better signal."

She scrutinized a jar on a shelf. "Go ahead."

I walked into a room with better reception. "Why didn't you call sooner, Vassal?"

"If I had, you wouldn't have called Lady Ruth. She would've suspected treason on my part and meted out who knows what cruel punishment. As it is, I'm forced to use a dormmate's phone because she confiscated mine."

I rolled my eyes—and got creeped out all over again by the glass ones in the taxidermy animals. "Don't get caught up in the role play. You serve me, not Lady Ruth."

He cleared his throat. "Technically, I serve whoever is leading the office. My survival depends on it."

A valid position. Ruth would infect him like the virus she was if he didn't cooperate. "She told me the police think Sullivan's dead. Did you find reports of any sightings in Europe?"

"Negative. However, I located information about Richard Chanfray, alias the Comte de Saint Germain. The story about his body not being found after he committed suicide is an urban legend. He was found deceased in his car with the Baroness of Trintignant, Paula de Loos, who committed suicide, as well. Incidentally, her title was false."

A gruesome story. "Chanfray was a fraud too, as is whoever used his name at the Casanova Museum."

"Not necessarily. I found a documentary about him on YouTube that aired on French television in 1972, in which he claimed to be an alchemist who possessed the powers of transmutation and immortality."

Immortality. Is that what the jewel thieves are after? Or am I on the wrong track?

"He then stated that he was the Comte de Saint Germain and gave a live demonstration of turning lead into gold to prove it. The interviewer brought the lead himself to make sure that Chanfray didn't cheat, and a scientist tested the metal and confirmed it was Au." He took a mouth-breathing break. "That's the periodic table symbol for gold."

"Thanks for the clarification." My tone was terse even though I'd had no idea what Au meant. "I don't know how Chanfray pulled off that demonstration, but he was lying about his past life."

"He wasn't the only one doing so. During the documentary, he introduced two people from the eighteenth century who claimed to be alive because of his youth potion, Madame de Pompadour and Casanova."

I went as still as one of the taxidermy animals. *Were Perpetua and the counterfeit Casanova...?*

Noooo.

My neck tingled again, and The Vassal's mouth-breathing didn't help.

I spun and came face to chest with a gorilla skin on the wall, its stuffed head frozen in a scream. "Gotta run," I said like a loud librarian. "Literally."

Shoving the phone into my pocket, I hurried from the jungle room and took a wrong turn smack into a sea monster. "Oh, jeez!" I put my hand on my chest to calm my heart. On second glance, the sea monster was kind of comical. Someone had paired the back half of a fish with the papier-mâché head, arms, and ribs of Squidward from *SpongeBob Square Pants*. "Nevertheless, I need to leave before this place turns into a *Night at the Museum* movie."

I returned to the supply room. "Okay, where should I start?"

"Actually, I'm done." Stella wrinkled her lips and looked around. "If the potassium permanganate that killed Iona and Tosca was in this room, it's gone now."

"At least we checked. An aquarium on the site of the bell ringer's skeleton did seem a likely source."

"Hey, while we're here, let's check him out." She locked the door and motioned for me to follow. "He's in the Comparative Anatomy hallway."

I stayed put. "Isn't that pressing our luck? Someone could've tipped off the police that we're here."

She grinned. "We Vegas girls like to roll the dice."

The only things we New Orleans girls liked to roll was the good times, and seeing a skeleton in a natural history museum wasn't one of them. Plus, I didn't see how his bones would help the investigation. But, I ran to catch up.

We entered a hallway lined with tall wooden cases with glass doors filled with all manner of stuffed, dried, and fossilized creatures, as well as jars of wet specimens like the ones in Commissario Lucifero's office.

I shivered, more because of the inspector than the specimens. If he found out that I'd broken into the museum, he might live up to his last name.

Stella looked back at me. "At midnight, the bell ringer supposedly leaves the museum and goes to St. Mark's bell tower to ring the largest bell, the *Marangona*, twelve times before haunting the streets in search of change."

Good thing it's only eleven. "What does Marangona mean?"

"It's dialect for 'carpenter.' They rang it to signal the beginning and end of the workday for workers. It was the only bell that survived the tower collapse in 1902."

I didn't know the campanile had collapsed, but I would've bet it sounded the death knell for the practice of selling wine in the shadows of church towers.

Stella swept her hair from her shoulders. "There were four other bells, but the most infamous was the *Maleficio*. It announced an execution at the Palazzo Ducale with a single toll."

Funny she'd mention that under my current threat. I had no idea how the Maleficio sounded, but I was sure the hair on my arms would recognize it.

She stopped at a glass case. "The *campanaro*, aka, the bell ringer." She gave a laugh as dry as his skeleton. "I'd say 'in the flesh,' but it's 'in the bones.'"

I didn't laugh with her. I was reliving the moment on the canal when the man dressed as the bell ringer had extended his cup and revealed a skinless hand and wrist.

Because the screwed-together bones on the seven-foot skeleton before me were their dead ringers.

"HERE WE ARE. PIAZZETTA SAN MARCO." Stella, rowing upright from the stern of the batela while Madge rowed from the bow, steered to a gondola service station. It was ten minutes to midnight, so the gondoliers had gone home.

"Oh, the Christmas tree." Midge squeezed my hand from her seat beside me in the middle of the boat. "It's so lovely, isn't it?"

Madge looked behind her at her sister. "It's as magnificent as the one in Trafalgar Square."

"And the one at Caesar's Palace," Stella said.

The tree was beautiful, sparkling white, but I couldn't enjoy it. The screws from the bell ringer's skeleton were drilling into my skull, or maybe it was the thorns from the "Roses Are Red" poems.

Stella gripped her oar. "Do you want us to walk you to your hotel, Franki?"

I did, but the last thing I wanted was for one of them to get hurt—or worse—on my account. Besides, I had police training in self-defense. "No, I can manage." I climbed off the boat. "I'll be in touch as soon as I talk to Father Festin to find out where the Valpolicella was purchased."

Madge saluted. "Jolly good."

Stella shoved off, and she and Madge guided the batela into the lagoon.

Midge waved. "Pleasant dreams, Francesca."

I forced a smile, but I feared a nightmare awaited me—and not in my sleep. To get to my hotel, I had to walk past the Palazzo Ducale, the Basilica di San Marco, and the campanile where the bell ringer would soon appear.

But not to ring the Marangona.

To wring my neck, instead.

"It's just a short distance." My voice was soft to soothe my nerves. "And not many places to hide...except the twenty or so columns across the façade of the palace, the nooks and crannies of the basilica, and the sides of the bell tower." I breathed in. "Not a problem."

The heels of my boots echoed in the piazza like a clock ticking.

Was my time running out?

"Stop freaking yourself out, Franki."

As I walked the length of the Palazzo Ducale, my eyes darted to the two red columns on the loggia. There was no sign of anyone and, most importantly, no noose.

The moonlight waned, which was odd. Clouds had covered the moon like a shroud. "Lousy timing."

My gaze shifted to the campanile. Nothing out of the ordinary, and all was quiet except for my shoes.

Too quiet.

I would've even welcomed the pigeons.

The piazzetta opened into the main piazza as I began walking along the Basilica di San Marco. "I've learned one thing for sure. Venetian Gothic architecture is all wrong when you're alone and being stalked by a maniac. But on the bright side, you're halfway to the hotel. You're going to be fine."

A bell tolled.

The hair on my arms told me not to wait for eleven more. That bell wasn't the Marangona striking midnight.

It was the Maleficio announcing my execution.

"You had to run your mouth, didn't you? Now run your feet." I broke into a sprint. The bell ringer, or whoever was in the tower, had to make it down over three hundred feet of stairs to catch me.

Unless he's not alone.

I made it to the end of the basilica.

And the bell ringer stepped from the shadows in his black tabarro cloak. The lowered hood obscured his face, and in place of a cup for change to buy back his skeleton, he held a dagger in a black-gloved hand.

"*Chi sei?* Who are you?"

He remained immobile. And eerily silent.

I backed in the direction of the lagoon. *Those screwed-together bones were just a coincidence. He's not the bell ringer. He's just a loser in a seven-foot skeleton costume.*

As if he could hear my thoughts, he raised the blade.

I opened my mouth to call for help, but the Marangona began to strike midnight.

The bell ringer lunged, and I leaped back, stunned. He was surprisingly agile under those fake bones.

Without giving myself a chance to fear the consequences, I leaned back on one leg and kicked the dagger.

It clattered to the ground.

We both lunged, and a struggle ensued. He stooped and reached for the knife, and I yanked back his hood.

My bones went cold.

The bell ringer of Venice had a skull for a head and eyes that glowed red like the pasties Glenda gave Shona.

The Christmas tree began to spin.

Or was it an angel in a dress made of stars?
The lights merged into an all-consuming white.
It wasn't an angel. It was the Empyrean.
Heaven.
I gazed in wonder at the white light of God.
Until it went black.

16

My head swayed. *Am I in a swing?*

No, I couldn't be. My arms swayed too.

Because I'm hanging.

The two red columns of the loggia flashed before my eyes like warning signs. *Has the Palazzo Ducale's executioner strung me up and left me to rot?*

But I was upside down, so he couldn't have—unless he'd hanged me by my heels like the partisans had done to Mussolini and his mistress.

My eyes opened.

To bones.

My encounter with the bell ringer flooded back like acqua alta in a crypt—his dagger, his skull, the glowing red eyes. *Why hasn't he stabbed me? And where are we going?*

His boots dragged across an old stone floor. I turned my head and saw columned archways covered in wire grating and coin-operated tower viewers, and my heart sank—or rather, rose. We were somewhere high. I looked at the ceiling.

Giant bells.

Fear sliced through me like a dagger. That's why the bell

ringer hadn't stabbed me. He planned to make my death look like a suicide dive.

From St. Mark's campanile.

What I didn't know was how he'd gotten me to the top of the tower. *Is he actually superhuman?*

I couldn't let my head injury fool me. The bell ringer was just a guy in a costume.

But if that's true, why does he have exposed rib bones?

Whatever the reason, I had to get away from him. I kicked and writhed, and he dropped me skull-first onto the stone.

Perfect, Franki. You helped the bell ringer ring your bell. Again.

As I lay on my back trying to get my bearings, a clipping sound broke through the chaos in my brain. The bell ringer's gloved hand held wire cutters he was using to make a hole in the grate.

Big enough to throw me through.

Frantic, I looked for a potential weapon. But my head hurt, and my arms ached thanks to Shona and her ballet-slipper-whacked bicep. My gaze landed on a poster of the golden statue of Archangel Gabriel that adorned the top of the bell tower, and I instantly thought of my nonna. She'd once vetoed my mother's suggestion of Gabriel statuettes for my *bomboniere*, or wedding favors, saying she didn't want to wait for him to blow his horn before I got married. If I didn't know better, I'd swear she hung the poster because this was clearly an Archangel-Michael-with-his-scales moment.

Bradley. Will we make it to the altar?

The bell ringer reached down to lift me, and I came face to face with his skull and glowing red eyes. I pushed and kneed him and managed to twist a rib from his padded black costume. As we struggled, I punched through the padding to a black-and-white striped shirt, like Glenda's gondola pole outfit, and a patch of scarred skin—a neck that had been burned.

Where have I seen that before?

He yanked me upright and turned me around.

An elevator was in the center of the campanile, surrounded by the bells.

That's how he got me up here. If only I could get to it. But in my condition, I was no match for the punk piazza pigeons, much less a seven-foot bell ringer with a dagger.

I made like dead weight, but he pushed me against the waist-high wall. I gripped the wire on either side of the remaining grate, desperate to keep my feet on the floor. If he pushed my lower body through the hole, I'd be hanging outside the campanile—that had once collapsed—by two thin wires. "You won't get away with this!"

A suffocated laugh erupted from the torso of his costume. Then he gripped my neck and shoved me backward over the Piazza San Marco.

Three hundred and twenty-three feet below.

My stomach flipped, and the Christmas tree resumed its spin.

I squeezed the grate and closed my eyes. I didn't want to see an angel, and definitely not the Empyrean. *I have to get justice for Iona and Tosca, talk to Bradley, see my best friend get married.*

The bell ringer released my throat and worked to lift my legs.

Eyes wide with fright, I held my feet to the floor and clung to the grate, but my biceps felt as though they were tearing. With the searing pain came a searing realization.

I'm not strong enough to stop him from lifting me.

He grabbed my knees and heaved, and my bottom went over the side.

An awful thought rang in my brain like the Maleficio—I'd predicted my Venetian demise with the slip to Father Festin about my date with death. A gasp-laugh escaped my lips. I had a dangerous job, and yet a wedding had turned out to be my funeral.

He pried my calves from the wall, and I steeled myself—both literally and figuratively—for what came next.

The elevator dinged.

A shout from Shona rang out, followed by a thud, and the bell ringer's skull sailed past me into the night.

Headless, he spun, surprised.

But I wasn't. I could've told him that Shona would show up.

Pulling myself inside, I fell to my knees. If we made it to the piazza in one piece, I'd kiss the ground, pigeon poop and all. Then I'd tell her that when a person was holding on for dear life, the last thing you wanted to do was startle them with your foghorn voice.

Shona whacked the bell ringer with her romance tote, knocking him off balance. "I got the front. You get the back." She got off another tote blow. "Just look at what books can do for you."

Despite my ravaged arms, I stood, grabbed hold of a bell clapper, and gave the bell ringer a kick that sent him sprawling. Then I dropped to the floor.

Shona jumped on the bell ringer, collapsing his costume. "This is what we do to the lurkers where I work."

Yet another reason to avoid the library in Screamer.

The bell ringer had gone still.

I rose and gave Shona a look. "We need to go."

"I'm not done teaching this hoodlum a lesson." She jumped. "Get it? *Hood*-lum?"

The pun was the last straw. I pulled her inside the elevator and punched a button. As I turned, I spotted a silver skull on the heel of the bell ringer's boot.

Like the one on the man who met Casanova and Perpetua at the Caffè Florian.

The doors closed, and I slumped against the elevator wall, too tired to process what I'd just learned. I could've used an ombra, but not in the shadows of Saint Mark's bell tower.

Shona put her hands on her hips. "I thought you were going to bed early."

I wanted to whack her with her romance tote. "Uh, I kind of got hijacked on my way to the hotel."

"I know." She pulled my purse from her tote. "I found this when I was coming back from Glenda and Casanova's date, and then wire started falling from the tower. By the way, those two put the 'red' in Red Light District. They—"

"Never mind them." I pulled out my phone. "We need to call the police."

"Did it before I came up." She flashed a grin. "Incidentally, 9-1-1 is 1-1-3 in Italy. Also, I wanted to tell you—"

"Shona, we just fought off a killer. This is not the time for an information dump."

Her dimples deflated. "Pardon me, but I don't dump information. I provide useful knowledge, not to mention handy resources and helpful tips."

Maybe under normal circumstances, I thought. *Actually, not always even then.*

The floor location indicator above the doors showed that we were a third of the way down. "We have to think about what to do if someone is waiting for us on the ground, like Perpetua or Casanova."

Her lids lowered lustily. "Oh, he won't be down there. When I left him with Glenda, she'd taken one of the nunchucks and—"

"What was it you wanted to tell me?"

"The Screamers found Tosca's birth certificate in Venice's *Archivio di Stato*. That means 'State Archive' in Italian."

I was so surprised that I overlooked the translation.

"Iona was her mother, but no father was listed. And Rosa at

Dogaressa Flowers, which I still think is a weird word, was right about Iona's necklace referring to a child. Tosca's birth name was Violet."

Lucrezia's favorite color. But did it have some other significance?

I glanced at the floor indicator—over halfway down. I massaged my neck where the bell ringer had grabbed me, and I remembered who I'd seen with a burn scar.

The guard in the torture chamber.

It all made sense. After Shona had spotted me at Caffè Florian and shouted my name and profession to the piazza, the cloaked jewel thief had left Casanova and Perpetua at the table and followed us to the Secret Itineraries tour. What I didn't know was whether he actually worked at the Palazzo Ducale.

"Shona, when we get off this elevator, get your quad scull, and I'll meet you at the hotel's private jetty."

"Oh, I can't row. The big race is in less than forty-eight hours, so I have to rest."

I bared my teeth. "Get the boat, or when these doors open, I'll get out and send you back up."

She flattened against the side of the elevator. "Someone's a cranky pants."

I gave her a bell-ringer's-skull stare and glanced at the floor indicator. Almost at ground level. I leaned against the opposite wall, and braced myself for another battle.

The elevator lurched to a stop.

The doors opened.

And my stomach fell to hell.

"Commissario Lucifero." My voice sounded as sinfully guilty as the time a nun at my Catholic school caught me eating a cupcake intended for a church bake sale. In my defense, the cupcake was devil's food.

The inspector shifted eyes as fiery as the bell ringer's from me to Shona, who let out an odd cry that belied both her Screamer and Belchertown origins, shot from the elevator, and exploded through the tower exit.

And that caterwauling coward had the nerve to point out my shortcomings.

"I told you to be careful, Signorina Amato."

My arms would have flailed at his victim-shaming, but they were too sore. "I was walking to my hotel when the man posing as the campanaro came at me with a knife and then tried to throw me from the tower."

"And where, *precisamente*, were you walking to the hotel from?"

Leave it to Lucifer to know the devil is in the details. "He's still in the tower," I said, sidestepping the devilish detail of my museum break-in. "Are you going to go up and arrest him, or are you going to stay down here and blame me for that maniac's actions?"

"My men are on their way via the stairwell." His tone had cooled, but his gaze remained icy hot. "I chose to greet whomever had taken the elevator."

Lucky me. The man was so hateful that I almost preferred being hunted by the bell ringer and my shark mom and nonna.

An officer entered the building, and the inspector rattled off orders.

My head throbbed, so the only thing I caught was *Pronto Soccorso.* "I don't need to go to the emergency room."

The officer ignored my protest and took me by the arm, as though I was some kind of criminal. We exited the campanile and walked briskly across the piazzetta to a police boat at the gondola service station. He loaded me inside, slammed the cabin door, and barked instructions at the driver.

The boat sped off, and I sank into the cushioned seat. The ache in my head turned drill, and the adrenaline rush left me drained. After a concussion it was best to stay awake, but my medical knowledge was no match for the rhythmic bounce of the boat and the hum of the engine.

The boat slowed to a stop, and I opened my eyes—to the bronze statue of Dante's Barge, journeying through inferno.

I clamped my eyelids shut. As omens went, it wasn't the best.

My eyes opened again, and I was in a bed surrounded by a white curtain. The ER. I looked down. Someone had dressed me in a gown marked *Ospedale SS Giovanni e Paolo*, the hospital where aquatic hearses and funeral gondolas took bodies to the San Michele cemetery.

Another not-so-great omen. But I didn't dare close my eyes again for fear of where I'd find myself next, e.g., in a tomb in the flooded crypt.

Someone in the bay next to me moaned.

The bell ringer? Did the police bring him in too? Pushing myself to a sitting position, I listened for clues to the moaner's identity.

The regular beeps of a vital signs monitor escalated to an alarm.

"*La pressione sta calando!*" a nurse shouted.

His pressure is dropping? Panic pierced me like an IV. If the bell ringer died, there was a strong chance the inspector would lock Shona and me in a jail cell together.

Clutching my hospital gown closed, I slid from the bed and peered through the curtain. I was at the end of a row of ER bays across from a supply closet.

A male nurse approached the bay next to me and opened the curtain.

My already dizzy head went into a tailspin.

Madge Maven lay in the bed, as Midge looked on.

A hand covered my mouth and pulled me backward into the closet. *The bell ringer come to finish me off?*

I thrashed and twisted as the door closed. My captor let me go, and I spun ready for a final showdown.

Stella Di Stefano stood before me with her finger pressed to her lips.

"What are you doing?" I whisper-shouted. "Madge's blood pressure just nosedived out there."

"Keep your voice down. It's a diversion." She turned to the shelves and rummaged among boxes of gauze. "After we dropped you off, Madge decided that we needed to check the hospital for the poison. Feigning a heart issue was the easiest option."

"So, what, she can slow her heartbeat on cue?"

"That was Midge's doing."

Either my concussion was playing tricks on me, or Stella had been hitting the hospital's rubbing alcohol.

She pulled a box from a shelf. "By the way, I'm glad to see you upright. I overheard a police officer telling a nurse that you were attacked in the campanile. Which one of the jewel thieves did it?"

"The bell ringer, who's hopefully been arrested. But could we go back to the Midge-stopping-Madge's-heart thing?"

"You've heard of McAfee, the software security company, right?"

I nodded. "Virus protection. Two young guys I work with are big fans."

Stella put the box back and grabbed another. "Well, I told Midge about a live demonstration they did at a Defcon hacker event I went to in Vegas in 2018. They were reporting on North Korean malware and how it's being used to target critical corporate systems, including those in hospitals."

I sat on the lid of a five-gallon bucket. Madge, malware, and North Korean hackers sent my battered brain into overload.

She opened a container that reeked of antiseptic. "McAfee's researchers showed in real-time how the malware can be used to hack into medical networks and falsify vital signs. So Midge replicated their methods with her Raspberry Pi."

Raspberry pie? Forget the rubbing alcohol. Stella was on something stronger, like medicinal marijuana or opioids. "Like, the pie you eat?"

She bit her lip to keep from laughing. "You really got your bell rung, didn't you?"

I refrained from comment. I'd rather go with the bell-ringing than admit that I wasn't the most tech-savvy of PIs.

"A Raspberry Pi is a computer the size of a phone. Midge is using it to manipulate the patient monitor to create a distraction, so I can search the supply closet for the poison."

Miss Marple didn't have a thing on Midge Maven. Nor did James Bond. But the distraction technique convinced me that the jewel thieves had used it with the flaming coffin. They dressed up in costumes that evoked spooky Venetian legends to distract from what they were really doing—committing crimes in the name of religion.

The bucket semi-collapsed under my weight. I got up, and the lid popped off.

Stella and I gaped at the bucket's contents.

Violet crystals.

But was it the potassium permanganate that killed Iona and her daughter?

SHONA SHONE her flashlight in my face from the quad scull. "Whoa. You look like death warmed over."

I didn't flinch at seeing her outside the hospital at 3:00 a.m. —by now it was a given that she'd show—but I did flinch at the light, which burned into my head like a laser. "That's because I barely escaped it."

She watched me climb into the seat behind her. "So ironic you'd say that because the bell ringer escaped."

The boat rocked—or maybe it was my brain in my skull. "How?"

"All I know is that when I was waiting for you to meet me at the hotel jetty, the police started combing the streets for him."

If I hadn't torn the hole in the bell ringer's costume, I would've half-wondered whether he really was supernatural. There were three ways out of the tower—two had been blocked by police, and the other wasn't survivable.

Shona grabbed the oars. "Then I overheard the inspector mentioning you and the hospital to another officer."

"He was probably telling him to alert the staff in case the bell ringer came looking for me." I texted Stella a warning. She and the Mavens were still inside, awaiting Madge's release.

"Should we go back to the hotel until they find him?"

"We're going to the San Zaccaria archives at the Carabinieri station. We've got to find a reference to the jewels in Lucrezia's necklace."

"Smart thinking. If the bell ringer comes and tries to push you from the tower at the San Zaccaria church, the Carabinieri are already there."

Somehow that wasn't comforting.

A story-telling-time smile crossed her face, and she leaned on an oar. "Hey, did I ever tell you that at my library they call me 'Mistress of the Archives?'"

The only thing Shona was mistress of was the motormouth. "Listen, I've got a screaming headache," I stressed *screaming* as a hint about her decibel level. "Can we be quiet for a while?"

Shona sniffed and spun in her seat. She rowed angrily across the black lagoon to the Rio dei Mendicanti where the bell ringer had begged for money to buy back his skeleton.

We glided past dark, decaying palazzos and shops that threatened to succumb to the sea. I spotted the creepy Carnival mannequins, and their masks reminded me of the disturbing black oval moretta worn by Ghost Lucrezia. And her elaborate walking stick.

What was up with that doll in the cage?

We turned onto a canal on the route the coffin had traveled, past the Libreria Acqua Alta bookstore. I kept eyes peeled for the familiar candle flames, but I suspected the diversionary tactic had died with Tosca, aka Violet.

How had Iona's daughter found out about Lucrezia's crucifix necklace? Either she was in contact with Iona or someone else told her about it, like one of the other jewel thieves. *But who were they to her?*

More importantly, who was I to Violet and Iona? And were the jewel thieves planning to wait until I was dead to steal the jewel from the Pala d'Oro? Whatever the answers, I had to find out what kind of stone was missing from that necklace.

My life depended on it.

Shona was in such a huff that we traveled for another twenty minutes without even a *heave!* before docking near the S. Zaccaria pontile. She climbed out, but I struggled because of my ravaged arms.

Shona stared down her still-out-of-joint button nose. "First I have to row to the hospital and wait outside for three hours. Then I have to row you to the Carabinieri station. And now you expect me to haul you out of the quad scull, when you know I have a race coming up?"

I didn't remind her that my current physical state had started when she made me row her from the cemetery after I'd whacked her delicate bicep with the ballet slipper. No matter what I said or did, Shona would stay a pain in the arse *and* the arms.

When I finally exited the boat, we walked through the covered portico and along the row of shops to the Carabinieri station. Because of the grilled windows on the building, there were few entry options except for a ventilation grate high on the wall. "We're probably going to have to circle the building to look for a way in."

"We could try that air vent. Want me to give you a boost?"

No way I was falling for that after she'd slingshotted me over the cemetery wall and waltzed in through a gate. "This time I'm following you in."

"Fine by me." She sauntered through the station entrance.

My fingers curled—the ones that still could. *And that lunatic librarian was going to push me through the grate.*

The station appeared deserted, but inside an office, a carabiniere with his back to us spoke at Shona-volume on the phone.

We tiptoed down a hallway, following a sign with an arrow. The archives were around a corner. The door had a window, and the locking mechanism on the handle was loose. My credit card got us inside.

The room was small, packed with shelves, and smelled of dust and decaying books. I spotted the word *Testamenti* above a shelf of deteriorating leather containers. "The nuns' wills."

Shona browsed books on a shelf. "A fellow librarian told me that they also have inventories of the dotal alms."

"What are those?"

"The dowries women had to give to the church to enter the convent."

I was stunned that nuns had to have a dowry. Then again, they *were* marrying Jesus. "Were they large amounts?"

"Enough to make them cost-prohibitive for most women.

That's why Venetian nuns were mainly from wealthy families. Women without dowries couldn't marry or take the veil, so they usually became prostitutes."

Or lacemakers at the Le Zitelle almshouse, thanks to donations from the likes of the Duchess Von Leipold. The dowry talk made me wonder about the going rate for a desperate Sicilian count with a Habsburg chin. If I didn't work things out with Bradley, I might be in the market for one.

I scanned the boxes of wills for nuns whose last names began with *p.* It took a few minutes, but I found the box and pulled it from the shelf. I turned to head out of sight of the doorway and noticed Shona at a table, typing furiously into her phone. "Did you find something?"

Her eyes were feverish. "According to Google translate, this is a trial transcript of two nuns who snuck their lovers into the convent through a hole they made in a wall."

"Was one of them Lucrezia?"

"No, Laura and Zaccaria, like the saint."

"Then why do we care?"

She lay across her romance tote. "Because the story is sizzling, sister."

Sleuthing Shona had once again been sidelined by Lusty Librarian. At least it would keep her out of my hair. I carried the box to the opposite side of the shelf and knelt beneath a grilled window overlooking the Campo San Zaccaria. I removed the lid, and Lucrezia Pavan's will was on top.

Had someone read it recently? If so, my guess was Perpetua, because she volunteered at the church.

As I unfolded the yellowed document, my pulse pounded and my head spun. I felt as if I were about to commune with the dead. And in a way, I was.

The will was written in old Italian and an ornate cursive, both of which made it difficult to read. Lucrezia began with a preamble, stating that as a young woman, she'd had many hopes for her life, hopes dashed by the ambitions of her late sister, Ludovica. And yet, she bore her no ill will. The next sentences caught my attention. *Women's cross to bear is that our only value is our bodies. And as we are exploited, we must also exploit, lest we be locked in cells and left to die.*

I sat on my heels. *What did that mean? That Ludovica had played a part in Lucrezia's banishment to the convent?*

A faint moan came from the other side of the shelf.

My eyes gravitated to their corners and then back to the will. I didn't want to know what was going down with Shona and that trial testimony.

The next sentence was partially illegible, but one phrase was clear...*known as I was in the convent, by the name of a virgin and martyr from Verona, Santa Violetta.*

"Lucrezia took the name Violetta," I whispered. That explained why she wore the color, and why Iona chose the name for her daughter.

For my funeral, I desire to be buried in a modest habit with the crucifix necklace given to me by Giacomo Casanova, as that is the purpose for which it was intended.

"For which it was intended?" I repeated. It seemed strange that a man who was known for lavishing his lovers with jewels would give her a necklace for her burial. And it was stranger still that a woman who was known for her anti-nun sentiment and lavish clothing would want to be buried in a simple habit. *The Fair Nun Unmasked* came to mind. In this case, the habit didn't reflect the wearer. *Or did it? Was I beginning to unmask Lucrezia?*

The moaning grew louder, but I couldn't take my eyes off the final sentences.

I bequeath a gold sphere necklace to Duchess Genevieve Magritte Von Leipold. May it protect her from the unjust attacks of my suocero, Annibale Bragadin.

"How did Lucrezia get the gold sphere necklace?" I whispered to myself. "And why her brother-in-law?" Madge said that Ludovica's husband had squandered the family fortune, but I couldn't understand why he would've attacked the Duchess *before* Lucrezia left her the necklace, or why Lucrezia felt obliged to protect her.

The moaning became groaning.

Annoyed, I crawled to the end of the shelf. "For crying out loud," I began, since the expression was particularly pertinent to Shona, "we're in a Carabinieri station. Could you keep it down so we don't get arrested?"

She tore her eyes from the trial document, her forehead glistening. "I thought that was *you*."

"Why would I be moaning?"

"Uh, head injury? Sore arms?"

An awful thought penetrated to my skeleton. *Is the bell ringer in the library?*

Another groan sent me back below the window.

Shona dropped and rolled as though she were on fire, and from the sound of that trial testimony, she probably was. She came to a stop beside me. "That groan came from outside."

Swallowing hard, I inched up toward a corner of the window, until one eye peered out.

The doll in the cage hung from the grille, and any question I'd had about her significance was gone.

Because she had long brown hair and cat-eye eyeliner, just like me.

17

My eyelids opened, and my body went as taut as a rope—because I was dangling from the one in the Torture Room at the Palazzo Ducale!

The concussion I'd gotten from the bell ringer was serious, but how had I missed being hanged by the hands tied behind my back? Ghost Lucrezia must've caught up with me outside the convent and whacked me with her Venetian Voodoo Priestess walking stick.

I looked at the floor, and panic coursed through my veins. Water was pouring in.

Acqua alta.

Terrified, I looked for something, anything, to free myself. But the only things in the room were the antique desk and chairs and the three steps that led to my rope. I tried wresting my wrists, but that sent electric shocks through my shoulders.

My fear grew as fast as the water level.

Am I doomed to a tomb at San Michele? If so, Glenda would have to be Veronica's maid of honor, and Bradley would move to Boston.

No, I couldn't let that happen. I had to be there for my best friend's wedding and for my own. And besides, I had murders to solve.

I checked the water level.

Somehow, I was no longer in the Torture Room. I was in the flooded crypt at the Church of Murders.

In a shark cage?

The cage began to lower accompanied by a soundtrack—the theme from *Jaws*.

Two lemon sharks surfaced above the foamy water—that I hoped was seafoam and not bone broth scum—and started snapping. One of the sharks wore a tiara and the other a rosary.

A man-eater shark all whored up like Madame de Pompadour swam in, and she was joined by a screamer shark with a romance tote and cleaver oars for fins.

This nightmare had to be a dream—either that or the concussion and the canal water had done crazy things to my head. *Oh, God. What if I really do have a brain amoeba?*

As the cage approached the water, a Habsburg jaw shark appeared beside a vampire shark, which opened its mouth. But instead of shark teeth, it had the long, gnarly chompers of Maurizio Bonsignore.

That was my cue to wake up, because there was no way those snaggleteeth were touching me. Focusing my energy on my eyelids, I forced them open.

And I screamed like a librarian from Screamer, Alabama.

Mom and Nonna sat across the Caffè Florian table from me. Even though I was wide awake, the *Jaws* soundtrack still played in my head.

"Honestly, Francesca. Dozing off in public?" My mother glanced around to make sure no one was staring, and I did the same to make sure the museum guard, aka bell ringer, wasn't lurking.

My mother pulled her fur wrap around her. "You need to get more sleep."

Nonna raised a knobby finger. "Not-a so fast, Brenda. *Chi dorme non piglia pesci.*"

It was the Italian equivalent of *you snooze, you lose*, but a key implication was lost in translation. Its literal meaning was *one who sleeps doesn't catch fish*, as in, fish in the sea. And I hazarded a guess that the Habsburg jaw shark of my nightmare had been a premonition.

"True, Carmela, but Francesca can't catch fish without her beauty rest."

"Eh," Nonna waved off the notion, "that's-a what a dowry is-a for."

Asian tiger moms couldn't hold a coffin candle to these Italian sharks. Even the pigeons kept their distance, as well they should, because apparently my mom used them in her pasta sauce. "FYI, I didn't come to Venice to catch fish. I came to be my best friend's maid of honor, and on top of that, I have to solve two homicides."

My mom clutched her clutch as though it was my future fish husband that she'd just caught with her bare hands. "You'd best get in the fish market, Francesca, because like I said, Sheilah hasn't moved on, she's moved back. And if you don't do something, the next thing to die will be your relationship. Bradley standing in as Dirk's best man is the perfect opportunity to show him what he could be missing, starting with the rehearsal at the Church today."

I looked for the waiter in desperate need of the espresso and Cioccolata Casanova I'd ordered before I'd nodded off so that I could ditch my bloodthirsty shark family and go to the basilica.

Nonna followed my gaze and spotted Ambrosio. "Oo mamma mia! Forget-a Bradley, we get-a him."

"You can't just tell the guy to marry me, Nonna."

"I know-a that-a." She folded her hands in her lap. "We buy-a him."

Sicilian nonne had been treating both women and men as commodities long before Venice and its nuns had come into being, but she sounded ready to make a marriageable-man purchase. "Wait. Do I actually have a dowry?"

"*Sì, signorina*," Nonna blustered through pursed lips. "It's-a big enough to get a conte from-a Sicilia or three average Giuseppes."

Money *did* afford one options. "Where'd this windfall come from?"

"Never you mind, Francesca." My mother pulled a compact and lipstick from her clutch. "The important thing is that we've found a Count."

The Habsburg jaw shark resurfaced, only to be crowded out by the Compte de Saint Germain. The nagging fear of whoever had posed as Richard Chanfray at the Casanova Museum hovered over me like a Torture Room rope.

"Since your father's not here," she paused to apply Dolce & Gabbana's Sophia Loren lipstick, "the Count will be my plus one to the rehearsal dinner and the wedding."

Time to break out of this shark cage. "You've got the dowry and the date, so you're all set." I rose and pushed in my chair. "But someone should break the news to Dad that you're buying yourself a Count."

"Francesca Lucia Amato, you come back here."

Ambrosio approached with my order.

I met him halfway and deposited some euros on his tray. Then I shot the coffee, let the Cioccolata Casanova slide down my throat, and grabbed the Nutella cornetto. "Grazie."

He let his gaze slither to my chest. "My pleasure."

Good thing Nonna's out of earshot, or she'd try to negotiate a dowry discount.

The pigeons postured at my feet.

"I feel you. Since I've been in Venice, I've been surviving off street food too." I tossed them some crumbs out of empathy. Then I remembered that Dr. Pimple Popper compared cyst contents to food and threw the whole cornetto. "Damn Ruth ruined the Nutella center. She's worse than the plague—she's a black hole of death."

My stomach roared like the winged lion of Venice as I crossed the piazza to the Basilica San Marco, keeping an eye on the Palazzo Ducale for the bell ringer.

A middle-aged tour guide in a tweed suit skirt directed the attention of a group of tourists to a mosaic on the exterior. "This one depicts sailors covering the body of Saint Mark with a layer of pork and cabbage leaves."

The lion in my stomach was as silent as Saint Mark's corpse, and I thought of my upcoming food tour with Stella. Based on her enthusiasm for the legend, I might have to row her batela to the next town to get a decent meal.

Bradley and Dirk came around a corner of the basilica, and I stopped short. Dirk went inside, but Bradley headed for me.

I couldn't beat him to the entrance, so I stopped near another tour guide and a crowd of women wearing t-shirts that said, "I came to Italy to find a husband. *Sposami!*"

You can't make this stuff up, I thought.

The tour guide, a young male wearing a pink Prada scarf, clapped his hands to get their roving eyes back on him. "*Attenzione*, please-a. As I was saying-a, the Arcangelo Michael on the basilica symbolize the war, but-a the Arcangelo Gabriel on the Palazzo Ducale symbolize the politics."

He also symbolizes my unmarried state, as do the women's t-shirts.

In an epic case of bad timing, Bradley walked up. "Franki, we need to talk."

My stomach fluttered. He looked handsome in tight jeans and a black turtleneck, but then I remembered what he and Sheilah had been wearing in the hallway and got mad all over again. "I'm investigating."

"This will only take a minute."

A full-figured woman from the t-shirt crew licked her well-glossed lips. "I've got all the time in the world, handsome."

"Aren't you here to land an Italian?" I snapped.

She avoided my sizzling stare—in favor of a final ogle at my fiancé—and rejoined her group.

I turned to Bradley, who had wisely kept his eyes on me during the exchange. "You were saying?"

His jaw set. "Sheilah loves her husband. That's why she wanted to talk to me."

"This isn't about Sheilah and Ted. It's about that job interview in Boston."

He sighed. "I told you, Franki, I just wanted to hear the offer."

"What if it had been an offer you couldn't refuse? If we're going to build a life together, I need to know where that is."

"I want our life to be in New Orleans, but it's not solely up to me. The job market plays a role too."

A couple of women from the husband-hungry crew eavesdropped on us. I pointed at the Caffè Florian. "Have y'all seen the waiter at that café? His name means 'nectar of the gods,' and it doesn't do him justice."

The women fled to Florian like a flock of pigeons, and the pink-Prada-scarf-wearing tour guide fled with them.

I turned to Bradley, whose brow hadn't unfurrowed from my nectar-of-the-gods assessment. "You're an accomplished bank president. Any New Orleans bank would be thrilled to get you."

"I'm working on it." His voice was suspiciously quiet.

"Does that mean you have some irons in the fire I don't know about?"

"It means just what I said. You're going to have to trust me."

If he was going to run his jobs by Sheilah, I wasn't sure I did.

Monsignor Meneghello passed by in his black robe en route to the basilica.

"I have to go."

Bradley took my hand. "Are we okay?"

"I really hope so." I pulled my hand away and entered the basilica, my head clouded with concern for our future—and with the Pontifical Incense, which was smoking like the chimney of the Sistine Chapel when the cardinals elected a new pope. I sneezed.

"Bless you, child."

I froze at the Monsignor Meneghello's blessing, afraid he'd think I was allergic to the scent of Christ's suffering. "Um, I was just coming to talk to you. This might be a strange question, but are any of the stones on the Pala d'Oro more significant than the others?"

He looked at me askance, as though I planned to steal a few. "Perhaps the jewels on the Christ Pantocrator panel."

"Pantocrator?"

"It's Greek, but the term is in the Book of Revelations and the New Testament. In English, the panel is called 'Christ in Majesty.'"

We walked to the bejeweled altar cloth, and the panel he spoke of was the largest, positioned in the center. Christ sat on a throne with a book, probably the Bible. He had a crown of stones that circled his head and ended on his shoulders, and within it was a stone beside each ear and one on the top of his head. "What are the jewels?"

"Heavens, I can't name all of them."

I studied him for a few seconds, not because he didn't know the stones but because it occurred to me that if he'd replaced "heaven" with "hell," it would have been a curse word.

Dirk sauntered up. "Mind if I answer that, Monsignore?"

"Not at all."

Dirk leaned forward and inspected the cloth. "Apart from the pearls, there are some emeralds, but the stones on his crown and book are sapphires."

The monsignore gave a jolly grin. "The stones replace the words of Scripture to emphasize their precious nature."

The sapphires were pink, lavender, and two shades of purple. "Would you call any of them violet, Dirk?"

"The ones with more blue than red."

There were quite a few of those on the crown and the book, but the missing stone on Lucrezia's necklace could have been any color since it had been a gift. "Are there any other distinguishing features of the stones?"

Dirk's face went taut. "To be honest, yes. You can spot the ones that were replaced after Napoleon stole the originals because they're faceted, as opposed to polished. For instance, the stones on the book are the originals, but a few of the ones in the crown are newer, as is the one on his head." He paused. "And some are glass."

I expected Monsignor Meneghello to be shocked by the revelation, especially since he'd told me the story of the priest who'd tried to trick Napoleon into thinking the jewels were glass, but his face remained serene. "Do these stones have any religious significance, Monsignore?"

He clasped his hands beneath his belly. "Most certainly. One school of thought believes that rubies and sapphires are the most divine since they derive from metamorphic rock, which could only have been created during catastrophic times when God judged the Earth."

That must be what the counterfeit Casanova had been referring to when he told Glenda they were the most divine stones.

Dirk touched my arm. "Forgive me, but I have to run. See

you at the rehearsal."

"Looking forward to it," I said, hoping that the monsignore —and God—couldn't tell I was lying. I was in no mood to practice a trial run at the altar with Bradley. "I've heard that the ruby signifies the blood of Christ and the divine sacrifice of Christ on the cross, but what about the sapphire?"

"Hebrew tradition holds that Moses was given the Ten Commandments on tablets of sapphire, so it's the gemstone of choice of kings and priests, and in Ezekiel 1:26, God's throne is made of sapphire. We also know from Hrabanus Maurus, a Frankish Benedictine monk in the ninth century, that for early Christians, sapphires symbolized heaven and their hope for eternal life."

Eternal life. If the jewel thieves belonged to a cult of light, then the stone from the necklace had to be a sapphire. *But which one?*

The crown?

The book?

Or neither?

"Monsignore, is there a book on the doge who added more stones to the Pala d'Oro?"

"Andrea Dandolo? I would imagine so. He is an important figure in Venetian history and the last doge to be interred in the basilica in 1354."

"What can you tell me about him?"

"He was from a prominent patrician family, a benefactor of the arts, and a friend of the poet Petrarca."

I knew from college that Petrarca was a contemporary of Dante. *Does that matter?*

"Unfortunately, Venice experienced a series of misfortunes during his rule. An earthquake in 1348, and that same year the Black Death. Then the city fell to Genoa. He died of a broken heart because he blamed himself for the tragedies."

I was surprised he hadn't blamed the nuns. Everyone else in Venice did. "Why did he think those things were his fault?"

"He believed, as did his contemporaries, that the tragic events happened because one of his acquaintances stole a pair of sacred necklaces from the Church."

My nose tingled. I knew the answer to my question, but I had to ask. "What necklaces?"

"One was a gold sphere that was thought to be the model for Dante's Empyrean."

So Dante *was* a factor, and it explained why Lucrezia gave the necklace to the Duchess—it symbolized the abode of God, and therefore his protection. But I still didn't know how Lucrezia had gotten the necklace or why she wanted to protect the Duchess from her brother-in-law. "And the other?"

The monsignore coughed, and it wasn't from the incense— although the air was so thick with the stuff that it had to be a factor. "The one rumored to have been stolen from Lucrezia Pavan's grave."

I'd been right to think he was hiding something the first time I asked him about the necklace. "Who stole them?"

"His name has been lost to history, but he swindled the doge by claiming to be a nobleman from Transylvania."

My body shuddered. The Comte de Saint Germain had claimed to be a nobleman from Transylvania.

Did one of his ancestors steal the necklaces and pass them down to him? Or did he steal them himself—four hundred years before Casanova won them from him in the gambling match?

"Damn Gothic windows." Although it was only 11:00 a.m., black storm clouds cast a dark pall inside the Chiesa di San

Zaccaria, which didn't bode well for a trip to the flooded crypt. *Hopefully, Father Festin's in his office, for once.*

As I walked through the vestibule to the back of the church, the gold-and-glass caskets of Saint Athanasius and Saint Zecheriah gleamed in the somber light. I hadn't thought about it before, but it was weird that the giant angel statues held Athanasius's corpse up to the heavens, while Zecheriah, the father of John the Baptist and church namesake, was relegated to the space below.

"Who does this saint think he is?" I pulled out my phone and googled Athanasius. He was the first defender of the divinity of Christ, and his name was from the Greek *Athanasios*, which meant...

Immortal.

My head shot up. The candles burning beside his casket looked exactly like those on the coffin that Iona's daughter Violet, dressed as Tosca, led down the canal.

"The cult of light," I whispered. *Did the inspiration for this madness come from the Church of Murders?*

Since Perpetua was a volunteer, she could've eavesdropped on Iona's confession to Father Festin, read Lucrezia Pavan's will in the convent archives, and plotted the jewel thefts and murders, justifying all of it through a twisted interpretation of the various symbols and relics associated with the Church. For a deranged mind, it wouldn't be hard to distort the promise of immortality into that of eternal life.

"Franki?" Veronica came up the black-and-white marble aisle in an ivory pantsuit.

"Oh, God," I said—and made the sign of the cross to atone for the ill-timed outburst. "Did I miss the rehearsal?"

Her lips tightened. "I just told Father Festin that it's off."

The news sent my concussed head reeling. "The wedding?"

"No, the walk-through."

Relief flooded my chest, followed by remorse for not wanting to do the rehearsal with Bradley. "If this is about me and—"

"It's not." She sat in a pew. "Glenda and her Russian oligarch offered to be your stand-ins."

My head went into a tailspin. "This Russian oligarch wouldn't be connected to Nadezhda Dmitriyeva, would he?"

A wan smile briefly graced her lips. "Relax. Nadezhda can't come because she has to run the liquor store."

"Don't forget the waxing services she offers in the back." I certainly hadn't after I'd let that penny-pinching Communist give me a bikini wax so I could question her about a case. "Are you sure about canceling?"

Veronica rested her head on the back of the pew. "I'm not up to a rehearsal, but we're still going to have the dinner tonight for our guests."

Seeing her stress, I couldn't tell her about my close call with the bell ringer. But I was even more determined to get answers about Iona and Violet's deaths before the wedding. I slid into the pew beside her. "I feel awful that I haven't seen your parents yet, especially after they paid for my room."

"They know you're investigating, and they're grateful. So are Dirk and I." She lifted her head. "By the way, Dirk said you talked to Bradley today. How are you two?"

My guilt level, which was always high to overflowing when I was in a church, could have flooded the crypt. It was so like Veronica to put my worries above her own. "That depends on where his next job is. When he quit the bank to spend more time with me, I thought it was the most romantic gesture ever. Now I'm afraid it'll be our ruin."

"Don't worry about the job, Franki. It's going to work out."

I wasn't so sure, but I wasn't going to add to her stress by telling her that Bradley might take a job in Boston. Private Chicks had recently lost a PI, so I didn't want her to worry about losing me as well. "Your wedding is going to work out too. If I can just figure out which jewel the thieves are after and how they're connected to one another, then I could finally piece together their plan and ID the killer—or killers."

Father Festin came down the aisle rolling his dark-circled eyes at Veronica. "Is Francesca going on about murder again?" Except for the British accent, his voice could have belonged to Vincent Price. "So morbid."

Talk about the priest calling the kettle black. The day I met him, he blathered on about murdered doges, suffocated nuns, and saints' corpses—as gifts, no less. But I didn't dare talk back to a clergyman. Venice was already hell, so I didn't want to go to the real one—for eternity.

Veronica pulled a Bible from the pew in front of us. "We were discussing the missing jewel from Lucrezia Pavan's necklace."

"I'm almost positive it's a sapphire, and it might've been violet."

Father Festin threaded his fingers. "Violet sapphires have been worn throughout the centuries for protection. And the color has considerable religious significance. It symbolizes the modesty of the Virgin Mary, spiritual wisdom, and humility." He cast a bagged eye on me. "It is also associated with repentance from sin."

I shot him a lidded look because that sounded like a veiled jab at my violet maid-of-honor dress. "That must be why Lucrezia took the name in the convent."

Veronica's forehead crinkled. "She took the name Violet?"

"After a saint."

The father harrumphed—with a haunting hum. "An obvious attempt to seek redemption for her sins. Another strategy was to follow Mary Magdalene's example."

I half-wondered whether she'd made lace at Le Zitelle with the other prostitutes. "What do you mean?"

"Mary Magdalene redeemed herself through modest dress, and nuns who'd worn all manner of scandalous attire tried to emulate her. Even some noblewomen asked to be buried in habits because they believed they could use them to cast off vanities of the world and reacquire an ideal virginity."

The salvation strategy could explain the "purpose" of the crucifix necklace that Lucrezia had alluded to in her will. Casanova had once called the Comte de Saint Germain a liar, so I doubt he would have believed the necklace was the key to eternal life. But as a religious man, he would have believed it could restore Lucrezia's virtue and ensure a heavenly afterlife. But why would he do that for her? And why had Lucrezia given the sphere necklace to the Duchess for protection?

"Father, do you have any idea why Lucrezia was buried in a prominent place at the cemetery?"

"It's unfathomable. To think that an impious nun would have received a funeral procession through the streets before being carried by gondola, complete with a wax effigy, to San Michele cemetery...it's a sacrilege." His pale lips curled. "Incidentally, wax effigies were all the rage at funerals of the era."

I was surprised he hadn't called them a graveyard smash.

"While I'm on the subject, the first effigy in Venice was that of Doge Giovanni Mocenigo in 1485. He died of the plague, so they didn't parade him through the streets because the Black Death caused necrosis of the skin." He stared into space and scratched his arm.

I did too, and I thought of Ruth.

"The doge's effigy was of his entire body, but sometimes they were only a head and hands on a dummy, and other times a mere death mask." He gave a ghoulish giggle. "You can see some of them at the Museo Correr. They're a scream."

I shot a warning look at Veronica. Getting married on a Friday in the Church of Murders by this guy was *not* a good idea.

Veronica returned the Bible to the holder in the pew. "Well, whatever Lucrezia did, it must've been important."

Father Festin rubbed his head. "It would have been monumental. Something that benefited all of Venice."

I stared at the Bible and stood. "That's it."

Veronica rose and grabbed my hand. "You figured it out?"

"It was right in front of me the entire time. Lucrezia donated a sapphire from the crucifix necklace to the Pala d'Oro to replace one that Napoleon stole. That's why she was honored in death. Nuns' behavior was thought to be a factor in God's favor toward Venice, so by donating the stone, she atoned for her sins and helped restore God's protection for the city."

For the first time since Iona was poisoned, Veronica's eyes sparkled. "Franki, you're so smart! How can we find out which violet sapphire she donated?"

I rubbed the back of my neck. "That's the problem. I was hoping that Shona or one of the Hos," I stopped and crossed myself again, "I mean, the Screamers, would've found the answer in the archives by now."

"What if that information doesn't exist?"

"It must. How else would the jewel thieves know which stone to steal?" I glanced at Father Festin, who studied the ceiling fresco in the apse, *San Zaccaria in Gloria*, as though he'd never seen it before. "Unless, they're still trying to figure that out too, or...Iona figured it out and shared it with a priest in confession."

Father Festin didn't turn around.

Iona had told him something, but he wasn't going to break his vow of silence. I had to press him on another matter, the reason I'd come to the church. "Father, before I forget, did you find out where Perpetua bought the Valpolicella?"

He turned away from the fresco. "At the Enoteca Schiavi, near the costume shop where she works."

My hands trembled as I pulled out my phone and texted Stella to prepare the batela for the cicchetti tour. Perpetua was Ghost Lucrezia, and she'd been outfitting the other jewel thieves. "Is she here today?"

"She's on leave indefinitely."

I pocketed my phone. "What happened?"

"Oh, the usual." He fiddled with the crucifix at his neck. "A death in the family."

The sparkle left Veronica's eyes. "I'm sorry to hear that."

I was too, but I was more focused on why the father was acting nervous. "Do you mind if I ask who died?"

He looked at Veronica. "Told you she was morbid."

This from a guy who'd gushed about wax funeral effigies, death masks, and necrosis of the skin. "Are you avoiding my question?"

Another tug at the crucifix. "It was her stepdaughter."

I knew what Iona had told him in confession, and it had nothing to do with the stone that Lucrezia donated to the Pala d'Oro. "Her name was Violet, wasn't it?"

"Oddly enough."

Veronica's blue eyes met mine, and they were as dark as the lagoon. She knew what I did—that it wasn't odd at all. Perpetua's stepdaughter was the baby Iona Parsons gave up for adoption. "Who is her father?"

Father Festin released the crucifix. "If you must know, his name is Ubaldo Falsetti. He's a guard at the Palazzo Ducale."

The Maleficio tolled in my head.

Perpetua's husband, Ubaldo, was also the bell ringer.

And Iona's teenaged fling on that family trip to Venice.

And the source of the information about Lucrezia's crucifix necklace that kicked off a cult crime spree.

18

"Why would a Latin Lover like Casanova want to save Miss Lucrezia's soul?" Glenda asked from the stern of the batela. She'd convinced Stella to let her try standing rowing, and she'd taken to it like a duck to canal water—because it involved a pole.

"I wish I knew the answer." I stared straight ahead from my seat next to Stella in the middle of the boat to avoid Glenda's stripper gondolier look. She had the straw hat and red waist sash, but she'd replaced the black pants with a thong. Even worse, she'd swapped gondola-sticker pasties for the light-up kind she'd given Shona, claiming it was so cloudy out that the batela needed a pair of headlights. Needless to say, despite those headlights, gondolas and boats were crashing all around us.

Madge pulled the bow oar. "Redemption was Casanova's obsession toward the end of his life. He proclaimed himself a Christian with his dying breath."

I'd heard that from Ruth, who'd been suspiciously quiet the past couple of days. But even though she hadn't called, she was under my skin, spreading silently like bacteria—or festering like a boil on *Dr. Pimple Popper*. Instinctively, my eyes did a quick check of my exposed flesh for any issues.

Stella gazed at a pale pink palazzo with inflected arches. "Didn't Casanova's fixation on redemption have something to do with Mozart?"

"Historical record indicates as much." Madge adjusted the brim of her navy-and-white tricorn hat. "Mozart based the opera *Don Giovanni* on the legend of Don Juan, and his librettist, Lorenzo Da Ponte, used Casanova as their model. After Casanova moved to Dux, he met Da Ponte in Prague and contributed to the libretto—unaware of the opera's unfavorable ending." Madge raised her nose. "When he attended the premiere and learned that Don Giovanni went to hell for his crimes, among them lust, he found it an outrage that seducing women would deserve such a fate. The incident planted the proverbial fear of God in him and sparked his quest for atonement."

Some people took entertainment way too seriously. "But that would have been after he gave Lucrezia the necklace, so it doesn't explain why he would've been worried about saving her soul."

Madge's chin jutted forward. "He was well past his prime, so I rather suspect he'd worried about his fate in the afterlife before he moved to Dux. My guess is that the necklace was part of a calculated plan. Saving a nun would go a long way toward one's redemption."

Her theory was plausible, but there had to be more to the story. If Casanova believed the necklace would save Lucrezia, why not keep it for himself? I stared at a palazzo with double rows of white cross-like structures lining the roof like lace. And who gave Lucrezia the gold sphere necklace that she left to the Duchess?

The batela glided from the mouth of the Grand Canal.

Madge filled her lungs with the salty-scented air of the lagoon. "Ah, open sea."

We were headed for the sestriere Dorsoduro on the south-western side of the island. Despite my battered physical state, I didn't want Madge to help Glenda row the entire way. "I'll take over, Madge."

"Nonsense, my dear girl. You must rest. And you're lucky Midge stayed at the hotel to research other sources of the poison. Otherwise, I'm afraid she'd tire you with our genealogy. We come from a long line of seamen."

A problematic-sounding statement.

Her bosom swelled with pride. "Our father was an admiral in the navy, and his father before him."

That accounted for her tricorn hat and matching sailor suit skirt.

As if to demonstrate her seafaring lineage, Madge propped a foot on the bow of the batela with the solemnity of a British George Washington crossing the Delaware.

"*Heave!*" blasted across the lagoon like a musket shot, and my gut took the hit. Shona and the Hos were in the vicinity.

"Ho!"

"Ho!"

"Ho!"

In desperation, I looked at Glenda, outfit and all. "Can you row any faster?"

"*Heave!*"

"Sugar, I once escaped the crew of the USS New Orleans in a dingy with a broken paddle."

"Ho!"

"Ho!"

"Ho!"

Glenda gave a saucy smile. "Oh, hell, who am I kidding? I let those sex-starved sailors catch me."

"Heave!"

Panic pelted my chest like microscopic musket balls. The enemy was closing in.

"Row!"

"Row!"

"Row!" I shouted over the Hos.

Glenda gripped the oar with one hand and a cigarette holder adorned with a tiny red gondolier sash in the other. Then she dug in the heels of the black velvet stripper fetish shoes she'd swapped for the traditional black velvet Friulane slippers of gondoliers, and squatted so low she could've scooped up dollar bills.

"Heave!"

The quad scull emerged from a canal. Shona had her head lowered, but the Screamers gaped at Glenda's gondolier getup.

"Whoa!"

"Whoa!"

"Whoa!"

Their cries caught the attention of a passing gondolier, who got a glimpse of Glenda and fell off his boat.

"Man overboard!" Shona squalled.

Glenda tutted as the gondolier climbed back onto his gondola. "I told Miss Franki those Friulane slippers were dangerous. Feet can't function in shoes that flat."

Hers couldn't. Like the lotus feet of Chinese women who'd been subjected to foot binding, Glenda's feet were also misshapen—in six-inch-stripper-platforms position.

Shona maneuvered the quad scull alongside the batela, her round perky face had turned pouty. "Why didn't you guys tell me you were doing the tour? I'm even wearing my *Screamers on the Rowd* touring sweatshirt."

I'd already noticed and hoped that all 'rowds' on that tour led to Venice and not New Orleans.

Stella checked to be sure no other boats were in earshot. "I'm sorry, Shona. I didn't think. It was a last-minute thing, after Franki made a discovery."

"You found the poison?" Shona brayed.

I ran my fingers through my hair and tried not to rip it out. "Did you not just see Stella making sure no one was around?"

"Yeah, and no one is."

"But your voice carries long distances, across the lagoon—and entire oceans."

"Fine, I'll use my library voice."

My teeth clenched because she was still shouting. "Great, you could start now."

"Uh, I already am." She huffed and looked at the Hos. "Sheesh. She needs to get her hearing checked."

They nodded.

I pitied the poor patrons of the Screamer library. "To answer your question, yes, I found some potassium permanganate, but I can't say for sure whether it was the poison that killed Iona."

"Then why do the tour?"

"Because it's suspicious that Perpetua recommended the Valpolicella to Iona, so I want to go to the Enoteca Schiavi where she ordered it to see what I can find out."

Stella looked at the Screamers. "You're welcome to come along for un'ombra and cicchetti."

Dena, Gena, or Lena wrinkled her brow. "Is cicchetti a kind of gum?"

Madge's jowls frowned. "I should say not. Cicchetti are similar to Spanish tapas. The word derives from the Latin *ciccus*, meaning 'little' or 'nothing.'"

Thunder rumbled—or maybe it was my stomach, which had eaten little or nothing since I'd been in Venice.

Shona rose from her seat. "Hold her steady, Screamers. I'm going on board."

Nope, that rumble was thunder, sending me a warning.

Shona clambered onto the boat and stood in front of me, shifting her weight from one foot to the other.

Fearing another deadly December dip, I gripped my seat. "Surely you've heard the expression 'don't rock the boat?'"

She glanced over her shoulder. "I'm trying to get my sea legs."

"What for? You can sit on the hull."

"Are you kidding?" She gestured to her wetsuit. "This bod was born for *voga alla veneta*."

I braced myself. With Glenda and Shona womanning the batela, I'd be safer using the flaming coffin as a kayak.

Shona took the oar from Madge. "I'm up for the cicchetti, but I can't day-drink wine before the big race."

Glenda blew out a disgusted drag. "In NOLA it ain't day-drinking unless it's before noon, Miss Shona."

"You're so wild, Miss Glenda." Shona pawed at her like a lioness. "*Roar*. Or maybe I should 'meow' since I'm going to wear a *Gnaga* costume to Veronica's rehearsal dinner tonight."

The news that she'd been invited sent a jolt through me that rocked the batela. *What was my best friend thinking by getting married in the Church of Murders on a Friday in Italy with Shona in attendance?* When the 'speak now, or forever hold your peace' time came, the large-lunged librarian was likely to get up and give the guests an info dump on the history of Catholic weddings.

Stella grinned. "Have you seen the Gnaga, Franki?"

"I haven't," I said, but I knew what it looked like—Shona following me around the rehearsal dinner, meowing.

"It's a traditional cat mask that men wore to dress as women."

Glenda cackled. "That's why it sounds like 'nag.'"

Madge took Stella's seat next to me. "The mask wearer wore

an ordinary dress, a feather hat with a type of hood that covered all but the face and carried a kitten in a basket, wandering about as a plebian courtesan uttering mocking meows and shrill sounds."

"I didn't know thaaat," Shona shrilled. "I'll have to start practicing."

My eyes lowered to a duck feather floating on the murky water. *Should I throw myself in now? One way or another, I'm going down anyway.*

Stella gestured to a rio. "Turn right there. Before we go to the enoteca, we'll stop at the osteria across from the *Squero di San Trovaso* to make this look like a real tour."

"I've been wanting to see a squero," Shona belly-waulered.

I braced myself for the wave of info to come.

"It's one of the three remaining gondola boatyards in Venice. The gondola-makers are called *squeraroli*, and they've been in existence since the eleventh century. At one time, fifteen thousand gondolas sailed the canals of Venice, whereas today there are around three hundred and fifty but four hundred gondolieri."

I didn't dare ask why there were fifty gondola-less gondolieri for fear of feeding the handy-resources-and-helpful-tips monster.

Stella pointed at a boatyard. "That's the squero."

The old boatyard resembled a set from a period movie. It had a centuries-old work shed and a two-story brick building with graffiti and an old chimney. Amid stacks of lumber, four black gondolas lay on their sides. Two squeraroli stood before two sawhorses, while one waved flames from a lit bundle of brush underneath a curved plank of wood.

"Any idea why they're burning it?" I asked.

Stella nodded. "It's an ancient technique. They wet the top of the plank and use heat underneath to make the wood curve like the bottom of a boat, and—"

"Each gondola is made of two hundred and eighty pieces of wood," Shona blurt-dumped, taking over the tour, "oak, fir, walnut, cherry, elm, mahogany, larch wood, white pine, and lime tree."

I was only half-listening—to either of them. My eyes were locked on a young man in a black-and-white-striped shirt, who warmed his hands over a fire in a rusty oilcan. The shirt was like the one the bell ringer had worn beneath his costume, and I realized that it was the one worn by members of the *Associazione Gondolieri di Venezia*.

The young man looked up, and our eyes met.

"Casanova!" I dropped to the hull before Shona had a chance to voga alla veneta me overboard.

The batela reached the dock in seconds, but Casanova was long gone. I climbed out and approached the two squeraroli and asked them who he was in Italian to increase the odds of a response. "*Mi scusino. Chi era quel ragazzo?*"

The older of the two wrinkled the grooves on his weathered face. "*Chi? Fabio?*"

It figured that fake Casanova's name was Fabio, like the infamous square-jawed blond Italian who'd appeared shirtless on the cover of hundreds of romance novels. My mom had read every one, and she still had them in a walk-in closet that seemed to need weekly reorganization.

The younger man with massive eyebrows, who watched his senior coworker heat the plank, crossed his arms with a grunt. "Fabio is *baloso*, like last name."

"Baloso?" I repeated, unsure of the meaning.

"Venezia word," he said, referring to the local dialect. "He no like-a work."

Weathered Face gave a gruff laugh and shoved the burning

brush into a bucket of water, happy to take a break from work himself.

"A good-for-nothing," I said.

Massive Eyebrows nodded. "He let girl-a-friend make-a the moneys."

That was no surprise. A guy couldn't keep himself in frock coats and man heels on tourist tips alone.

"Sì, Flora," Weathered Face said.

"No, no." Massive Eyebrows wagged his finger. "*Quella che lavora da adetta alle pulizie all'ospedale, Violetta.*"

His words had the same effect on me as the bucket of water had on the flaming brush, and my abdomen collapsed like the lid on the bucket of potassium permanganate that I'd sat on in the Ospedale SS Giovanni e Paolo supply room. Because I could now definitively connect that poison to a person.

The one who works as a cleaning lady at the hospital, Violet.

A SHRILL SCREAM PIERCED the polite chatter in the Museo Correr ballroom like the bell ringer's dagger.

I didn't have to turn around to know it was Shona doing her Gnaga number, but I did—so I could kill her. "If the bell ringer had spent one minute listening to her in the campanile," I muttered, "he would've tried to throw *her* over the edge."

Shona pranced up covered from head to toe in a feathered hat, hood, and a puffy commoner's dress. I wouldn't have known it was her were it not for the white cat mask with gold lips and ears and the basket containing a plush toy kitten. "*Meow.* That's spelled m-i-a-o in Italian."

The woman was unable to speak without tacking on a fact, even dressed as an animal. "You know the old saying 'there's more than one way to skin a cat?'"

"I've always thought it was awful."

"It is, and what'll be more awful is you making Gnaga noises during Veronica and Dirk's dinner, and me showing you all the ways I can skin you."

She hissed and took a swipe at me. Then she skipped away swinging her kitten basket to annoy the hell out of the other guests.

I'd come early to chat with Veronica's parents, but the Maggios hadn't arrived. Veronica's mother had picked the perfect location for the rehearsal dinner—the Empire-style ballroom was wedding-white with gold accents. On either end, there were loggias for an orchestra, and along the sides, gilded capitals of fluted columns lined the windows. Below a stunning ceiling fresco and exquisite crystal chandeliers, a long dining table spanned the length of the black-and-white marble floor.

My mom and Nonna entered, and unlike Shona's costume, their identities were clear. Nonna had glammed up her mourning dress with a shawl and a rosary and carried a black mask on a stick, whereas my mother wore a rhinestone mask to match her tiara with a silver-gray dress that accentuated her shark nature. A man lurked behind them whose identity was equally obvious. He wore a tricorn hat and tabarro cloak with a bauta—the white mask with the protruding chin. "Someone should really tell the desperate count about the Habsburg stereotype."

Before the school of predators spotted me, I turned and pretended to check my updo in a gilded mirror. My gondola mask brought me back to the squero. *Why had the counterfeit Casanova fled?* Sure, he wasn't in his eighteenth-century finery, but he'd never run from us before. Something had changed.

What was it?

Seeing us at the gondola yard could have clued him in that we were hunting down the poison, although, that didn't seem likely. The Enoteca Schiavi had turned out to be a bust—except for the cicchetti, and I'd eaten a boatload. The other possibility was that he assumed we'd traced him to the squero to find out more about him. Either way, if the killer thieves' next target was one of the violet sapphires on the Pala d'Oro, then seeing me at the squero might have accelerated their plan to steal it.

"The Politi fresco is a masterpiece," a woman exclaimed.

A man in a plague doctor mask leaned backward to admire the ceiling, tipping his champagne flute at a precarious angle. "It's a clear reference to the restoration of the Habsburgs after the fall of Napoleon."

I eyed the Sicilian count—and the pointed chin of that mask.

"Yes, Peace surrounded by the Virtues and the Geni of Olympus."

Virtues? They were a common theme in the Republic of Venice, as was protection. And I suspected that they played a role in Iona's and Violet's deaths.

"There you are, Miss Franki." Glenda sashayed toward me shaking her Virtues in a Venetian stripper version of the Playboy Bunny costume. She wore a gold rabbit mask and bowtie. And judging from the way her ponte delle tettes drooped in her fishnet bunny suit, she needed to retire the nunchuck pasties —pronto.

"You should've told me you were going to wear a gondola mask, sugar. I would've lent you my gondolier costume."

My gaze lowered to the Valentino dress I'd splurged to buy on clearance. "I figured this black ball gown would do."

"Well, I found out that Venetians have been wearing rabbit masks to Carnival for centuries, so my costume choice was clear."

Yes, a fishnet bunny suit is exactly what one would wear to a rehearsal dinner.

A masked man joined Glenda with two glasses of champagne, and I recognized his black eyes and model bone structure as those of Ambrosio, the waiter who served me Cioccolata Casanovas at Caffè Florian.

He looked at me and shrugged.

She'd gotten her Ambrosio after all. *But who was she bringing to the wedding? And why wouldn't she tell us who it was?* Then again, maybe Glenda's mystery wedding date was exactly that—a mystery to her too until the day of the event.

Glenda drained her champagne and took his. "Ambrosio says that after Napoleon was run out of town, this museum was home to the emperor and empress of Austria."

The empress got my attention. According to Midge, the Duchess Von Leipold's husband was a relative. "Ambrosio, is there an archive here?"

"A library, in the *Procuratie Nuove*."

"Who cares about a dusty old library, sugar? The empress redecorated Napoleon's apartments and turned one into her boudoir and another into a bed chamber." She polished off her second champagne. "Come on, Ambrosio, honey. I want to see if you live up to your name." She led him away, shaking the cotton tail on her suit and the ones on the backs of her stripper shoes.

For Veronica's sake, I didn't try to stop her.

I turned to go to the marble staircase, and ran into a kid.

"*Ahia, mamma!* My head, he is-a broken."

He was no kid. He was the mini marriage broker, Maurizio Bonsignore, pressing a gloved hand to his skull. Because of the black half-mask he'd chosen, he no longer looked like the phantom of the opera but a wee Zorro in a top hat and little brown loafers. "Serves you right for trying to hit me with a lamp in your hotel room—and calling me a donkey."

"It is-a normal for the couple to have-a the squabble, no?"

"Couple?" I shouted like Shona on steroids.

"You have seen-a my nightshirt. In-a Sicilia, we are betrothed."

"No, we are not, in any country or region."

He bared vampire shark teeth. "Technically, you are-a correct, signorina. But I have compromised your honor, and as a good gentleman, I must make-a the amends."

I smelled a rat—doused in Sicily perfume. Despite his surname, the 'good gentleman' was anything but. "This is about my dowry, isn't it?"

He whipped out a rose instead of a rapier. And with a flourish of his cape, he removed his hat and bent on one knee. "I would-a never equate the *amore* with money, cara mia."

"Uh, that's what you do for a living, and since my nonna stole a page from your little black book and found her own desperate Sicilian count, you're out some bucks."

"Excellent points." He touched a gloved finger to his lips. "So, before I pop-a the question, precisely how much-a dowry are-a we talking?"

My eyes narrowed to the width of sword blades. "Get up."

"You are-a certain? The marriage broker make an excellent match—for the right-a price, of course."

"There is no one I want to marry less."

"That's a relief." He rose. "Because-a my knee, he is-a screaming."

A shrill cry sliced through the ballroom.

So is Shona.

I checked to see if Bradley had arrived and witnessed the near-proposal. A little competition wouldn't hurt him, but I would rather be passed through a pasta maker than admit that to my mom and nonna. I checked the entrance, and my mouth fell open.

Sheilah waltzed in—sans Ted—dressed as a modern-day Madame de Pompadour. Her blonde hair was piled high, and she wore an embellished cleavage dress with a half-mask and lots of beauty marks—in all the man-eater places.

It's like she walked straight out of my nightmare.

Shona pranced up with a mighty meow. "Do you see that crocodile bag on Sheilah Kensington? It's a Versace Virtus that retailed for twenty-five grand."

Virtus? That was an even weirder coincidence than her being dressed like Madame de Pompadour. "It's the cat's meow," I said drily. "Did you know there's a library in the Procurator's offices that belonged to Napoleon?"

"That's what I was coming to tell you. I saw a sign for the library when I came in and texted Dena, Gena, and Lena. They reached out to our contacts, and it turns out that the Museo Correr has the Duchess Von Leipold's papers. I have their catalog number on my phone."

"We have to get in there."

"Me-*ow*. Not with all these people around. If word got back to my boss that I broke into a library, my career would be over."

Because of her loud-talking, it should have been over long ago. "Then I'll do it myself. Just tell me where to find the papers."

She hissed and took a swipe. "Curiosity killed the cat."

"You know what else killed that cat?"

"I'd rather not. Although," she leaned forward, "I'm a little curious."

Could this woman hear herself? "It was me. I killed the cat. Because the one time I actually wanted information from the fickle feline, she didn't give it to me."

She pulled her phone from her kitten basket, and flashed the display.

After I'd memorized the catalog number, I skirted the sharks by walking along the windows to the exit. My pulse pounded as I headed for the marble staircase at the museum entrance.

Something told me that the Duchess's papers held the missing piece I needed to make sense of the killer thieves' mad plan.

A shrill sound sent me stumbling into the stairs.

"Seriously, Shona?" I spun to shoo—and maybe skin—her, and my concussed head took a spin. Because Bradley was behind us dressed like a contemporary Casanova in a sleek Italian suit à la Marcello Mastroianni in *La Dolce Vita*, and his blue eyes were just as black.

He turned to Shona. "Will you excuse us? I need to speak to my fiancée alone."

She fled like a female cat in a Pepé Le Pew cartoon.

Bradley watched her scamper off. "Why won't she talk to me?"

"Cat's got her tongue."

His jaw tightened. "Is that your excuse too? You're barely speaking to me because of things I didn't do, and when I went to your room to escort you to dinner, your nonna said you'd be attending with a Sicilian count. What the hell is going on?"

My eye scanned the area. I was enjoying his jealous outburst, but if he caught sight of Pint-Sized Zorro or Pointy Chin Mask, he might burst into laughter. "After the Sheilah hallway incident, my mom and nonna went into full-on matchmaking mania, and they'll stay that way until there's a wedding date, or maybe even a ring on my finger."

A pang crossed his face, and one crossed mine too. Because when I mentioned that finger, it ached like it had when I'd jammed it in the hotel's revolving door.

A Tosca legend omen?

A group of guests entered the building, and Bradley pulled me aside. "Franki, the dinner starts in less than thirty minutes. Let's focus on Dirk and Veronica's wedding, and as soon as it's over, we'll work this out."

He was right to put our friends first, and he'd reminded me

that the clock was ticking on finding the Duchess's papers. "Agreed. I'll see you inside. I need to visit the ladies' room."

"I'll save you a seat?"

By the time I realized that was a question, I was halfway down the hall. I forged ahead to the Museo Correr Library and checked the door handle.

It opened.

"M-kay. That's some horror movie stuff right there." Nevertheless, I crossed the floor of the *Procuratie Nuove*, conscious of my heels clicking on the polished marble. The library books were behind wooden cases with glass doors similar to the ones at the Museo della Storia Naturale with the bell ringer's skeleton, which reminded me that I didn't want to run into any of the wax death masks that Father Festin mentioned.

Using my phone light, I scanned the antique books until I located a bound collection of papers titled *Duchess Genevieve Magritte Von Leipold*. Page after page was written in German. Discouraged, I flipped to the last document and discovered a court transcript in Italian from 1800, two years after Lucrezia's death.

Annibale Bragadin vs. the City of Venice.

"Lucrezia's brother-in-law." Transfixed, I lay the document on a glass display case beneath an enormous frosted-glass chandelier.

The transcript was written in an elaborate script that was difficult to decipher. But the opening remarks made two things abundantly clear—Venetians blamed the sinful behavior and dress of its nuns for the fall of their city to the French and subsequently the Austrians, and Annibale blamed Lucrezia for the loss of his fortune. In compensation, he sought two precious necklaces, the crucifix from her tomb and the gold sphere from the Duchess Von Leipold.

The defense maintained that Lucrezia owed Annibale nothing, and especially not the necklaces as the former was a gift from Casanova, and the latter was part of her proceeds from a gambling match with the Comte de Saint Germain.

"So that's how Lucrezia got the gold sphere necklace. Stella will be impressed with her skills." I imagined Lucrezia in a scandalous nun dress cleaning out the high rollers in Vegas and smiled.

A bell tolled in the piazza, and the smile fled from my face. *The Marangona marking the end of the workday?*

Or the Maleficio marking my murder?

"Don't do that, Franki. Focus."

The prosecution claimed that Lucrezia's gambling proved she was as big a scoundrel as Casanova and the Comte, who, it turned out, had been the subject of a dossier maintained by Napoleon. However, said dossier had burned in a mysterious fire.

The hair on my arms rose. "The Comte burned that dossier. Was it because Napoleon had proof he was a vampire?"

My eyes traveled to the side, and my body followed to see over my shoulder. A dark library in a Venetian palace was exactly the sort of place where one would get their blood sucked.

And my hair was in an updo.

Covering my neck with my hands, I returned to the text. The prosecution confirmed that Lucrezia had been intimate with Casanova and that the affair was revealed to her parents and fiancé by Annibale and her late sister, Ludovica. To get even with the couple, Lucrezia and Casanova concocted a gambling scheme to cheat Annibale out of all his money—that of her family and his.

"The words from Lucrezia's will!" *And as we are exploited, we must also exploit, lest we be locked in cells and left to die.* "She wasn't just referring to her sister exploiting her to avoid the convent, she was talking about herself."

The defense countered by asserting that Annibale was a willing participant in the gambling and was attempting to blame a nun for his lack of gaming skills.

"Ha! That's a huge LOL."

The Duchess was then called to the stand, and I held my breath as I read.

Lucrezia's vices did not invalidate her virtues, which were many. She gave me the money she won from Annibale so that I might help the poor and disgraced women of Le Zitelle. She also bequeathed the gold sphere necklace to me as protection from Annibale, who maltreats me for her generosity, and who unjustly persecutes Lucrezia even in death. For Lucrezia saved Venice by donating a precious stone to the Pala d'Oro, ruining a necklace intended to guarantee her heavenly repose.

The Fair Nun Unmasked painting flashed before my eyes. The Venetian habit was not reflective of the wearer. Lucrezia had slept with Casanova, but she wasn't a whore. She was noble, and a nun.

My text tone beeped, and my skeleton almost pulled a bell ringer and shed its skin. "The unexpected noises aren't working for me in this dark, empty wing."

The message was from Bradley, asking where I was and telling me the dinner was about to start.

I replied, "Be right there" and returned to the Duchess's testimony.

Presently I shall read the Bible verse that Lucrezia recited on the occasion of donating the stone so that it might illustrate her service to God and Venice and remind those who question her virtues of their true purpose, to serve Him and spread His word. Rightfully, Lucrezia recited a verse from Zechariah, the patron saint of her convent and church, the Chiesa di San Zaccaria, where his relics rest in peace.

"*Pff!* Does *anyone* rest in peace in that waterlogged boneyard? The church has a murderous past *and* present, thanks to that zealot, Perpetua."

A roar of thunder shook the palazzo.

"All right," I looked at the wood-beamed ceiling. "Message received." I turned the page to Zechariah 9:16.

AND THE LORD *their God shall save them in that day as the flock of his people: for they shall be as the stones of a crown, lifted up as an ensign upon his land.*

"SAVE," I whispered. "The stones of a crown..."

The blood drained from my body.

"Oh my God." My hands moved from my neck to my cheeks. "The violet sapphire is the one crowning Christ's head."

"*Miau.*"

I was so angry I went rigid. That meow sounded German, and if Shona thought I had the time or inclination to take a tour of the world's cat noises, she had another thing coming. I spun on her with the eye of the tiger. "If you don't stop with the Gnaga nonsense, you're going to lose all nine of your lives—tonight."

She raised her mask, and if I'd been a cat, I would've lost at least eight of mine.

The Gnaga wasn't Shona.

It was Perpetua, and her face was that of lioness about to pounce.

Perpetua pulled a dagger from her kitten basket. "You make peep, I make kill."

"Understood," I said, but as soon as we turned, I planned to run.

She pressed the blade into my back and gripped my arm. "Ve valk." She turned me toward the door. "You try someting, friend die."

Friend? Does she have Veronica?

Thunder rumbled and a crack of lightning lit the room.

Now I was trapped. I had to cooperate and try to reason with her—if she wasn't too far gone. "My friend is expected in the ballroom for her rehearsal dinner. If you don't let her go, Commissario Lucifero will have the entire police force looking for her."

Perpetua pushed me into a dark hallway. "Not bride, idiot. How you tink I get Gnaga costume?"

I relaxed, as much as one could at knifepoint, and resisted the really strong urge to tell her that Shona and I weren't friends.

She guided me away from the ballroom and shoved me toward a door. "Open."

I obeyed.

We exited into the Piazza San Marco. Because it was after nine, Venice had emptied out for the night. And it was cold and raining, so only a handful of tourists from nearby hotels were around the Christmas tree.

For a second, the strands of lights spun in my head, creating a golden sphere.

The Empyrean. Is that where I'm headed?

As much as I wanted to yell to the tourists for help, I couldn't for fear of what Perpetua *et al.* would do to Shona. So I walked the length of the piazza without asking where we were going, but I already knew—to the Palazzo Ducale where her husband, Ubaldo Falsetti aka the bell ringer, worked as a museum guard.

We turned right into the piazzetta, and I eyed the two red columns of the loggia.

Are they going to hang me between them, as Venetians did during the reign of the doges?

We continued walking, and ahead of me was the gondola service station on the lagoon. A cruel final image, given how I'd longed to ride in a gondola with Bradley.

Perpetua forced me inside a side door of the Palazzo Ducale. I was wet from the rain, and my ball dress was ruined, but it didn't matter.

I wasn't going to Veronica's dinner.

I was going to my funeral.

We came to the same stairs Shona and I had taken for the Secret Itineraries tour.

Turns out a Thursday rehearsal dinner in Italy is unluckier than a Friday wedding.

"Shtep!"

I interpreted that as German English for *climb*. "Where are we going?"

"Shtanza della Tortura."

Where the Council of Ten tried alleged criminals. I'd come to Venice for a romantic wedding and vacation, but the theme had been death from start to finish—*my* finish included.

And why was torture necessary when the Palazzo Ducale had so many options for killing—the red columns, the Piombi, the Pozzi, the new prisons across the Bridge of Sighs? A better question was, why couldn't they just put potassium permanganate into my Valpolicella, like they'd done to Iona and Violet?

On the flip side, this way I had a chance to escape.

Perpetua jabbed the blade between my shoulder blades, as though she'd read my thoughts. "No trick."

"What have you done with my friend?"

"You see."

I envisioned Shona hanging by hands tied behind her back. If her rowing shoulders were broken, I'd never hear the end of it. That loud librarian would shout it from the rooftops of Screamer, and her voice would carry clean to New Orleans.

If we survived.

We arrived at the next flight of stairs, and I was already winded. But not Perpetua. Underneath Shona's puffy commoner dress, she was lean and mean. She was a shorter, less muscular version of Petra the Pretzelmaker, the German wrestler that my cheating ex Vince had hooked up with. Even her name was similar.

And wow, Vince. I hadn't thought of him in ages. His name rhymed with prince, but he was as big a louse as Annibale had been to Lucrezia, and Ubaldo had been to Iona. The one positive thing about our relationship was that his one-night stand with Petra had prompted my move to New Orleans, where I'd met my real prince.

Bradley.

I imagined him waiting for me in the ballroom and got dizzy. *Did he think I'd left him?*

No, he knew that I'd never pull a stunt like that at Veronica's rehearsal dinner.

But if I die tonight, will he know how much I loved him?

Tears fell like the rain. No matter what happened to me, I didn't want Bradley to live with that doubt. *I have to figure out a way to save Shona and myself from our deaths in this ducal dungeon.*

We exited the stairwell and entered the Stanza della Tortura.

Ubaldo stood stoically at his museum guard post, which seemed weird. He spotted me, as if coming out of a trance, and grabbed a rope from the ancient desk. Without a word, he tied my wrists behind me.

I gave him a piece of my mind with a steady glare. Out of his seven-foot skeleton costume, he was a small man, and definitely not noble. He'd obviously lied to Iona about his identity when she was a teen. *But is he the ringleader of this crackpot cult? Or is it Perpetua?*

And who is the counterfeit Casanova to either of them?

"Mm! Mm!"

Startled, I looked over my shoulder.

Shona was in her Sherpa suit, tied to one of the hand-carved chairs in a corner. Her arms were bound behind her back, and she was gagged—something I should have thought to do the day she'd showed up at Caffè Florian and blasted my name and profession to the piazza. Her loudness had put me on the killer thieves' radar and gotten me those lion's head boxes with the *Roses Are Red* death threats.

A door closed, and I turned.

The counterfeit Casanova, otherwise known as Fabio Baloso, had entered in a black sweater and pants.

He nodded to Ubaldo, who led me to the top of the three steps in front of the dangling rope.

Casanova Fabio sat at the desk. "The trial of Private Investigator Francesca Amato shall commence."

A trial?

"MM! MM mm MM MM mm!"

I didn't know what Shona was grunting, but I was glad she was gagged for my court appearance. She was totally the type to add a few crimes to their list. "What am I charged with?"

"Offenses against God and La Serenissima. You're a heathen whore, like Lucrezia Pavan, the nun from whom you are descended."

I worked my wrists—and my patience. "I'm none of those things. And neither was Lucrezia. While we're on the subject, I'm not even sure that she and I are related."

He kicked up his feet on this desk, and even his contemporary boots had heels. "Why did you come to Venice, if not?"

"To stand at the altar with my best friend and her fiancé, and the love of my life."

Perpetua moved behind him. "Und now you stand at altar of justice."

She sounds like a German Ruth Walker. "And what crime has my friend supposedly committed?"

Shona's eyes went *Puss-in-Boots* at the word *friend*.

"She is your accomplice, no?"

"It's funny you would treat us like criminals and talk about justice when you've desecrated graves, stolen jewels, and most egregiously, killed two women."

Shona's eyes popped, and she shook her head. "MM mm! MM mm!"

Casanova tapped his fingers together. "Violet killed Iona."

"And you killed *her*."

He remained impassive, and my eyes darted to Ubaldo, who had no reaction to the mention of his daughter's death.

The killer cult leader cleared his throat. "We seek to right the wrongs that began with your ancestor, at any cost. Lucrezia and Casanova stole sacred necklaces from the Basilica."

"The one who stole them was the Comte de Saint Germain."

Perpetua's eyes glowed. "Der Wundermann."

"The Wonder Man?" I guess-translated. "Is that what they call the Comte in Germany?"

Casanova's eyelids lowered, as though I'd insulted her. "My *mutter* is Austrian, and the Comte is no thief."

So that's how he's connected to Perpetua and Ubaldo. Since his last name was Baloso, not Falsetti, he wasn't Ubaldo's biological son. And that was good. It was bad enough that Fabio had dated his stepsister, Violet.

I wiggled my wrists. "But the three of you are thieves. You have no plans to return those necklaces to the church. You stole them from the Duchess and Lucrezia's graves, and now you plan to steal the violet sapphire from Christ Pantocrator's crown on the Pala d'Oro. And all because you think they'll grant you eternal life."

"The Comte is still very much alive, is he not?"

I snorted, even though I still wondered if the old vampire was trailing me. "Have you met him?"

"That is not necessary. He is like God. We know he exists."

Theirs wasn't a cult of light as much as it was a cult of the Comte. "Isn't it a sin to worship false idols, especially one who's undead?"

"We do not worship him, and the vampire legend is preposterous." He put his man heels on the floor. "The necklaces were his youth potion."

"Uh, no. If the necklaces *were* the source of his eternal youth, and they weren't, then he would have died when he lost them gambling with Casanova and Lucrezia in the casinos."

"You know nutink!" Perpetua shouted so loud that even Shona was taken aback.

"I know this," I said with a hiss, "if your objective is getting closer to God and, hence, immortality, then killing Iona and Violet, and now me and my friend, is completely counter-productive."

"Mm HM!" Shona nodded. "Mm HM!"

Casanova silenced her with a glacial glower. "My mutter is correct. Our actions have precedent throughout history. Catholics killed Christians during the Roman Inquisition to punish heresy."

"Sure, but we don't know how that worked out for them in the afterlife, do we?"

Casanova pounded his fist on the desk. "You will not mock this court. I declare you guilty of treason against God, the city of Venice, and your heritage."

"You do that. But I refuse to be convicted by a bunch of cult criminals."

Shona threw her head to one side. "MMMMMmmmmm!"

His full lips thinned. "Remove her from my sight."

Ubaldo pulled me from the steps toward the exit, and I shot a look of solidarity at Shona, imploring her not to lose hope.

Shona used her lips to move the gag. "Don't let him take you to the Leads, Franki! Casanova said in his autobiography that the rats up there are as big as rabbits."

For a split second, I regretted that look of solidarity and hoped she'd be strung up on that rope. Then I remembered the religious principles that the killers had lost and forgave her—but not before I pointed out the obvious. "Does it look like I have a say in the matter?"

Perpetua whispered something to her son, who nodded. "Pozzi."

Shona looked from me to Perpetua. "But it's raining cats and dogs. She'll drown when the tide comes in tomorrow."

If my hands had been free, I would've returned that gag to its proper place—or crammed it down her throat.

Because the counterfeit Casanova's lips had curled into a smile that made the Commissario Lucifero's seem warm and inviting. "That, cara mia, is the idea."

THE MARANGONA TOLLED, marking the start of the workday.

Friday, December 24. I shivered, because I was freezing on the block of stone that served as a bed in my Pozzo cell, and because I knew that no one in Italy would come to work that day and find me. "I can't die on Veronica's wedding day."

But conditions didn't bode well. Overnight, a foot of water had entered my cell, like the crypt at the Chiesa di San Zaccaria. And because the Pozzi were half the height of regular cells, it wouldn't be long before they flooded.

My only solaces were that I'd freed my hands and Ubaldo hadn't confiscated my cell phone when he'd locked me inside, probably because there was no chance of reception in a prison beneath the Palazzo Ducale.

And no chance of survival.

My hand went to my throat. Whatever had caused the burn scar on Ubaldo's neck had damaged his voice, and maybe his mind. But I suspected the latter had been taken by the counterfeit Casanova, his cult leader stepson. Fabio was a narcissist who used charisma and unpredictable behavior to brainwash otherwise rational people into believing he was working for a higher power—instead of stroking his ego.

Why else would Ubaldo condone the murder of his own daughter?

Shuddering more from the crime than the cold, I used my phone light to scan my cell once more. I'd jiggled the bars on the window overlooking the corridor, but they were solid. And while I could get my arm through the large peephole on the low wooden door, I needed something long and pointed to move the peg-like handle protruding from the round bar, and my bobby pins wouldn't do it.

Meanwhile, the water was rising.

What time did the tide come in?

The light landed on an image of Christ on the crucifix that a prisoner had carved into the wall. I thought of Lucrezia's necklace and the violet sapphire on the crown of Christ Pantocrator. The killer thieves had stolen it from the Pala d'Oro by now.

Would they ever be found?

Or would Iona and Violet be denied justice?

And what about me and Shona? I hadn't seen her since the Stanza della Tortura, but I feared she was there, hanging by wrists tied behind her back.

My text tone sounded.

I gasped and bolted upright in the calf-deep water, banging my head on the low ceiling. A blinding white obscured my vision.

The Empyrean.

"No, Franki. It's a blow to an already concussed head."

When my sight returned, I tried to text Bradley, but it wouldn't go through. Nor would a call. Frustrated, I checked the message I'd received.

By the way, I'm still expecting a Santa-on-a-gondola ornament. If I don't get it, I'll pop you like one of Dr. Pimple Popper's cysts and squeeze until the Nutella comes out.

If I didn't need my phone so badly I would have thrown it.

"The one text I get is freaking Ruth trying to ruin my chocolate-hazelnut spread?"

A sob escaped my lips. It was ironic—but not outrageous—that the loss of Nutella is what pushed me over the edge. It was supposed to be my bomboniere at my wedding.

This must've been how Lucrezia felt in her convent cell while wearing a fabulous dress like my Valentino, as though life's pleasures had been taken from her, and she wasting away, waiting to die.

A sloshing sound shook me from my self-pity.

Feet, plodding through water.

And a light.

Are they coming to hang me between the red columns of the loggia? Or is it Commissario Lucifero? This cellhole is his kind of place.

Stooping, I stood in the now knee-deep water. "*Aiuto!* I'm locked in a cell."

"Mm MM! MM mm!"

I dropped onto the stone block. It was Shona, showing up.

But at least she's alive.

Ubaldo shoved her, still gagged and bound, into the cell.

I rushed him, but he'd already slammed the door. We listened as he slid the round bar across it and splashed away, and then I shone my phone light in her eyes like she'd done to me with her damn flashlight on the quad scull.

"MM mm! MM mm!"

She wanted me to take off her gag, and I weighed my options like the Archangel Michael weighed souls on his scales. Trapping me in a cell with the loud librarian was a Council of Ten terror tactic. But as much as I wanted to sh Shona, she was a fact machine and could have information that would help us escape from our prison.

I untied the gag.

"Whew!" She shook out her stringy hair. "I tried to tell you it was me, but I don't think you could understand me with that rag in my mouth."

"Mona with a 'mm' would have worked better."

"Right?" She smacked her mouth. "I need to get the blood back in my lips. They were going all numby tingly, and I was afraid I'd have permanent nerve damage, and then I wouldn't be able to talk right ever again. Can you imagine?"

I could, and I liked what I saw—and didn't hear. "Where have you been?"

"In the Piombi. But this morning I got my gag off and yelled for help. They heard me down in the piazza, so they moved me underground."

That was one move the killers and I could agree on. "What are they still doing here? I thought they made off with the violet sapphire last night."

"I don't know if they've stolen it yet. The police came not long after the bell ringer guard took you away."

"Who called them so soon?"

"Beats me. I've been locked up."

I leaned the back of my head on the cold stone. "Everyone must be so worried."

"The Screamers are for sure having a fit. I know from the Marangona that the race is in half an hour. We trained for a year, and we have cute Santa and elf sweatsuits that we'll never get to wear."

Santa Shona and the Screamin' Ho Elves. "There's still time for you to make that race. Do you have anything long and pointed on you, maybe a pencil?"

"No, I wore this Sherpa under my dress, and all my stuff was in the kitten basket."

I sighed. "Then rack your resource brain for anything you can think of to get us out of here."

"Can I borrow your phone light?"

I couldn't hand it to her fast enough.

She shone it on the walls.

The water had risen another couple of inches.

"Hey, I read about this place. We're in Cell X, and that carving of Christ is the work of a fresco artist, a guy named Riccardo Perucolo. He was imprisoned here in the sixteenth century during the Roman Inquisition, and he made it out."

She turned off the light, but I saw a glimmer of hope. "How'd he do it?"

"He confessed."

It was a good thing the Pozzi were as black as a Venice night, because my face was no less dark. And deadly.

A light came on, and the sloshing started.

I shoved the gag into her mouth—which gave me immense satisfaction in my possible last moments—and held my hands behind my back.

"Don't you push me, you filthy brute!"

My hands dropped to my sides. *Sheilah?*

Ubaldo appeared with Bradley's ex in her modern Madame de Pompadour gown.

She saw me and gasped. Then she turned to Ubaldo and pounded his chest. "The police are looking for her, you horrible fool. Let us go!"

He shoved her into the cell as Shona rushed the door. Ubaldo met her rush with a shoulder block, and she flew backward to the stone block. Sheilah attended to her.

I glared through the bars. "God wouldn't want you to treat a woman that way."

He barred the door and trudged away, and I turned on my phone light.

Shona spat the gag. "I think I sprained my shoulder."

"Let me untie your hands." I sat beside Shona and untied

her wrists. "What are you doing here, Sheilah?"

She sat on the stone and pulled her feet from the water. "Ted didn't come back to our suite last night, so I went out to look for him and saw that oaf and two others coming out of the Basilica. He grabbed me and brought me here."

The violet sapphire. "You caught them stealing a stone from the Pala d'Oro."

Sheilah puckered, causing her coquette beauty mark to protrude. "I knew they were thieves, but I thought they were after my bag, so I hid it in my bodice." She paused and pulled it from her dress. "There was no way I'd let him touch genuine crocodile with those dirty mitts."

Shona retracted the finger she was just about to run along the leather. "That Versace bag protected you. Virtus was the Roman goddess of bravery and military might."

I got halfway into an eye roll and stopped. *Virtue and protection—there they are again.* "What about Bradley? How is he?"

"How do you think? You've completely emasculated him."

Sheilah was another one I'd like to sh, but it was my fault for asking her the question. "That's kind of harsh."

"Is it? He knows you're in danger but can't do a thing to help you. And then there's your best friend who is frantic on what should be the happiest day of her life, not to mention your poor family. Despite that strong jaw on your father, I could tell he's really shaken."

Evidently, the count's Habsburg chin wasn't the effect of that bauta mask.

"Honestly," she said, rummaging in her bag, "I don't know how any of them tolerate your investigations."

I didn't expect her to understand my work. Sometimes I didn't understand it myself.

Shona shot me a semi-side-eye. "You know, it *is* a lot for Bradley to handle."

Sheilah and Shona both needed to sh. I stooped and stood in the thigh-deep water. "What about me and what I'm handling? Like now, for example. I'm trying to do good in the world, but I'm stuck in this Venetian prison with the two of you. One of you outed me to the killers, and the other tried to sabotage my relationship."

Sheilah put a hand to her amply exposed bosom. "How did I do that, pray tell?"

"By crashing my best friend's wedding and cavorting with my fiancé in your lingerie."

"Ted was Veronica's father's college roommate, so we were invited. Plus, I needed Bradley to turn down that job in Boston. The position is ideal for Ted."

Sheilah always had an ulterior motive. "Well, since I had no idea about the job interview, you can see how I would've gotten mad."

"Oh, I can. Because you're a hot-headed Italian."

Shona side-eyed Sheilah. "That's a stereotype."

They both had a point.

Sheilah put on gloves from her purse. "Bradley turned down seven figures to stay in New Orleans with you, and now Ted is so furious with me he might not take the job, even if it's offered to him. And he needs it because his company went under."

I returned to the stone block, shaken by the news of that seven-figure salary and the 'went under' expression, given that the water was rising at an alarming rate.

Sheilah leaned around Shona. "You seem shocked, Franki. Don't you know that men's identity is their professions?"

She was right. I had other identities besides PI—friend, daughter, fiancée, future wife and mother. I could give up my job and find satisfaction in other things, like creating a home, raising our children, and eating Nutella—if Ruth didn't destroy it for me. And it started with breaking out of the cell and being my best friend's maid of honor. Bradley would be at Dirk's side, and it wouldn't hurt for Sheilah to see us at an altar, just in case.

My eye went to the Versace bag. *Virtus.* Virtue, and protection. I had to fight for our lives like a Roman goddess—and a Venetian nun. "What do you have in your purse?"

Sheilah folded her hands. "That's none of your business."

"Clearly, I'm not trying to snoop into the contents of that dead crocodile. I need something to get us out of here, like a nail file."

"I have one of those. Diamond dust."

Shona's brows arched. "Ooh. Fancy."

Sheilah handed it to me, and I got up and trudged to the door. Then I gritted my teeth and shoved my still-sore left arm through the peephole, shaving off skin.

"Dear God," Sheilah murmured.

"That's kind of sick," Shona said.

My head lowered. "Listen. I have to flip the peg-handle down, and then I can slide the bar open with my hand. So, I could use some encouragement here."

Shona stood in the waist-high water. "H-O-T-T-O-G-O! Franki Amato," clap! "is hot to go! WHOOP! Hot to go! WHOOP WHOOP!"

After that cheer, I *was* 'hot to go.' Because I had to get the hell out of this cell to finally shake the woman. I shoved harder, screaming. Then I extended the nail file to the peg handle.

It didn't quite reach.

I shoved harder and jammed my sprained ring finger on a piece of wood.

A flash of white exploded before my eyes.

But it wasn't pain or a vision of the Empyrean.

It was a wall of water, surging down the corridor.

Aqua alta.

We were all going down like the *Death in Venice* book.

20

"Tide!" Fueled by sheer terror, I flipped the peg-handle, rolled back the bar, and held on as the water hit us like a liquid hammer.

We were submerged.

My phone was on the cell floor with the light shining.

Shona and Sheilah's feet dangled above.

A wave of horror hit me like the tide.

Did they have air?

Or were they dead?

I tried to pull my arm from the peephole, and pain zapped oxygen from my lungs.

It was stuck.

I yanked.

It had swollen.

My cell light went off.

I was trapped underwater in the pitch black, in desperate need of air.

Positioning my feet against the door, I wrested my arm free with a silent scream and discovered that I was still holding the nail file. I shoved it inside my bodice as I floated to the ceiling and gulped in a breath.

"Franki?" Shona shrieked. "Are you here?"

The good news, we had around six inches of air. The bad news, Shona's volume elevated in a crisis.

Sheilah wrenched out a sob. "We're going to diiiie, like Fraaaankiiii."

Clearly, that sob wasn't for me. "I'm not dead yet, Sheilah. But if you don't stay calm, we all will be. Now, we're going to form a chain. I'll dive and open the door. Shona, after I tug your hand twice, you and Sheilah take a deep breath and swim behind me into the corridor."

Filling my lungs for what I hoped wasn't the last time, I went under. Because there was no handle inside the cell, I used the peephole. The door was heavy, but it was completely underwater, so it opened. I tugged Shona's hand two times, and she squeezed—as hard as she was loud.

I gritted my teeth and went through the doorway. I waited until I felt Shona rise, and then I followed. We rose to the ceiling, gasping, in several feet of air.

"My Versace Virtus," Sheilah wailed. "It's ruined."

She'd been clinging to that damn crocodile the entire time. "Worry about saving your life, not your bag."

"Remember," Shona said, in a story-time-at-the-library voice, "crocodiles live in water, and Virtus is a brave warrior."

She was fast with facts, even under duress. One fact she didn't share—we were as dead as that crocodile if we didn't hurry. Water was coming in so fast that we would have drowned if I hadn't freed my arm when I did.

"Float on your backs and kick," I said. "Make sure you feel the feet of the person in front of you so we're going in the same direction."

We started kicking.

"Is this the right way?" Sheilah called.

The hard answer was, I don't know.

"My inner compass says yes," Shona shouted.

That made me feel better. What didn't—we were already down to a foot of air.

Water lapped my cheeks as I traveled up the corridor, and I slammed into stone, sending shock waves through my brain. "Stop!" Dazed, I felt the object. "There's an archway above a door. We have to swim under it."

We reformed the chain, and as I dived down, I flashed back to Iona in the Grand Canal, and other images of watery graves followed.

The flooded crypt.

The floating coffin.

The island cemetery, San Michele.

I came up and resumed kicking. And I thought of Dante's Barge in the middle of the lagoon and its solar panel. Its white light filled my core with warmth.

A mirage from the new blow to my head?

Or was I headed to the Empyrean?

I tilted my head back and extended my arm to feel for another archway.

The white light was neither.

It was the sun streaming through an opening.

"Kick," I screamed. "The stairwell is ahead."

"I'm scared," Sheilah said. "We're almost out of air."

I was well aware of that. The tip of my nose touched the ceiling, and water was at the corners of my mouth. "Kick harder."

My head turned into the stairwell, and my body followed. The ceiling opened to a vast reserve of air.

Shona came next, then Sheilah.

Relief flooded my body like the ray of light. But we had to walk up old stone steps while water cascaded at us, and after hours in the cold with no sleep and nothing to eat, that was no easy task. "Find the railing."

"I can't," Sheilah cried.

Bradley's ex was not good in a crisis. "Grab Shona's hand. We've got to plow through this."

"My feet," Shona spat a mouthful of water, "can't touch the steps."

The two of them were dead weights, which was not a comforting metaphor—or a comforting reality, for that matter. I had to motivate them to keep going.

I grabbed Shona's hand. "*Heave!*"

"H—" Shona coughed. "Ho!"

Silence followed.

"Say 'ho,' Sheilah," I ordered.

"No."

"C'mon," Shona spat-coughed, "Sheilah! I'll say it twice, and you'll be the third." She coughed and gagged a little. "Go, Franki!"

"*Heave!*"

"Ho! Ho!"

"No."

Despite the lack of enthusiasm on Sheilah's part, we made it to the upper floor of the Pozzi prison and found the water source. The entire corridor of cells was lined with windows.

Shona stared at the glass. "That's not fair that these get light, and ours don't."

For once I agreed with her.

We continued to the first floor of the Palazzo Ducale, and I pushed open the *Porta del Frumento*, the main door overlooking the lagoon, and basked in the light of the sun.

But only for a second. The killer cult members were on the loose.

"Let's get to the hotel and call the cops."

We walked the piazzetta on high alert, as pale as zombies and just as battered. Our updos looked as though we'd spent decades in a mausoleum. Shona, on the other hand, looked like a soggy sheep in her Sherpa.

The piazzetta opened onto the main piazza, and we witnessed a Christmas Eve Day miracle—Veronica and Glenda, still in her fishnet bunny suit, were at the Caffè Florian.

And it was open for business.

Their backs were to us, so they didn't notice us coming up. I flopped into a chair at their table.

Veronica went as white as her tracksuit and screamed, and I couldn't blame her. In our wet, bedraggled ball gowns, we looked like Venetian ghost legends freshly risen from the canal —with a random sheep.

Veronica stood and threw her arms around me.

I hugged her back, hard. "I'm ready for your wedding."

Her face contorted, probably because Glenda in her bunny suit would've been a more suitable maid of honor than I was at the moment. "You have to go to the hospital, and we'll see what the doctor says."

Shona's eyes filled with panic. "She can't. Sheilah saw the thieves leaving the Basilica an hour ago. They could still be in Venice."

"And this is personal, Veronica, whether I'm related to Lucrezia or not."

Sheilah lifted her head from the table. "It's personal for me too. They're going to pay for what they did to me and my bag."

Veronica shot me a questioning look, and I replied with a half-lidded look and a shake of my head. "Have the police checked the Christ Pantocrator panel on the Pala d'Oro?"

Her jaw contracted. "They have, and a violet sapphire has been stolen from his crown. But leave that to the police, okay?

You've already told them who these people are, so let them handle it from here."

I snort-huffed. "Like they did our disappearance? I didn't hear them searching the Palazzo Ducale for Shona and me."

Glenda lit a cigarette. "They didn't, sugar. But they checked the empress's bed chamber and saw one hell of a performance."

Shona scooted her chair next to Glenda's. "Could I get a recap?"

Veronica grimaced. "After the police searched the Museo Correr, they went to the campanile and the Basilica. Then a gondolier reported his gondola stolen, and they thought the killers had taken you and Shona by boat."

Glenda leaned in, her breasts hanging from her suit. "I stole that gondola, sugar. I took Ambrosio to the Casanova Museum to look for you."

With the legendary lover's canopy bed on display, we all knew she took him there for something else. "What about Bradley?"

"He's beside himself." Veronica pulled out her phone. "I'll call Dirk. Stella took him and Bradley on the batela to search the buildings at the squero, while Midge and Madge check the Museo della Storia Naturale and the hospital."

I wished he was here.

Veronica placed the phone to her ear. "Hm. It's not going through."

Why did that not surprise me?

She got up and pushed in her chair. "Let's call from the hotel. We need to tell your mom and nonna you're okay."

Ambrosio exited the café with a tray of cornetti, espresso, and the nectar of the Gods—Cioccolata Casanova.

"Hold that thought." It was a dog eat dog world, or maybe a Gnaga eat Gnaga one, and I needed sustenance to survive it. So did the pigeons, who postured around me like protective friends.

After throwing them some Nutella-stuffed cornetto, I shot the espresso. Then I leaned back and savored the luxurious Cioccolata Casanova. I refused to allow a killer cult leader to ruin it for me. And I wasn't going to let Ruth ruin my chocolate-hazelnut spread, either.

That justice-obsessed nutjob would have enjoyed my trial—and seeing the counterfeit Casanova squeeze me like a Dr. Pimple Popper cyst. *She'll get that Santa-on-a-gondola ornament when Venice freezes over.*

I took another swallow of the warm mint chocolate and gazed at the gondolas at the service station.

Then I sat up in my seat.

Casanova might use the Santa event to escape Venice.

"Shona, we've got to get to that race. The killers might try to sneak out of town in a gondola."

She looked at Veronica. "Can I borrow your phone to call the Screamers?"

Glenda, who had her arm around Ambrosio's backside, stubbed out her cigarette. "The Screamers already went to the race, Miss Shona. They thought you might show up."

A logical assumption based on my experience with her.

Glenda rose and adjusted her cottontail. "I'll take you in the gondola. The gondoliere already thinks it's stolen."

Veronica's lips compressed. "I'll notify the police that you're safe and headed to the race, but I'll leave out the details of your transportation method."

As I rose to follow Glenda Cottontail to the gondola, Veronica touched my forearm. "I'm not getting married without you, so please be careful."

"You know it," I said, as I gave her another hug.

But I didn't 'know it.' Because if I found Casanova and his cult, they would do anything to save their precious necklaces, starting with sinking me for eternity.

"S<small>EE ANY CULT KILLERS</small>, <small>SUGAR</small>?" Glenda called from the stern of the stolen gondola.

I scanned the sea of Santas packed in boats on the Venetian lagoon. "Not yet." I turned to Sheilah, who sat beside me in the red heart-shaped seat for two, still clutching her crocodile bag. I'd wanted a gondola ride with Bradley, but it was looking like I'd have to settle for one with his ex and my ex-stripper landlady. "Anything in the crowd?"

She shook her head, threatening to topple the rest of her updo. "Just tourists."

To doublecheck, I surveyed the riva walkway. Instead of watching the Santas, most of the spectators watched us. And I could see why. In our bedraggled ball gowns and fishnet bunny suit, we looked like a bawdy band of prostitute pirates, which one didn't see at just any Christmas Eve Day race.

"*Heave!*"

"Ho!"

"Ho!"

"Ho!"

Shona and the Screamers were behind us in sparkly Santa and elf sweatsuits, weaving the quad scull among boats and gondolas to sniff out the killers.

Tuning them out as best I could, given Shona's heightened hunting-a-killer hollering, I scoured the Jolly Saint Nicks again and spotted something odd—instead of the usual white wig, one had a rolled curl above each ear.

And a ponytail with a bow.

No self-respecting Santa had eighteenth-century hair, and especially not in Italy, where Kris Kringle was a relatively recent import. That was Fabio the good-for-nothing in his counterfeit

Casanova wig with Ubaldo and Perpetua, who were also shoddy Santa Clauses.

"That's them!" I pointed.

Sheilah stood. "They're getting away with the violet sapphire and the necklaces!" She looked around helplessly. "And after they kidnapped us and ruined my crocodile handbag!"

Shona's face turned as red and glistening as her sequined Santa hat, and the Screamers' eyes were mean green like evil elves.

"*Hell!*"

"No!"

"No!"

"No!"

The killer Casanova Santa heard the Screamers, and shouted at Ubaldo and Perpetua, who paddled faster.

Glenda veered the gondola toward them, and as they passed by, she raised her pole and knocked Ubaldo off the boat.

Sheilah cheered, and I rose and gave my landlady a high five. "You don't call yourself a polecat for nothing, Glenda."

She took a drag off a cigarette holder that she'd deftly managed during the clubbing. "That's right, sugar. We're anti-social bandits, until it comes to mating."

Without Ubaldo, the Casanova Santa and his mad mutter were no match for Shona and the Screamers. The quad scull pulled alongside their boat, and Shona took out Perpetua with a whack of her cleaver oar.

Watching the awful woman fly into the water was almost as satisfying as shoving the gag into Shona's mouth.

Casanova Fabio jumped into the lagoon. Instead of saving his mother, he swam for the shore.

I dived in after him and did the crawl as fast as my injured arms would take me.

He made it to a dock, and I was on him like white on wig.

A police boat siren wailed, but I couldn't wait for the police. Casanova Fabio was on the move, and the dark and twisted Venetian streets offered too many opportunities to hide and escape.

As I gave chase along the rio, I realized we were near the Chiesa di San Zaccaria, where my nightmare vacation began.

Is this where it would end?

Where I would end?

Casanova crossed a bridge, and I followed.

We entered a maze of streets.

No, I won't end. I hadn't slept, and I was battered. But I'd loaded up on Italian super fuel—espresso, a Nutella cornetto, and a Cioccolata Casanova. I was primed to catch a cult-leader killer and stand at the altar with my BFF and my fiancé.

But only for about five more minutes. *Seriously, how far is this guy going to run?*

He dashed down a short, narrow street and hooked a right.

I ran after him.

And I skidded to a stop. Because Casanova was waiting for me around the corner—with an all-too-familiar dagger.

My chest heaved from shock and the long haul.

The street was shaped like a closed L, so I had to back out. But my legs had turned to spaghetti because something about the encounter seemed staged. From the corner of my eye, I stole a glance at the tall walls surrounding me and spotted a sign.

And I understood how the Council of Ten had tricked so many into their untimely demise. Because a Council of Three had just tricked me.

"The infamous Calle della Morte," Casanova Fabio drawled.

It figures Death Alley is by the Church of Murders. Because this Casanova wasn't a lover. He was a killer, and he'd led me here to make sure I died.

He crept toward me, his shoes crunching on the damp stone.

As I backed away, my gaze lowered for a split second. The freak had worn his eighteenth-century man heels with his Santa suit.

His dark eyes softened into a Casanova-canopy-bed-bedroom look. "It is a shame that it should end this way between us. In another circumstance, we could have been lovers."

A laugh erupted from my overworked lungs. I looked like I'd come from the tomb, which I basically had, and he looked like a deranged, cross-century-dressing Santa Claus. "Not with you wearing those girly shoes with cute brass buckles."

His eyes went from soft sensual to fiery furious.

"What's the matter?" I taunted. "Did I offend your monstrous cult-leader ego?"

Father Festin was right about evil spirits being created on Fridays. Casanova was already diabolical, but after my insult, he morphed into demonic. He had actual evil in his eyes.

I backed from the L-shaped street.

And fell from a small step at the entrance, sprawling onto my back.

He leapt on top of me and raised the knife, and I kneed him in the original Casanova's favorite private parts.

The dagger clattered to the street.

I reached for it, but he reached for my throat.

And squeezed.

I grabbed his hands and tried to pry them off, but he was too strong.

And too enraged.

As he strangled me, his face went from red to violet.

A poetic color.

Thrashing only enraged him further and intensified his grip.

My lungs screamed for air, and a pain stabbed my chest.

But it wasn't the dagger.

A white light flashed in my head. Not the light of a concussion or the Empyrean.

The light of realization.

I released his left hand and reached into the bodice of my ballgown.

Before the killer Casanova could react, I plunged Sheilah's diamond dust nail file deep into his neck.

21

W   ith a flourish of his black satin wedding-reception
        cape, Maurizio Bonsignore bowed before me.
        "May I have-a this dance?"

I frantically searched Hotel San Marco ballroom for Bradley,
who'd been mysteriously absent since our trip to Veronica and
Dirk's wedding altar.

The Sicilian count caught my gaze and bowed. As he rose,
his chin kept coming.

Glaring at Maurizio to discourage any ideas, I grumbled,
"Let's get this over with."

He took my hands, which were covered with the stratagliati
gloves Glenda had loaned me to cover the bandages and bruises
on my arms, and led me to the dance floor as the next song
began.

'Tiny Dancer'? My gaze shot heavenward. Are you putting
me on?

Maurizio nestled into my abdomen—and pinched my
bottom.

I pushed him away, and his eyes smoldered. The 'good
gentleman' was seriously shady.

Shona flounced toward us in a ruffled blue dress.

This time I was glad she showed up.

Maurizio removed his hat. "And-a who is-a this flower?"

She lowered her eyes like a shrinking violet.

I recognized that bashful behavior and yanked her away from the mini marriage broker-groper.

Shona stared at Maurizio over her shoulder. "He's dreamy."

"Did you not see his tombstone teeth?"

"Yeah, he's like an Italian Donny Osmond in an opera star outfit. A potent combination."

It was potent, all right, but not in the way Shona meant.

The hotel manager, Gaspare, approached with a chest as padded as a Santa.

Studying the shirt beneath his suit coat, I noted the outline of a bulletproof vest. The guy still thought I was a Mafia princess.

He shoved an envelope of cash into my hands.

"I'm not the one getting married."

"You take, and do not come-ed back." He serpentined through the crowd, probably for fear of being shot.

"Child," Glenda drawled as she watched his backside, "I'd like to gasp with Gaspare."

I turned and gasped myself. Not because of her reception outfit, although Murano glass pasties and a thong were quite breathtaking, but because her mystery date had arrived, fashionably late—actually, unfashionably. But it wasn't the German beermaker with the moth-eaten lederhosen.

He, dressed as a she, grasped Shona's hand. "Ben Dover, or Carnie Vaul in art."

Shona's mouth gaped as though she'd never seen a drag queen in Screamer or Belchertown—either that, or she was preparing to scream or belch.

"Close your mouth, hunty," Carnie commanded at full-blown Shona-tone. "You never know who might come up and stick something in it."

Pleasant wedding chitchat. I turned to tell Shona that "hunty" was drag-queenese for friend or comrade, but she'd already scurried off. If you asked me, she was frightened in part by Carnie's costume—a busty pink ballgown, an enormous white wig with a saloon-girl-style feather, and a mustache sprouting through her white pancake makeup. "So, the masked ball was last night. But who are you supposed to be?"

"I'm surprised you don't recognize me. I came straight from my last show in Paris and wore this for you." She leaned in and her blue-glittered eyelids went frosty. "I'm Marie-I-Just-Can'-Toinette."

"That's ironic, because I just can't, either."

She batted her eyelids, but her three-inch painted-on lashes didn't move. "And why is that, Miss Thing?"

"Because with your mustache showing, you look like the ghost of Freddie Mercury dressed as Dolly Parton."

The Over-It Marie Antoinette twisted a curl around her finger and turned to Glenda. "I'd say, 'Let her eat cake,' but it would go straight to her Italian hips."

My Italian hips started walking to find Bradley. Carnie Vaul was proof that getting married on a Friday in Italy was unlucky after all.

"Franki!" A hand with violet coffin nails grabbed my arm, and for a moment my head spun.

"Whaaat? You don't recognize me?" she asked in a Philly accent.

Green leopard-print dress, dyed red curls, and tarted-up makeup to match the lips, eyeliner, and CarLashes on her VW Bug. "Ladonna Cucuzza."

"I told yous and Veronica that I wouldn't miss the wedding."

She grabbed the huge hand of a man whose chin rivaled that of the Sicilian count. "This is my Rocco."

He gave my arm a hard shake. "Nice ceremony."

Guessing Ladonna was the conversationalist in the family, I smiled and casually massaged my bicep. The ceremony had been surprisingly nice for a Friday in Italy in the Church of Murders—except for the dead saints in glowing caskets and Father Festin, who should've followed Elvira's lead and gone into the Halloween business.

Ladonna popped her gum. "So I was tawkin' to Veronica, and she told me that she's not going to hire another PI to replace me. Instead, she's looking for someone to head up a fraud department, so's she can spend more time with Dirk now that they're married and all."

Veronica hadn't mentioned that, but we hadn't seen much of one another lately. "That makes sense. I can handle the homicide cases myself."

Someone tapped me on the shoulder. "May I have a word, signorina Amato?"

Commissario Lucifero. I thought it was hot in here. "Excuse me. Duty calls."

"Sure, hon." Ladonna winked. "That duty must be murder."

The double meaning was clear. Lucifero was as handsome as hell, but he had the personality to match.

The inspector led me to a corner table. "I am sorry to interrupt the joyous occasion, but I felt I should tell you that we have recovered the necklaces and the violet sapphire, and Signor Baloso is resting comfortably in hospital."

My mind went to Violet and the potassium permanganate. I was relieved that I hadn't killed him, but the cult creep should have been resting on the stone bed in the Pozzi prison. "Is there anything else you can tell me?"

His nostrils flared. "I shall tell you what I am able to share and no more."

"That's understandable."

He took a breath. "Ubaldo Falsetti has worked as a guard at the Palazzo Ducale for many years. A few months ago, he saw Iona as he was crossing the piazza. They spoke briefly, and then he informed his wife, Perpetua, that his daughter's mother had returned to Italy and that she had an interesting ancestry."

I took a glass of champagne from a waiter passing with a tray. "Lucrezia and the necklaces."

"Precisely. Perpetua told her son, Fabio, who convinced her to volunteer at the Chiesa San Zaccaria. He correctly assumed that Iona would attend the church because of its connection to Lucrezia, and he wanted his mother to access the convent archives to research the necklaces."

Perpetua had read Lucrezia's will.

"One day as Iona was leaving the confessional, Perpetua engaged her in conversation. Iona mentioned that she intended to cook risotto alle violette for an upcoming wedding, and Perpetua recommended the Valpolicella."

"Because she wanted to make sure that Violet knew which wine to poison in the hotel kitchen."

He nodded.

I twirled my champagne flute on the table. "What did Fabio get out of this, besides control?"

"Signor Baloso's sole ambition had been to buy his own gondola until he learned of the necklaces. At that point, he devised a plan to deceive his mother, Ubaldo, and Violet into helping him obtain the precious jewelry so that he could eventually sell it. He exploited their piety. However, he has no belief in God, or in the Comte de Saint Germain."

Like all con men, he'd put on one hell of an act. "Did Iona know Violet was her daughter?"

"According to a source at the Chiesa di San Zaccaria, she did. She also knew that Violet hated her because she'd been abandoned."

The source at the church was Father Festin. Iona had confessed to him, and he'd confessed to the devil inspector.

"Perhaps the greatest tragedy is that Chef Parsons believed that Violet planned to kill her, and yet she did nothing to prevent it. I suspect, out of guilt."

There wasn't enough champagne in my glass, much less the ballroom, to drink away the memory of that revelation.

Commissario Lucifer rose and pushed in his chair. "Now I must go. As you say, duty calls."

Drained like my glass, I stayed in my seat.

The inspector's black gaze contemplated me like one of his wet specimens. "My men assured me that you are no relation to Lucrezia Pavan. Otherwise, I would have arrested you on suspicion of murder. Arrivederci, Signorina Amato."

Nice of Lucifer to launch some firebombs at me and leave. "A scintillating personality." I swigged champagne and stared at my violet maid-of-honor dress. My mom would be disappointed that she wasn't a noble, but I was relieved. There was too much sadness in that family.

Someone tapped silverware on a wine glass, and I looked for the culprit. To my surprise, it was my nonna's friend, Luigi Pescatore.

Per custom, the bride and groom, who were seated at a banquet table, responded to the tapping with a kiss.

Bradley was still MIA. Was he mad at me? Had he left?

He wouldn't do that at Dirk and Veronica's reception. There had to be some other explanation.

Dirk rose with a microphone. "Veronica and I would like to thank everyone for traveling all this way and turning what began as a difficult time into a happy day."

Veronica gave me a little wave.

Dirk extended a hand to his new bride. "Now, if you'll all follow us out of the hotel to the Piazzetta San Marco, a gondola awaits."

A gondola. I sighed and searched again for Bradley. There was no doubt about it. He wasn't in the ballroom.

I stood and ran smack into Shona. *I really need to start watching for her, because she's going to show up.*

She held a plate of bigoli al ragù d'anatra, recommended by my duck-pasta-sauce-loving mother to replace the risotto alle violette, and two plates of tiramisù and Napoleons from the Venetian table. "I forgot to tell you that the Screamers and I have an early flight out tomorrow morning."

"Well, I guess this is goodbye."

"Don't worry. We'll see each other again soon."

Worry pierced my chest like the bell ringer and Casanova Fabio's dagger. "We will?"

"Suuure," she sonic-boomed. "The Screamer Scullers didn't win today, so we're going to show the Bayou Rowing Association in New Orleans what we've got. That's why we have the 'Screamers on the Rowd' sweatshirts. Did you notice that instead of r-o-a-d, we spell it like 'row?'"

My sigh was deeper than that of any prisoner to ever cross the Bridge of Sighs. I might not know where Bradley was, but one thing was certain—Shona would always be there. So, she might as well be my wedding date. "Would you escort me to the piazzetta?"

"I'd be delighted." She put down her pasta plates—but not the ones with the desserts—and slid her free arm through mine.

Something metal jabbed my Italian hip—the clasp on Sheilah's waterlogged handbag. "What are you doing with that dead crocodile?"

"Ted got that seven-figure job, so Sheilah gave it to me. I hope you two will be friends. She's pretty great."

I spotted Bradley's ex as we headed for the stairs. She smiled and then clutched Ted's arm as though she thought I might come for him now that Bradley and I were having problems. "Maybe not friends, but good acquaintances."

Shona and I followed the crowd through the lobby. Caterina waved, while Gaspare peered from beneath the counter.

Out in the piazzetta, a gleaming black gondola waited at the service station. At the stern was Venice's first female gondoliera, who thankfully wore the traditional uniform instead of a Glenda gondolier getup.

Stella approached from the piazza with the Mavens. "I'm glad we found you."

Midge pulled a lace shawl around her neck. "We're all leaving for Rome in the morning. We've received a tip about a mystery concerning our father, the admiral."

"I didn't realize there was one."

Madge puckered and clasped her hands behind her back. "Indeed, and it's quite complex. Should you ever wish to take on the challenge, we would appreciate your investigative insights."

"As long as it's not in Venice, I might be able to help."

"Sorry to interrupt, ladies." Luigi jiggled a car-motor-sized hearing aid. "I wanted to say hello to Franki before she left."

"I'm not going anywhere yet."

"You're right, kid." He tapped his temple. "What was I thinking?"

"What are you doing here, anyway?"

"I wouldn't miss Veronica's wedding. And your nonna won't let me take her out, so I've gotta seize these opportunities."

I chuckled and then looked for my best friend. I didn't want to miss her leave.

Veronica came toward me, beaming. Despite the awful start

to her wedding week, she was every bit the glowing bride. A gorgeous—not ghostly—vision in white.

She took my hand. "Excuse us, Luigi. It's time for Franki to come with me."

"Why?" I hesitated. "Where are we going?"

She dragged me behind her. "To the gondola."

"Uh, I know we're close, Veronica, but I'm not going to be a third wheel on your boat ride."

She let go of my hand and stepped aside.

Bradley stood in front of the gondola with a bouquet of roses —yellow, no violets.

Confused, I stayed glued to the spot—until my mother shoved me forward.

"Don't keep him waiting, Francesca," she whisper-shrilled. "Everyone is staring, and he might leave."

My father emerged from the crowd.

"Dad!" I didn't even know he'd arrived, but it explained why I hadn't seen the Sicilian count and his Habsburg chin lurking.

He gave me a peck on the cheek. "Go on, Franki. Bradley's a good man."

Nonna shuffled up. "Listen to your patri, Franki. I like-a Brad-a-ley too." She shielded her mouth with her handbag. "And your mamma made up-a that big-a dowry."

At the words "big-a dowry," Maurizio Bonsignore appeared with flustered cape flourish. "Let's-a not-a be hasty, Francesca." He pressed a gloved hand to his chest. "My heart, you don't-a want-a to break him."

I wanted to say, No, just your vampire shark fin that pinched my bottom, but the whole crowd had gone silent, waiting for my next move.

Slowly, and with sharks circling, I walked toward Bradley, certain that I gleamed as bright as the white lights on the Christmas tree.

He dropped to one knee.

My heart stopped. "We're already engaged. What are you doing?"

He flashed his dazzling smile. "Who says I can't propose twice?"

Acqua alta had nothing on the tears that flooded my cheeks.

He gave me the bouquet and took my hand. "Francesca Lucia Amato, will you marry me on January eleventh?"

The anniversary of the day we met. I'd been wrong on two counts. Venice was the city—not the tomb—of love, and it was as romantic as a movie. "I can't wait."

The crowd erupted in cheers.

"Carmela!" my mother shrieked. "The wedding is in two-and-a-half weeks!"

Bradley's head tilted at the time span, and I rushed him into the gondola and signaled for the gondoliere to shove off. If my mom and nonna figured out that he was talking about January eleventh the following year, they were likely to hop into the stolen gondola with Glenda and have her whack us with the pole.

The gondoliera steered toward the mouth of the Grand Canal.

Bradley took my hand and looked into my eyes. "Franki, I'm so sorry I wasn't there for you last night. When I think of what could've happened—"

"Bradley, investigating is my job, not yours. And if I'd told you I was going to the library instead of the ladies room, you would've come with me and saved me from my abductor."

"That's not all I would've done." He ran a hand through his hair to release pent-up tension. "But we can talk about this another time. Let's enjoy our gondola ride."

He didn't have to tell me twice. I'd been longing for this

moment the entire trip. I snuggled up to him, and he slid his arm around my shoulders. "Where are we going, anyway?"

"Where else would I take my fiancée after second-proposing in Venice? The Bridge of Sighs."

"But it's the opposite way."

He nuzzled my neck. "I told her to take the scenic route."

I squirmed as he nipped my ear. "What happened to waiting to set a date until you figure out your work situation?"

"The Sicilian suitors had been summoned, and I got a job offer this morning." He squeezed my hand. "With your permission, I'd like to accept."

I bit my lip. If he needed my permission, the job was probably outside New Orleans. But I'd made the decision in the Pozzi to support him no matter where his career took us. "Bradley, wherever you want to work is fine with me, even if it's in another city. I want you to be happy."

He ran his thumb across my cheek and gave me a peck on the lips. "In that case, I'll be working with you at Private Chicks."

The job Ladonna mentioned.

"Veronica offered it to me this morning, and thanks to the money Luigi invested in the company last year, it's quite a deal. But if you're worried we'll be one of those couples who can't work together, I can turn it down."

"No, it's great. It solves the problem of us never getting to see each other because of our hectic schedules, and I don't have anything to do with the fraud stuff. So, technically, we won't be working together."

"Then it's settled."

"It is. Perfectly."

We kissed again, and I nestled into his side, marveling at the turn of events. My Venetian nightmare was turning into a Venetian dream. And for the first time since I'd come to La Serenissima, I was serene.

"Oh," he rested his hand on my thigh. "Ruth Walker called me today, and I'm going to hire her as my assistant."

The gondola listed, or maybe that was a holdover from the concussion. Either way, we were on troubled canal waters. "R... r...r...Rrrruth?"

"Yeah, she let me know she's on the market, and I've always felt bad that she lost her job when I quit the bank."

I knew that wack woman had been too quiet. And the timing of her call was suspicious.

Somehow she'd sniffed out the job offer. But he'd just heard about it today, and Veronica wouldn't have shared that kind of information.

My heart chilled in the love seat. Was Ruth in Venice?

My fingers flew to my mouth. I'd never nailed down who sent the "Roses Are Red" threats, or who used the name Richard Chanfray at the Casanova Museum. I didn't believe that the Comte de Saint Germain was still alive—or Wesley Sullivan, for that matter. If the ex-detective had been skulking around Venice, he would've already surfaced. Ruth, on the other hand, was alive and obsessive enough to come to Italy to haunt me

I gripped the side of the gondola. The gondoliera. I hadn't gotten a good look at her face. What if...?

Using my hair as a shield, I stole a glance at the gondoliera.

She stared at the canal, oblivious to my fear.

Ruth wasn't in Italy. She was a bacteria—omnipresent and perpetually infecting my life.

But I'd vowed not to let her ruin my Nutella, and she wasn't going to ruin my gondola ride. When Bradley and I got back to NOLA, I'd deal with Ruth in a professional manner—by disinfecting her. In the meantime, precautionary measures were in order.

I turned to the gondoliera. "If there's an after-hours gift shop on the way, could you please stop?"

"Certo, signorina."

Bradley pulled away. "You want to shop? Now?"

"I have to get two Santas, one in a gondola ornament, and the other is a medallion of Santa Francesca, the patron saint of plagues."

Bradley's brow furrowed.

The Marangona tolled to mark the midnight hour.

Or is it the Maleficio?

No, I'm being paranoid. And who could blame me after this trip?

Bradley gazed at me with love in his eyes. "Buon Natale, babe."

Entranced, I kissed him. As we glided down the Grand Canal in the hazy moonlight, I put my head on his shoulder and sighed. "Venice is hauntingly beautiful at night."

PREORDER TUACA TAN!

Preorder *Tuaca Tan*, Franki Amato's 8th mystery!

Here are the details on the investigation:
When PI Franki Amato was invited to watch her sixty-some-

thing landlady, Glenda, compete at the French Quarter's annual kickoff to Mardi Gras weekend, she had reservations. After all, the event is called the Greasing of the Poles, and Glenda is an ex-stripper. But she never expected the fun event to turn her world upside down—and, literally, the victim's. Now instead of hunting for a wedding venue with her honey, Franki's hunting down a killer. The trail seems to lead to the wealthy board of the Krewe of Clotho, a carnival organization of women whose character is nowhere near as impeccable as their blonde hair, tan outfits, and old New Orleans ancestry. As members begin dropping like beads from Bourbon Street balconies, Franki must decipher clues as murky as the krewe's signature milk punch brunch drink. Otherwise, this Mardi Gras parade could be her last.

Tuaca Tan is book 8 in the Franki Amato Mysteries, but it can be read as a standalone. If you like zany characters and laugh-out-loud humor with a splash of suspense, then you'll drink up this fun series by *USA Today* Bestselling Author Traci Andrighetti. Cheers!

FREE MINI MYSTERIES OFFER

Want to know what happens to Franki after *Limoncello Yellow*?
Sign up for my newsletter to receive a free copy of the *Franki
Amato Mini Mysteries*, a hilarious collection that contains
"Prugnolino Purple" (Franki #1.5) and five other fun short
mysteries. You'll also be the first to know about my new releases,
deals, and giveaways.

Here's the blurb for "Prugnolino Purple:"

It's springtime in New Orleans, and Franki Amato's BFF and
boss, Veronica Maggio, has dragged her to an art auction at one
of the city's historic house museums. Up for sale, a provocative,
not to mention peculiar, painting of their sixty-something ex-
stripper landlady that is anything but priceless. Franki thinks
the only crime at play is the image on the canvas until a cocktail
waitress is found unconscious in front of an empty easel. After
Franki finds a purple splotch on the presumed weapon, she and
Veronica spring into action to ID the attacking art thief and
locate the missing painting. But Franki's biggest surprise isn't the

culprit—it's the "blooming idiot" who bought the portrait before the auction started.

And don't forget to follow me!

BookBub
https://www.bookbub.com/authors/traci-andrighetti

Goodreads
https://www.goodreads.com/author/show/7383577.
Traci_Andrighetti

Facebook
https://www.facebook.com/traciandrighettiauthor

BOOK BACKSTORY

When I was debating which book to write next—either Franki Amato 7 or something new—I saw a man wearing a *Medico della Peste* (Plague Doctor) costume at seven a.m. while walking my dogs. He was standing on a tiny bridge that goes over a creek behind the Elisabet Ney Museum in Austin, Texas. The sighting was so bizarre and unexpected that I took it as a sign to write *Valpolicella Violet* in Venice.

A few other oddities occurred while writing this book. One involves the Comte de St. German, who I first wrote about in Franki 4, *Campari Crimson*. I didn't plan to write about the Comte in *Valpolicella Violet*, but like Shona, he just keeps showing up. Case in point: When I was doing the research, I discovered that Giacomo Casanova actually knew the Comte de St. Germain, and he said so in his autobiography. Also, Napoleon really did have a dossier on the Comte that was burned in a fire. Odd, isn't it?

Incidentally, Richard Chanfray was a real person too. On YouTube, you can watch an infamous documentary interview with him from French TV in the 1970s. He talks about being the Comte and even turns lead into gold during the interview. Not only that, he brings in two people who claim to be none other than Casanova and Madame de Pompadour. Wow.

Another strange thing that happened during my research: I found the Biblioteca Andrighetti Marcello in the Piazza San Marco online. On a previous trip to Venice, I walked past the library countless times without knowing it (it's inside a palazzo, and there's no sign). Anyway, I contacted the library, because I'm pretty sure I'm related to the family, and I have a standing invitation to visit.

Other fun facts about *Valpolicella Violet*: The ghost stories are all actual Venetian legends, and yet the only book I know of on the topic is out of print—*Venetian Legends and Ghost Stories: A guide to places of mystery in Venice* by Alberto Toso Fei. The places I reference are also real, although I changed the name of the hotel. And the historical details about the Venetian nuns are all true— except for Lucrezia Pavan, herself. I made her up, but her last name is part of my family tree. If you'd like to read more about these fascinating women, two of the best historical studies are *Forbidden Fashions: Invisible Luxuries in Early Venetian Convents* by Isabella Campagnol and *Virgins of Venice* by Mary Laven. Oh, and Casanova did have affairs with Venetian nuns. He goes way too much into detail about them in his autobiography!

Speaking of Casanova, the Caffè Florian really does make a mint hot chocolate named Cioccolata Casanova that is one of the most sinfully seductive drinks to have ever passed my lips. I dream of it. I honestly do.

Next up for Franki and me are two adventures, *Tuaca Tan* (Franki Amato 8), which involves a murderous all-female Mardi Gras krewe, and a collaboration called *Four Sleuths and a Bachelorette*. Leslie Langtry, Arlene McFarlane, Diana Orgain, and I decided to bring our sleuths together to solve a mystery. And one of the funniest things to come out of it, besides the book itself, is that the initials of our last names spell *LMAO*.

You can't make this stuff up, y'all—at least, not all of it!

Cin cin (Cheers)!

Traci

A COCKTAIL AND A DISH

RED WINE WHISKEY COCKTAIL

Although this cocktail is sometimes called the "Dolce Vita," I think of it as a Venetian Sunset. It's a layered drink with a whiskey colored bottom, a violet middle, and a creamy white froth. It's both dark and romantic, like Venice.

Ingredients
  1 ounce Rye Whiskey
  1/2 ounce Amaro Montenegro
  3/4 ounce Amontillado Sherry
  3/4 ounce cinnamon syrup
  3/4 ounce freshly squeezed lemon juice
  1 egg white
  Valpolicella, to float
  Ground cinnamon, to garnish

In a cocktail shaker, shake all ingredients except the wine. Add ice, shake again, and double strain into a coupe glass. Using the back of a bar spoon, gently layer in the wine, making a zigzag design. Garnish with cinnamon and serve.

Cin cin!

RISOTTO ALLE VIOLETTE

In Northern Italy, rice dishes are more common than pasta, and risotto with flowers is a real thing. For *Valpolicella Violet*, risotto with violets was the obvious choice. This dish is usually made with white wine, but you can substitute with red. But if you use Valpolicella, make sure it hasn't been poisoned!

Ingredients

    1 quart vegetable stock
    2.5 ounces unsalted butter
    1 small shallot, finely chopped
    11 ounces Arborio or Carnaroli rice
    1 cup dry white or red wine at room temperature
    1/3 cup heavy cream
    1 ounce violet petals
    2 tablespoons grated Parmigiano-Reggiano cheese
    Sea salt and freshly ground black pepper

Directions

In a saucepan over medium heat, warm the vegetable stock.

In a large saucepan, heat about 3 tablespoons of the butter. Add the chopped shallot and sauté for 2 to 3 minutes over medium heat. Add the rice and stir thoroughly for about 3 minutes to "coat" it with the butter and shallot mixture. Add the wine, and stir over medium-high heat until completely absorbed.

Add a soup ladle or two of the stock until the rice is just

covered. Stir continuously with a wooden spoon. When the stock is almost completely absorbed (the rice on top should not be dry), repeat this process.

After 16 to 18 minutes, remove the risotto from the heat when the rice is al dente and the liquid has been mostly absorbed (the risotto should still seem a bit "soupy"). Add the remaining butter, the cream, and Parmigiano-Reggiano. Stir the risotto until thoroughly blended. Add all but a few of the violet petals, leaving some for garnish, and mix gently. Add salt and freshly ground pepper to taste, and serve immediately.

Buon appetito!

ALSO BY TRACI ANDRIGHETTI

FRANKI AMATO MYSTERIES

Books
Limoncello Yellow

Amaretto Amber
Campari Crimson
Galliano Gold
Marsala Maroon
Valpolicella Violet
Tuaca Tan (preorder now!)

Box Sets
Franki Amato Mysteries Box Set (Books 1–3)
Franki Amato Mysteries Box Set (Books 4–6)
The Franki Amato Mysteries Big Box Set (Books 1–7)

Short Stories
Franki Amato Mini Mysteries
(short mysteries free to newsletter subscribers only)

Nocino Noir (a novella)

Franki Amato also investigates with the sleuths of Leslie Langtry, Arlene McFarlane, and Diana Orgain in the

KILLER FOURSOME MYSTERIES

Books
4 Sleuths & A Bachelorette
4 Sleuths & A Burlesque Dancer
4 Sleuths & A Barnstormer (preorder now!)

DANGER COVE HAIR SALON MYSTERIES

Books
Deadly Dye and a Soy Chai
A Poison Manicure and Peach Liqueur
Killer Eyeshadow and a Cold Espresso

ABOUT THE AUTHOR

Traci Andrighetti is the *USA Today* bestselling author of the Franki Amato mysteries and the Danger Cove Hair Salon mysteries, and she is a co-author of the Killer Foursome mysteries. In her previous life, she was an award-winning literary translator and a Lecturer of Italian at the University of Texas at Austin, where she earned a PhD in Applied Linguistics. But then she got wise and ditched that academic stuff for a life of crime—writing, that is. Get news of Traci's upcoming books and latest capers at www.traciandrighetti.com.

Speaking of capers, Traci and one of her Killer Foursome co-authors, Diana Orgain, take published and aspiring authors on writing retreats to Italy through LemonLit. If you're up for an Italian adventure, then *andiamo*! But be careful. Traci and Diana are a lot like their sleuths, so you never know what—or who—might go down on the trip...

SNEAK PEEK

If you liked *Valpolicella Violet*, read the first chapter of:

DEADLY DYE AND A SOY CHAI
Danger Cove Hair Salon Mysteries Book 1

2016 Daphne du Maurier Award Finalist
2016 Mystery & Mayhem Award Finalist
2016 Silver Falchion Award Finalist

by
Traci Andrighetti
&
Elizabeth Ashby

CHAPTER 1

"That statue's not wearing any panties!"

My body tensed at the outrage in Donna Bocca's voice. As the preeminent gossip of Danger Cove, not to mention a women's undergarment salesperson, she'd spread the news of this latest Conti family calamity all over town.

"And a child is watching," PTA member Mallory Winchester added through clenched teeth.

I stole a glance over my shoulder at the crowd gathering in the street. Besides Donna and Mallory, there was an elderly couple, an attractive thirty-something male with a camera, and Reverend Vickers's wife, Charlotte, with the members of her Bible study group. Even worse, a ten-year-old boy was speaking into a walkie-talkie with the intensity of a CIA agent on an intelligence-gathering mission.

I looked at my watch. It was a quarter after one on a Thursday in September. Why wasn't that kid in school?

I took a deep, calming breath of the crisp ocean air and then tried to convince myself that the situation wasn't really that bad. I mean, sure, there was a wooden statue of a gold rush era prostitute hovering, like a ghost of times past, from a rope in front of my home slash hair salon. And yes, she was skirtless and spread-eagle on a chair, displaying her intricately carved wares for all to see. But at least she had a shirt on.

"Beaver shot!" a young boy shouted.

I turned and saw packs of prepubescent males speeding up the sidewalk on bikes, alerted to the sex show, no doubt, by the CIA wannabe.

Okay, if little boys were ditching elementary school, then the situation *was* that bad.

I looked up on the roof. "Tucker," I began, trying to control the rising anxiety in my voice. "You need to get down and bring that statue with you. *Now.*"

"Mellow out, Cassidi," he replied, giving me a half-lidded look. "I told you, the pulley's stuck."

Tucker Sloan was the owner of One Man's Trash, a junk

shop on the outskirts of Danger Cove that dealt in antiques, used furniture, and eclectic decorative items, like my late Uncle Vincent Conti's—*ahem*—art collection. As Tucker's hippie-speak indicated, he was all about peace, love, and understanding. But right then, I wasn't about any of those things. When he'd bought the statue from me, he'd said that because of its "splayed style," it would be easier to move it out of a second-floor window than to try to take it down the spiral staircase. So much for that idea.

I cupped my hands around my mouth and whisper-shouted, "People are getting upset. Can't you unstick it?"

He shook his thick dreads. "Looks like old Sadie's not going to leave without a fight."

"Sadie?"

"Sexy Sadie's what your Uncle Vinnie used to call her. He nicknamed all of his women, real or otherwise." He grinned. "That cat was far out."

That was one way to describe him. "Could you please just try yanking the rope again?"

"Okay, but I don't think it'll do any good." Tucker braced himself with his legs and pulled until veins bulged in his neck and the fringe on his moccasins shook.

The pulley didn't budge, but Sadie did. She began to move back and forth like a swing. Each time she swung toward the street, the onlookers let out a collective gasp—and it wasn't because they were afraid that she was going to hit them.

"Seriously, Tucker?" I cried.

"I told you so, man," he replied.

I put my head in my hands—that is, until I heard one of the boys yell "Boobies!" followed by cheers from the rest of the under-twelve crowd.

I looked up and saw Tucker's temporary helper, Zac Taylor,

pushing the ship's figurehead from my second-floor apartment out the double doors of the salon. It was also the likeness of a woman, but instead of baring her nether region, this one was baring her breasts. And Zac's face was buried right smack between them.

"That's a sight for sore eyes," a deep female voice said.

I turned and saw Amy Spannagel, the assistant librarian, dismounting her bike.

"You mean, an eyesore."

She pushed up her glasses. "I'm talking about Zac's ripped biceps. What are you talking about?"

I gave her a blank stare. For a PhD student, Amy could be kind of dense. But, as much as I hated to admit it, Zac's muscles were kind of distracting. Repairing boats at the Pirate's Hook Marine Services had done his body good. "I'm talking about my Uncle Vinnie's antique porn."

"It's not porn." She tucked a strand of mousy brown hair behind her ear. "It's art."

"Psh," I said with a flick of my hand. "You're from Seattle."

She arched her quasi unibrow. "So?"

"So, it's a lot more open minded than where I'm from. Trust me. In Fredericksburg, Texas, this stuff is straight-up smut. And apparently," I began, glancing back at the scowling faces in the crowd as Zac pulled the bare-breasted wench down the steps of the porch and into the yard, "it's smut in Danger Cove too."

Amy inclined her head to one side and nodded, conceding my porn point.

"Zac," Tucker shouted, "Sadie's putting up a fight. Come and give her a tug from below."

"Sure thing," he replied. "Just let me put Pearl on the truck."

"Who's Pearl?" Amy asked.

"That figurehead," Tucker replied. "She was the apple of Vinnie's eye."

I frowned at Pearl's cupless corset. "She's a real peach, all right."

Zac pushed Pearl up a ramp and into the bed of Tucker's old pickup. Then he walked between Sadie's legs, jumped up, and grabbed onto her thighs.

I was less than thrilled about the suggestive scene, but I was more than happy that he was blocking the va-jayjay view.

"Now that's what you call eye candy," Amy breathed, ogling the backside of Zac's tight jeans.

"Hello!" I gave her a shove.

"What?" She lurched to the side and stumbled out of a penny loafer.

"I'm trying to clean up the image of The Clip and Sip and the Conti family name, and your gawking isn't helping."

Avoiding my gaze, Amy put her shoe on and pulled her socks high, as though suddenly ashamed of her naked knees.

"She's starting to drop," Zac announced as he let go of Sadie's massive thighs. But instead of lowering to the ground, she began to rock left and right.

The little boys began whistling and fist pumping like budding wannabe strip-club patrons.

"Sadie sure is kicking up a fuss," Tucker commented.

"She's kicking, all right," I yelled. "A burlesque version of the cancan."

No sooner had I spoken than a woman in the crowd let out a muffled cry.

Amy turned toward the street. "Looks like Charlotte Vickers just went down."

I threw my hands in the air. "That's it," I shouted. "Cut the rope."

"But Sadie's over a hundred and fifty years old," Tucker protested. "She might not survive the fall."

"Then you can take comfort in the fact that she's had a good, long life." I pointed at the offending item. "Now, you promised me that this would be a quick job, so you've got ten more minutes to get this junk off my property."

Tucker pulled a pocketknife from the front pouch of his Mexican Baja jacket and began cutting. "This is a real drag, man."

After a few seconds, the rope snapped, and Sadie hit the ground. But she didn't have the decency to fall on her face. She landed upright, lascivious grin and all.

Tucker hurried down the ladder and ran to Sadie's side. After he was sure that her parts were intact, he breathed a sigh of relief. "Groovy."

"Yeah, outtasight." I put my hands on my hips. "You dig?"

His face was expressionless. Then a light went on in his burned-out brain. "Grab a leg, Zac. Let's get Sadie on the truck."

Zac ran a hand through his thick, brown hair and flashed me a mischievous smile. "Did you want us to take Hope, Faith, and Charity too?"

My face turned as pink as my Blushing Berry lip gloss. He was referring to a painting-sized photograph from the late 1800s of three prostitutes on their backs with legs splayed, clothed only in socks and shoes.

"We'd be happy to take them off your hands," he added, winking a sexy, steel-blue eye.

"I'm sure you would," I intoned as he turned to help Tucker with Sadie.

"Hey," Amy said, punching my arm.

"Ow." I glared at her as I rubbed my bicep. "What did you do that for?"

"Because you promised me that picture."

"You can have it. But why would you want that hideous thing?"

"It's vintage erotica." She adjusted her beige cardigan. "And not everyone can have blonde hair and a petite figure like you. Some of us girls need a little help with the opposite sex."

I pretended to be absorbed in the loading of Sadie onto the truck. Amy and I had become friends a couple of months ago when I started studying for my online accounting class at the library. And if there was one thing I'd learned (it wasn't accounting), it was that she liked to talk about her nonexistent love life. As much as I wanted to be there for her, now wasn't the time. I had a staff meeting to plan and a quiz to study for. Besides, truth be told, talking about Amy's man troubles reminded me of mine, and that was something I'd rather forget.

"The girls are ready to go," Tucker said as Zac slammed the door of the truck bed shut. "Later, Cassidi."

Now that Sadie and Pearl were covered by a tarp, I turned to the sizable crowd. "Peep show's over, folks."

The townspeople began to disperse, and Tucker climbed into the driver's seat and started the engine. Zac saluted and got into the truck.

"Wait," I said, approaching the passenger door. "How much do I owe you for helping Tucker move the, uh, things?"

He leaned out the window. "Nothing. I used to work for Tucker in high school, so I was happy to help." He paused. "Especially since it meant coming to your place."

Flustered by his comment, I pulled some cash from the pocket of my jeans. "I insist."

"Okay." He gave an opportunist smile. "Then how about dinner?"

I felt my face flush. "I...I'd rather pay you for your time." I shoved three twenties into his hand. "That should cover it."

He looked from the money to me. "For now."

I nodded and then did a double take when I processed what

he'd said. But before I could respond, Tucker flashed the peace sign out the driver's window and sped away.

"Can you believe that Zac guy?" I asked as I stared after the truck.

Amy punched me in the arm—again. "He was hitting on you."

"*You're* hitting on me," I corrected. "What's up with you today?"

"Someone has to knock some sense into you." She put her hand on her hip. "Zac Taylor is one of the most sought-after guys in town. You owe it to those of us who'll never get a date with him to go for it."

I crossed my arms. "I told you. I'm not interested in dating right now."

She looked me straight in the eyes. "It's because of whatever happened between you and that guy back in Fredericksburg, isn't it?"

"That has nothing to do with it," I fibbed, wishing I'd never alluded to the unfortunate incident. "You know that between the hair salon and my class, I've got more on my plate than I can handle."

"That reminds me," Amy said as she reached into her messenger bag. "Here's that textbook you wanted."

"Thanks." I took the accounting tome, and the sheer weight of it served as a reminder of the burden of school. "If I don't make a C or better on that quiz in the morning, I'll have to drop the course."

"You can do it." Amy straddled her bike in her blue pencil skirt. "Are we still on for girls' night tomorrow?"

"Absolutely." I frowned at the textbook. "Pass or fail, I'm going to need to get my drink on. This has been a hard week, and the statue striptease just now didn't help."

She wrinkled her forehead. "Is everything okay?"

I shrugged. "Business has been especially bad. I can count the number of clients that Lucy, Gia, and I've had on two hands."

"Well, you've only been in town for a few months. The customers will come."

"Yeah." I stared at the pink-and-orange plaid pattern on my shirt. "I'm sure they will."

Amy looked at her watch. "My lunch hour's almost up. I'd better get back to the library."

"'K. See you tomorrow night." I watched Amy ride away and wondered whether the customers really would come. In the four months that I'd been in Danger Cove, I'd gotten a real education, and it had nothing to do with my degree. The people of the town were nice but wary of me and my salon. And now that I knew why, I couldn't say that I blamed them. As much as I'd wanted to escape small-town Texas, I might have stayed put if I'd known the truth about Uncle Vinnie and this building.

I stared at the bank balance on my laptop screen. That couldn't be right, could it? The clock was showing the correct time, 2:30 p.m., so my computer was working properly. I blinked in case something was clouding my vision. Nope, still the same number. I tried closing my weak eye, but it was no use. Any way I looked at it, I had three months of money before my inheritance from Uncle Vinnie ran out. I sighed and rested my head on the back of the wooden chair.

"I hear I missed quite a show today," my step-cousin, Gia Di Mitri, said from the doorway of the salon break room.

I turned my head to glare at her but winced instead. I didn't know which was more blinding—the afternoon sun shining through the bay window or Gia's bright-blue stretch top, pink cheetah-print tights, and neon-yellow stilettos. "Who told you that?"

"Woman Mouth," she replied, translating Donna Bocca's name from Italian. "I was shopping at Lily's Lingerie when she came in for her shift. She told everyone in the store that the statue gave Zac Taylor a lap dance." She opened the refrigerator and pulled out a can of lemon soda. "Which is pretty funny if you think about it."

"Yeah. Hilarious." Despite my sarcasm, I *could* see the humor. It was a tragic comedy.

Gia popped the tab on the can and flopped into a chair. "Just remember, Cass, there's no such thing as bad publicity."

"No?" I spread my arms to emphasize the emptiness of the salon.

Lucy O'Connell rushed into the room, her curly red tendrils flying. "Sorry I'm late," she said as she took a seat at the table. "Since we didn't have any clients, I babysat for Mallory Winchester while she ran an errand, but it took longer than she expected." She bit her lip. "She said it was because she had to stop by here to see your porno yard sale with her own two eyes."

"Yard sale?" Now I took offense to that but not to the "porno" part. I was hardly the type to sell the girls—and by that I mean "the merchandise"—on the front lawn.

Gia's shiny lips straightened into a flat line. "Yeah, I'll bet she wanted to see it—every square inch."

"Oh, Mallory wouldn't have any interest in those statues," Lucy said. "She's into Pennsylvania Dutch art."

Gia rolled her eyes.

"Let's just start the meeting," I interjected. As upset as I was about Mallory's take on the event, I had to brush it off—just like I'd brushed off the news that the Victorian home I lived and worked in had a hundred-year history as a brothel for local lumberjacks. "Now," I began, glancing at my notes, "the plan is still to grow The Clip and Sip to fill the three empty salon chairs and hire a receptionist, despite the lack of customers."

Lucy cleared her throat. "Yeah, about that..."

I looked up.

"Um, if business doesn't pick up soon..."

"Yeah?" Gia prodded, tapping the silver-glittered tips of her French-manicured nails on the table.

Lucy looked like a deer caught in the headlights. "Well, I'll have to find another job."

My heart sank. I couldn't lose Lucy. I'd had to lure Gia from New Jersey with the promise of free room and board after Lucy was the only hairstylist in Danger Cove who'd answered my ad. "I understand."

"I'm sorry," Lucy said, big blue eyes welling with tears. "It's just that I won't ever be able to save enough money to marry Sven."

Sven Mattsun was a Swedish exchange student from Stockholm whom Lucy had fallen head over heels for two years ago during their senior year at Danger Cove High School. Ever since he'd returned home last year, Lucy had been scrimping and saving to pay for her to move to Sweden and their wedding.

Gia snorted. "What do you really know about the Swedish Fish, anyway?"

"Gia!" I scolded. "Sven's not a piece of candy."

"Too bad for Lucy," she said, examining a lock of her hair for split ends.

Lucy's chin trembled. "I know that I love him, no matter what you think."

Gia tossed the lock of hair to the side and shook her head.

"I met Sven when he came for a visit, and he's very nice," I said in a soothing tone for Lucy's benefit. Then I turned to Gia. "He's way better than those brainless bodybuilder types you go for. They can barely carry on a conversation."

She flipped her silky black hair over her shoulder. "Who needs to talk?"

I smirked. "Men aren't just for sex, you know."

"Who said anything about sex? I just meant that men aren't exactly known for their conversational skills."

She had me there. "Give it a little more time, Lucy. I have some ideas to bring in more business."

"Really?" Her eyes widened. "Like what?"

"For starters, The Clip and Sip now serves alcohol." I handed each of them a copy of the new drink menu. "Every customer gets either a free glass of wine or one of my homemade liqueurs."

Lucy's face brightened. "This is awesome. It'll feel more like a spa experience."

Gia took a sip of soda as she perused the drink list. "And a little Texas moonshine might help to alleviate the bitter taste in people's mouths about the building's past."

I shot her a look. "Peach liqueur hardly qualifies as moonshine. Anyway, Gia, you'll also offer a complimentary manicure to our customers."

She dropped the menu. "How will I get paid?"

"I'll have to cover your commission during the promotion." I couldn't afford it, but it was the least I could do. Even though my aunt Carla had married Gia's father, Frank, ten years before when we were both sixteen, my Uncle Vinnie hadn't left Gia so much as a mention in his will. Apparently, he hadn't been as into family as my dad, Domenic. But now that I thought about it, ever since my dad had divorced my mom last year and moved back to his native New Jersey, he didn't seem too interested in family, either, because I'd hardly heard from him since.

Gia patted me on the back. "Thanks, Cass."

"Also," I began, "since we're so close to Seattle, we're going to offer coffee drinks. I bought a professional-grade espresso machine by Nuova Simonelli."

"Those are like twelve grand!" Gia exclaimed. "I knew your Uncle Vinnie was loaded."

"He wasn't. I bought the machine on credit." My stomach turned as I admitted that last part. "Anyway, I'm glad you're excited about the machine, because you're going to make the drinks."

"I'm going to make cawffee too?" she squawked, her New Jersey accent rearing its colorful head. "Why do all of your new promotions involve me?"

"Because you have skills that Lucy and I don't," I replied. "Plus, your makeup services haven't exactly taken off."

Her eyes narrowed. "It's not my fault that the nature-loving ladies of Danger Cove don't appreciate the smoky eye."

The smoky eye was the unofficial state look of New Jersey. But the combination of purple, blue, and even green eye shadow with smudged eyeliner would be more appropriately named "the sickly eye." "No, but it is your fault that you don't apply makeup that's suited to the client."

"But the whole point of makeup is to look made up, not"— she wrinkled her mouth—"*natural.*"

"The *whole point* is to make the client happy," I snapped. "Now, starting today, we're running an ad about our new services in the *Cove Chronicles*. In the meantime, I need the two of you to spread the word, especially you, Lucy. Tell all of your girlfriends and their moms."

She nodded. "I'm sorry to bring this up, but..."

Gia exhaled loudly. "For crying out loud—just spit it out."

"Is there any update on getting the ceiling fixed?"

Gia and I exchanged a look.

"I know it's a sensitive subject," Lucy continued, "and I

wouldn't normally bring it up, but it's starting to sag. And since it's right above my chair..."

I shifted in my seat. "Well, I'll have to get police permission for a plumber to go into Uncle Vinnie's room. I can stop by the station today."

"Thanks, Cassidi."

An uncomfortable silence fell over the room.

Gia turned to me and cocked a well-plucked brow. "Is that it?"

I looked at my meeting agenda. "That's all I have."

"No, I mean, is that all you have planned to bring in new clients? Because, if you ask me, we need something bigger."

Of course, I hadn't asked Gia, but I knew from experience that she was going to tell me exactly what she thought. "What do you have in mind?"

"Egypt." Her face beamed brighter than her outfit.

I blinked. "I'm not following you."

Gia stood up and started to pace. "Think Cleopatra, the most regal and seductive queen of all time."

"O-kay," I said.

"We want to make women feel like her. You know, spread out all sexy on a gold chaise lounge."

I was pretty sure that the chaise lounge was a modern French invention, but whatever.

"So, picture this," Gia continued, motioning like a movie director. "We give the clients blowouts. But instead of the smoky eye, we do the Cleopatra eye. And the whole time they're in the chair, tanned bodybuilders are fanning them with those big feather-duster things and feeding them with their hands."

I stared at Gia openmouthed, and Lucy went pale.

"You do realize, don't you, that using sex to sell the salon is exactly what I *don't* want to do?" I paused for effect. "For obvious reasons."

"Gawd!" Gia threw her head back in frustration. "Sex sells, Cassidi. It sold when this place was a brothel, and it sold when your Uncle Vinnie ran his hair salon here. That's why his business was so successful."

"Yes." I met her gaze straight on. "But that's also what got him murdered."

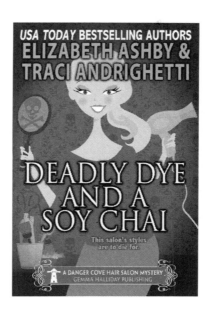

Made in the USA
Las Vegas, NV
04 January 2023

65019512R00195